P9-DNW-107

Jonathan Lethem

THE VINTAGE BOOK OF AMNESIA

Jonathan Lethem is the author of the novels *Gun, with Occasional Music, Amnesia Moon, As She Climbed Across the Table, Girl in Landscape,* and *Motherless Brooklyn,* as well as a collection of stories, *The Wall of the Sky, the Wall of the Eye.* He lives in Brooklyn, New York.

ALSO BY JONATHAN LETHEM

Motherless Brooklyn
Girl in Landscape
As She Climbed Across the Table
Gun, with Occasional Music
Amnesia Moon
The Wall of the Sky, the Wall of the Eye

THE VINTAGE BOOK OF

AMNESIA

THE VINTAGE BOOK OF

AMNESIA

AN ANTHOLOGY

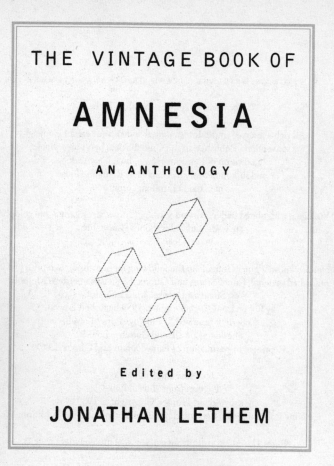

Edited by

JONATHAN LETHEM

Vintage Crime / Black Lizard
Vintage Books
A Division of Random House, Inc.
New York

A VINTAGE CRIME/BLACK LIZARD ORIGINAL, NOVEMBER 2000

Copyright © 2000 by Jonathan Lethem

All rights reserved under International and Pan-American Copyright
Conventions. Published in the United States by Vintage Books,
a division of Random House, Inc., New York,
and simultaneously in Canada by Random House
of Canada Limited, Toronto.

Vintage is a registered trademark and Vintage Crime/Black Lizard and colophon
are trademarks of Random House, Inc.

Grateful acknowledgment is made to the following for permission to reprint previously
published material: Farrar, Straus and Giroux, LLC: Excerpt from "Memories of
West Street and Lepke" from Life Studies
by Robert Lowell. Copyright © 1959 by Robert Lowell.
Copyright renewed © 1987 by Harriet Lowell,
Sheridan Lowell, and Caroline Lowell.
Reprinted by permission of Farrar, Straus and Giroux, LLC.

Ice Nine Publishing Co.:
Excerpt from "Box of Rain,"
lyric by Robert Hunter. Copyright © 1980 by
Ice Nine Publishing Co. Reprinted by permission of Ice Nine Publishing Co.

Pages 411–414 constitute an extension of this copyright page.

Library of Congress Cataloging-in-Publication Data
The vintage book of amnesia : an anthology / by Jonathan Lethem, editor.
p. cm.
ISBN 0-375-70661-5
1. Amnesia—Miscellanea.   2. Anthologies.   I. Lethem, Jonathan.
RC394.A5 V55 2000
616.85'232—dc21   00-020649

www.vintagebooks.com

Printed in the United States of America
10 9 8 7 6 5 4 3 2

For Cara O'Connor

ACKNOWLEDGMENTS

Thanks to Richard Parks, Bill Thomas, Marty Asher, Carter Scholz, Pamela Jackson, Alan Michael Parker, Gordon Van Gelder, Laura Miller, Bryan Cholfin, Michael Seidenberg, Nicky Roe, John Clute, Johan Kugelberg, Chris Offutt, and Dan Barden.

And especially to Zoë Rosenfeld and Edward Kastenmeier, each in a way co-creator of this book.

CONTENTS

INTRODUCTION

A writer sat in a featureless white room trying to remember a genre which had never existed.

REAL, diagnosable amnesia—people getting knocked on the head and forgetting their names—is mostly just a rumor in the world. It's a rare condition, and usually a brief one. In books and movies, though, versions of amnesia lurk everywhere, from episodes of *Mission Impossible* to metafictional and absurdist masterpieces, with dozens of stops in between. Amnesiacs might not much exist, but amnesiac characters stumble everywhere through comic books, movies, and our dreams. We've all met them and been them.

This book of literary amnesia began as an observation of certain resemblances in two or three novels I admired—a passing notion, a reader's list. I had no intention of editing a book, let alone identifying a genre. But amnesia turned up more the harder I looked, and meant more the harder I thought about it. At first it was the obvious, gaudy cases, amnesia breaking out into an overt premise or plot symptom—there were more of these than I'd ever imagined (in fact, I'd written more than one myself). Elsewhere amnesia appeared pulsing just beneath the surface, an existential syndrome that seemed to nag at fictional characters with increasing frequency, a floating metaphor very much in the air. Amnesia, it turned out when I began to pay attention, is a modern mood, and a very American one.

Not that there's any question that literary amnesia has European grandfathers: Franz Kafka and Samuel Beckett. If it's usually felt that every compelling novel is in some sense a *mystery*, the examples of Kafka and Beckett suggest that *amnesia* can be seen as a basic condition for characters enmeshed in fiction's web. Conjured out of the void by a thin thread of sentences, every fictional assertion exists as a speck on a background of consummate blankness. There's a joke among writing teachers that apprentice writers, at a loss for an idea, will usually commit some version of the story that begins: "A man woke alone in a room with bare white walls—" unconsciously replicating their plight before the blank page and hoping that compositional momentum will garb the naked story in identity, meaning, and plot. Our hero might have blood on his hands, or answer a ringing phone, or find himself wiggling an antenna—we'll improvise as we go along. Kafka and Beckett dance beautifully at the edge of that void which has always loomed for fiction, has always been waiting to be noticed and flirted with. They're the very soul of amnesia.

The body that soul would come to inhabit, however, was provided by pop culture's appropriation of Freud. The explosion of psychotherapeutic metaphors into the narrative arts in the twentieth century is so complete and pervasive it would be hard to overstate; a profound sense of before-and-after is traceable in nervous jokes about how well Gissing or Poe might have responded to a course of Prozac. Or, say, try imagining Emily Brontë if she'd scrutinized her characters with the neurological vocabulary available to writers like Philip K. Dick, Lawrence Shainberg, and Dennis Potter. The ease with which these writers— and their audiences—grasp those new vocabularies for human perceptual life creates fresh textures in fiction, both particular and universal. Anyone's been Heathcliff on a bad day, but, unlike Heathcliff we've had our brooding shaped by diagnosis or its rejection; had romance and faith decanted into symptom, codependence, and past-life trauma; seen childhood sexual abuse converted into alien abduction and back again.

But what about that sharp blow to the head? And who fired this smoking gun in my hand if it wasn't me? Amnesia is film noir, too, a vehicle made of pure plot, one that gobbles psychoanalysis passingly, for cheap fuel. Cornell Woolrich and John Franklin Bardin are collected here to stand for many others: David Goodis and Richard Neely and Orson Welles (in *Lady from Shanghai* and *Mr. Arkadin*), plus another thousand haunted, desperate protagonists wandering the black-and-white streets of the Noir Metropolis wondering if they really did something terrible during their boozy binge and trying to persuade the cops to give them a chance, like O. J. Simpson, to hunt for the real killers and redeem the memory of that tragic, unworkable love affair. Amnesia plots are, however inadvertently, often stories about guilt—a trail that leads right back to Kafka, of course. (Maybe Kafka's the real killer!)

Beckett's Amnesia, to give another strain its diagnostic name, is characterized by meditation on the absent, circular, and amnesiac nature of human existence, as well as on the vast indifference of the universe to matters of identity. His novella *The Lost Ones* is an eerily dispassionate meditation on the plight of a group of bereft human bodies stuck in a cramped metal cylinder. It prefigures the disembodied-brains-dreaming subgenre of amnesia, which often arises in science fiction. In stories like A. A. Aattanasio's *Solis* and Joseph McElroy's *Plus*, brains implanted into machines are plagued into malfunction by sticky emotional residue from their forsaken human lives. Ambrose Bierce's "Occurrence at Owl Creek Bridge" is the most famous version of a closely related amnesia archetype, where a character discovers that the bewildering events of his story were only the strobelike hallucinations of a dying brain. A couple of the novels excerpted here or listed in the bibliography adopt this *darn, I was dead the whole time* template, but to name them would be to give away the endings to several wonderful ontological mystery stories—even if those endings are all essentially the same.

Perhaps an even more disheartening realization for an amnesiac is that he's *only a fictional character*. Call it Pirandello's Syndrome. Those elusive memories never existed, because the author never bothered to imagine them, having abandoned the mimetic pretense— which is hard on those of us who prefer to believe we live in a three-dimensional world. Thomas Disch, Paul Auster, and Vladimir Nabokov are among the writers prone to tipping their hands metafictionally—confessing authorial whim as readily as a Warner Brothers animator depriving Daffy Duck of the ground he stands on, instead warping the edge of his celluloid prison inward to reveal the sprocket holes.

Another form of amnesia is the collective political type, identified by Orwell, Huxley, and Yvgeny Zamyatin and extended, refined, and watered down by an army of science fiction writers ever since ("Soylent Green is—people!"). Taken in its direst and dryest sense, this version of amnesia points to theories of social or institutional knowing and forgetting, to theorists and critics like Michel Foucault, Marshall McLuhan, Frederic Jameson, Allan Bloom, and G. W. S. Trow. Obviously, I risk spilling my precious and only-recently-distilled vial of amnesia fiction into the broad streams of dystopian writing and cultural critique, but, well, that's what genres *do* under study: merge and disappear into others. (Noir, dystopia, theory, metafiction: watch amnesia swirl and be lost in them like James Stewart in *Vertigo*'s dream sequence.) Anyway, any good dystopian tyrant knows the use and value of controlled collective amnesia, or he loses his job.

As I reread and weighed the fiction on my list, it was possible at times to enter into a state of forgetting what I'd meant by distinguishing *amnesia* from *fiction*—by declaring one the modifier of the other—in the first place. Genres are also like false oases, only visible in the middle distance. Get too close and they atomize into unrelated particles. Eventually, though, I achieved editorial déjà vu, remembering what I couldn't have already known: I had in mind fiction that, more than just presenting a character who'd suffered memory loss, *entered into an amnesiac state at some level of the narrative itself*—and invited the reader to do the same. Fiction that made something of the white spaces that are fiction's native habitat or somehow induced a dreamy state of loss of identity's grip.

I knew I'd identified a genre—even if I was its whole audience as well as its only scholar—when I came across Helen Schulman's *The Revisionist*. That excellent book contained a scene of literal amnesia yet didn't actually fit my parameters, not even well enough to include in my bibliography of amnesia fiction. In the same week I came across another novel that struck me on the whole as precious and airless yet provided a thrill of discovery: it perfectly *exemplified* the *principles* of amnesia fiction. Now I was an amnesia nerd!

In gathering these stories, essays, and excerpts I willfully ignored the boundaries of my new genre. There's some real science in here, as well as cryptoscience, and reverse amnesia, and one straight-up alcoholic blackout. I followed the higher principle of pleasure, tried to end where I'd started: with writing I loved and wanted to recommend to someone else. That is to say, you. Let this introduction be a ghostly scrim in front of the stories, then, a vanishing scroll of words like the preamble of backstory before the start of an engrossing movie, or like the rantings of the captive amnesiac in Thomas Disch's "The Squirrel Cage," which vanish into air as they are typed. What good is a genre? Genres should vanish and be forgotten, this one especially—it was made for it. Forget this introduction. Here are some stories. Here's a book.

THE VINTAGE BOOK OF

AMNESIA

THOMAS PALMER

Dream Science

POOLE had begun to give an ironic inflection to the phrase "in my former life." Sitting at the long laminated-plastic table in his socks and blue pajamas (even though he wore them all day, they were still pajamas), he would glance at Mac, who was working across the room at the terminal, and begin some casual reminiscence with these four words— then pause significantly, as if the idea itself were a doubtful one and did not deserve its habitual introductory status. Having made his point, he would go on to talk about his wife, his job, the small coastline town where he lived; at other times he concentrated on his childhood, his family, or his years in school. It was hard to tell if Mac was listening, since he continued punching keys with his blunt, thick-nailed fingers, dropping his head down between his heavy shoulders to peer at the screen. He would make a comment now and then but he never offered any stories of his own. Mac was more likely to talk to the machine, pushing his wheeled chair back against the wall and cursing it steadily under his breath or banging the ivory-colored case with his meaty hand. He was a powerful man. Poole had fought with him several times without inflicting any damage, though he himself had been beaten almost senseless.

Poole reminisced to pass the time. He was amazed by how much he could remember. One thing led to another—if he could see, for instance, a motel cottage in Florida where he had spent two nights at the age of nine, then a little further effort might bring back a woman in a straw hat he had seen by the pool, or maybe the exact shade of red of the vinyl upholstery in his family's rented car. And so his stories tended to wander and lose themselves in detail; sometimes he would stop talking altogether. He wanted to catch these memories, fix them, and add them to the growing edifice of his past. Some, he suspected, had been sweetened and rubbed smooth by the intervening years, and his determination to identify them and dig out the truth in them occasionally struck him as quixotic, even perverse, in the light of his current circumstances—after all, if Mac had chosen to argue that he had no past at all, how could he have proven him wrong? He had no photographs, no letters, nothing—only the memories themselves, which hardly proved anything, as comforting as they might be.

For now, however, the world was nothing like what he remembered. To begin with, it was much smaller—it had shrunk to a single room. This room was built like an interior office, with bare white walls, yellow-green carpeting, fluorescent lights, and a bathroom at one end. It was about the size of a small conference room and contained the sort of furniture familiar to Poole from his days as a fund manager for a Connecticut bank—two office desks, two black vinyl chairs on casters, the long, bare table, a file cabinet, and various smaller items: wastebaskets, ashtrays, staplers, and a telephone. Pushed into one corner was the large bed on a hospital-type frame where Poole slept on bleached white sheets.

He and Mac were the sole inhabitants, and Mac was there only during working hours. Poole guessed he was ten or fifteen years older than himself—maybe in his late forties. He wore jeans, work boots, and knit shirts in various solid colors—not typical business attire, but Mac looked more like a bus driver than an executive. Balding, he had a few dried-out clumps of pale gray hair that he slicked back from his forehead and a dour, fleshy face with lots of color. His eyes were small, blue, and weary. When he stood after sitting for a long time, he would spread his feet, press both hands into the base of his spine, and rock from side to side, with an evil look on his face, his bones audibly cracking.

Mac was Poole's tie to a larger world—a world he still believed in, though he never saw it. The office had no windows; the only door was in the center of the longest wall. It opened onto a corridor that went completely around the office. This corridor was unique in Poole's experience in that it had no exit—no fire door, no elevator, not even a heating duct. After months, Poole had still not discovered how Mac got in and out of it.

The critical area was the long stretch farthest from the door to the office. When Mac left for the day he went back there and vanished; he was big enough to keep Poole from following him. And when he arrived in the morning at a quarter to nine, Poole had to be at least as far away as the front corridor or he wouldn't come in at all.

This situation was deeply frustrating for Poole; he could not accept it. Why should Mac be able to come and go but not him? In his more energetic days he had spent much of his time in the rear corridor looking for a way out. He had pried back the wall panels and shone a flashlight behind them; he had dug up the linoleum and chopped holes in the plywood underneath. Whenever he penetrated more than an inch or two he came up against a solid wall of cinder blocks set in mortar. He had picked away at them also—he had laboriously carved his way through an entire block with a pair of scissors only to find another one behind it.

Poole now saw this belief in a hidden or secret exit as a remnant of certain mental habits that were no longer useful to him. The hours he had spent searching for it had been wasted in a futile attempt to deny the truth of what had happened to him. That truth, plainly stated, was that his life had changed; there was no reason to expect that prior assumptions should apply. It was easier, in fact, to suppose that Mac simply vanished into thin air than to dream up theories about trapdoors and concealed passages, theories that couldn't stop there but had to go on to explain why someone would build and operate this elaborate prison—in short, theories that had to force rationality on an irrational situation.

Yes, it must be admitted—Poole had lost faith in actuality. He regarded his surroundings as a function of his own mental condition rather than as a separate and independent background. He was like a balloon that had slipped through a child's grasp—the world where he had spent his first three decades, the world he had shared with millions, had floated away when he wasn't looking. It wasn't enough, he now knew, to live in that world—you had to embrace it, you had to hold it close, or you would lose it.

Poole often tried to think back to the exact moment when he had departed from his former life. Had he been in a car wreck? Was his body in a coma somewhere? Unfortunately, he couldn't pin down the time with any certainty; there was no clean break. All he could remember was that it was sometime in the early spring—the lawns were cold and green, the streets were full of potholes, and he'd been spending his evenings working on IRS forms. The last specific event he felt sure of was a five-mile road race on the last Saturday in March. He also had the impression, hard to account for, that much time had passed between that day and his arrival here—time when he had perhaps hurried, barely conscious, through other possible worlds.

At any rate, time had a different meaning for him now. The watch Mac had given him—a digital one, on which the hour and minute appeared in figures made of black, bacilli-like rods that showed dark against a smooth, oyster-gray background—did not display either the day or the month. This was an ominous sign. It suggested that every week turned back on itself, that each of them started from the same eternal Monday morning. Poole had counted seventeen of these identical weeks since he landed in this place. Even so, he found it hard to convince himself that time was passing. How could it, when there was no change? In his former life time had carried him forward into the future; now he had gotten stuck somewhere and it was slowly wearing him away.

Occasionally, after Mac had left, he would turn out all the lights and wander. He would reach out for the wall and follow it like a blind man in a maze, imagining that he could go places and explore areas that were denied to him otherwise; he even hoped that he might stumble across a narrow chink where a light shone through. Who could say? The dark had no depth to it and therefore no boundaries; the walls he could no longer see might cease to exist. He shuffled along the corridor in his socks, barely breathing, the blackness thick around his eyes. Sometimes he would see things—pale, elusive thinnings of the air. Sometimes, pursuing them, he would move too quickly and bump into the walls. He often got caught up in long, cloudy discussions of his fate, which he addressed to an imaginary listener, a listener who did not choose to answer but who heard him just the same. When he had had enough he would find his way back to the switches and turn them on. He slept with at least a few lights.

Mac always arrived in the morning with a cafeteria-style plastic tray loaded with two large polystyrene cups of coffee and some sort of breakfast for Poole—doughnuts, grapefruit, oatmeal, eggs. At noon he went out again and came back an hour later with sandwiches and soup, chili, or some other hot food. Poole could ask for whatever he liked, but the selection was limited. He could get cigarettes but no liquor, candy bars but no newspapers or magazines. The only books Mac would bring him were cheap paperbacks with the covers torn off—war stories, astrological guides, pornographic fantasies, celebrity bios—twenty or thirty at a time.

At first Mac's apparent indifference to his predicament had outraged Poole. "I fail to understand," he remembered saying, "how anyone who claims to be human can stand by and allow this to continue." On some occasions he had gone on in this vein, his voice rising, until he shouted himself hoarse. Mac remained bent over the terminal and pretended not to hear. At the time, Poole had not realized that he was working himself up for more drastic measures—that he was in effect giving off warning signals. He soon learned that he could get better results by sudden, unexpected outbursts—hurling objects against the walls and screaming choice obscenities. Mac's shoulders would stiffen as his fingers stopped moving on the keyboard. He would lift his head slightly and look up at Poole from under his gray eyebrows. That look made Poole's heart swell with fear and pride. If he had gone too far—if the chair or stapler or whatever he had thrown had come too close—Mac would get up slowly, back him into a corner, and administer a thorough and methodical beating with his fists that centered on Poole's midsection and continued long past the point where any resistance had ceased. Poole had discovered that he could escape into the corridor, but he didn't like being run out of the office and there was something horribly satisfying about the inevitability of his fate once Mac got hold of him.

So they became enemies. Poole convinced himself that Mac was responsible for all his troubles and learned to hate his wrinkled, leathery eyelids, the click of his teeth as he chewed a sandwich, the sagging slope of his round, thick shoulders, his muffled belches, his aches and pains, his sour breath, even the ashy smudges on the toes of his work shoes. He looked back on that period now with a mixture of remorse and embarrassment; he felt that it had cost him Mac's trust. It ended with an event he classed with the five-mile road race in that it immediately preceded a foggy interval of uncertain duration. One morning he had crouched in wait just inside the door to the office with a long, daggerlike splinter of glass that he had broken out of the mirror in the bathroom, its blunt end wrapped in a towel. He intended to learn all of Mac's secrets. It was time, he thought, to show that he would not shrink from extreme measures.

As it happened, he was more successful than he had anticipated. Mac was still drowsy and went down hard when Poole hit him from the side, hot coffee soaking his chest and collar. For a few critical instants he was on his back and powerless, with Poole's knee holding him down, the shard of glass poised at his throat. But Poole had lost his nerve and couldn't go on. It was that sense of unreality again; it seemed to him that his situation was too bizarre and unsettled for murder to be an appropriate response. So he hesitated, and that hesitation was decisive; it was nearly the last thing he remembered.

The most painful aspect of his recovery—he still didn't know whether it had taken a few days or many—was his gradual realization that nothing had changed. At first the pallid, bare walls and the recessed fluorescent panels of the office seemed to him only one view, one window out of many that he looked through on his travels, and not one of the most attractive. Later he became aware that he was lying in bed and that he was often in pain. As his better dreams receded— dreams where these four walls couldn't hold him—he tried to withdraw with them, to inhabit them rather than observe them from a distance. It was a losing struggle. He was less and less able to disregard the sight of Mac working across the room or the tray of food on the floor by the bed. One day, at last, he surrendered—he pushed the covers aside, sat up, and let his feet down onto the carpet.

Poole was changed. The idea of escape no longer quickened him. All his feelings lost their sharpness. He would lie in bed for hours, smoking, or sit at the table and study his hands. He lost his appetite; he couldn't read. He craved sleep but it didn't restore him; he looked forward to it only because it reduced his waking hours. He stopped trying to talk to Mac. Every motion required enormous effort—even the tally he kept of the passing weeks seemed to him too difficult to maintain.

At night he lay in the bathtub for hours with his head on a pillow and the water running.

He spent much of his time in the back corridor, though he no longer tried to dig his way out. Instead, he would sit against the wall with his eyes shut and his blue-and-white-striped quilt wrapped around him. The idea that this was perhaps the place where he had come into this world comforted him. Now and then he would hear Mac swearing at the terminal.

Though they rarely spoke, he was always glad to see Mac arrive in the morning. If he was more than a few minutes late Poole got restless and hung around the door, listening—not because he was hungry, but because the day could not begin until he came. If he didn't, as sometimes happened, Poole would spend hours pacing the corridor and trying to calm himself. His great fear, which he was reluctant to admit to himself, was that Mac wouldn't come back at all and he would be left alone.

This is not to say that he had lost hope. He thought of his reduced existence as a sort of hibernation, a waiting period, a necessary adaptation to an environment where action led nowhere. He had too much pride to involve himself with the toys provided for him here—paper and pencil, sleeping and waking, eating and crapping. They weren't enough; he remembered a larger world.

He often wondered what he had done wrong. Until his arrival here he had been a success by most standards. The people he came from— longtime citizens of the USA, Yankees and German Protestants, salesmen, sailors, lawyers, and engineers—had found themselves, toward the end of the century, belonging to a nation that in its size and collective power had come to dominate the world. Who threatened them? Who was likely to dislodge them? It seemed to Poole that as their heir he had reason for confidence and might be excused for not expecting to wind up where he was now.

His own history was, he believed, quite typical. He had grown up in a large, tree-shaded house in a wealthy suburb of New York with his parents, his brother, and his sister, and he had weathered all the challenges this life had offered—he had left at eighteen to go to college and within ten years he had an M.B.A. and a healthy salary and was living in a similar house just up the Connecticut shore with a wife and their child. He had not achieved all this by accident. He gave himself credit; he had worked for it. When you were as tightly wedged in as that, surrounded by family, willingly bound by a mortgage and marriage vows, strapped down with your whole life's baggage packed in beside you, it ought to take a good hard kick to spring you loose—a bad illness, say, a divorce, a death. There was nothing like that. There was no forewarning. Here he was.

There was something, then, that he had not accounted for—some weakness or soft spot in his assumptions. He had been too literal-minded. He had put too much trust in appearances. The world he had accepted without question as a constant, an independent factor—the world of day and night, summer and winter, rain and sunshine—had not survived him. He was still here; it was gone.

News like this could not be absorbed all at once. Poole believed that he was just beginning to realize how bad it was. To think that he was not bound by time and place—to think that he could vanish without warning and reappear in any imaginable heaven or hell—this was enough to make you wonder whether life was truly a gift.

Poole started leaving on the office lights at all hours. At night he tried to make his dreams go to work for him. Lying in bed, half awake, he would imagine that he was back in his own home on a Saturday morning and that he could smell the fresh coffee Carmen, his wife, was making downstairs; he could see the sun glowing on the yellow curtains and the blue sky outside. And while he pretended to sleep, there was a struggle going on, a struggle to make that imaginary world linger and grow. What he hoped for was the moment when the skin on his carefully blown bubble would find a life of its own and swell outward dramatically, gathering strength as it took in walls, furniture, the entire house, the neighborhood, and more. Always, however, the wish failed—the dream that survived and became real was the one containing this hateful box and the corridor around it. These efforts exhausted him and he rarely got up after Mac came in without a feeling of defeat.

Mac had grown warier since Poole's attempt to ambush him. He had set up his desk so that it blocked the entrance to the nook alongside the bathroom; from his seat behind it he could see the entire room and he stood up if Poole got too close. He also seemed to be under pressure from the higher-ups—the phone hooked up to the terminal rang several times a day and he was always making excuses to someone on the other end. During these calls his face reddened and he squeezed the edge of the desk between his thumb and knuckles; it was plain that he took his job seriously. Poole always listened in but he never heard himself mentioned.

Every now and then Pool convinced himself that he could use that phone to get help, even though he had long since discovered that both it and the terminal were protected by a nine-digit access code that Mac was careful to keep hidden from him. On evenings and weekends he whiled away hours taking the phone apart and putting it back together again. He made a list of all the numbers he could remember and tried each of them in turn; he never succeeded in getting so much as a dial tone.

One afternoon the phone rang while Mac was in the bathroom. Poole answered immediately.

"Mac?" a bored voice said.

"Yeah." Poole did his best to mimic Mac's scratchy growl. "Listen, it's good you called. I need help. The kid went nuts—he's bleeding all over the place. I can't get near him. Send me some help, quick."

After a long pause the voice said evenly, "Call it yourself."

"I can't. I tried; I can't get through."

"So let him bleed. What do you care?" A click; the line went dead.

Mac was snickering and shaking his head as he came out of the bathroom. By then Poole had tried and failed to get the operator, the police emergency number, and a few others. "Here, like this," Mac said. He punched a few quick numbers. Poole still had the receiver to his ear; he heard two rings, and the same impatient voice answered.

"Who's this?" Poole said in his own voice.

"'Who's this?'" the voice echoed, incredulous. "Are you kidding?" The line went dead again.

"I'm in trouble now," Mac said, punching up the sequence again, his face grim and amused.

Poole listened for two rings. When the voice answered, he said, as calmly as he could, "You've got to help me."

"Why should I?"

"Because"—he ground his teeth together—"because I *need* help."

"Yeah, yeah. Let me talk to Mac."

"No—*listen* to me. There's been a mistake. I'm not supposed to be here. My name is Poole and I'm from Rowayton, Connecticut."

"How do you spell that?"

"R-O-W-A . . ." Poole had turned toward the wall and was holding the receiver tight against his ear.

"Not that. Your name."

"P-O-O-L-E."

"What makes you think you're in the wrong place?"

"I didn't do anything. I don't want to be here."

"Why didn't you tell me this before?"

"I couldn't. Mac won't let me use the phone."

"Put him on."

Poole started to obey and then hesitated. "What're you going to do?"

"I said put him on."

Poole gave up the receiver.

Mac held it to his ear, his other arm crossed on his shirt. He leaned back on one leg and looked at the ceiling. "Yeah?" He nodded. "OK . . . yeah, OK . . . all right." He pushed out his lower lip, shook his head, and hung up. Then he turned to Poole, his large face bland and thoughtful. "Dial 292," he said. After a moment he turned and went out.

Poole stood motionless for a few seconds and then dashed after him, shouting. He was too late. As he cut around the first corner he saw Mac turning at the second; by the time he reached that one Mac was gone and the corridor was empty. Groaning deep in his chest, Poole lurched back to the office and punched 292, stabbing the buttons with a stiff finger.

It was the same voice again, sharp and unmusical. "Yeah?"

"This is Poole."

"OK, good. I've got some questions for you. Would you mind telling me what kind of work experience you've had?"

"Wait a minute," Poole said. "First of all, what am I doing here?"

"How should I know?"

"There's been a mistake. I can't stay—I've got responsibilities."

He heard papers rustling in the background. "What's your first name, Poole?"

"Rockland." Poole thought he heard the voice talking to someone else but couldn't make out the words.

"Rockland, Rockland . . . Well, I was going to say that I might have a job for you, but you don't sound like you want it."

"Do you know where I am right now?"

"What?"

"Right now—do you know where I am?"

"You're in Mac's office."

"Yes—have you ever been here?"

"Uh—no, I haven't."

"Then could you do me a big favor? Could you come over and talk to me here?"

"Why?"

"It's very important. I'll tell you then."

Poole was staring, as he had been throughout the conversation, at the screen of Mac's terminal. Three unbroken columns of bluish numbers were marching upward, entering at the bottom and disappearing at the top.

"I'm all tied up right now," the voice said.

"I promise you it'll be worth your while."

"What do you mean by that?"

The voice had dropped a bit. Poole twisted one of the broad, flat buttons on his pajama top. "I'd rather see you in person," he said.

After a silence the voice said, "What exactly is going on there?"

Poole had run out of ideas; the truth itself seemed to him lacking in credibility. "Look," he said, "I want to talk to you—I am *eager* to talk to you—because I have been living in this office for over four months. Were you aware of that?"

"No, I wasn't."

"That figure is only an estimate. I've been cut off completely from the outside. I haven't seen a newspaper or a TV broadcast. I eat only what Mac brings me. I don't know why I was brought here—I don't know when I'll get out. Mac is my keeper—he takes out the trash, brings me my laundry, and leaves on weekends. I've heard him talk to you—I assume it was you—about his work. Am I clear so far?"

"Uh-huh."

"Then can you see why I'm dissatisfied? Would you agree that I have a legitimate grievance?"

"Just a second."

Poole heard him put the phone down. This time he was sure there was a conversation. His heart was racing; he crushed the receiver against his ear.

"Mr. Poole?"

"Yes."

"Would you consent to answer a few questions?"

"Why?"

"We're trying to straighten things out here. It's possible, as you said, that there's been a mistake."

"What kind of mistake?"

"We don't know yet." He cleared his throat. "You are troubled, you say, by your confinement."

"Yes."

"You remember an earlier time, a period of relative freedom and happiness. Your present life seems empty and frustrating by comparison."

"That's right."

"You had not expected this change and you resent it—it seems unfair to you."

Poole was losing patience. "Listen," he said, "aren't you missing the point? It seems to me that—"

"Just a few more," the voice said, cutting him off. "Now, in reference to this change, this transformation we were talking about, do you know why it happened? Something you did, maybe? Something you didn't do? You've had time to think it over, right?"

Poole sat down heavily in Mac's chair. "I'm still working on that one."

"So you don't have any idea."

"No, I don't."

"All right, Mr. Poole. Hold on—I'll get back to you."

Poole listened to the line hiss faintly. His hands were sweating; his moist breath bounced back from the receiver. Please, he thought, let this be the one. Let the doors open for me now. On the terminal the three columns of numbers kept jigging upward.

"Mr. Poole." The voice had a new edge of authority.

"Yes."

"We can't account for you. We haven't been able to trace you."

"What do you mean by that?"

"I mean that as far as we're concerned, you're on your own—your problem is outside our jurisdiction."

"So?"

"So we've got nothing to talk about. I'm sorry, but that's the way it is."

"Wait a minute." Poole's voice cracked as he hunched over, sheltering the receiver. "You said—"

"You said yourself that you didn't know why you were here. We don't know either. Therefore it's our view that you ought to seek help elsewhere."

Poole was stunned. His eyes turned hot and salty. "Elsewhere?" he said. "There isn't any elsewhere."

"Maybe not. Good-bye, Mr. Poole." He hung up.

Poole immediately punched the three numbers again. The voice answered. "I can't let you do this," Poole said.

"I heard you before. You don't seem to understand—there's nothing to be done."

"What's your name?" Poole asked.

There was no answer except for a faint clicking. "You hear that?" the voice said. "I'm changing the number here. You won't be able to call us anymore.'

The line went dead again and didn't ring when Poole tried it. He punched it in again—nothing. It seemed to him impossible that the episode was already over; it had barely begun. He sat still for a moment, then slammed the receiver down and jumped to his feet. "No!" he shouted, his head thrown back. "No!" he bellowed again, drawing it out, assaulting the silence. The walls drank up his voice without echo. He yelled again, filling the room with sound, his gut tightening and his bent legs trembling. He had a sense, however, that it was just noise, just an exercise, since his mind was already working in another direction.

Mac didn't come in until almost an hour later. Poole was sitting at the long table with a spiral-bound notebook, writing down an account of the conversation. Mac looked subdued. He trudged over to the terminal and sat down, though he seemed in no hurry to log himself in. Instead, he rubbed his face slowly with one hand, pulling his cheeks back with the heel of his palm.

Poole tossed down his pen and turned to him. "Mac," he said, "I've got to talk to you. Now."

"So talk."

Poole pulled his chair closer. "I've been blind, Mac. I couldn't see a damn thing. I thought that you were against me—that you were keeping me prisoner." He leaned forward, his hands on his knees, his eyes hungrily searching the other man's face. After a moment he went on. "I know better now, Mac. Now I'm asking for your help."

Mac braided his fingers behind his head and tilted up his large face. "Sure, OK," he said, his eyelids closing briefly.

"Show me the first step, Mac. Show me the way out."

Mac coughed behind closed lips, then sighed, his chest sagging. His powerful arms hung from his laced fingers. "I wouldn't do it before. Why should I now?"

"I wasn't ready. I would have been lost out there."

"Out where?" Mac said.

Poole hesitated. "Out there," he said, "where you're alone with yourself."

Mac shook his head as if disappointed. "You think I don't want you out of here? You're nothing but trouble."

"That's just it, Mac. It wouldn't have worked even if you'd tried to show me. But it's different now. I can do it."

Mac was eyeing Poole critically when the phone rang. He made a sour face and picked it up. "Yeah," he said, "he's still here . . . No, that's all right . . . The what?" His voice rose. "What do you want, you want my fucking head? . . . All right, I'll tell him." He hung up, sat back, and crossed his arms. "They got their eye on you now, kid," he said. "They're coming after you—they're gonna wear you down." He scratched an eyebrow with his thumbnail and clapped his hand on his arm. "Maybe you'll wish you never picked up that phone."

"I don't get it," Poole said.

"It was the guy you talked to before. He says he changed his mind—he says maybe he has a job for you after all."

"What kind of job?"

Mac nodded at the terminal with his chin. "Something like that."

The phone rang again. Mac didn't move. "Don't answer it," he said.

Poole had to fight to keep still. After five rings the phone was quiet.

"They got your scent now," Mac said. "They're gonna run you down."

"But why?"

"For this." Mac tapped the terminal with two fingers. "Forty hours a week. Bodies are scarce around here."

Poole was confused. "But you work for them, right?"

"I need the money."

Poole looked to one side. "I thought—"

"You thought," Mac said softly. "Tell me what you thought."

The mockery in his tone discouraged Poole, but he went ahead anyway. "All right," he said. "I asked for your help—I'll tell you why." He was excited; in the last hour he had built up an argument that he hoped would change everything.

"While you were gone," he began, "I was talking to that guy on the phone—your boss. I guess. I was describing my situation to him. After all this time, to talk to someone outside this room, someone besides you . . . anyway, he wasn't interested in my problems. He couldn't care less."

Poole was watching Mac closely. Though his face was almost expressionless, he looked as if he was listening.

"He sounded," Poole continued, "as if he'd heard it all before." He leaned closer. "*Before*. Mac! As if what happened to me had happened to other people around here. As if it was strictly routine."

Poole wanted a Winston. He patted his pajama pocket, found none, and crossed the room to get one, lighting it on his way back. "OK," he said, sitting down again, "so I said to myself, let's suppose everybody—I say everybody even though I haven't met any of them—let's suppose everybody gets dumped in here by surprise just like I did. It's a different world. The rules are different. The boundaries are different. Take this office, for example—it looks ordinary enough. But it's not—it's very strange. When you go out to the back of the hallway, there's a door there—you can come and go. When I go back there—nothing. I know; I looked. I'm convinced that even if I had a jackhammer, a cutting torch, and fifty pounds of quality explosives, I still wouldn't be able to find a door back there. You with me so far?"

Mac looked thoughtful. He shifted in his seat.

"Good," Poole said. "Now how is it that you can come and go and I can't? This is the question that was killing me. And the reason I couldn't get past it was that I was too dumb to see what was staring me in the face the whole time—namely, that all this crap about doors and openings was beside the point. *I* was the problem. *I* was the one who couldn't get out. And the reason I couldn't was that I had locked myself in!"

Poole was on the threshold of his main argument. He crushed out his half-smoked cigarette. "When I first came here," he said, "it didn't seem real to me—I thought it was a bad dream and I was waiting to wake up. I thought that you, for instance, weren't genuine, but just something I imagined. Now I know better. Now I know that the main difference between this place and the place I came from is that there is no big picture. Get it? There's no setting, there's no background that's the same for all of us—there's just you and me. It's like the world had been chopped up into little bits. Each of us has one—each of us lives in one. This office is mine; that's why I can't follow you when you go out. We can be here together but we can't meet anywhere else, because this office is the only place where your world and mine overlap."

Poole sat back, a little dizzy. His heart was thumping. He looked up at Mac. "That's how it is, isn't it?"

Mac took a toothpick out of a white cardboard box beside the terminal and started cleaning his teeth at a slow, methodical pace that was torture for Poole.

"It happened to you too, didn't it?" Poole asked. "You used to live in the big world."

Mac pulled the toothpick from his mouth and peered at the end, then leaned down and tossed it in the wastebasket.

"I know this is true," Poole said, lying.

"Suppose it was?" Mac said. "Then what?"

"I know you can help me, Mac. I want to make my world bigger. You've got to show me how."

Mac sat still and stared at him for a moment. "Let me get this straight," he said. "You think it's different here. You think we've lost touch. You think we're all locked up in our heads, or something."

"That's right, Mac. Remember the real world? It's gone." Poole rapped on the desk with his knuckles. "Hear that? That's a ghost knocking on a windowpane. We've been changed into spooks and we're living on memories. This place isn't real, Mac—it wouldn't be here if we hadn't imagined it."

Mac creaked back in his chair. "So you think we're dead, then."

"Something like that."

Mac shook his head and looked away.

"Admit it," Poole said. "You've been acting as if there's nothing peculiar about this place. But when you leave here I *know* you don't go back to some little house you bought twenty years ago. You're a ghost, too. Confess."

Mac seemed reluctant to answer, and Poole sensed an advantage. "Look," he said, "I know it hasn't been easy to put up with me. A new arrival, a nobody. Why should you have to clue me in? Until this moment I probably wouldn't have believed you. But I'm letting go, Mac—I can handle it now. You've got nothing to hide."

Poole gathered from the other man's silence that he was on the right track. "If I had to guess what you're thinking," he said, "I'd say you're wondering what the guy on the phone will say when he finds out I'm gone. He wants to nail me down, right? He wants to hook me up to one of these goddamn boxes." He slapped the plastic side of the terminal. "Well, I don't want to join his operation. I want to travel—I want to stretch my legs. I know you can help me."

He was barely conscious of what he was saying. He didn't care; all that mattered was whether Mac agreed. He felt, now, that he had said all he could. "So what about it? Are you listening? You want to give me a fighting chance?"

Mac glanced around the room, then leaned forward and shut off the machine. His voice was low and distinct. "I think you're in trouble, kid. I think you're becoming unbalanced."

"One more reason to help me, Mac."

"What makes you think I can?"

Poole lowered his voice also. "I know you, Mac. I can tell you've made your peace—you've settled for what you have. But if you decided to change things, I can tell you'd know where to start. Give me some of that knowledge, Mac. I need it. I'm asking you. Give it to me."

Poole rejoiced at the signs of conflict in Mac's face: the pushed-down brow, the frozen jaw, the restless eyes. He felt he had the upper hand. He was afraid to give Mac that one last shove; it might be one too many. So he waited, afraid to breathe, his chest tight as a fist.

"You better hope it works," Mac said quietly. "Things can go wrong."

"Then you'll do it?" Poole said, his voice rising.

Mac ignored him. "And if it does," he went on, "you may be sorry. I can think of worse places than this. This may look like heaven next to where you're going."

"And where might that be?" Poole asked, giddy in spite of himself.

"I don't know." Mac had a doleful look. He got to his feet, his eyes avoiding Poole's, and went through his rocking motion, making his bones creak. "I'll come back in the morning, we'll eat breakfast, and we'll do it." He slid past and stopped a few steps away, his back to the doorway, his shoulders slumped.

Poole had turned in his seat and was looking at him; he had never studied Mac so closely. There was something new in his blunt, weather-beaten face, something he had not seen even at the moment when he had him down on the carpet, helpless, with the shard of glass inches from his throat. The sight of it subdued him. "Why are you afraid?" he asked.

"I'm not afraid," Mac said. "There's nobody to be afraid for." He turned and went out.

JULIO CORTÁZAR

The Night Face Up

And at certain periods they went out
to hunt enemies; they called it the
war of the blossom.*

HALFWAY down the long hotel vestibule, he thought that probably he was going to be late, and hurried on into the street to get out his motorcycle from the corner where the next-door superintendent let him keep it. On the jewelry store at the corner he read that it was ten to nine; he had time to spare. The sun filtered through the tall downtown buildings, and he—because for himself, for just going along thinking, he did not have a name—he swung onto the machine, savoring the idea of the ride. The motor whirred between his legs, and a cool wind whipped his pantslegs.

He let the ministries zip past (the pink, the white), and a series of stores on the main street, their windows flashing. Now he was beginning the most pleasant part of the run, the real ride: a long street bordered with trees, very little traffic, with spacious villas whose gardens rambled all the way down to the sidewalks, which were barely indicated by low hedges. A bit inattentive perhaps, but tooling along on the right side of the street, he allowed himself to be carried away by the freshness, by the weightless contraction of this hardly begun day. This involuntary relaxation, possibly, kept him from preventing the acci-

*The war of the blossom was the name the Aztecs gave to a ritual war in which they took prisoners for sacrifice. It is metaphysics to say that the gods see men as flowers, to be so uprooted, trampled, cut down.—ED.

dent. When he saw that the woman standing on the corner had rushed into the crosswalk while he still had the green light, it was already somewhat too late for a simple solution. He braked hard with foot and hand, wrenching himself to the left; he heard the woman scream, and at the collision his vision went. It was like falling asleep all at once.

He came to abruptly. Four or five young men were getting him out from under the cycle. He felt the taste of salt and blood, one knee hurt, and when they hoisted him up he yelped; he couldn't bear the pressure on his right arm. Voices which did not seem to belong to the faces hanging above him encouraged him cheerfully with jokes and assurances. His single solace was to hear someone else confirm that the lights indeed had been in his favor. He asked about the woman, trying to keep down the nausea which was edging up into his throat. While they carried him face up to a nearby pharmacy, he learned that the cause of the accident had gotten only a few scrapes on the legs. "Nah, you barely got her at all, but when ya hit, the impact made the machine jump and flop on its side . . ." Opinions, recollections of other smashups, take it easy, work him in shoulders first, there, that's fine, and someone in a dustcoat giving him a swallow of something soothing in the shadowy interior of the small local pharmacy.

Within five minutes the police ambulance arrived, and they lifted him onto a cushioned stretcher. It was a relief for him to be able to lie out flat. Completely lucid, but realizing that he was suffering the effects of a terrible shock, he gave his information to the officer riding in the ambulance with him. The arm almost didn't hurt; blood dripped down from a cut over the eyebrow all over his face. He licked his lips once or twice to drink it. He felt pretty good, it had been an accident, tough luck; stay quiet a few weeks, nothing worse. The guard said that the motorcycle didn't seem badly racked up. "Why should it," he replied. "It all landed on top of me." They both laughed, and when they got to the hospital, the guard shook his hand and wished him luck. Now the nausea was coming back little by little; meanwhile they were pushing him on a wheeled stretcher toward a pavilion farther back, rolling along under trees full of birds, he shut his eyes and wished he were asleep or chloroformed. But they kept him for a good while in a room with that hospital smell, filling out a form, getting his clothes off, and dressing him in a stiff, grayish smock. They moved his arm carefully, it didn't hurt him. The nurses were constantly making wisecracks, and if it hadn't been for the stomach contractions he would have felt fine, almost happy.

They got him over to X-ray, and twenty minutes later, with the still-damp negative lying on his chest like a black tombstone, they pushed him into surgery. Someone tall and thin in white came over and began to look at the X-rays. A woman's hands were arranging his head, he felt that they were moving him from one stretcher to another. The man in white came over to him again, smiling, something gleamed in his right hand. He patted his cheek and made a sign to someone stationed behind.

It was unusual as a dream because it was full of smells, and he never dreamt smells. First a marshy smell, there to the left of the trail the swamps began already, the quaking bogs from which no one ever returned. But the reek lifted, and instead there came a dark, fresh composite fragrance, like the night under which he moved, in flight from the Aztecs. And it was all so natural, he had to run from the Aztecs who had set out on their manhunt, and his sole chance was to find a place to hide in the deepest part of the forest, taking care not to lose the narrow trail which only they, the Motecas, knew.

What tormented him the most was the odor, as though, notwithstanding the absolute acceptance of the dream, there was something which resisted that which was not habitual, which until that point had not participated in the game. "It smells of war," he thought, his hand going instinctively to the stone knife which was tucked at an angle into his girdle of woven wool. An unexpected sound made him crouch suddenly stock-still and shaking. To be afraid was nothing strange, there was plenty of fear in his dreams. He waited, covered by the branches of a shrub and the starless night. Far off, probably on the other side of the big lake, they'd be lighting the bivouac fires; that part of the sky had a reddish glare. The sound was not repeated. It had been like a broken limb. Maybe an animal that, like himself, was escaping from the smell of war. He stood erect slowly, sniffing the air. Not a sound could be heard, but the fear was still following, as was the smell, that cloying incense of the war of the blossom. He had to press forward, to stay out of the bogs and get to the heart of the forest. Groping uncertainly through the dark, stooping every other moment to touch the packed earth of the trail, he took a few steps. He would have liked to have broken into a run, but the gurgling fens lapped on either side of him. On the path and in darkness, he took his bearings. Then he caught a horrible blast of that foul smell he was most afraid of, and leaped forward desperately.

"You're going to fall off the bed," said the patient next to him. "Stop bouncing around, old buddy."

He opened his eyes and it was afternoon, the sun already low in the oversized windows of the long ward. While trying to smile at his neighbor, he detached himself almost physically from the final scene of the nightmare. His arm, in a plaster cast, hung suspended from an apparatus with weights and pulleys. He felt thirsty, as though he'd been running for miles, but they didn't want to give him much water, barely enough to moisten his lips and make a mouthful. The fever was winning slowly and he would have been able to sleep again, but he was enjoying the pleasure of keeping awake, eyes half-closed, listening to the other patients' conversation, answering a question from time to time. He saw a little white pushcart come up beside the bed, a blond nurse rubbed the front of his thigh with alcohol and stuck him with a fat needle connected to a tube which ran up to a bottle filled with a milky, opalescent liquid. A young intern arrived with some metal and leather apparatus which he adjusted to fit onto the good arm to check something or other. Night fell, and the fever went along, dragging him down softly to a state in which things seemed embossed as through opera glasses, they were real and soft and, at the same time, vaguely distasteful; like sitting in a boring movie and thinking that, well, still, it'd be worse out in the street, and staying.

A cup of a marvelous golden broth came, smelling of leeks, celery, and parsley. A small hunk of bread, more precious than a whole banquet, found itself crumbling little by little. His arm hardly hurt him at all, and only in the eyebrow where they'd taken stitches a quick, hot pain sizzled occasionally. When the big windows across the way turned to smudges of dark blue, he thought it would not be difficult for him to sleep. Still on his back so a little uncomfortable, running his tongue out over his hot, too-dry lips, he tasted the broth still, and with a sigh of bliss, he let himself drift off.

First there was a confusion, as of one drawing all his sensations, for that moment blunted or muddled, into himself. He realized that he was running in pitch darkness, although, above, the sky criss-crossed with treetops was less black than the rest. "The trail," he thought, "I've gotten off the trail." His feet sank into a bed of leaves and mud, and then he couldn't take a step that the branches of shrubs did not whiplash against his ribs and legs. Out of breath, knowing despite the darkness and silence that he was surrounded, he crouched down to listen. Maybe the trail was very near, with the first daylight he would be able to see it again. Nothing now could help him to find it. The hand that had unconsciously gripped the haft of the dagger climbed like a fen scorpion up to his neck where the protecting amulet hung. Barely moving his lips, he mumbled the supplication of the corn which brings about the beneficent moons, and the prayer to Her Very Highness, to the distributor of all Motecan possessions. At the same time he felt his ankles sinking deeper into the mud, and the waiting in the darkness of the obscure grove of live oak grew intolerable to him. The war of the blossom had started at the beginning of the moon and had been going on for three days and three nights now. If he managed to hide in the depths of the forest, getting off the trail farther up past the marsh country, perhaps the warriors wouldn't follow his track. He thought of the many prisoners they'd already taken. But the number didn't count, only the consecrated period. The hunt would continue until the priests gave the sign to return. Everything had its number and its limit, and it was within the sacred period, and he on the other side from the hunters.

He heard the cries and leaped up, knife in hand. As if the sky were aflame on the horizon, he saw torches moving among the branches, very near him. The smell of war was unbearable, and when the first enemy jumped him, leaped at his throat, he felt an almost-pleasure in sinking the stone blade to the haft into his chest. The lights were already around him, the happy cries. He managed to cut the air once or twice, then a rope snared him from behind.

"It's the fever," the man in the next bed said. "The same thing happened to me when they operated on my duodenum. Take some water, you'll see, you'll sleep all right."

Laid next to the night from which he came back, the tepid shadow of the ward seemed delicious to him. A violet lamp kept watch high on the far wall like a guardian eye. You could hear coughing, deep breathing, once in a while a conversation in whispers. Everything was pleasant and secure, without the chase, no . . . But he didn't want to go on thinking about the nightmare. There were lots of things to amuse himself with. He began to look at the cast on his arm, and the pulleys that held it so comfortably in the air. They'd left a bottle of mineral water on the night table beside him. He put the neck of the bottle to his mouth and drank it like a precious liqueur. He could not make out the different shapes in the ward, the thirty beds, the closets with glass doors. He guessed that his fever was down, his face felt cool. The cut over the eyebrow barely hurt at all, like a recollection. He saw himself leaving the hotel again, wheeling out the cycle. Who'd have thought that it would end like this? He tried to fix the moment of the accident exactly, and it got him very angry to notice that there was a void there, an emptiness he could not manage to fill. Between the impact and the moment that they picked him up off the pavement, the passing out or what went on, there was nothing he could see. And at the same time he had the feeling that this void, this nothingness, had lasted an eternity. No, not even time, more as if, in this void, he had passed across something, or had run back immense distances. The shock, the brutal dashing against the pavement. Anyway, he had felt an immense relief in coming out of the black pit while the people were lifting him off the ground. With pain in the broken arm, blood from the split eyebrow, contusion on the knee; with all that, a relief in returning to daylight, to the day, and to feel sustained and attended. That was weird. Someday he'd ask the doctor at the office about that. Now sleep began to take over again, to pull him slowly down. The pillow was so soft, and the coolness of the mineral water in his fevered throat. The violet light of the lamp up there was beginning to get dimmer and dimmer.

As he was sleeping on his back, the position in which he came to did not surprise him, but on the other hand the damp smell, the smell of oozing rock, blocked his throat and forced him to understand. Open the eyes and look in all directions, hopeless. He was surrounded by an absolute darkness. Tried to get up and felt ropes pinning his wrists and ankles. He was staked to the ground on a floor of dank, icy stone slabs. The cold bit into his naked back, his legs. Dully, he tried to touch the amulet with his chin and found they had stripped him of it. Now he was lost, no prayer could save him from the final . . . From afar off, as though filtering through the rock of the dungeon, he heard the great kettledrums of the feast. They had carried him to the temple, he was in the underground cells of Teocalli itself, awaiting his turn.

He heard a yell, a hoarse yell that rocked off the walls. Another yell, ending in a moan. It was he who was screaming in the darkness, he was screaming because he was alive, his whole body with that cry fended off what was coming, the inevitable end. He thought of his friends filling up the other dungeons, and of those already walking up the stairs of the sacrifice. He uttered another choked cry, he could barely open his mouth, his jaws were twisted back as if with a rope and a stick, and once in a while they would open slowly with an endless exertion, as if they were made of rubber. The creaking of the wooden latches jolted him like a whip. Rent, writhing, he fought to rid himself of the cords sinking into his flesh. His right arm, the strongest, strained until the pain became unbearable and he had to give up. He watched the double door open, and the smell of the torches reached him before the light did. Barely girdled by the ceremonial loincloths, the priests' acolytes moved in his direction, looking at him with contempt. Lights reflected off the sweaty torsos and off the black hair dressed with feathers. The cords went slack, and in their place the grappling of hot hands, hard as bronze; he felt himself lifted, still face up, and jerked along by the four acolytes who carried him down the passageway. The torchbearers went ahead, indistinctly lighting up the corridor with its dripping walls and a ceiling so low that the acolytes had to duck their heads. Now they were taking him out, taking him out, it was the end. Face up, under a mile of living rock which, for a succession of moments, was lit up by a glimmer of torchlight. When the stars came out up there instead of the roof and the great terraced steps rose before him, on fire with cries and dances, it would be the end. The passage was never going to end, but now it was beginning to end, he would see suddenly the open sky full of stars, but not yet, they trundled him along endlessly in the reddish shadow, hauling him roughly along and he did not want that, but how to stop it if they had torn off the amulet, his real heart, the life-center.

In a single jump he came out into the hospital night, to the high, gentle, bare ceiling, to the soft shadow wrapping him round. He thought he must have cried out, but his neighbors were peacefully snoring. The water in the bottle on the night table was somewhat bubbly, a translucent shape against the dark azure shadow of the windows. He panted, looking for some relief for his lungs, oblivion for those images still glued to his eyelids. Each time he shut his eyes he saw them take shape instantly, and he sat up, completely wrung out, but savoring at the same time the surety that now he was awake, that the night nurse would answer if he rang, that soon it would be daybreak, with the good, deep sleep he usually had at that hour, no images, no nothing . . . It was difficult to keep his eyes open, the drowsiness was more powerful than he. He made one last effort, he sketched a gesture toward the bottle of water with his good hand and did not manage to reach it, his fingers closed again on a black emptiness, and the passageway went on endlessly, rock after rock, with momentary ruddy flares, and face up he choked out a dull moan because the roof was about to end, it rose, was opening like a mouth of shadow, and the acolytes straightened up, and from on high a waning moon fell on a face whose eyes wanted not to see it, were closing and opening desperately, trying to pass to the other side, to find again the bare, protecting ceiling of the ward. And every time they opened, it was night and the moon, while they climbed the great terraced steps, his head hanging down backward now, and up at the top were the bonfires, red columns of perfumed smoke, and suddenly he saw the red stone, shiny with the blood dripping off it, and the spinning arcs cut by the feet of the victim whom they pulled off to throw him rolling down the north steps. With a last hope he shut his lids tightly, moaning to wake up. For a second he thought he had gotten there, because once more he was immobile in the bed, except that his head was hanging down off it, swinging. But he smelled death, and when he opened his eyes he saw the blood-soaked figure of the executioner-priest coming toward him with the stone knife in his hand. He managed to close his eyelids again, although he knew now he was not going to wake up, that he was awake, that the marvelous dream had been the other, absurd as all dreams are—a dream in which he was going through the storage avenues of an astonishing city, with green and red lights that burned without fire or smoke, on an enormous metal insect that whirred away between his legs. In the infinite lie of the dream, they had also picked him up off the ground, someone had approached him also with a knife in his hand, approached him who was lying face up, face up with his eyes closed between the bonfires on the steps.

—*translated by Paul Blackburn*

MARTIN AMIS

Other People

"**MORE** tea, love?"

"Yes please," said Mary.

"How you getting on then?"

"Fine, fine. I feel better all the time."

"Coming back to you, is it, dear?"

"Well—a little," Mary lied.

"It's just a matter of time," said Mrs. Botham thoughtfully, "—purely a matter of time."

Watched and smiled at by Mary, Mrs. Botham limped back to her seat—her inviolable armchair, wedged into the corner by the fire with toy flames. *Limp* hardly did justice (Mary coolly reflected) to the spectacular unevenness of Mrs. Botham's gait: she walked like a clockwork hurdler. Mary attributed this to the fact that one of Mrs. Botham's legs was roughly twice the length of the other. The standard limb sported its special extension, like a black brick; but that scarcely made up the disparity; and her longer leg seemed embarrassed by its own profligacy, bending outwards in a sympathetic arc. Mr. Botham—and Gavin, too, naturally—spoke of something going wrong with Mrs. Botham's leg a long time ago in her life. Something with a dark name had come and stretched it for her. No one said how or why.

"I knew a lady from the clinic," said Mrs. Botham, her head angled solicitously, "she took a knock on the head one night, said that she couldn't remember, you know, hardly anything."

"She was probably pissed," said Gavin, who sat nearby on the couch, gazing, as was his habit, at a magazine full of glaring, near-naked men.

They had all built their own bodies, and had all made a terrible mess of it.

Mrs. Botham's head twisted round towards her son. "She was *not* pissed, Gavin! I mean drunk," she added, returning to Mary with her smile. "She had *amnesia*. Her mind was a complete blank! In the morning she couldn't recognize a soul, not even her own husband who was cradling her in his arms or even her own little children, Melanie and Sue."

"That's not amnesia, Ma," said Gavin.

Mrs. Botham's features, which until that moment seemed poised for resigned and melancholy sleep, hardened watchfully. ". . . What is it then?" she asked.

"It's called a hangover," said Gavin without looking up.

"Why do you behave in this way to your own mother, Gavin? Why? Please tell me why, Gavin."

Gavin turned another page of his magazine, and another tiny head beamed out from its fortress. "Because you're an alcoholic, Ma," he said.

"No she's not," said Mr. Botham, who as usual had been sitting in cheerful silence at the table. "She's an ex-alcoholic."

"Ah, no my dear," said Mrs. Botham, her face all abrim again, "now that is where *you* are wrong. There is no such thing as an ex-alcoholic . . ."

"Only an alcoholic."

"Only an alcoholic."

"Only an alcoholic," they all said at once.

"And she was an *amnesiac!*" Mrs. Botham told her son.

" . . . And you're just a queer anyway."

"That's right, Ma" said Gavin, and turned a page.

"You see, Mary," said Mrs. Botham, "once an alcoholic, always an alcoholic. Oh, if I could've just got Sharon to come to Al Anon! But she'd never come. She was too drunk all the time. Do you know, Mary, that the true alcoholic"—and here she closed her eyes—"they fear nothing. Nothing. Oh, I've had the lot, I admit it, Mary. Methylated spirits. Turpentine. After-shave. The lot. Silver polish. Weed killer. Paint remover. Washing-up liquid. Everything. Disinfectant. 4711. Cough mixture. Nasal decongestant. Windowlene Optrex. I've had them all. You see, Mary, that was before I came to value my sobriety above all things. I *treasure* my sobriety. Have you ever looked up *sobriety* in the dictionary, Mary? Have you? You see, it doesn't only mean not being drunk. It means honesty, quietude, moderation, tranquillity, sanity, dignity, temperance, modesty, honesty . . ."

Mary settled herself more comfortably. Mrs. Botham had already explained to Mary about sobriety, half an hour ago; but Mrs. Botham was so drunk by now that she either couldn't remember or perhaps didn't care anyway. Mary wasn't about to mind. She fixed her eyes on Mrs. Botham's lost numb face, seeing Sharon everywhere, and employed a skill she had learnt to perfect over the past few days. When Mrs. Botham was talking to you, you just looked her way without really listening. Mrs. Botham wasn't about to mind. As far as she was concerned, talking was the main thing. It wasn't really to do with you; it was to do with her. Mrs. Botham acknowledged as much, quite frequently. She kept saying how nice Mary was to talk to. She said that was what she really liked—someone to talk to.

Mary even glanced around the room from time to time, or she sent her restless senses out on their patrol. There on the table was the empty blue plate, the teapot and its family. At nine o'clock every night Mrs. Botham would lollop into the kitchen and shut the door behind her. She said she hated the Nine O'clock News. Mary didn't blame her. Mary feared the television too. It was a window with everything happening on the other side—it was too much and Mary tried to keep it all out. At half past nine Mrs. Botham would emerge in processional triumph, bearing the small metropolis on her tray: the twin stacks of toast woozy with butter, the boiling pink tea so powerful that it made the mouth cry, the fanned brown biscuits like the sleeping dogs on the tin from which they came. According to Gavin, Mrs. Botham always got drunk again while she was in the kitchen alone. Mary believed him. Mrs. Botham was certainly very anxious to talk about sobriety on her return. But Mary didn't mind. She was very grateful to Mrs. Botham for everything she had done in making her so welcome here.

"Don't worry," Gavin told Mary on the first night. "I'm queer."

They were to share a room and a bed. Mary was still terrified, seeing no good reason why she shouldn't get fucked again.

"What does that mean exactly?" she asked.

"It means, I like men. I don't like women."

"I'm sorry," said Mary.

"Don't worry," he said again, looking at her with his knowledgeable eyes, "I like *you*. I just don't want to fuck you or anything."

"That's good," said Mary to herself.

"It's a drag actually," said Gavin, taking off his shirt. He had built his own body too, but he hadn't done it quite so badly as the people in his magazines. "It's supposed to be okay liking men. I don't like it. I don't like liking men."

"Why don't you stop?"

"Good thinking, Mary. I'll pack it in tomorrow." He sighed and said, "I know a man who's queerer than me. He only likes Spanish waiters. Only them. I mean he doesn't even like Italian waiters. I said, 'That's funny. I like all sorts.' He said—then you're very lucky. But I'm not lucky. I'm just not as unlucky as him. Do you, can you remember who you like?"

"No," said Mary.

"That'll be interesting, won't it?"

"Perhaps I'll like men too."

"That won't make you queer."

"Won't it?"

"We'll see. Good night, Mary."

"I hope so," she said.

Queers like men more than women because they liked their mothers more than their dads. That's one theory. Here is another: queers like men more than women because men are less demanding, more companionable, and above all cheaper than women are. Queers, they just want shelter from the lunar tempest. But *you* know what queers are like.

Soon, Mary will know too. She will learn fast here, I'm sure. The Bothams were just what she needed. She isn't alarmed by them and, more importantly, they aren't alarmed by her.

Mrs. Botham is, in fact, alone in her conviction that Mary is an amnesiac—hence her constant spearheading of this unpopular view. Gavin, who spends more time with her than the others, has vaguely formed the opinion that she must be somehow retarded; Mary had the mind, he thought, of an unusually bright, curious, and systematic twelve-year-old (she would be very clever when she grew up, he often found himself thinking). Mr. Botham, finally, and for various potent reasons of his own, is secretly under the apprehension that Mary is quite normal in every respect. Granted, Mr. Botham is something of an enigma. A lot of people—neighbors and so on, Mary, perhaps you yourself—assume that he must be a man of spectacularly low intelligence. How else has he managed to live with an alcoholic for thirty years? The answer is that Mr. Botham himself has been an alcoholic for twenty-nine of them. *That's* why he has stuck to Mrs. Botham's side during all these years when she's been drunk all the time: *he's* been drunk all the time.

But Mary will gain ground fast now. If you ever make a film of her sinister mystery, you'll need lots of progress-music to help underscore her renovation at the Bothams' hands . . . Ironically, she enjoys certain advantages over other people. Not yet stretched by time, her perceptions are without seriality; they are multiform, instantaneous, and random, like the present itself. She can do some things that you can't do. Glance sideways down an unknown street and what do you see: an aggregate of shapes, figures, and light, and the presence or absence of movement? Mary sees a window and a face behind it, the grid of the paving stones and the rake of the drainpipes, the way the distribution of the shadows answers to the skyscape above. When you look at your palm you see its five or six central grooves and their major tributaries, but Mary sees the numberless scratched contours and knows each of them as well as you know the crenellations of your own teeth. She knows how many times she has looked at her hands—a hundred and thirteen at the left, ninety-seven at the right. She can compare a veil of smoke sliding out of a doorway with a particular flourish of the blanket as she strips her bed. This makes a kind of sense to her. When the past is forgotten, the present is unforgettable.

Mary always knows what time it is without having to look. And yet she knows hardly anything about time or other people.

But she was gaining ground fast now.

She got to know her body and its hilly topography—the seven rivers, the four forests, the atonal music of her insides. By watching Mr. Botham, who did it often and expressively, she learned to blow her nose. Her body ceased to surprise her. Even the first glimpse of lunar blood left her unharrowed. Mrs. Botham talked constantly about these things and Mary was prepared for almost any disaster. (Mrs. Botham was obsessed by her grisly torments during what she ominously called "the Change." The Change didn't sound worth having to Mary and she hoped it wouldn't get round to her for a long time to come.) She told Mrs. Botham about the blood, and Mrs. Botham, in her unembarrassable way, told Mary what she had to do about it. It seemed an ingenious solution. On the whole, yes, Mary was quite pleased with her body. Gavin himself, who was a body-culture expert, announced that she had a good one, apart from her triceps. Conversely, Mary didn't think that Gavin's body was all it was built up to be—Gavin, with his dumb-bells, his twanging chest-flexers, and his stinking singlets. But she assumed he must know what he was talking about. There were many really bad bodies round where they lived, with bits missing or added, or twisted or stretched. So Mary was pleased with hers, and it was certainly all very interesting.

She started reading in earnest.

At first she was inhibited by not knowing how private reading was. She kept an eye on all the things the others read and secretly read them too.

Mr. Botham read a dirty sheath of smudged gray paper that came and went every day. It was never called the same thing twice. There were pictures of naked women in it, and on the back pages men but not women could be bought and sold; they cost lots of money. In the center pages someone called Stan spoke of the battle between cancer and his wife Mildred. Cancer won in the end, but heroism such as Stan and Mildred's knows no defeat. It was all about other places, some of them (perhaps) not too far away. It told of atrocious disparities of fortune, of deaths, cataclysms, jackpots. And it was very hard to read, because the words could never come to an agreement about the size or shape they wanted to be. Mrs. Botham read pamphlets sent to her by Al Anon, of whom she always spoke most warmly. The pamphlets were all about alcoholics and sounded just like Mrs. Botham did. They had scales and graphs of what alcoholics got up to: they drank alone, they lied and stole things, they trembled and had visions of mice and shell-fish. Then they forgot everything. Then they died. But if you put your faith in A.A. and God, it would all turn out right in the end.

Gavin spent a lot of time gazing disdainfully through his slippery magazines, but he had some other things in a cupboard in his room which he would occasionally consult or sort through. They were books, and books turned out to be where language was kept. Some were from school; others were acquired for a night course that Gavin had got too disheartened to complete; still others had been pressed on him by a friend of his, a poet, a dreamer. Mary was rather dashed to discover that Gavin had gone to school for eleven years and yet even now considered himself to be lamentably ill-educated. She never knew there was so much to know. Gavin said she could help herself to his books, and so, slackly prompted by his nods and scowls, Mary got started straightaway.

Books were difficult. She read *The Major Tragedies of William Shakespeare*. It was about four men made up of power, mellifluous-ness, and hysteria; they lived in big bare places that frightened them into speech; they were all cleverly murdered by women, who used an onion, a riddle, a handkerchief, and a button. She read *A Dickens Omnibus*. It was about parts of London she had not yet seen. In each story a nice young man and a nice young woman weaved through a gallery of grimacing villains, deformed wags, and rigid patriarchs until, after an illness or a separation or a long sea voyage, they came together again and lived happily ever after. She read *Rhyme and Reason: An Introduction to English Poetry*. It was about an elongated world of elu-sive vividness and symmetry; there was a layer, a casing on it, that she found nowhere else and knew she would never fully penetrate; the words marched to the end of their rank, sounded a chime, darted back again, and marched forward cheerfully, with renewed zest, completely reconciled to whatever it was that determined their role. She read *The Jane Austen Gift Pack*. The six stories it contained spoke more directly to her than anything else had done. The same thing happened in every book: the girl liked a bad man who seemed good, then liked a good man who had seemed bad, whom she duly married. What was wrong with the bad men who seemed good? They were unmanly, and lacked candor, and, in at least two clear instances, fucked other people. Mary reread one of these stories and was anxious that things would turn out the same way as they had before. They did, and she found this very comforting. She read *The Rainbow, What Maisie Knew,* and two fat shiny works about natural disaster and group jeopardy . . . At one point it occurred to her that books weren't about other places; they were about other times, the past and the future. But she looked again and saw that Shakespeare's book, for instance, was much newer than Lawrence's, and that couldn't be right. No. Books were about other places.

Where were they? How far did life stretch? It might go on forever, or it might just stop dead a few corners away. There was a place across the river called the World's End. For a long while in Mary's mind this was the limit of life. (Similarly she once half heard from the television that there was fighting in Kentish Town—with machine guns and tanks. When she discovered that the fighting was actually taking place in Kurdistan, she didn't know how relieved to be about this.) She wondered where the end of the world was and what the world ended with—with mists, high barriers, or just the absence of everything. Would you die if you went there? Often she nauseated herself by sending her mind into the sky, past the bloated nursery toys of the middle-air, ever upwards into the infinite limey blue. She knew a little about death now. She knew that it happened to other people, to every last one of them. It was a bad thing, obviously, and no one liked it; but no one knew how much it hurt, how long it lasted, whether it was the end of everything or the start of something else. It couldn't be that bad, Mary thought, if people did it all the time.

With Gavin, with Mrs. Botham, and sometimes alone, Mary walked the streets of London, London South, as far up as the River, as far down as the Common, carving a track of familiarity from the grid of ramshackle streets, eviscerated building sites, and the caged sections of high-wire concrete. You needed to walk through somewhere seven times before it ceased to be frightening. Knowing other people helped, and Mary was getting to know quite a few of them these days. They waved at her as she moved past them in the streets, or talked in her direction when she went to the shops and exchanged money for goods under Mrs. Botham's stern-eyed but unsystematic tutelage. Mary invested inordinate emotion in these routine sallies. A courtly particularity from the greengrocer could make her smile all afternoon; an unreturned glance from the milkman could bring the beginnings of tears to her eyes and sink the whole day in mist. At the newsagent's one morning Mary got briefly excited by all the magazines called things like *People, Life, Woman,* and *Time.* But they weren't what she had hoped for. They were still all about other places instead.

In shops everyone talked about money. Money had recently done something unforgivable; no one seemed to be able to forgive money for what it had done. Mary secretly forgave money, however. It appeared to be good stuff to her. She liked the way you could save money as you spent it. Mary developed a good eye for bargains, especially in the supermarket where they openly encouraged you to do this anyway. Mrs. Botham was always saying how much money Mary saved her. Pretty good going, she thought, considering that all she ever did was spend it. But Mrs. Botham still couldn't find it in her heart to forgive money. She hated money; she really had it in for money. She would repetitively abuse money all day long.

So on top of all this and one way or another, Mary learned a little about glass, desire, voodoo, peace, lotteries, libraries, labyrinths, revenge, fruit, kings, laughter, despair, drums, difference, castles, change, trials, America, childhood, cement, gas, whales, whirlwinds, rubber, oblivion, uncles, control, autumn, music, enmity, time.

Life was good, life was interesting. Only one thing worried her, and that was sleep.

"Good night," said Gavin, still panting rhythmically from the fifty press-ups he always did last thing.

"I hope so," said Mary.

"You—why do you always say that? I hope so."

"Well I do. I hope they're going to be all right. They haven't been good so far."

"What, you have nightmares, do you?"

"Yes, I think that's what I have."

She had expected sleep to be ordered and monotone. It wasn't. She lived through the days on tracks because that was what other people did. But her nights were random, and full of terror.

Mary knew other people had bad dreams but she was pretty certain they weren't as bad as hers. Incredible things happened to her while she was asleep. For hours in the darkness her mind struggled fiercely to keep the dreams away, when Mary would as soon have given up and let the dreams begin. But her mind wouldn't listen to her; it thrummed on its own fever, dealing her half images of graphic sadness and fluorescent chaos, setting her hurtful tasks of crisis and desire, trailing before her that toy alphabet with its poisonous p's and q's. And then the dreams came and she must suffer them without will.

She felt that the dreams came from the past. She had never seen a red beach bubbled with sandpools under a furious and unstable sun. She had never felt a sensation of speed so intense that her nose could remember the tang of smoldering air. And the dreams always ended by mangling her; they came down like black smoke and plucked her apart nerve by nerve.

And she asked for it, and wanted more.

SHIRLEY JACKSON

Nightmare

IT was one of those spring mornings in March; the sky between the buildings was bright and blue and the city air, warmed by motors and a million breaths, had a freshness and a sense of excitement that can come only from a breeze starting somewhere in the country, far away, and moving into the city while everyone is asleep, to freshen the air for morning; Miss Toni Morgan, going from the subway to her office, settled a soft, sweet smile on her face and let it stay there while her sharp tapping feet went swiftly along the pavement. She was wearing a royal blue hat with a waggish red feather in it, and her suit was blue and her topcoat a red and gray tweed, and her shoes were thin and pointed and ungraceful when she walked; they were dark blue, with the faintest line of red edging the sole. She carried a blue pocketbook with her initials in gold, and she wore dark blue gloves with red buttons. Her topcoat swirled around her as she turned in through the door of the tall office building, and when she entered her office sixty floors above, she took her topcoat off lovingly and hung it precisely in the closet, with her hat and gloves on the shelf above; she was precise about everything, so that it was exactly nine o'clock when she sat down at her desk, consulted her memorandum pad, tore the top leaf from the calendar, straightened her shoulder, and adjusted her smile. When her employer arrived at nine-thirty, he found her typing busily, so that she was able to look up and smile and say "Good morning, Mr. Lang," and smile again.

At nine-forty Miss Fishman, the young lady who worked at the desk corresponding to Miss Morgan's, on the other side of the room, phoned in to say that she was ill and would not be in to work that day.

At twelve-thirty Miss Morgan went out to lunch alone, because Miss Fishman was not there. She had a bacon, tomato, and lettuce sandwich and a cup of tea in the drugstore downstairs, and came back early because there was a letter she wanted to finish. During her lunch hour she noticed nothing unusual, nothing that had not happened every day of the six years she had been working for Mr. Lang.

At two-twenty by the office clock Mr. Lang came back from lunch; he said, "Any calls, Miss Morgan?" as he came through the door, and Miss Morgan smiled at him and said, "No calls, Mr. Lang." Mr. Lang went into his private office, and there were no calls until three-oh-five, when Mr. Lang came out of his office carrying a large package wrapped in brown paper and tied with an ordinary strong cord.

"Miss Fishman here?" he asked.

"She's ill," Miss Morgan said, smiling. "She won't be in today."

"Damn," Mr. Lang said. He looked around hopefully. Miss Fishman's desk was nearly empty; everything was in perfect order and Miss Morgan sat smiling at him. "I've got to get this package delivered," he said. "Very important." He looked at Miss Morgan as though he had never seen her before. "Would it be asking too much?" he asked.

Miss Morgan looked at him courteously for a minute before she understood. Then she said, "Not at all," with an extremely clear inflection, and stirred to rise from her desk.

"Good," Mr. Lang said heartily. "The address is on the label. Way over on the other side of town. Downtown. You won't have any trouble. Take you about"—he consulted his watch—"about an hour, I'd say, all told, there and back. Give the package directly to Mr. Shax. No secretaries. If he's out, wait. If he's not there, go to his home. Call me if you're going to be more than an hour. Damn Miss Fishman," he added, and went back into his office.

All up and down the hall, in offices directed and controlled by Mr. Lang, there were people alert and eager to run errands for him. Miss Morgan and Miss Fishman were only the receptionists, the outer bulwark of Mr. Lang's defense. Miss Morgan looked apprehensively at the closed door of Mr. Lang's office as she went to the closet to get her coat. Mr. Lang was being left defenseless, but it was spring outside, she had her red topcoat, and Miss Fishman had probably run off under cover of illness to the wide green fields and buttercups of the country. Miss

Morgan settled her blue hat by the mirror on the inside of the closet door, slid luxuriously into her red topcoat, and picked up her pocketbook and gloves, and put her hand through the string of the package. It was unexpectedly light. Going toward the elevator, she found that she could carry it easily with the same hand that held her pocketbook, although its bulk would be awkward on the bus. She glanced at the address: "Mr. Ray Shax," and a street she had never heard of.

Once in the street in the spring afternoon, she decided to ask at the newspaper stand for the street; the little men in newspaper stands seem to know everything. This one was particularly nice to her, probably because it was spring. He took out a little red book that was a guide to New York, and searched through its columns until he found the street.

"You ought to take the bus on the corner," he said. "Going across town. Then get a bus going downtown until you get to the street. Then you'll have to walk, most likely. Probably a warehouse."

"Probably," Miss Morgan agreed absently. She was staring behind him, at a poster on the inside of the newspaper stand. "Find Miss X," the poster said in screaming red letters, "Find Miss X. Find Miss X. Find Miss X." The words were repeated over and over, each line smaller and in a different color; the bottom line was barely visible. "What's that Miss X thing?" Miss Morgan asked the newspaper man. He turned and looked over his shoulder and shrugged. "One of them contest things," he said.

Miss Morgan started for the bus. Probably because the poster had caught her eye, she was quicker to hear the sound truck; a voice was blaring from it, "Find Miss X! Win a mink coat valued at twelve thousand dollars, a trip to Tahiti; find Miss X."

Tahiti, Miss Morgan thought, on a day like this. She went swiftly down the sidewalk, and the sound truck progressed along the street, shouting, "Miss X, find Miss X. She is walking in the city, she is walking alone; find Miss X. Step up to the girl who is Miss X, and say 'You are Miss X' and win a complete repainting and decorating job on your house, win these fabulous prizes."

There was no bus in sight and Miss Morgan waited on the corner for a minute before thinking, I have time to walk a ways in this lovely weather. Her topcoat swinging around her, she began to walk across town to catch a bus at the next corner.

The sound truck turned the corner in back of her; it was going very slowly, and she outdistanced it in a minute or so. She could hear, far away, the announcer's voice saying ". . . and all your cosmetics for a year."

Now that she was aware of it, she noticed that there were "Find Miss X" posters on every lamppost; they were all like the one in the newsstand, with the words running smaller and smaller and in different colors. She was walking along a busy street, and she lingered past the shopwindows, looking at jewelry and custom-made shoes. She saw a hat something like her own in a window of a store so expensive that only the hat lay in the window, soft against a fold of orange silk. Mine is almost the same, she thought as she turned away, and it cost only four ninety-eight. Because she lingered, the sound truck caught up with her; she heard it from a distance, forcing its way through the taxis and trucks in the street, its loudspeaker blaring music, something military. Then the announcer's voice began again: "Find Miss X, find Miss X. Win fifty thousand dollars in cash; Miss X is walking the streets of the city today, alone. She is wearing a blue hat with a red feather, a reddish tweed topcoat, and blue shoes. She is carrying a blue pocketbook and a large package. Listen carefully. Miss X is carrying a large package. Find Miss X, find Miss X. Walk right up to her and say 'You are Miss X,' and win a new home in any city in the world, with a town car and chauffeur, win all these magnificent prizes."

Any city in the world, Miss Morgan thought, I'd pick New York. Buy me a home in New York, mister, I'd sell it for enough to buy all the rest of your prizes.

Carrying a package, she thought suddenly, *I'm* carrying a package. She tried to ease the package around so she could carry it in her arms, but it was too bulky. Then she took it by the string and swung it as close to her side as she could; must be a thousand people in New York right now carrying large packages, she thought; no one will bother me. She could see the corner ahead where her bus would stop, and she wondered if she wanted to walk another block.

"You are Miss X," the sound truck screamed, "and win one of these gorgeous prizes. Your private yacht, completely fitted. A pearl necklace fit for a queen. Miss X is walking the streets of the city, completely alone. She is wearing a blue hat with a red feather, blue gloves, and dark blue shoes."

Good heavens, Miss Morgan thought; she stopped and looked down at her shoes; she was certainly wearing her blue ones. She turned and glared angrily at the sound truck. It was painted white, and had "Find Miss X" written on the side in great red letters.

"Find Miss X," the sound truck said.

Miss Morgan began to hurry. She reached the corner and mixed with the crowd of people waiting to get on the bus, but there were too many and the bus doors were shut in her face. She looked anxiously down the long block, but there were no other buses coming, and she began to walk hastily, going toward the next corner. I could take a taxi, she thought. That clown in the sound truck, he'll lose his job. With her free hand she reached up and felt that her hat was perched at the correct angle and her hair neat. I hope he *does* lose his job, she thought. What a thing to do! She could not help glancing over her shoulder to see what had become of the sound truck, and was shocked to find it creeping silently almost next to her, going along beside her in the street. When she looked around, the sound truck shouted "Find Miss X, find Miss X."

"Listen," Miss Morgan told herself. She stopped and looked around, but the people going by were moving busily without noticing her. Even a man who almost crashed into her when she stopped suddenly said only "Excuse me," and went on by without a backward look. The sound truck was stopped by traffic, up against the curb, and Miss Morgan went over to it and knocked on the window until the driver turned around.

"I want to speak to you," Miss Morgan said ominously. The driver reached over and opened the door.

"You want something?" he asked wearily.

"I want to know why this truck is following me down the street," Miss Morgan said; since she did not know the truck driver, and would certainly never see him again, she was possessed of great courage. She made her voice very sharp and said, "What are you trying to do?"

"Me?" the truck driver said. "Look, lady, I'm not following anybody.

I got a route I gotta go. See?" he held up a dirty scrap of paper, and Miss Morgan could see that it was marked in pencil, a series of lines numbered like streets, although she was too far away to see what the numbers were. "I go where it tells me," the truck driver said insistently. "See?"

"Well," Miss Morgan said, her voice losing conviction, "what do you mean, talking about people dressed like me? Blue hats, and so on?"

"Don't ask me," the truck driver said. "People hire this truck, I drive where they say. I don't have nothing to do with what happens back there." He waved his hand toward the back of the truck, which was separated from him by a partition behind the driver's seat. The traffic ahead of him started and he said quickly, "You want to know, you ask back there. Me, I don't hear it with the windows all shut." He closed the door, and the truck moved slowly away. Miss Morgan stood on the curb, staring at it, and the loudspeaker began, "Miss X is walking alone in the city."

The nerve of him, Miss Morgan thought, reverting to a culture securely hidden beneath six years of working for Mr. Lang, the goddamn nerve of him. She began to walk defiantly along the street, now slightly behind the sound truck. Serve them right, she thought, if anyone says to me, "Are you Miss What's-her-name?" I'll say "Why, yes, I am, here's your million dollars and you can go—"

"Reddish tweed topcoat," the sound truck roared, "blue shoes, blue hat." The corner Miss Morgan was approaching was a hub corner, where traffic moved heavily and quickly, where crowds of people stood waiting to cross the street, where the traffic lights changed often. Suppose I wait on the corner, Miss Morgan thought, the truck will have to go on. She stopped on the corner near the sign "bus stop," and fixed her face in the blank expression of a bus rider, waiting for the sound truck to go on. As it turned the corner it shouted back at her, "Find Miss X, find Miss X, she may be standing next to you now."

Miss Morgan looked around nervously, and found she was standing next to a poster that began "Find Miss X, find Miss X," but went on to say, "Miss X will be walking the streets of New York TODAY. She will be wearing blue—a blue hat, a blue suit, blue shoes, blue gloves. Her coat will be red and gray tweed. SHE WILL BE CARRYING A LARGE PACKAGE. Find Miss X, and claim the prizes."

Good Lord, Miss Morgan thought, good Lord. A horrible idea crossed her mind: Could they sue her, take her into court, put her in jail for dressing like Miss X? What would Mr. Lang say? She realized that she could never prove that she wore these clothes innocently, without criminal knowledge; as a matter of fact, she remembered that that morning, out in Woodside, while she was drinking her coffee, her mother had said, "You won't be warm enough; the paper says it's going to turn cold later. Wear your heavy coat at least." How would Miss Morgan ever be able to explain to the police that the spring weather had caught her, made her take her new coat instead of her old one? How could she prove anything? Cold fear caught Miss Morgan, and she began to walk quickly, away from the poster. Now she realized that there were posters everywhere: on the lampposts, on the sides of the buildings, blown up huge against the wall of a high building. I've got to do something right away, she thought, no time to get back home and change.

Trying to do so unobtrusively, she slid off her blue gloves and rolled them up and put them into her pocketbook. The pocketbook itself she put down behind the package. She buttoned her coat to hide the blue suit, and thought, I'll go into a ladies' room somewhere and take the feather out of my hat; if they know I tried to look different, they can't blame me. Ahead of her on the sidewalk she saw a young man with a microphone; he was wearing a blue suit and she thought humorously, put a blue hat on him and he'd do, when she realized that he was trying to stop people and talk about Miss X.

"Are you Miss X?" he was saying. "Sorry, lady, red topcoat, you know, and carrying a package. Are you Miss X?" People were walking wider to avoid him, and he called to ladies passing, and sometimes they looked at him curiously. Now and then, apparently, he would catch hold of someone and try to ask them questions, but usually the women passed him without looking, and the men glanced at him once, and then away. He's going to catch me, Miss Morgan thought in panic, he's going to speak to *me*. She could see him looking through the crowds while he said into the microphone, loudly enough so that anyone passing could hear, "Miss X is due to come down this street, folks, and it's about time for Miss X to be passing by here. She'll be along any minute, folks, and maybe you'll be the one who walks up to her and says 'Are you Miss X?' and then you'll get those beautiful awards, folks, the golden tea service, and the library of ten thousand of the world's greatest books, folks, ten thousand books, and fifty thousand dollars. All you have to do is find Miss X, folks, just find the one girl who is walking around this city alone, and all you have to do is say 'You are Miss X,' folks, and the prizes are yours. And I'll tell you, folks, Miss X is now wearing her coat buttoned up so you can't see her blue suit, and she's taken off her gloves. It's getting colder, folks, let's find Miss X before her hands get cold without her gloves."

He's going to speak to me, Miss Morgan thought, and she slipped over to the curb and signaled wildly for a taxi. "Taxi," she called, raising her voice shrilly, "taxi!" Over her own voice she could hear the man with the microphone saying, "Find Miss X, folks, find Miss X." When no taxi would stop, Miss Morgan hurried to the other side of the sidewalk, next to the buildings, and tried to slip past the man at the microphone. He saw her, and his eyes jeered at her as she went by. "Find Miss X, folks," he said. "Find the poor girl before her hands get cold."

I must be crazy, Miss Morgan thought. I'm just getting self-conscious because I'm tired of walking. I'll definitely get a taxi on the next corner.

"Find Miss X," the sound truck shouted from the curb next to her.

"She's gone past here now," the man with the microphone said behind her, "She's passed us now, folks, but she's gone on down the street, find Miss X, folks."

"Blue hat," the sound truck said, "blue shoes, carrying a large package." Miss Morgan went frantically out into the street, not looking where she was going, crossed directly in front of the sound truck, and reached the other side, to meet a man wearing a huge cardboard poster saying "Miss X, Miss X, find Miss X. CARRYING A LARGE PACKAGE. Blue shoes, blue hat, red and gray tweed coat, CARRYING A LARGE PACKAGE." The man was distributing leaflets right and left, and people let them fall to the ground without taking them. Miss Morgan stepped on one of the leaflets and "Find Miss X" glared up at her from the ground under her foot.

She was going past a millinery shop, when she had a sudden idea; moving quickly, she went inside, into the quiet. There were no posters in there, and Miss Morgan smiled gratefully at the quiet-looking woman who came forward to her. They don't do much business in *here*, Miss Morgan thought, they're so eager for customers, they come out right away. Her well-bred voice came back to her; "I beg your pardon," she said daintily, "but would it be possible, do you think, for you to let me have either a hat bag or a hatbox?"

"A hatbox?" the woman said vaguely. "You mean, empty?"

"I'd be willing to purchase it, of *course*," Miss Morgan said, and laughed lightly. "It just so happens," she said, "that I have decided to carry my hat in this beautiful weather, and one feels so foolish going down the street *carrying* a hat. So I thought a bag . . . or a hatbox . . ."

The woman's eyes lowered to the package Miss Morgan was carrying. "Another package?" she asked.

Miss Morgan made a nervous gesture of putting the package behind her, and said, her voice a little sharper, "Really, it doesn't seem like such a *strange* thing to *ask*. A hatbox or a bag."

"Well . . ." the woman said. She turned to the back of the shop and went to a counter behind which were stacked piles of hatboxes. "You see," she said, "I'm alone in the shop right now, and around here very often people come in just to make nuisances of themselves. There've been at least two burglaries in the neighborhood since we've been here, you know," she added, looking uneasily at Miss Morgan.

"Really?" Miss Morgan said, her voice casual. "And how long, may I ask, have you been here?

"Well . . ." the woman said. "Seventeen years." She took down a hatbox, and then, suddenly struck with an idea, said, "Would you like to look at some hats while you're here?"

Miss Morgan started to say no, and then her eye was caught by a red and gray caplike hat, and she said with mild interest, "I might just try *that* one on, if I might."

"Indeed, yes," the woman said. She reached up and took the hat off the figure that held it. "This is one of our best numbers," she said, and Miss Morgan sat down in front of a mirror while the woman tried the hat on her.

"It's lovely on you," the woman said, and Miss Morgan nodded. "It's just the red in my coat," she said, pleased.

"You really ought to wear a red hat with that coat," the woman said.

Miss Morgan thought suddenly, what would Mr. Lang say if he knew I was in here trying on hats when I'm supposed to be going on his errands. "How much is it?" she asked hastily.

"Well . . ." the woman said. "Eight ninety-five."

"It's *far* too much for this hat," Miss Morgan said. "I'll just take the box."

"That's eight ninety-five *with* the box," the woman said unpleasantly.

Helplessly, Miss Morgan stared from the woman to the mirror to the package she had put down on the counter. There was a ten-dollar bill in her pocketbook. "All right," she said finally. "Put my old hat in a box and I'll wear this one."

"You'll never be sorry you bought that hat," the woman said. She picked up Miss Morgan's blue hat and set it inside a box. While she was tying the box she said cheerfully, "For a minute I was afraid you were one of the sort comes into a shop like this for no good. *You* know what I mean. Do you know, we've had two burglaries in the neighborhood since we've been here?"

Miss Morgan took the hatbox out of her hand and handed her the ten-dollar bill. "I'm in rather a hurry," Miss Morgan said. The woman disappeared behind a curtain at the back of the shop and came back after a minute with the change. Miss Morgan put the change in her pocketbook; I won't have enough for a taxi there and back, she thought.

Wearing the new hat, and carrying the hatbox and her pocketbook and the package, she left the shop, while the woman stared curiously after her. Miss Morgan found that she was a block and a half away from her bus stop, so she started again for it, and she was nearly on the corner before the sound truck came out of a side street, blaring, "Find Miss X, find Miss X, win a Thoroughbred horse and a castle on the Rhine."

Miss Morgan settled herself comfortably inside her coat. She had only to cross the street to get to her bus stop, and the bus was coming; she could see it a block away. She stopped to get the fare out of her pocketbook, shifting the package and the hatbox to do so, when the sound truck went slowly past her, shouting, "Miss X has changed her clothes now, but she is still walking alone through the streets of the city, find Miss X! Miss X is now wearing a gray and red hat, and is carrying *two* packages; don't forget, *two* packages."

Miss Morgan dropped her pocketbook and the hatbox, and stopped to pick up the small articles that had rolled out of her pocketbook, hiding her face. Her lipstick was in the gutter, her compact lay shattered, her cigarettes had fallen out of the case and rolled wide. She gathered them together as well as she could and turned and began to walk back the way she had come. When she came to a drugstore she went inside and to the phones. By the clock in the drugstore she had been gone just an hour and was only three or four blocks away from her office. Hastily, her hatbox and the package on the floor of the phone booth, she dialed her office number. A familiar voice answered—Miss Martin in the back room, Miss Walpole?—and Miss Morgan said, "Mr. Lang, please?"

"Who is calling, please?"

"This is Toni Morgan. I've got to speak to Mr. Lang right away, please."

"He's busy on another call. Will you wait, please?"

Miss Morgan waited; through the dirty glass of the phone booth she could see, dimly, the line of the soda fountain, the busy clerk, the office girls sitting on the high stools.

"Hello?" Miss Morgan said impatiently. "Hello, hello?"

"Who did you wish to speak to, please?" the voice said—it might have been Miss Kittredge, in accounting.

"Mr. Lang, please," Miss Morgan said urgently. "It's important."

"Just a moment, please." There was silence, and Miss Morgan waited. After a few minutes impatience seized her again and she hung up and found another nickel and dialed the number again. A different voice, a man's voice this time, one Miss Morgan did not know, answered.

"Mr. Lang, please," Miss Morgan said.

"Who's calling, please?"

"This is Miss Morgan, I must speak to Mr. Lang at once."

"Just a moment, please," the man said.

Miss Morgan waited, and then said, "Hello? Hello? What *is* the matter here?"

"Hello?" the man said.

"Is Mr. Lang there?" Miss Morgan said. "Let me speak to him at once."

"He's busy on another call. Will you wait?"

He's answering my other call, Miss Morgan thought wildly, and hung up. Carrying the package and the hatbox, she went out again into the street. The sound truck was gone and everything was quiet except for the "Find Miss X" posters on all the lampposts. They all described Miss X as wearing a red and gray cap and carrying two packages. One of the prizes, she noticed, was a bulletproof car, another was a life membership in the stock exchange.

She decided that whatever else, she must get as far from the neighborhood as she could, and when a taxi stopped providentially to let off passengers at the curb next to her, she stepped in and gave the driver the address on the package. Then she leaned back, her hatbox and the package on the seat next to her, and lit one of the cigarettes she had rescued when her pocketbook fell. I've been dreaming, she told herself, this has all been so silly. The thing she most regretted was losing her presence enough, first, to speak so to the driver of the sound truck, and then to drop her pocketbook and make herself conspicuous stooping to pick everything up on the street corner. As the taxi drove downtown she noticed the posters on every lamppost, and smiled. Poor Miss X, she thought. I wonder if they *will* find her?

"I'll have to stop here, lady," the taxi driver said, turning around.

"Where are we?" Miss Morgan said.

"Times Square," the driver said. "No cars getting through downtown on account of the parade."

He opened the door and held out his hand for her money. Unable to think of anything else to do, Miss Morgan paid him and gathered her hatbox and package together and stepped out of the taxi. The street ahead was roped off and policemen were guarding the ropes. Miss Morgan tried to get through the crowd of people, but there were too many of them and she was forced to stand still. While she was wondering what to do, she heard the sound of a band and realized that the parade was approaching. Just then the policeman guarding the curb opened the ropes to let traffic cross the street for the last time before the parade, and all the people who had been standing with Miss Morgan crossed to the other side and all the people who had been on the other side crossed to stand on Miss Morgan's side, turning in order to cross again on the side street at right angles to the way they had crossed before, but the policeman and the crowds held them back and they waited, impatient for the next crossing. Miss Morgan had been forced to the curb and now she could see the parade coming downtown. The band was leading the parade; twelve drum majorettes in scarlet jackets and skirts and wearing silver boots and carrying silver batons marched six abreast down the street, stepping high and flinging their batons into the air in unison; following them was the band, all dressed in scarlet, and on each of the big drums was written a huge X in scarlet. Following the band were twelve heralds dressed in black velvet, blowing on silver trumpets, and they were followed by a man dressed in black velvet on a white horse with red plumes on its head; the man was shouting, "Find Miss X, find Miss X, find Miss X."

Then followed a float preceded by two girls in scarlet who carried a banner enscribed in red, "Win magnificent prizes," and the float represented, in miniature, a full symphony orchestra; all the performers were children in tiny dress suits, and the leader, who was very tiny, stood on a small platform on the float and led the orchestra in a small rendition of "Afternoon of a Faun"; following this float was one bearing a new refrigerator, fifty times larger than life, with the door swinging open to show its shelves stocked with food. Then a float bearing a model of an airplane, with twelve lovely girls dressed as clouds. Then a float holding a golden barrel full of enormous dollar bills, with a grinning mannequin who dipped into the barrel, brought up a handful of the great dollar bills, and ate them, then dipped into the barrel again.

Following this float were all the Manhattan troops of Boy Scouts; they marched in perfect line, their leaders going along beside and calling occasionally, "Keep it up, men, keep that step even."

At this point the side street was allowed open for cross traffic, and all the people standing near Miss Morgan crossed immediately, while all the people on the other side crossed also. Miss Morgan went along with the people she had been standing with, and once on the other side, all these people continued walking downtown until they reached the next corner and were stopped. The parade had halted here, and

Miss Morgan found that she had caught up with the float representing the giant refrigerator. Farther back, the Boy Scouts had fallen out of their even lines, and were pushing and laughing. One of the children on the orchestra float was crying. While the parade halted, Miss Morgan and all the people she stood with were allowed to cross through the parade to the other side of the avenue. Once there, they waited to cross the next side street.

The parade started again. The Boy Scouts came even with Miss Morgan, their lines straightening, and then the cause of the delay became known; twelve elephants, draped in blue, moved ponderously down the street; on the head of each was a girl wearing blue, with a great plume of blue feathers on her head; the girls swayed and rocked with the motion of the elephants. Another band followed, this one dressed in blue and gold, but the big drums still said X in blue. A new banner followed, reading "Find Miss X," with twelve more heralds dressed in white, blowing on gold trumpets, and a man on a black horse who shouted through a megaphone, "Miss X is walking the streets of the city, she is watching the parade. Look around you, folks."

Then came a line of twelve girls, arm in arm, each one dressed as Miss X, with a red and gray hat, a red and gray tweed topcoat, and blue shoes. They were followed by twelve men each carrying two packages, the large brown package Miss Morgan was carrying, and the hatbox. They were all singing, a song of which Miss Morgan caught only the words "Find Miss X, get all those checks."

Leaning far out over the curb, Miss Morgan could see that the parade continued for blocks; she could see green and orange and purple, and far far away, yellow. Miss Morgan pulled uneasily at the sleeve of the woman next to her. "What's the parade for?" she asked, and the woman looked at her.

"Can't hear you," the woman said. She was a little woman, and had a pleasant face, and Miss Morgan smiled, and raised her voice to say, "I said, how long is this parade going to last?"

"What parade?" she asked. "*That* one?" She nodded at the street. "I haven't any idea, miss. I'm trying to get to Macy's."

"Do you know anything about this Miss X?" Miss Morgan said daringly.

The woman laughed. "It was over the radio," she said. "Someone's going to get a lot of prizes. You have to do some kind of a puzzle or something."

"What's it for?" Miss Morgan asked.

"Advertising," the woman said, surprised.

"Are *you* looking for Miss X?" Miss Morgan asked daringly.

The woman laughed again. "I'm no good at that sort of thing," she said. "Someone in the company of the people putting it on always wins those things, anyway."

Just then they were allowed to cross again, and Miss Morgan and the woman hurried across, and on down the next block. Walking beside the woman, Miss Morgan said finally, "I think I'm the Miss X they're talking about, but I don't know why."

The woman looked at her and said, "Don't ask *me*," and then disappeared into the crowd of people ahead.

Out in the street a prominent cowboy movie star was going by on horseback, waving his hat.

Miss Morgan retreated along a quiet side street until she was far away from the crowds and the parade; she was lost, too far away from her office to get back without finding another taxi, and miles away from the address on the package. She saw a shoe repair shop, and struck by a sudden idea, went inside and sat down in one of the booths. The repair man came up to her and she handed him her shoes.

"Shine?" he said, looking at the shoes.

"Yes," Miss Morgan said. "Shine." She leaned back in the booth, her eyes shut. She was vaguely aware that the repair man had gone into the back of the shop, that she as alone, when she heard a footstep and looked up to see a man in a blue suit coming toward her.

"Are you Miss X?" the man in the blue suit asked her.

Miss Morgan opened her mouth, and then said, "Yes," tiredly.

"I've been looking all over for you," the man said. "How'd you get away from the sound truck?"

"I don't know," Miss Morgan said. "I ran."

"Listen," the man said, "this town's no good. No one spotted you." He opened the door of the booth and waited for Miss Morgan to come.

"My shoes," Miss Morgan said, and the man waved his hand impatiently. "You don't need shoes," he said. "The car's right outside."

He looked at Miss Morgan with yellow cat eyes and said, "Come on, hurry up."

She stood up and he took her arm and said, "We'll have to do it again tomorrow in Chicago, this town stinks."

That night, falling asleep in the big hotel, Miss Morgan thought briefly of Mr. Lang and the undelivered package she had left, along with her hatbox, in the shoe repair shop. Smiling, she pulled the satin quilt up to her chin and fell asleep.

LAWRENCE SHAINBERG

Memories of Amnesia

LIKE so much brain damage, the first symptoms mine produced were almost indistinguishable from normal behavior. In a man less sensitive to his neurology they might have gone unnoticed; or if noticed, filed away among that enormous class of behavior (sometimes called, for want of a better word, *psychological*) one does not associate with the brain. For me, however, such dismissal was impossible. Twenty-one years a neurosurgeon, I had seen hundreds, even thousands, of people with brain damage, and I knew all too well that the early symptoms were often so unremarkable as to leave no trace, even in brains unafflicted with amnesia, in the memory. Brain damage isn't always as grotesque as normal brains expect it to be. It's true that it can strike like a hurricane, but sometimes it's more like a gentle breeze, a subtle change of vectors that leaves you headed not in the opposite direction, but almost exactly where you were headed before. A charming eccentricity becomes obnoxious, private habits go public, it gets a little harder to keep things to yourself. I've seen it begin with farting or belching, nose-picking, cursing, bragging, talking or laughing too much or not at all, a lean to the left or a lean to the right, too many adjectives, self-absorption, visions of grandeur, arrogance, dogmatism, indecision or its opposite. In one patient the first symptom his tumor produced was an inability to admit mistakes. Another qualified everything he said. "It's only one man's opinion, but it seems to me that . . ." There's nothing the brain can't use when it turns against you. Why should we be surprised that when it goes askew it proceeds at first along familiar routes, taking the line of least resistance, like water flowing down a mountain or an artist painting portraits of his friends?

At that time, I was operating on a young woman named Lucinda Roosevelt. She was conscious on the table, maybe that had something to do with it. It was only five years that I'd been doing this particular operation, and even though I was good at it—one of the best, to be frank about it—I'd never quite got used to it. When a patient is unconscious, his brain, as far as neurosurgeons are concerned, is flesh and nothing more. We build drapes around the incision so as not to see his face, avoid every thought of emotion, personality, etc. The reason is obvious: it's almost impossible to work with tissue if you grant it powers beyond itself. With conscious patients, patients like Lucinda, there's no way to hide from those powers, no way to deny that the cells you're invading are fundamentally the same as those that guide the invasion. Circularity, we call it, excessive reflection within the brain about the brain itself. You find yourself thinking that the tissue you're looking at is looking back at you. Nothing is more dangerous in a neurosurgeon, and as I see it, something in my brain found it, circularity, I mean, irresistible. In fact, ever since I'd begun performing this operation, I'd had the fantasy of performing it on myself, watching it all with mirrors, forcing my brain, in other words, to process images of itself. I don't agree with those who believe that fantasies of this sort, or circular thought in general, caused my disintegration (it's much more likely, in my opinion, that they were caused by it), but the fact that my neurology tended in this direction cannot be denied. The sad part is that my brain was never so quiet and focused, so convinced of its own omnipotence as when engaged in speculation concerning, for example, the source within itself of the speculation in which it was engaged.

Lucinda was epileptic, her seizures so frequent and violent and uncontrollable that we had no alternative but surgery. She had to remain conscious because in seizure surgery the brain was mapped— using low-voltage electrical probes—and this required that she report on her responses. Only local anesthetic was administered. Her skull and scalp were deadened to counteract the pain of craniotomy, her brain (itself devoid of sensation) left free of all medication so as not to distort her perceptions. The idea was to locate the tissue that caused her seizures, defining its function so that we could excise it and cure her seizures. We had a rough idea of the target tissue, but before we could take it out we had to be precise about it, making sure not to take

too much, and to convince ourselves that she could live without it—
that we wouldn't leave her mute or paralyzed or with some other dysfunction ranking higher on the scale of neurological catastrophe than
epileptic seizures.

Twenty-four years old, Lucinda was an undersized (pituitary dysfunction) black woman whose brain had betrayed her on every level.
Besides the seizures, her pituitary problem, and a retardation that had
left her with the intellect of an eight-year-old, she was also what we call
an "idiot savant." Articles had been written about her not only in scientific journals but also in the popular press. Only recently, in fact, she
had appeared on a television special devoted to those with her condition, demonstrating the useless memory skills that allowed her to recall
quantities of text or lengthy mathematical equations or almost any
other form of linear information ingested by her brain. She didn't
understand what she was reading, but given a minute to study a page of
printed matter, she could recite it years later, backward or forward.
Filled with useless information, her memory prevented her learning
such tasks as dressing herself or finding her way about the house, but
from what we could see, her incapacities—like her seizures—did not
disturb her. Despite her dysfunctions, she was gentle and charming
and not without a sense of humor. Almost everyone on our staff, myself
included, had grown more fond of her than we generally liked to do
with patients. I'd even found myself stopping to see her when I wasn't
making rounds. I enjoyed her memory tricks and her malapropisms as
if they were signs of intelligence and wisdom. Was this an early sign of
my condition? I think so. I can't say that my problems began with
Lucinda, but it seems to me that what I felt for her was a sign that my
brain—long before its grosser symptoms made their appearance—had
lost its capacity to limit its curiosity and keep me apart from that which
aroused it. What could be more dangerous, for a man in my profession,
than a breakdown of those particular neurological faculties that separate us from what we're supposed to study?

Diagnostic tests had determined that Lucinda's seizures originated
in an area near the center of her Left Hemisphere. She had been posi-
tioned on her right side so as to turn her left side upward for surgical
access. Her head rested on a thin black leather cushion and a system of
clamps secured it, gripping it front and back with small foam-covered

plates that my assistant, Eli Stone, had tightened with a pair of pliers. Altogether it took me nearly three hours to prepare her for mapping. The craniotomy was a large one, requiring an opening in her scalp and skull—what we called a "flap"—that stretched from the crown of her head backward toward her hairline, then forward on a line just above her ear to a point two centimeters in front of the ear, then upward on a slight diagonal to the crown of the head again. When I'd completed the superficial craniotomy and cut through and clamped apart the four layers of muscle and tissue that cover the brain, I placed my forceps on the instrument stand and with a quick sweep of my hand removed the drapes that had separated me from her face. Suddenly, Lucinda's left eye and ear and the left-hand corner of her mouth were visible below the opening I had carved in her skull. It was unclear whether she was smiling or whether the left side of her mouth had been drawn on an upward slant by the trauma to which she had just been subjected. Then too the disease that produced her seizures was located in cells not too far removed from those that controlled her mouth and cheeks. An inappropriate smile was one of her most common symptoms. "Hello, Sarah," I said. "Remember me?"

Lucinda's answer—a broader smile—made it clear that her first had not been inappropriate. Then again, even if it had been inappropriate, it would have remained, in all likelihood, an accurate indication of her mood. As I've noted, her condition was such that her spirits never sank. Along with the largest part of her intelligence, her pathology had eliminated, as far as we could discern, all sense of future time from the repertoire of her neurological functions. With no capacity for expectation she had none for fear or dread, and, except for moments of physical pain, no ostensible dissatisfaction with any circumstance in which she found herself.

Standing on my left, Eli nudged me with his elbow. "'Lucinda,'" he whispered. "Name's 'Lucinda,' boss."

"Of course, it's 'Lucinda.' Why are you telling me that?"

"You called her 'Sarah.'"

"'Sarah'?" I could not deny that the name rang a bell. And once the bell was rung, others rang as well. That's the miracle of the brain. No bells ring alone. All at once the act of calling her "Sarah," unconscious until that moment, was everywhere I looked, a memory so clear I could not pretend I had invented it. What astonished me, however, was not my mistake but the fact that, as far as I was concerned, I had *chosen* it. The act of calling her "Sarah" had been anything but involuntary. This is why I say that this first symptom, the first, I mean, of my visible symptoms, was unremarkable to me. In fact, if anything was remarkable, it was the fact that the symptom did not disturb me. Knowing full well that "Lucinda" was her name, I had decided, with all my wits intact, to call her "Sarah"! The mistake was no mistake! This is not to say that it was normal but that *choice* was the symptom, not language. In other words, my problem was not in the cells that had *produced* "Sarah" but in those that had *made them do so*. What we often forget about brain damage is that it affects intention as well as behavior, wish as well as fulfillment. Sometimes it makes you do what you don't want to do, but just as often it makes you want to do what you shouldn't. Both conditions are grave, of course, but the odd thing that I discovered then was how much better a man can feel if he can locate his problem in the second category rather than the first. With all my experience, I certainly knew that dysfunctions of will are no less serious than dysfunctions of language, but once I concluded that I had chosen "Sarah," my mistake became not only insignificant but just slightly, though I was far from ready to admit it, exhilarating.

During seizure surgery we used no respirator, so there was much less noise than during other procedures. The ceilings in the operating room were high and the walls of course very thick, so at times the room felt like a church or perhaps a spaceship, anything but ordinary time and space. When things were really quiet, the silence had a pulse that pounded like a drum. Except for that pounding, the only sound came from the instrument stand above the table, where a nurse named Ruth was rearranging the tools in preparation for stimulation. Overhead, the drumlights shown like the sun on a hazy summer day. I did not answer Eli. Not because I did not want to but because I'd forgotten what he'd asked. Instead I requested an instrument called a "rongeur" and made small adjustments at the edge of the flap, then adjusted the headlight strapped on my head, then turned my back to the table and studied Lucinda's X rays, which were mounted on a light-box on the wall. Not one of these actions was necessary. My brain, like an army in retreat, was seeking positions where it could regroup. But signs of dysfunction proliferated. Twice in succession, I forgot what I was thinking about, and several disconnected phrases—"It seems to me," for example, and "Unless I'm mistaken," and (a happy sound) "No doubt about it!"— passed through my mind for no apparent reason. More disturbing, the urge to laugh aloud was often upon me, and I had begun to notice within myself feelings of exaltation. To see one's brain become dysfunctional is one thing, but to exult in that dysfunction is another. Only once or twice in my career had I seen patients who suffered from this syndrome—a need to celebrate their own disease, a belief that brain damage is a happy condition—but of all the nightmares the brain can produce, none is worse, and none—God, how well I knew this—is more difficult to treat. No physician can help a patient who rejoices in his disease. Even if you could locate, through the magic of brain mapping, the cells that produce this type of distortion, what right have you to excise them when the patient himself does not desire it?

Sarah's vital signs were excellent. On the opposite wall an oscilloscope tracked her pulse and blood pressure, and electroencephalographic leads, taped to her skull, provided a constant display of her brain wave pattern, which would be used to track epileptic activity, when and if it arose. Leaning close, I palpated her brain with a fingertip to get a rough sense of her intracranial pressure. For all her symptoms, it looked like any other brain. Oyster-gray with streaks of red and black, marked like a map by the lines of its convolutions, its surface rose and fell with her pulse like gently boiling water. An ordinary brain, as I say, but I stared at it as if I'd never seen one before. Naturally, the fact that it startled me so was startling in itself. Was it possible that the pathology I'd noticed earlier was focused in the cells now engaged in processing this image? No one had to remind me that if the Optic Lobe lacks access to visual memory it is sometimes incapable of distinguishing between the familiar and the unfamiliar. Of course, such problems can be caused by memory alone, even if the Optic Lobes are perfectly normal. Whatever the reason, I could not avoid the suspicion that my memory was impaired in some way, so much so that all the other brains on which I'd operated were no longer available to remind me, by comparison, that Lucinda's was not extraordinary. Had I lost the habit that in the past had ordered my perceptions? Was I about to enter, like so many of my patients, a world devoid of history? A life in which everything encountered would astonish me? If so, why did I continue to feel exuberance and exhilaration? Had amnesia caused me to forget the horror of such conditions, or had it caused me to invent such horror when in fact it did not exist?

Far from distracting me, such questions passed me by before I could pursue them. One of the pleasures of brain damage is the way in which it interrupts the normative relationship between questions and answers, the freedom it grants one to ask questions without concern for answers, or to delight in answers for which no question is apparent. Disconnection of this sort, which I was only now beginning to discover, was of course the reason for my exhilaration, which—I know now—was all the more intense because I could not understand it. Nothing exemplifies neurological bondage like the need for answers or the anxiety that follows questions that do not produce them, and it was this bondage which, without realizing it, I was beginning to escape. The way in which my exhilaration increased when I could not answer the question, "Why am I exhilarated?"—that alone should have alerted me to the severity of my condition, but of course, if it had, my exhilaration might have diminished for the very reason it had increased. The resilience of the brain is never so apparent as in its ability to produce, from unanswered questions, answers to larger ones, and in this manner, to transform a position of weakness into one of even greater strength. Only reasoning as confused as that on which this paragraph is based will guard against such transformation and prevent the brain from accomplishing the miracle for which it is justly famous, snatching victory from the jaws of defeat or, more precisely, illusions of clarity from illusions of incoherence.

I covered the flap with a towel and declared a short break before stimulation began. Orange juice was brought on a plastic tray, the straws extending from each cup bent so as to fit behind our operating masks, and we put some country music (Merle Hagard and Hank Williams) on the sterilized tape deck we kept in the instrument case. Except for the fact that voices were muted and nothing but eyes visible on our faces, our conversation might have taken place in the cafeteria.

We spoke about a new Chinese restaurant that had opened near the hospital and a recent Swiss conference called "Neurology and Religion" where Eli, who was something of an authority on the subject, had delivered a paper called "Brain Wave Patterns in Experienced Meditators." He was a reasonable man, a first-rate neurosurgeon, and a good researcher, but when it came to this sort of thing he was a bit excessive, to my mind, the kind of surgeon who liked to explain religious epiphany as neurochemical pathology. As far as he was concerned, people like Jesus and Buddha and Mohammed were neurological freaks whose inspiration had been produced by abnormal brain metabolism. He'd once published a paper, called "Brain Damage in Literature," which investigated the "symptoms" of characters like Ahab, Don Quixote, Molloy, and of course all the heroes of Faulkner and Dostoevsky. Fortunately, his greatest obsession wasn't neurology but food, so we barely skirted the conference before returning to the Chinese restaurant. Both Eli and the anesthetist, an old friend of mine named Harry Marks, had eaten there recently, and a ridiculous argument developed between them as to whether the place was worthy of their patronage.

Remembering that all of this was audible to Sarah, I was suddenly embarrassed and not a little angry. Leaning forward, I addressed her in a whisper. Only after I had begun did I realize I had no idea what I meant to say. The words and phrases circulating earlier had assumed a higher volume and a dogged continuity. In effect, they were full-fledged voices now, the sort of thing my patients had told me about for years. They were beginning to nag me, interrupting my thoughts on the one hand, masquerading as them on the other. They were concrete sounds, muted but clearly external, like conversations on which I was eavesdropping. Sometimes they were coherent and sometimes not, sometimes impersonal and sometimes—as in the case of my father's voice, and my wife's—completely recognizable.

"No doubt about it!" I whispered.

"What?" said Sarah.

Clara Finch, the supervising nurse, came to my rescue. "What about you, Sarah? Do you like Chinese food?"

"What's Chinese food?"

"It's real spicy, with everything chopped up and covered with sauces."

Sarah though it over for a minute. "I don't like nothing chopped up. I likes my food in little pieces."

"What Sarah likes," said Clara, "is Milky Ways. Isn't that right, sweetheart?"

A dreamy expression appeared on Sarah's face. "Oh, Lord, yeah. Sometime a Snickers, but them Milky Ways—"

"What about Three Musketeers?" Eli said.

"I don't know no Three Musketeers."

"Baby Ruth?"

Sarah groaned. "Baby Ruth! I hate Baby Ruths!"

"Too bad for you," said Eli, who was deadly serious about his food. "Three Musketeers, in my opinion, is the only great candy bar made in America. I'm not talking about Swiss chocolate, mind you, but—"

Harry interrupted him. "Tell you what, Lucinda. You decide for yourself. Later, in the Recovery Room, I'll get you one from the machine."

"One what?"

"Three Musketeers."

"I told you—I likes Milky Way."

"You got it, sweetheart. To hell with Three Musketeers."

"She knows all the ingredients in Milky Ways," Clara said. "Isn't that right, Lucinda?"

"What's 'ingredients'?"

"What it's made of. What you read on the wrapper. Tell them what's on the Milky Way wrapper."

"Oh, that." Lucinda's eye—the one visible to us—rose in its socket until all but a tiny portion of the pupil had disappeared beneath the lid. Pausing as if to collect herself, she cleared her throat and licked her lips, and then, speaking in a monotone that sounded almost exactly like a computer, gave us what we had to believe was every word that could be found on the wrapper of a Milky Way. I don't remember all of it but I do recall, "Milk chocolate, corn syrup, sugar, milk, and partially hydrogenated vegetable oil," as well as the address of the company: "M&M Mars division of Mars, Inc., Hackettstown, New Jersey, 07840, U.S.A." Tell me, please, if it's more astonishing that her brain retained such information then than that mine should retain it now. Tell me how the brain decides what to offer us and what to withhold. Can any neurologist explain why I know the phone number of my high school girlfriend? The entire pitching staff of the 1977 New York Yankees?

"Hydrogenated vegetable oil"! "07840"! Who can measure the malice of an organ that generates such distraction? By what irony or fate did a few misdirected neurons determine that Lucinda, who could not remember her own mother's name, should remember "Hackettstown, New Jersey"?

I finished my orange juice and removed the towel that covered the flap. My moods and thoughts were shifting fast, almost equally divided between excitement and fear. One moment I felt disorganized, bereft; the next intrigued with these very sensations. The voices continued, my mother's especially, but they remained fragmentary and for the most part incomprehensible. Visible again, Lucinda's brain astonished me more than ever. The idea that the flesh at which I was gazing contained all the information on a Milky Way wrapper was alternately wondrous, infuriating, and a matter of indifference to me. In any case, my feelings for Sarah were very intense. Waves of affection, sadness, pity, and even, to my astonishment, envy. Yes, at moments it seemed she could teach me everything I needed to know, that she alone could protect me from the symptoms my brain had in store for me.

Father couldn't believe it. "What are you talking about? After all these years of treating brain-damaged patients, how can you be so romantic about the disease?" Naturally, I was embarassed. Twenty-one years a neurosurgeon, acting like a first-year medical student. Then Mother reminded Father how often tumors, aneurysms, epilepsy, etc., reveal themselves precisely in such romanticism, and my embarassment disappeared. Why? Because calling yourself romantic is a lot more upsetting than calling your brain romantic. Because it's easier to think of one's romanticism as a symptom than as a form of lazy thought or insufficient understanding. After all, a weakness of mind is embarassing, but a weakness of brain is simply a matter of fate. Even if it frightened me, it had no effect on my conscience.

"How's the EEG?" I said.

"Normal fluctuation," Harry said.

"Pressure?"

"One hundred over sixty."

"Okay, then, let's get on with it." I lifted my hand toward the instrument stand. "Stimulator, please."

While I adjusted the electrode, Eli inserted the jack that linked it to the generator. We used a bipolar electrode, two platinum wires two millimeters apart, passed through a glass tube that served as a holder. The generator was a foot-controlled device that produced rectangular pulses .2 to .5 milliseconds in duration, one to five volts in strength. Nerve cells are good electrical conduits. Stimulation activates not only the cell touched by the electrode but also other cells along the same path, eventually reaching the end of that path to produce whatever behavior that particular circuit controls.

Mapping began, as usual, in the motor region, at the rear of the flap, just about the center of Lucinda's head. Even more than in other forms of neurosurgery, I had to keep my hand steady, so we used a bracing device, a sort of tripod that steadied my wrist. When a particular charge produced a particular response, a small label or ticket, as it was called, was placed in her brain at the point where the charge had been produced. We used different colors for different functions—white for motor behavior, blue for language, and orange for psychic affect. The logistics looked simple, but they required a great deal of cooperation among the staff. The labels, kept in sterilized containers on the instrument stand, were gripped with tiny forceps and passed by Ruth to Eli, who then placed them beneath the tip of the electrode, at the point that I'd just stimulated. Clara kept the operation's log, entering the ticket number and its corresponding behavior on the charts. Since that behavior was not always easy to define, it was often left for me to decide how to enter it on the chart, dictating aloud to Clara, as when the first ticket was installed: "White ticket number one: right thumb tremor."

The cells that controlled somatic function were situated, as I say, more or less in the center of the brain, describing a vertical line above Lucinda's ear. In this area, located at the rear of the flap, stimulations continued to produce unequivocal responses that could be transferred to the chart with almost no elaboration. Ascending from ticket #1, we developed movement and/or sensation in the index, then the middle, then the ring finger, etc. Tickets #6 through #11 produced tremors in the hand; #12, #13, and #14 in the wrist, elbow, and shoulder; #15 through #19 the hip, knee, ankle, and toes. Number 17 caused a jerk in the right leg, #19 a tickling sensation on the inside of the right calf. Moving down from the point that had caused the thumb response, sensations were above the shoulders. Number 20 was in the neck, #21 the chin, #22 through #25 the cheeks and nostrils. Number 26 produced a twitch in the right eyebrow, #27 a fluttering of the right eyelid, and finally, #29 produced the same "inappropriate" smile we had seen so often on the ward.

I placed the electrode on the instrument stand, stepped back from the table, and sang several bars of a song that had long been one of my favorites: "Oh Susannah!" Given the fact that I was known to be a bit eccentric, and that as chief of the department I was given wide berth in general with respect to my behavior, this did not elicit any comment from the staff. My pitch was too high and my voice too loud to be considered, as we say, "appropriate," but though eyes turned, no one except Mother said a word, and she came to my defense.

"One hums or whistles to himself. What's wrong with singing?"

But I knew my voice had an independence it wasn't meant to have. As far as I could see, nothing in what I took to be my will, nothing of what I called "myself," had initiated this behavior. At this realization, a heady sense, very near to intoxication, came upon me. I felt as if I were embarking on a journey for which all my life had been a preparation. Even as I warned myself against such absurd conclusions (reminding myself, as always, of patients who had presented similar delusions), I told myself that nothing before now had mattered, that nothing from now on would not.

Moving away from the Motor Region, we entered language tissue. We knew this because, at tickets #1 and #2, Lucinda's speech was slurred. We used blue tickets now, and photographs to test identification. At labels #3, #4, and #5, we showed Lucinda, respectively, pictures of a woman, a tree, and an airplane, all of which she identified correctly. At label #5 she called a house "a horse," and at #6, a shoe produced an inarticulate stammer: "Sha-sho-sha-shapper." Stimulations #7–#10 left her mute, with no response to the photographs, but at each of them, once the electrode was removed, she said, "I had it right, but I couldn't get it out." Sometimes we went back to a previous stimulation, and while the electrode was activated, asked her to count for us. At labels #1–#5, she did fine, but at #6–#9 she had difficulty pronouncing numbers ("three" was "throw," "six" "sags," etc.), and #10 through #14 produced a confusion of counting itself ("One, two, seven, nine, four . . .").

With motor and language-area sufficiently demarcated, and with no sign yet of epileptic activity, I knew that the pathological tissue for which we were searching would be found where we had expected, below a large convolution, the so-called Fissure of Sylvius, in an area we called the "Interpretive Cortex." We used orange tickets there. Because cells in this area were not always, like those above them, specifically allied to function, the first five stimulations produced no dysfunction at all. The first "psychical" response occurred at orange ticket #7: "Oh, there's Mama!" Lucinda cried. "She comin' up the hill with the baby in her arms. Looka there! Uncle Jimmie behind her, and—"

She stopped because I had deactivated the electrode, thus interrupting the process through which the memory had been produced. Her voice was available of course, and words as well, but we knew from previous patients how quickly and completely such memories could be deleted from consciousness. Sometimes patients remembered what they'd seen even as they reported that they could no longer see it, and sometimes, as in Sarah's case, the electrode's removal produced an almost perfect void. I placed the electrode in the same spot and activated it again with the foot switch. Once again Lucinda saw her mother coming up the hill. The memory progressed from past to future like a film clip. She had a projector in her brain, no doubt about it, and I was turning it on and off with my foot. At label #9 she found herself at the dinner table with her younger brother, and at labels #10–#13, the electrode produced sensations she described as "spinning," "floating," or "flying."

For the first time, Harry Marks, watching the readouts from the electroencephalogram, noted that abnormal electrical activity in her brain was continuing after the electrode was deactivated. This first indication that the target area had been reached was supported by the fact that most of Lucinda's seizures began with sensations—spinning, flying, etc.—of the sort I had just produced. "Auras," they're called. Seizures like those from which Lucinda suffered—so-called Psychomotor Seizures—could announce themselves with fear or anger, a distorted sense of time, changes in colors, dizziness, ringing in the ears, noxious odors, giddiness, a feeling of insects crawling on one's skin, or any of a hundred other sensations. An aura can be nothing more than a vague sense that something is wrong. Your home seems unfamiliar, or you feel at home in a stranger's house. No one understood the mechanism that initiated seizures, but there were as many triggers as auras: light flickering at a particular frequency, sound of a certain pitch, frustrating thought, painful memories, atmospheric conditions, emotions high or low, etc. Seizures could be hereditary, too, or caused by fevers or infections or birth injury or tumors or abscesses. But sometimes—we called this "Ideopathic Epilepsy"—they appeared for no reason at all.

What we did know, as a result of our surgical experience, was that stimulation of any brain could induce seizures, and therefore, that any brain could become epileptic if subjected to the right sort of irritation. That is to say, there is no brain so strong that certain cells within it cannot be induced to fire when they're not supposed to.

For the previous four months, Lucinda's seizures had lasted approximately ninety seconds and had occurred between ten and fifteen times a day. We couldn't be sure that all of them originated from a single source, but we had no doubt that a good deal of her problem emanated from the tissue we were stimulating now. Sometimes you can see signs of pathology around an epileptic focus—discoloration, for example, or a scar—but in Lucinda's case there was no visible difference between this tissue and that which surrounded it. Realizing that a seizure could come at any moment, I altered my pattern of stimulation, circling the region I thought most volatile. We didn't want our patients having seizures on the table, but we had to produce their auras to identify the tissue to be removed. I wanted a circle of labels if I could get it, a clear pattern to define the peripheries of the epileptic region. Ten of the next twelve stimulations produced after-discharge on the electroencephalogram, and eight of them produced auras such as dizziness and nausea and once—#9—a burst of laughter and the feeling she called "flying." Stimulation at tickets #15 and #16 produced not only the dizziness but also darting movements in the eyes, a dilation of the pupils, and slight tremors in the right hand. Number 17 and #20 caused her to laugh aloud and exclaim, in a happy, childlike voice: "That's it, Mama!" When the next stimulation, at #21, produced a convulsive tremor in the right leg, I placed the electrode on the instrument stand. "Okay," I said. "I think we've got enough. Suction, please."

The suction device was electrically powered, a thin transparent tube that operated like a vacuum cleaner. Over the years we had perfected its use so that we could control how much tissue it would draw. Naturally, in operations such as this, we wanted a minimal draw, one that would take no tissue beyond a depth of .05 millimeters and allow me to control the radius of excision by altering the suction tube's angle relative to the surface of the brain. I held it just off the perpendicular, about eighty degrees, then slowly cleared the area—some two millimeters in diameter—that lay within the circle of orange labels. Tissue and blood snaked quickly up the tube and flesh at the point of suction moved as if a wind had blown across its surface.

Crucial though it was, excision was the easiest part of this sort of operation. Five minutes after the last orange label had been placed, I returned the suction device to the instrument stand, disconnected my headlight, removed my gloves, offered my thanks to the staff, and, leaving Eli to close the flap, headed for the door. I said good-bye to Sarah, of course, but while her eyes flickered with obvious comprehension, she made no sound in reply. That did not surprise me. Even when language cells had not been removed, this sort of surgery often produced temporary muteness. Not only did swelling develop in the area adjacent to that excised, but also the routes and circuits of brain cell connections were subjected to interruptions by the trauma of surgery in general. Something like short circuits in an electrical system. I felt ninety percent sure that she'd be speaking again within forty-eight hours, and I estimated her chances of being seizure-free at somewhere between thirty and forty percent. Thinking back on it now, in fact, to the degree that thinking back is possible for me, or believable, I'd say that her prognosis then was not too much worse than my own.

ROBERT SHECKLEY

Warm

ANDERS lay on his bed, fully dressed except for his shoes and black bow tie, contemplating, with a certain uneasiness, the evening before him. In twenty minutes he would pick up Judy at her apartment, and that was the uneasy part of it.

He had realized, only seconds ago, that he was in love with her.

Well, he'd tell her. The evening would be memorable. He would propose, there would be kisses, and the seal of acceptance would, figuratively speaking, be stamped across his forehead.

Not too pleasant an outlook, he decided. It really would be much more comfortable not to be in love. What had done it? A look, a touch, a thought? It didn't take much, he knew, and stretched his arms for a thorough yawn.

"Help me!" a voice said.

His muscles spasmed, cutting off the yawn in mid-moment. He sat upright on the bed, then grinned and lay back again.

"You must help me!" the voice insisted.

Anders sat up, reached for a polished shoe, and fitted it on, giving his full attention to the tying of the laces.

"Can you hear me?" the voice asked. "You can, can't you?"

That did it. "Yes, I can hear you," Anders said, still in a high good humor. "Don't tell me you're my guilty subconscious, attacking me for a childhood trauma I never bothered to resolve. I suppose you want me to join a monastery."

"I don't know what you're talking about," the voice said. "I'm no one's subconscious. I'm *me*. Will you help me?"

Anders believed in voices as much as anyone; that is, he didn't believe in them at all, until he heard them. Swiftly he catalogued the possibilities. Schizophrenia was the best answer, of course, and one in which his colleagues would concur. But Anders had a lamentable confidence in his own sanity. In which case—

"Who are you?" he asked.

"I don't know," the voice answered.

Anders realized that the voice was speaking within his own mind. Very suspicious.

"You don't know who you are," Anders stated. "Very well. *Where* are you?"

"I don't know that, either." The voice paused, and went on. "Look, I know how ridiculous this must sound. Believe me, I'm in some sort of limbo. I don't know how I got here or who I am, but I want desperately to get out. Will you help me?"

Still fighting the idea of a voice speaking within his head, Anders knew that his next decision was vital. He had to accept—or reject—his own sanity.

He accepted it.

"All right," Anders said, lacing the other shoe. "I'll grant that you're a person in trouble, and that you're in some sort of telepathic contact with me. Is there anything else you can tell me?"

"I'm afraid not," the voice said, with infinite sadness. "You'll have to find out for yourself."

"Can you contact anyone else?"

"No."

"Then how can you talk with me?"

"I don't know."

Anders walked to his bureau mirror and adjusted his black bow tie, whistling softly under his breath. Having just discovered that he was in love, he wasn't going to let a little thing like a voice in his mind disturb him.

"I really don't see how I can be of any help," Anders said, brushing a bit of lint from his pocket. "You don't know where you are, and there don't seem to be any distinguishing landmarks. How am I to find you?" He turned and looked around the room to see if he had forgotten anything.

"I'll know when you're close," the voice said. "You were warm just then."

"Just then?" All he had done was look around the room. He did so again, turning his head slowly. Then it happened.

The room, from one angle, looked different. It was suddenly a mixture of muddled colors, instead of the carefully blended pastel shades he had selected. The lines of wall, floor, and ceiling were strangely off proportion, zigzag, unrelated.

Then everything went back to normal.

"You were *very* warm," the voice said.

Anders resisted the urge to scratch his head, for fear of disarranging his carefully combed hair. What he had seen wasn't so strange. Everyone sees one or two things in his life that make him doubt his normalcy, doubt his sanity, doubt his very existence. For a moment the orderly Universe is disarranged and the fabric of belief is ripped.

But the moment passes.

Anders remembered once, as a boy, awakening in his room in the middle of the night. How strange everything had looked! Chairs, table, all out of proportion, swollen in the dark. The ceiling pressing down, as in a dream.

But that also had passed.

"Well, old man," he said, "if I get warm again, tell me."

"I will," the voice in his head whispered. "I'm sure you'll find me."

"I'm glad you're so sure," Anders said gaily, and switched off the lights and left.

Lovely and smiling, Judy greeted him at the door. Looking at her, Anders sensed her knowledge of the moment. Had she felt the change in him, or predicted it? Or was love making him grin like an idiot?

"Would you like a before-party drink?" she asked.

He nodded, and she led him across the room, to the improbable green and yellow couch. Sitting down, Anders decided he would tell her when she came back with the drink. No use in putting off the fatal moment. A lemming in love, he told himself.

"You're getting warm again," the voice said.

He had almost forgotten his invisible friend. Or fiend, as the case could well be. What would Judy say if she knew he was hearing voices? Little things like that, he reminded himself, often break up the best of romances.

"Here," she said, handing him a drink.

Still smiling, he noticed. The Number Two smile—to a prospective suitor, provocative and understanding. It had been preceded, in their relationship, by the Number One nice-girl smile, the don't-misunderstand-me smile, to be worn on all occasions, until the correct words have been mumbled.

"That's right," the voice said. "It's in how you look at things."

Look at what? Anders glanced at Judy, annoyed at his thoughts. If he was going to play the lover, let him play it. Even through the astigmatic haze of love, he was able to appreciate her blue-gray eyes, her fine skin (if one overlooked a tiny blemish on the left temple), her lips, slightly reshaped by lipstick.

"How did your classes go today?" she asked.

Well, of course she'd ask that, Anders thought. Love is marking time.

"All right," he said. "Teaching psychology to young apes—"

"Oh, come now!"

"Warmer," the voice said.

What's the matter with me? Anders wondered. She really is a lovely girl. The gestalt that is Judy, a pattern of thoughts, expressions, movements, making up the girl I—

I what?

Love?

Anders shifted his long body uncertainly on the couch. He didn't quite understand how this train of thought had begun. It annoyed him. The analytical young instructor was better off in the classroom. Couldn't science wait until 9:10 in the morning?

"I was thinking about you today," Judy said, and Anders knew that she had sensed the change in his mood.

"Do you see?" the voice asked him. "You're getting much better at it."

"I don't see anything," Anders thought, but the voice was right. It was as though he had a clear line of inspection into Judy's mind. Her feelings were nakedly apparent to him, as meaningless as his room had been in that flash of undistorted thought.

"I really was thinking about you," she repeated.

"Now look," the voice said.

Anders, watching the expressions on Judy's face, felt the strangeness descend on him. He was back in the nightmare perception of that moment in his room. This time it was as though he were watching a machine in a laboratory. The object of this operation was the evocation and preservation of a particular mood. The machine goes through a searching process, invoking trains of ideas to achieve the desired end.

"Oh, were you?" he asked, amazed at his new perspective.

"Yes . . . I wondered what you were doing at noon," the reactive machine opposite him on the couch said, expanding its shapely chest slightly.

"Good," the voice said, commending him for his perception.

"Dreaming of you, of course," he said to the flesh-clad skeleton behind the total gestalt Judy. The flesh machine rearranged its limbs, widened its mouth to denote pleasure. The mechanism searched through a complex of fears, hopes, worries, through half remembrances of analogous situations, analogous solutions.

And this was what he loved. Anders saw too clearly and hated himself for seeing. Through his new nightmare perception, the absurdity of the entire room struck him.

"Were you really?" the articulating skeleton asked him.

"You're coming closer," the voice whispered.

To what? The personality? There was no such thing. There was no true cohesion, no depth, nothing except a web of surface reactions, stretched across automatic visceral movements.

He was coming closer to the truth.

"Sure," he said sourly.

The machine stirred, searching for a response.

Anders felt a quick tremor of fear at the sheer alien quality of his viewpoint. His sense of formalism had been sloughed off, his agreed-upon reactions bypassed. What would be revealed next?

He was seeing clearly, he realized, as perhaps no man had ever seen before. It was an oddly exhilarating thought.

But could he still return to normalcy?

"Can I get you a drink?" the reaction machine asked.

At that moment Anders was as thoroughly out of love as a man could be. Viewing one's intended as a depersonalized, sexless piece of machinery is not especially conducive to love. But it is quite stimulating, intellectually.

Anders didn't want normalcy. A curtain was being raised and he wanted to see behind it. What was it some Russian scientists—Ouspensky, wasn't it—had said?

Think in other categories.

That was what he was doing, and would continue to do.

"Good-bye," he said suddenly.

The machine watched him, openmouthed, as he walked out the door. Delayed circuit reactions kept it silent until it heard the elevator door close.

"You were very warm in there," the voice within his head whispered once he was on the street. "But you still don't understand everything."

"Tell me, then," Anders said, marveling a little at his equanimity. In an hour he had bridged the gap to a completely different viewpoint, yet it seemed perfectly natural.

"I can't," the voice said. "You must find it yourself."

"Well, let's see now," Anders began. He looked around at the masses of masonry, the convention of streets cutting through the architectural piles. "Human life," he said, "is a series of conventions. When you look at a girl, you're supposed to see—a pattern, not the underlying formlessness."

"That's true," the voice agreed, but with a shade of doubt.

"Basically, there is no form. Man produces gestalts and cuts form out of the plethora of nothingness. It's like looking at a set of lines and saying that they represent a figure. We look at a mass of material, extract it from the background, and say it's a man. But in truth, there is no such thing. There are only the humanizing features that we—myopically—attach to it. Matter is conjoined, a matter of viewpoint."

"You're not seeing it now," said the voice.

"Damn it," Anders said. He was certain that he was on the track of something big, perhaps something ultimate. "Everyone's had the experience. At some time in his life, everyone looks at a familiar object and can't make any sense out of it. Momentarily the gestalt fails, but the true moment of sight passes. The mind reverts to the superimposed pattern. Normalcy continues."

The voice was silent. Anders walked on, through the gestalt city.

"There's something else, isn't there?" Anders asked.

"Yes."

What could that be? he asked himself. Through clearing eyes, Anders looked at the formality he had called his world.

He wondered momentarily whether he would have come to this if the voice hadn't guided him. Yes, he decided after a few moments, it was inevitable.

But who was the voice? And what had he left out?

"Let's see what a party looks like now," he said to the voice.

The party was a masquerade; the guests were all wearing their faces. To Anders, their motives, individually and collectively, were painfully apparent. Then his vision began to clear further.

He saw that the people weren't truly individual. They were discontinuous lumps of flesh sharing a common vocabulary, yet not even truly discontinuous.

The lumps of flesh were a part of the decoration of the room and almost indistinguishable from it. They were one with the lights, which lent their tiny vision. They were joined to the sounds they made, a few feeble tones out of the great possibility of sound. They blended into the walls.

The kaleidoscopic view came so fast that Anders had trouble sorting his new impressions. He knew, now, that these people existed only as patterns, on the same basis as the sounds they made and the things they thought they saw.

Gestalts sifted out of the vast, unbearable real world.

"Where's Judy?" a discontinuous lump of flesh asked him. This particular lump possessed enough nervous mannerisms to convince the other lumps of his reality. He wore a loud tie as further evidence.

"She's sick," Anders said. The flesh quivered into an instant sympathy. Lines of formal mirth shifted to formal woe.

"Hope it isn't anything serious," the vocal flesh remarked.

"You're warmer," the voice said to Anders.

Anders looked at the object in front of him.

"She hasn't long to live," he stated.

The flesh quivered. Stomach and intestines contracted in sympathetic fear. Eyes distended, mouth quivered.

The loud tie remained the same.

"My God! You don't mean it!"

"What are you!" Anders asked quietly.

"What do you mean?" the indignant flesh attached to the tie demanded. Serene within its reality, it gaped at Anders. Its mouth twitched, undeniable proof that it was real and sufficient. "You're drunk," it sneered.

Anders laughed and left the party.

"There is still something you don't know," the voice said. "But you were hot! I could feel you near me."

"What are you?" Anders asked again.

"I don't know," the voice admitted. "I am a person. I am I. I am trapped."

"So are we all," Anders said. He walked on asphalt, surrounded by heaps of concrete, silicates, aluminum, and iron alloys. Shapeless, meaningless heaps that made up the gestalt city.

And then there were the imaginary lines of demarcation dividing city from city, the artificial boundaries of water and land.

All ridiculous.

"Give me a dime for some coffee, mister?" something asked, a thing indistinguishable from any other thing.

"Old Bishop Berkeley would give a nonexistent dime to your nonexistent presence," Anders said gaily.

"I'm really in a bad way," the voice whined, and Anders perceived that it was no more than a series of modulated vibrations.

"Yes! Go on!" the voice commanded.

"If you could spare me a quarter—" the vibrations said, with a deep pretense at meaning.

No, what was there behind the senseless patterns? Flesh, mass. What was that? All made up of atoms.

"I'm really hungry," the intricately arranged atoms muttered.

All atoms. Conjoined. There were no true separations between atom and atom. Flesh was stone, stone was light. Anders looked at the masses of atoms that were pretending to solidity, meaning, and reason.

"Can't you help me?" a clump of atoms asked. But the clump was identical with all the other atoms. Once you ignored the superimposed patterns, you could see the atoms were random, scattered.

"I don't believe in you," Anders said.

The pile of atoms was gone.

"Yes!" the voice cried. "Yes!"

"I don't believe in any of it," Anders said. After all, what was an atom?

"Go on!" the voice shouted. "You're hot! Go on!"

What was an atom? An empty space surrounded by an empty space. Absurd!

"Then it's all false!" Anders said. And he was alone under the stars.

"That's right!" the voice within his head screamed. "Nothing!"

But stars, Anders thought. How can one believe—

The stars disappeared. Anders was in a gray nothingness, a void. There was nothing around him except shapeless gray.

Where was the voice?

Gone.

Anders perceived the delusion behind the grayness, and then there was nothing at all.

Complete nothingness, and himself within it.

Where was he? What did it mean? Anders tried to add it up.

Impossible. *That* couldn't be true.

Again the score was tabulated, but Anders couldn't accept the total. In desperation, his overloaded mind erased the figures, eradicated the knowledge, erased itself.

"Where am I?"

In nothingness. Alone.

Trapped.

"Who am I?"

A voice.

The voice of Anders searched the nothingness, shouted, "Is there anyone here?"

No answer.

But there was someone. All directions were the same; yet, moving along one, he could make contact . . . with someone. The voice of Anders reached back to someone who could save him, perhaps.

"Save me," the voice said to Anders, who lay fully dressed on his bed, except for his shoes and black bow tie.

BRIAN FAWCETT

Soul Walker

I was sitting in one of the bars at La Guardia Airport, waiting for a flight and trying to dig my way out of the vague depression I experience whenever I travel. Two men in business suits talking at the next table weren't helping.

"Did you get those futures under control before you left the office?" the older of them asked the other. I'm not normally an eavesdropper, but his peculiar use of the word *future* instantly captured my attention.

Both men were dressed in Akron Design Center standard combat issue: suits gray to blue, eyes gray to blue, underwear no doubt the same. Both were carrying briefcases with copies of *In Search of Excellence* placed to display conspicuously when opened. I noted the older one's suit was slightly darker, and that his voice exuded seniority if not quite authority. Or maybe it's just that I didn't like the idea of him controlling futures *and* wielding authority.

The other man seemed slightly uncomfortable with his question. "I tied down wheat and hog bellies, Hal," he answered, using the man's name as if it were a prayer rug he'd only recently gained the use of. "I've got the energies in my briefcase. They're all unstable as hell, Hal, and I thought we could work them over during the flight and wire our moves from Denver. I brought the laptop with me, so we can plug in my modem from the teleport terminal."

Hal grimaced. "Can't you handle this by yourself?" There was a slight edge of irritation in his voice.

"Hal, I need your help on this one," the younger man whined. "I just don't have enough experience in this kind of volatile market."

Hal gazed at the younger man, coiling his body in the chair as if he were about to impart a great truth—or to rip into his inferior's jugular. "Experience no longer exists, my friend," he said. "There's only data now, and the daring to recognize when it becomes profitable information."

Hal closed his briefcase as he said it, flipped a dollar bill into the center of the table, and placed his empty whiskey glass over it. The conference was finished and *In Search of Excellence* had triumphed over civilization once more. Both men slid out from behind the table, tugged the lapels of their suits straight, and walked to the entrance. The younger man walked just behind Hal's shoulder. He still didn't have a name.

The nameless asshole is openly displaying military deference, I thought, as I watched them disappear into the terminal crowd. Disgusting. I was glad they were leaving my universe. Then I realized that it was *their* universe *I* was in. At least I could be grateful that they were leaving the small part of it I was temporarily occupying, and I didn't want to know where they were going. Straight to hell, for all I cared. But with a stopover in Denver to manipulate the future.

To tell the truth, I didn't want to know where any of the grinning assholes still sitting in the lounge were going, where they'd been or why, or what they were calling themselves. I didn't want to be there. I wanted to be at home, where I could think straight.

Travel scrambles my brain circuitry, air travel more than any other kind. There's probably no other kind of place on earth I dislike more than airports. They make me grumpier than I normally am, and I'm a reasonably grumpy person. I'd been traveling for weeks and right then I'd have given quite a lot to be nonconscious, and more if I could be at home. I certainly didn't want to talk to anyone.

I wasn't to get my wish. An elderly man entered the bar and stood near the entrance, scanning the scattered clientele. Almost without hesitation, he focused on me. Our eyes met briefly. I broke contact first, developing a sudden urge to determine the species of wood used in the bar decor. I regretted that choice instantly. The table in front of me was walnut-grain Formica, a one-eighth-inch veneer over sawdust board. The wall panels were also ersatz walnut, the kind they photograph onto chipboard.

Unpleasant-looking old futzer, I decided as I gave in and watched the elderly man make his unerring way to my table. Something had gone dry in that face long ago, giving it a severity that masked his exact age. He might have been anywhere from his late fifties to early seventies. He moved easily enough, but there was nothing in his body language and demeanor that indicated the kind of weathering that creates the oaky wisdom that sometimes comes with age. He looked as if he were petrified.

The briefcase he carried intensified my instinctive dislike. It was an expensive leather one, neutral color, narrow and soft-sheened. No laptop in that one. This guy was from senior management.

Despite myself I wondered what was inside it. Plans for an industrial takeover? Plans for the end of the world? A leather-bound copy of *In Search of Excellence*?

There was a more immediate question. Why was he coming to pick on me? As he closed in, the expression on his face betrayed a strange sort of neediness. Well, then, he couldn't be an executive. The briefcase would therefore be filled with pamphlets. Pyramid sales, or some course on executive building. Or worse—religious pamphlets. He had the look of a man bent on saving someone.

As he approached, I almost wished the Akron Design Center slimeoids hadn't left. I could have pointed to them—see, look! Those guys need your literature, not me.

I would have had my objections brushed aside. He was fixed on me like the Ancient Mariner on the Wedding Guest. Oh, Christ, I thought as he closed in.

"Christ can't help you," he said in a crisp accent with German undertones. "But perhaps I might."

I'd have rolled my eyes if there'd been anyone around to do it for. There wasn't, and anyway, it was too late. My elderly assailant was staring at me as if he could see through me. Maybe he could. He'd already read my mind.

"Airports are horrible places," he said.

"That's what I've been thinking," I said before I could stop myself.

"I'm aware of that," he said, his mouth sucking on his cosmic lemon again. "You're impressionable. That's why I chose you."

"Go away," I said feebly. "I don't want to be chosen."

"Well," he replied, fixing me with his cold stare, "you've been chosen. Stop sniveling and listen."

Maybe, I calculated, a show of aggression will get him to leave me alone.

He cut that thought off. "Don't try aggression," he said. "It won't get you anywhere. I'm here to help you, and there's no avoiding it."

"I don't need help. I'm just fine. Let me wait for my stupid plane in ignorance."

"Stupid ignorance."

"Pardon me?"

"You heard me," he said. "Planes aren't stupid. They aren't anything at all, one way or the other. They're machines. But you're stupid if you desire ignorance."

Well, I thought, at least he's not a born-again Christian. They love ignorance. It's their operational precondition. "I desire you to leave me alone," I mumbled. "That's what I desire."

"You're already far too alone. That's why I'm here."

This time I did roll my eyes. To hell with him. "Go away," I said. "Cease and desist. Let me bear the agony of travel unmolested by your wisdom."

"Exactly," he said.

"What?"

"Travel is agony."

"You came here to tell me that?" I asked, interested despite myself.

He lowered himself gingerly into the chair opposite me. With our eyes at the same level I felt slightly less uncomfortable, but I still wanted him to go away. "No," he said solemnly. "I came to tell you why."

"You came to tell me why travel is agony?" I said. "I know why. It's because weird people are always hitting on me. Weird people like you."

The old man was unperturbed. "That isn't why, you ass, and you know it."

I didn't know, and I told him so. Then I repeated my request that he leave me to my discomforts.

"It's actually rather simple," he said. "It has to do with the travel abilities of the human soul."

Shit, I thought. "You're a Rosicrucian, aren't you?"

"No. Please listen carefully. The reason why you feel disoriented when you travel is because your soul isn't traveling with you."

"I don't have a soul," I said. That didn't sound right, so I corrected myself—better to discuss theology than personality. "There's no evidence for the existence of the soul."

At first he seemed to go for it. "There's no material evidence for the existence of the soul, you mean. Not conventional evidence, anyway. Don't underestimate me. *I'm* not a stupid man. We're both familiar with the philosophical arguments about the existence of the soul. They all proceed deductively from the phenomenon of human consciousness and memory. My argument is of a quite different sort."

"Go on," I said, curiosity overwhelming my misgivings.

"Let me give you an example you'll be familiar with. Some of the native cultures on the Northwest Coast have a saying. It's this: 'When a man (or a woman) abandons his home ground, he loses his soul.' Now, admittedly, that sounds like a syndicalist slogan until you examine a few illustrations."

"I'm listening." I *was* listening, against my will.

"If a multinational corporation were to purchase a plot of land next to the one you're living on, and announced that it intended to excavate a huge pit on it, what would you do?"

"Depends on what my piece of property was worth to me. And on how much the developer was willing to give me to get out."

"Multinationals don't give anything away. And how is value assigned to what you're calling property?" He paused for a second, as if to let the alternate taxonomies he was proposing penetrate. "Let me rephrase my question slightly. Imagine that there are two people living next to the target land. One was born on the spot, and his ancestors have lived there for at least several generations. The other has lived there for less than two years. Which one would be more likely to fight the multinational, and which one would be more effective?"

Those weren't very hard questions. "The homer, naturally. In both cases. He'd have reasons to stay and fight, and he'd be more likely to persist when the going got tough."

"Well," he said, "that's what the human soul is, and where it resides.

It's a relationship between consciousness and material objects. It is a sensibility created by familiarity and loyalty to places and things. This might sound like a new kind of materialism, but it's really very old."

"Interesting," I said. "But what's this got to do with flying, or with hanging around airports?"

"Quite a lot. Think of airports as generators of homelessness. Or as repositories of physical and intellectual landscape alienation, petri dishes of delocalizing despair. Think of them as soul debris depots. The first signal is that airports are much the same across the world. They're a home for the professionally homeless. But they're more than that, because of the alienated energies constantly passing through them and the residual buildup of that energy. They've become capable of creating alienation—actively disturbing and even destroying souls."

"This is getting awfully far-fetched," I muttered.

"It's merely unconventional. I could explain the physics to you, but you're not a physicist. I'm explaining it in urban design terms and in anthropological terms, which are within your range of nominal expertise."

Right again, I thought, wondering if he was from the CIA. Too old, I decided. And too accurate. Far too weirdly accurate.

He went on. "The technology for creating antilocalist experiential structures has existed now for some years. The motivation researchers inside the major consumer corporations have been using it for decades without really recognizing what they've got. They understand, for instance, that there is a fundamental human need for familiarity and solidarity, and they've learned to manipulate its focus from landscapes and kinship or social loyalty structures to consumer stereotypes. They're like terrorists with a neutron bomb they can't explode, but recognize that the more they tinker with it the more radiation will be released."

"Can you give me a concrete example?"

"Well, the Disney facilities are the most extreme ones."

"I've never been to one," I said. "Never will, either."

"Millions have, and millions more are going to go. Disney launders history, reshaping and cartoonizing its events and characters, and it does it to the world we're in. It encourages people to experience history and geography without any physical risk or threat to their values. But what it's really doing is translating the diversity of life into values designed to be easily digestible. Fish become fish sticks. Chickens become chicken nuggets. And then you go off to your local malls, which offer product simplifications that retool your everyday needs while you're shopping for them. Haven't you ever wondered why you feel odd after an hour or two at a mall?"

"I've thought about it quite often," I admitted. "I decided it was a result of being in an environment composed entirely of things other people *want* me to want without ever addressing what I might *need*. But what does this have to do with airports, or my soul? You're losing me."

"Well, think about Disney, the malls, consumerism in general, as an alternative to the human soul. Because there's no physical frame of reference or consequence in any of them, a soul can't find sustenance. It simply withers away."

"Uh-huh. That I can see. But maybe that's the way things are going. Maybe it's a natural evolution of the species."

"Oh, an evolution, perhaps. But not a natural one. It's closer to a devolution, or a convolution. And you'll have a hard time arguing that it's in the interest of the species. It will reduce our frame of reference in every conceivable way, wipe out our companion species, and eventually supplant nature itself with artificial technological environments. It will constrict the genetic pool and deactivate four-fifths of our earned intelligence. That's hardly a positive evolution."

"Those don't seem to be risks we can confront directly. They're happening. No way to stop them."

"I believe such a judgment is premature. I'm suggesting only that the alterations and the risks should be understood. Or rather, that *you* understand them."

The waiter was standing beside the table. "Is this man bothering you, sir?" he asked, motioning at the old man.

"No," I said. "Bring me another beer, will you?"

"What brand would you like, sir?"

The old man cut in. "Bring us two glasses of soda water. That will be just fine."

The waiter glanced sharply at me for confirmation. "Okay," I said. "He's my uncle. I'll drink soda water if he says it's good for me."

"Don't be impertinent," the old man snapped. "Now. Let's get back to our discussion."

"Do you think we might get a little more specific?"

"Fine," he said. "The human soul has a very specific property that makes it hostile to airports and air travel."

"And what's that property?"

"It doesn't fly."

He stared at me coolly, as if expecting a negative response. Laughter, probably. I wasn't laughing. Instead, I was sorting through the logic of his previous statements. It was consistent.

"Are you speaking metaphorically, or are you making a declarative statement to the effect that a human soul is prohibited from boarding an aircraft?"

"I see no difference."

"Well, I'd be interested to know why it can't board aircraft. There's nothing in the IATA regulations about it. I've read them. And surely it isn't the lack of seats."

"The soul is not a voluntary adjunct to your body," he answered, ignoring my witticism. "And it isn't an automatic possession. It can be earned and nurtured, just as it can be lost through inattention or destroyed by misadventure. And it is not automatically inherited. Several hundred million people, mostly in the industrial states, no longer have souls."

The confusion I was experiencing must have become visible, because he shifted his operating gloss from metaphysics to digital technology.

"Try to think of your soul as a database that by its nature can't be teleported, and is only transportable at speeds that allow it to be physically experienced in transit—at walking speed, in other words. It's only accessible *within* its specialized dataframe."

"Oh," I said, shifting in my chair as the waiter slid the two soda waters onto the table and smiled at me expectantly. I dropped him a five and he disappeared without making change. "That makes sense, I suppose. So where is my soul right now?"

The old man frowned and began to stare at the back of his hand as if it were a television screen. After a moment's consideration, he looked up again. "You've been traveling for thirteen days?"

I nodded. "About that."

"Then your soul is somewhere between Berwick, Pennsylvania, and Stroudsburg, depending on whether it followed Interstate Eighty or walked from Cleveland as the crow flies."

He said it with such authority that I couldn't laugh. "It's following me?"

"Of course. It followed you from Akron to Cleveland, and when you flew east it followed you. What else would it do?"

"You said that the soul is landscape-derived. Why wouldn't it stay on home ground and wait for me to return?"

"You're indulging in personification. You're ascribing self-consciousness to something which exists as an element of human consciousness. The soul is the relationship between a neurally housed body of understanding and a physical environment. Once created, it can't survive without its body of understanding, so to speak. So it follows it, tries to locate it."

"All the way from Akron? That's about three hundred and seventy-five miles."

"Your soul is quite a fast walker," he said without a trace of irony. "It would walk all the way here, unless you underwent a personality change, or a loss of memory, or you died."

"Then it would die?"

"Not exactly. It would try to return to the locations and conditions of its creation."

"And do what?"

For the first time, the old man seemed slightly embarrassed. "It would, er, haunt. For a while. Nothing nasty, mind you. You may have noticed that places where people have lived a long time have a certain eerie coldness after they've gone."

I have, but I didn't say so. After my mother and grandmother moved from the boardinghouse—it was redeveloped—the old neighborhood had that quality. It was very spooky, actually.

"That's right," he said. "Almost a sense of betrayal. But those old places have always welcomed you back."

He was right. I've managed to visit the old places fairly regularly since I left, and it has always felt good, despite the destruction and the changes.

"That's because while you're there you've taken care to visit each important location," he interrupted. "Paying your respects to the memories, as it were. You may not recognize this, but your behavior there is highly ritualized. The places sense the kinship of your present soul and nourish the connection."

I was getting used to having him read my mind. "I usually fly to get there. That means my soul isn't with me when I arrive."

"Smell," he answered. "The locations smell you, because you're from there."

"So what happens when I leave here and go home? Does my soul see me flying over it and start walking back?"

"Well, it senses your passage rather than sees you. That's why you feel disoriented for several weeks after a long trip. Your soul isn't there. And that's why there's a strong sense of mental disturbance for a few hours when it actually arrives back."

"Sort of like reentry impact? It must be pissed off when it arrives. All that walking for nothing."

"Yes," he said. "Quite. And of course I needn't add that touring is not recreation for the human soul. Its ability to move at all is a recent one. Three hundred years ago human souls had no such capacity. But like any other aspect of consciousness, it evolves to meet new conditions. During the tribal migrations of prehistory, for instance, the migrants lived for generations without souls. That accounts in part for the extraordinary brutality of the migrations. Fifty miles from home and a man was a barbarian."

A tall, good-looking man about my age sidled up to the bar and dropped his overnight bag at his feet. There was something familiar about him, but I couldn't quite place it. He was dressed in blue jeans and a weathered brown leather jacket, and was flipping an American Express card between his thumb and forefinger. Then it came to me: this was an Akron Design Center Visigoth. He looked even more exhausted and disoriented than I'd been feeling, but somehow I couldn't feel sorry for him.

My companion noticed my distraction and followed my gaze. "You shouldn't feel sympathy. He's one of those that deliberately gave up his soul."

"Look," I said. "All day I've had this sense that I might at any moment go spinning off my axis. Does this have anything to do with the temporary separation from my soul?"

"Definitely," he answered, shifting back to the computer tech gloss. "Most of your physical and emotional interface nodes—the points that process incoming data—are unavailable to you because they're created and maintained by your soul. You're relying on ego and stored intellectual fuel to keep you balanced right now. That's why the longer you travel, the more likely you are to commit purely selfish acts, or to make decisions on a purely abstract basis. Or other kinds of stupid behaviors I needn't spell out for you. There's nothing mystical about any of this. It's coldly pragmatic."

"You're suggesting that the soul is an inherent containment technology that operates in typical fashion, right? And that there are possible strategies for nurturing the soul—mine or anyone else's?"

"Yes. It's very simple. Travel as little as you can, for one. And never travel for purposes of avoiding the kinds of issues the soul is intended to help you with."

"Huh?"

"One of the singularly evil practices consumerism supports is the practice of traveling to exotic destinations in order to avoid the reality of everyday living. Most people do that precisely at the point where they should begin to investigate the particularities around them. And those pleasure ghettos are the worst. Two weeks at Club Med will kill a weak human soul, or preempt an incipient one. That's a far greater danger than herpes, which is what most people who go to those places worry about."

"I think most of them already have herpes, actually."

That got the smallest trace of a smile, but not for long. "That's your joke. I have no precise data on that question. As a matter of fact," he said, finishing his soda water and getting to his feet, "I'm pretty well out of relevant information."

I half expected him to vanish. I even closed my eyes to see if he would. "It's been, er, a slice," I said.

"No, it hasn't," he said. "This is not a mystical experience. Everything I've told you can be secured by evidence. It's a question of accurate processing. I've merely offered you the metaphoric software."

"Whatever you say."

I closed my eyes again, feeling weary and disoriented. When I opened them, the Akron Design Center Visigoth at the bar was gone. In his place was the old man I'd been talking to, dressed in the Visigoth's clothes. He was flipping the AmEx card, looking around the bar for someone else to hit on.

I had a plane to catch. And trudging along in the cool evening somewhere in the middle of Pennsylvania, I had a soul to placate. Or, for the first time in my life, a soul to believe in.

L. J. DAVIS

Cowboys Don't Cry

WHEN Clark Kent awoke he was on an airplane, sitting bolt upright. There were a great many cigarette burns on his clothing, especially the lap. He was fearfully hung over and he had no idea what he was doing on the airplane or where it was taking him. There was an elderly lady in the seat next to him and he asked her, the words forming in his mouth like dry big lumps of dough.

"Stewardess," she said. She craned around in her seat and started shouting it down the aisle. "Stewardess! Stewardess!"

A stewardess appeared as though by magic, smiling a tight little smile, her eyes like two tiny pistols trained at the center of Kent's forehead. "Well," she said. "Awake again, I see. Wouldn't you like to come to the back of the plane and freshen up? Of course you would."

She took his arm and maneuvered him out into the aisle, deftly grabbing his ankle with her other hand and manipulating his leg like a handle to prevent him from stepping in the old lady's lap. "Right this way, sir," she ordered. "Just come with me."

"He woke up again," said the old lady to an old man, apparently no relation, who had turned around in the seat ahead.

"That's too bad," said the old man.

People looked up from their magazines in an unfriendly fashion as Kent was led past them, and the attention of small children was directed out the windows. He wondered what he'd done, since it was so obvious he'd done it. Something pretty bad, by the look of things. A burly middle-aged man got up from his seat and blocked the aisle. "Listen, young fellow," he said, shaking his finger, "we've had about enough out of you."

"It's all right, Mr. Parker," said the stewardess. "I'm taking him to the rear of the plane."

"Good place for him," said Mr. Parker, resuming his seat. "Call me if you need help."

Kent noticed that the stewardess was wearing a heavy, sweet perfume. It went into his nostrils and stayed there like a heavy gas, shutting out the arid, plastic odor of the plane and threatening to suffocate him in a very short time.

"You're wearing perfume," he observed, hoping to win her favor.

"Yes, you mentioned it before," she replied, her voice as hard and musical as a radio. They reached the back of the plane. It was blue and there were three doors in it, along with an alcove about the size of a tenement shower. The stewardess stopped him and turned him around, an awful smile-shaped grimace distorting her face. "You said I smelled like a French whorehouse."

"Janice?" said another stewardess, sticking her head out of the alcove. Kent could have sworn there was nobody in there a second ago. "Oh Jesus. Him again."

"He's going to behave himself now," said Janice between her teeth, her smile now a snarl. "Aren't you, Mister . . . ah, Kent?"

He could see that she didn't believe his name was real. Nobody did at first, but that wasn't any reason why they shouldn't like him. It happened all the time. He wondered if they were planning to put him in the alcove and work him over with their high-heeled shoes.

"Where are we going?" he asked.

"Into the bathroom," said Janice. "I warned you."

Her friend took his other arm, and they put him in one of the bathrooms and locked the door.

"I didn't mean that," he said. "I meant the plane."

"The son of a bitch," said Janice on the other side of the door. "I could just cry."

The bathroom was a tiny cold windy place, barely large enough to turn around in, and enameled blue like the door. Its principal feature was a tiny aluminum toilet that had not been entirely cleansed by the last flushing. Kent sat down on it and tried to take stock of his situation, feeling more outside the plane than in it. There was a kind of shelf stuck into the wall in front of him, apparently for the perusal of squatting passengers. He rifled it, searching for something to help his hang-over, but all he found were some envelopes filled with manufacturers' samples of cosmetics and aftershave powder. They didn't do much good. Further search revealed a little cabinet containing a dozen sani-tary napkins. He took one of them, wet it in the fold-out washbasin, and tied it around his brow. It didn't do him much good either, but he liked to think that he was trying.

Apparently he had either smoked or lost all his cigarettes, but as he was searching the pockets of his jacket he found a shot glass. He put it on the little shelf with the envelopes and stared at it while portions of his memory came flooding back. He was running away from home. While doing so he'd evidently gotten very drunk indeed. He could only remember getting partly drunk, yelling at his wife, and throwing the furniture around. Beyond that point all was darkness, nor could he remember what had made him so mad. He also wished he knew where he was going. It was very bewildering. His brain felt bad, as though someone were standing on it.

Before he could speculate further or start feeling better, the door opened a crack and a tall man in a gray suit slipped through, carefully locking it behind him. The place was so small that their knees bumped.

"You can't come in," Kent told him. "This stall is busy."

"I know," said the man, gazing down at him with a pair of piercing blue eyes. "I'm a Protestant minister."

Kent wondered if they were going to give him last rites and throw him from the plane. It was absurd to think so, but it was also absurd to be on the plane in the first place and even more absurd to be locked in the bathroom with a wet Kotex around his head and all the passengers hating him like anything. He wanted to be home in his bath. That was where he really belonged right now, apologizing to his wife through the door, up to his neck in nice warm water, his desire to live restored by the smell of oils and lotions instead of the possibility of imminent death. He imagined the plane touching down without him, and all its occupants lying to the officials about this freak accident they'd had over the Grand Canyon.

"Where are we going?" asked Kent, figuring he might as well try it again.

"Son," said the minister, "you're going straight to Hell."

Kent scarcely knew how to answer that. "I'm Catholic," he heard himself say.

"Catholics go to Hell too, son, it don't make no difference what the Pope says. And the surest, straightest road to Hell is in the bottle, and you've been taking it. Carrying on like that. A grown man. Well, I've come to try and turn you aside from that wicked path and set your feet aright."

Kent came close to laughing idiotically right at the man's fly, but the plane began to buck before he could get started, the tail section describing a swift arc, and instead of laughing Kent grabbed hold of the minister's thighs and held on for dear life, a cold sweat breaking out on his forehead. The minister misinterpreted this desperate gesture and gently placed his hand on top of Kent's head.

"Our Heavenly Father," he intoned, "accept the contrition of this despicable sinner, the least of Thy children, as, sodden with booze, his breath reeking like a sewer, his stomach awash with the foul broth of Bacchus—"

"Jesus Christ," muttered Kent, swallowing hard.

"Oh, sweet Jesus Christ!" boomed the minister. "Hear how he calls upon You even now, even now from the stinking sink of iniquity, and though encased in sin like a tight leather garment, even so he calls upon Thy mercy. I know You won't forget about him, Lord, any more than You went and forgot about that sheep. Heed, Lord . . ."

There was a great deal more in the same vein but Kent, though definitely interested, had stopped listening. The plane was switching every which way, especially up and down, and he was taking his breath in great gulps.

"My father was a drunkard," the minister was saying when Kent was able to attend to him again. Apparently he'd finished his prayer and had fallen into the cadence of a favorite sermon. "I WAS A DRUNKARD!" he roared without warning. "I *know* the perils of booze! Son . . ."

"You don't happen to have a cigarette?" asked Kent, gazing up at the minister's tanned, closely shaven face. It was the sort of face that looked as though it had never had any hair on it. It didn't even seem to have any pores. The minister met his eyes, then pressed his head back down and held it there firmly. "Tobacco?" he demanded. "Son, tobacco is the second horseman of the Devil. Look at your clothes."

With his head pressed down the way it was, it was hard to look at anything else. Sure enough, there were all those burns like so many tiny hot hoofprints. For a moment he was tempted to ask if the Devil's second horseman wore a tight leather garment too, but he decided to let it pass. He thought wistfully of Father Brogan, the parish priest of his childhood, who smoked, drank, swore, killed eight Germans at Bastogne and bragged about it, and died before he was sixty at a sanitarium for alcoholics.

"It's not too late," suggested the minister. "Son, open your heart to the Lord and let His light shine in."

"This is ridiculous," said Kent. He ducked his head and got it free. "Why don't you get out of here and leave me alone?"

The minister's face beamed broadly, but his eyes went hard and mean. Kent wondered why people had suddenly taken it into their minds to smile at him when they were angry.

"Tell me, son," said the minister, leering and bending low as though to puncture Kent's neck with his teeth, "what exactly is your name?"

Kent had wondered how long it was gong to take him to get around to it. "They told you about that, huh?" he said. "Okay, I'll come clean. My name is Clark Kent. Always has been and always will be."

The minister's smile continued to broaden until it looked as though he was trying to nibble both his earlobes at the same time. "Come on, son," he said warmly. "I'm a minister. I hear all sorts of things. You can tell me your name."

Kent looked into the minister's eyes and decided that if he really had been his son, it would have been too bad for him right now. He could see that the minister was definitely not a nice man and in the days when he'd been a drunkard he'd probably been a very ugly one indeed. "You can shove it, buddy," Kent told him. "I really mean it. God can shove it too."

The minister straightened as though goosed, with a look in which outrage was curiously mingled with something akin to terror. Kent realized that he had never heard anybody suggest that God might shove it, not even in his drunkard's days, and he didn't know what to do with someone who had. "Stewardess!" he cried.

"See this thing I have around my head?" Kent asked. "It's a Kotex. What do you think of that?"

"Stewardess!"

"Dr. Brower?"

"Open the door. Let me out."

The door was opened a crack, and he slipped through it with remarkable agility for a man of his age. "You got a booby in there, miss," Kent heard him say. "A real basket case. The captain better radio ahead."

"My name really is Clark Kent," said Kent weakly, more to himself than to the world beyond the door. "Nobody ever believes it at first."

The rest of the trip passed without serious incident. Kent sat on his toilet, feeling funny doing it with his pants on but aware that he would feel even funnier if he took them off. The plane went up and down. Kent's stomach seemed to be suspended from a single fixed point in the air, and he spent most of his time trying to get back to it and stay there. He didn't succeed very well. Outside his door, halfhearted preparations for defense were made under the minister's direction. Mr. Parker and several other male passengers, all of them sounding about the age of Kent's father, came back with rolled-up newspapers and established a perimeter, but after about ten minutes, when Kent made no attempt to escape and it appeared that among Dr. Brower's sermons was a long one about card playing and Christian Manliness, they all drifted back to their seats. The plane landed shortly thereafter, the captain cautioning everyone to put out their cigarettes and fasten their seat belts. Kent, who had neither of these things in his bathroom, keenly felt the full measure of his exile from the affairs and hopes of normal men.

Nothing more was heard from Dr. Brower. The plane taxied to a halt and everyone got off. Kent wondered who would come to him next and what they would say. He almost felt as though they could say any damn thing they wanted, just so long as they would tell him where he was. The plane seemed remarkably silent and still, as though it had been landed some place where no noise was. Kent got up and tried the door, but it was still locked and he wondered if they had forgotten about him. He imagined the plane taking off with another crew and them finding him here and demanding his ticket.

Soon he heard footsteps and voices. They shook the fuselage and made it seem frail.

"Hello," he called.

"That's him," said one of the stewardesses.

"You in there," called a commanding male voice. "Open up."

"I can't. I'm locked in."

"I put him there," said the stewardess proudly. "He woke up and I put him in there and locked the door."

"He pinched my fanny black-and-blue," said the other stewardess, entering the conversation for the first time. "I just looked in the mirror in the ladies' room."

Although the spectacle her words brought to mind was an intriguing one, Kent was certain he was not responsible for it. He never pinched girls; men like Dr. Brower did. He was being framed, but before he could tell them so, the door was flung open and he found himself confronted by the entire crew. They were dressed in dark, trim uniforms and looked very stern. Kent suddenly felt odd, sitting there on the toilet in his pants, and he stood up hurriedly.

"Take that thing off your head," ordered the captain.

Kent took it off. He wanted to please the captain. "Where are we?" he asked.

The captain seemed to find in this question some kind of snide imputation of his flying ability. "Don't get wise with me, kid," he said. "You're in big trouble."

"Big trouble, Superman," put in the co-pilot, a skinny little man who was obviously the captain's cat's-paw. Kent immediately disliked him in a big way.

"I'm not a kid," he told the captain. "I'm twenty-eight years old."

The captain took out a little book and wrote this down. "Okay," he said grimly, "now tell us your real name."

"My real name," said Kent, remembering all the countless times he'd been held down and tortured by the big kids, all the oafish strangers at parties, all the dead looks in people's eyes, all the deliveries he had failed to receive, everyone demanding his name, his real name. "My real name," he repeated, "is Clark Kent. If you like, I will spell it for you, but it's really pretty simple."

"Give me your wallet," ordered the captain, indicating by his expression that he was prepared to take it by force.

"The wallet," said the co-pilot.

Kent handed it over, wondering if the co-pilot hadn't gone a little crazy from all those years of repeating the names of switches.

The captain returned Kent's wallet, his face stony, towers of rage and foolishness building in his eyes.

"What does it say, Ed?" asked one of the stewardesses. "Ed?"

"Take his picture."

The co-pilot whipped out a little Japanese camera and rapidly took Kent's picture several times.

"What's that for?" asked Kent.

"For our files," said the captain. "This picture and your name will be posted at our ticket desks all over this country and abroad. You aren't allowed to fly on Allied Airlines again."

"Don't be absurd."

"If you call for a reservation, they will tell you all the flights are booked."

"It's the shit list, Superman," said the co-pilot happily.

"Swell," said Kent. "Now can I go?"

"I think you'd better apologize to these girls first."

"Will you take me off the shit list if I do?"

"I think," said the captain quietly, "that you'd better apologize to these girls no matter what."

"Okay, I'm sorry. I'm sorry, I'm sorry."

"That wasn't nice enough," said the captain.

Kent gnashed his teeth but concealed his feelings. Not only were there more of them than there were of him, but the captain was a strong-looking man, especially in the hands.

"From the bottom of my heart," he said. "I apologize for my shameful conduct and beg your pardon."

"That okay with you girls?" asked the captain.

The girls slowly agreed that it was, while Kent mentally rehearsed postures of obsequious humility that would have shamed a Japanese Arab. He suddenly had to go to the bathroom as only a man with a hangover can, and the irony of having been locked up in one for an hour was not lost on him.

"All right," said the captain, a little grudgingly. "You can go."

They parted to let him pass and Kent put his head down and hurried toward the exit, trying not to look too swift or eager.

"Shazam!" yelled the co-pilot suddenly. Kent halted in his tracks and whirled around. This was something he knew how to handle. This was a time when he was in the right.

"Superman doesn't say Shazam," he raved. "Captain Marvel does that. Superman takes off his clothes. Like this!" With a manic cackle he gave his zipper a quick run up and down its track and bolted out the door before they could catch him.

WALKER PERCY

The Second Coming

1

IT was no trouble handling him until he came to and looked at her.
She could do anything if nobody watched her. But the moment a pair
of eyes focused on her, she was a beetle stuck on a pin, arms and legs
beating the air. There was no purchase. It was an impalement and a
derailment.

So it had been in school. Alone at her desk she could do anything,
solve any problem, answer any question. But let the teacher look over
her shoulder or, horror of horrors, stand her up before the class: she
shriveled and curled up like paper under a burning glass.

The lieder of Franz Schubert she knew by heart, backwards and for-
wards, as well as Franz ever knew them. But when four hundred pairs
of eyes focused on her, they bored a hole in her forehead and sucked
out the words.

When he landed on the floor of her greenhouse, knocking himself
out, he was a problem to be solved, like moving the stove. Problems are
for solving. Alone. After the first shock of the crash, which caught her
on hands and knees cleaning the floor, her only thought had been to
make some sense of it, of him, a man lying on her floor smeared head
to toe with a whitish grease like a channel swimmer. As her mind cast
about for who or what he might be—new kind of runner? masquerader
from country club party? Halloween trick-or-treater?—she realized she
did not yet know the world well enough to know what to be scared of.
Maybe the man falling into her house was one of the things that happened, albeit rarely, like a wood duck flying down the chimney.

But wait. Was he a stranger? Strange as he was, smeared with clay and bent double, there was something about the set of his shoulders, a vulnerability in their strength, that struck in her a sweet smiling pang. She recognized him. No, in a way she knew who he was before she saw him. The dog recognized him. It was the dog, a true creature of the world, who knew when to be affrighted and enraged, e.g., when a man falls on him, who therefore had attacked as before and as before had as quickly stopped and spat out the hand, the furious growl winding down to a little whine of apology. Again the dog was embarrassed.

Perhaps she ought to be an engineer or a nurse of comatose patients. For, from the moment of her gazing down at him, it was only a matter of figuring out how to do what needed to be done, of calculating weights and angles and points of leverage. Since he had crashed through one potting table, the problem was to get him up on the other one. But first make sure he wasn't dead or badly hurt. It seemed he was neither, though he was covered with bumps and scrapes and blood and clay. He smelled of a freshly dug ditch. A grave. Again her mind cast about. Had he been digging a well for her in secret, knowing her dislike of help? But how does one fall from a well? Perhaps he had found a water supply on the ridge above.

She tried to pick him up. Though she was strong and had grown stronger with her heavy work in the greenhouse and though he was thin, he was heavy. He was slippery. His long slack muscles were like straps on iron. When she lifted part of his body, the rest clove to the earth as if it had taken root. Now sitting propped against the wall, the dog's anvil head on her thigh, she considered. The block-and-tackle she figured gave her the strength of three men. Better than three men. Three men would have demoralized her. Her double and triple pulleys conferred mastery of energy gains and mechanical advantages. With pulleys and ropes and time to plan, one could move anything. Now that she thought of it, why couldn't anyone do anything he or she wished, given the tools and the time? It was hard to understand why scientists had not long ago solved the problems of the world. Were they, the scientists, serious? How could one not solve any problem, once you put your mind to it, had forty years, and people didn't bother you? Problems were for solving. Perhaps they the scientists were *not* serious. For if people solved the problems of cancer and war, what would they do then? Who could she ask about this? She made a note to look it up in the library.

She got him up by first rolling him onto a door from the ruin, then, using a single double-gain pulley, hoisted one end of the door enough to slide the creeper under it, then rolled him to her bunk, devised a rope sling for the door, a two-strand hammock, hoisted the door by two double-blocks hooked to the metal frame of the gambrel angle in the roof where the vents opened. The trick was to pull the ropes to both systems, then when the pulleys had come together take both ropes in one hand and stack bricks under the door with the other and start over. When the door was a little higher than the cleared bunk, she eased him over door and all, hoisted one end of the door, the head end, high enough to put three bricks under it so water would run off when she gave him a bath.

The only real trouble was getting his clothes off. Pulleys were no use. Man is pitiful without a tool. It took all her sweating gasping strength to tug the slippery khaki over his hips and to roll him over far enough to yank one elbow clear of a sleeve. Why not cut his clothes off? Then dress him in what? She considered his underwear shorts. She wouldn't have minded him naked but perhaps, later, he would. She covered him with her sleeping bag while she drew two pots of water, one for him, one for his clothes, the clothes first so they would have time to dry in the sun. No, the sun would take too long. Instead, she hung the shirt and pants on the nickel towel rack of the great stove. Quel pleasure, putting her stove to such good use!

It took all afternoon. She didn't mind bathing a man. How nice people are, unconscious! They do not glance. Yes, she should be a nurse of comatose patients. Again it was a matter of calculating weights and angles and hefts. The peculiar recalcitrant slack weight of the human body required its own physics. Heaving him over to get at his back, a battleground of cuts and scrapes and caked blood and bruises, she wondered: what had he done, fallen off a mountain? His face! With its week's growth of beard, a heavy streaked yellow-and-white stubble, and the lump above his jawbone, he looked like a covite with a wad of chewing tobacco. But only when she finished did she stop to gaze down at him. No, not a redneck. Except for the golfer's tan of his face and arms, his skin was white, with a faint bluish cast. The abdomen dropping away hollow under his ribs, the thin arms and legs with their heavy slack straps of muscle, cold as clay, reminded her of some paintings of the body of Christ taken down from the crucifix, the white flesh gone blue with death. The closed eyes sunk in their sockets and bluish shadow. The cheekbones thrust out like knees. He had lost weight. While his beard grew he had not eaten.

Exhausted, she cooked a supper of oatmeal and made a salad of brook lettuce and small tart apples from the ruined orchard and hickory nuts. Her back felt looks. She turned around. The dog and the man were watching her, the dog with his anvil head between his paws, the man with his cheek resting on his elbow. The looks did not dart or pierce or impale. They did not control her. They were shyer than she and gave way before her, like the light touch of a child's hand in the dark. The man looked one way, the dog the other, as if she were not there. Was she there?

The man could not sit up to eat. She fed him. He ate heartily but his eyes, like the dog's, only met hers briefly and went away as he chewed. She put hot oatmeal in the dog's dry meal from the fifty-pound sack, which she had packed from town by tying it like a blanket roll in the lower flap of the Italian NATO knapsack. Her strength surprised her. She could hoist anything.

2

IT wasn't bad taking care of him. To tell the truth, before he landed in the greenhouse, she had begun to slip a little. It surprised her. She liked her new life. Physically she was healthy and strong. The hard work of cleaning the greenhouse and moving the stove made her hungry and tired. She ate heartily and slept like a log. She gained weight. When she caught sight of herself in the shop windows of Linwood, she did not at first recognize the tan towheaded long-haired youth loping along.

But looks became more impaling. Some people, most Southern people, guard their looks as if they knew what she knew about looks: that they are not like other things. The world is full of two kinds of things, looks and everything else. Some people do not guard their looks. A woman met her eye in an aisle of the supermarket and looked too long. The look made a tunnel. The shelves of cans seemed to curve around the look like the walls of a tunnel. She knew she was not crazy because a can fell off.

Some people use their looks to impale. Once, as she walked down the street, her thighs felt a look. She turned around. A dark stout man perhaps from Florida (most visitors were from Florida), perhaps a Cuban, perhaps South American, was not only looking at her buttocks but had bunched his fingers under his chin and was shaking them and making a sucking noise, not a whistle, through his pursed lips.

Time became separated into good times and bad times. The nights and mornings were good times.

Then along comes late afternoon—four o'clock? five o'clock? she didn't know because she had no clock and lived by forest time—but a time which she thought of as yellow spent time because if time is to be filled or spent by working, sleeping, eating, what do you do when you finish and there is time left over? The forest becomes still. The singing and clomping of the hikers, the cries of the golfers, the sweet little sock of the Spalding Pro Flites and Dunlop Maxflys, the sociable hum of the electric carts die away and before the cicadas tune up there is nothing but the fluting of the wood thrush as the yellow sunlight goes level between the spokes of the pines. By now the golfers, sweaty and hearty, are in the locker room tinkling ice in glasses of Tanqueray, and Diz Dean briquets are lighting up all over Linwood. Forest time turned back into clock time with time going out ahead of her in a straight line as a measure of her doing something, but she was not doing anything and therefore clock time became a waiting and a length which she thought of as a longens. Only in late afternoon did she miss people.

She said to the dog: This time of day is a longens.

The dog turned his anvil head first one way then the other. What? In this longitude longens ensues in a longing if not an unbelonging. What? said the dog.

One way to escape the longens of clock time marching out into the future ahead of her was to curl away from it, going round and down into her dog-star Sirius serious self so there she was curled up under, not on, the potting table. The dog did not like her there. He whined a little and gave her a poke with his muzzle. Okay okay. She got up. No, it wasn't so bad and not bad at all when it got dark and clock time was rounded off by night. She lit a candle and the soft yellow light made a room in the dark and time went singing along with cicada music and not even the screech owl was sad except that just at dusk there rose in her throat not quite panic but something rising nevertheless. She swallowed it, all but the aftertaste of wondering: tomorrow will it be worse, even a curse?

But in the dark: turn a flowerpot upside down and put the candle on it to read by, the dog now waiting for her signal, which is opening the book, hops up he not she spiraling round and down but always ending with his big anvil head aimed at her, eyes open, tiny flame upside down in each pupil, watching her until she starts reading her book: then down comes his head on her knee heavy as iron. She read from *The Trail of the Lonesome Pine*:

Hand in hand, Hale and June followed the footsteps of spring from the time June met him at the school-house gate for their first walk in the woods. Hale pointed to some boys playing marbles.

"That's the first sign," he said, and with quick understanding June smiled.

Sign of what? Spring?

3

ONE morning she woke and could not quite remember what she was doing in the greenhouse. But she remembered she had written a note to herself in her notebook for just such an occasion. The note read:

The reason you are living here is to take possession of your property and to make a life for yourself. How to live from one moment to the next: Clean the place up. Decide on a profession. Work at it. What about people? Men? Do you want (1) to live with another person? (2) a man? (3) a woman? (4) no one? (5) Do you want to make love with another person? (6) "Fall in love"? (7) What is "falling in love"? (8) Is it part of making love or different? (9) Do you wish to marry?

(10) None of these? (11) Are people necessary? Without people there are no tunneling looks. Brooks don't look and dogs look away. But late afternoon needs another person.

What do I do if people are the problem? Can I live happily in a world without people? What if four o'clock comes and I need a person? What do you do if you can't stand people yet need a person?

For some reason when she read this note to herself, she thought of an expression she had not heard since grade school: "Doing it." Was "doing it" the secret of life? Is this a secret everyone knows but no one talks about?

She "did it" at Nassau with Sarge, the Balfour jewelry salesman, thinking that it might be the secret of life. But even though she and Sarge did everything in the picture book Sarge had, it did not seem to be the secret of life. Had she missed something?

On the days she walked to town she found herself sitting on the bench near the Happy Hiker. One day the marathon runner saw her and sat down on the bench beside her. Again he shook hands with his fibrous monkey hand. Again he asked her to crash with him in the shelter on Sourwood Mountain. Again she said no. Again he loped away, white stripes scissoring.

Another afternoon a hiker asked for a drink of water at the greenhouse. Unshouldering his scarlet backpack, he sat beside her on the floor of the little porch. Though he was young and fair as a mountain youth, his face was dusky and drawn with weariness. When he moved, his heavy clothes were as silent as his skin. He smelled, she imagined, like a soldier, of sweat and leather gear. They were sitting, knees propped up. His arm lay across his knee, the hand suspended above her knees. She looked at the hand. Tendons crossed the boxy wrist, making ridges and swales. A rope of vein ran along the placket of muscle in the web of the thumb. Copper-colored hair turning gold at the tip sprouted from the clear brown skin. The weight of the big slack hand flexed the wrist, causing the tendon to raise the forefinger like Adam's hand touching God's.

As she watched, the hand fell off his knee and fell between her knees. She looked at him quickly to see if he had dozed off but he had not. The hand was rubbing her thigh. She frowned: I don't like this but perhaps I should. Embarrassed for him, she cleared her throat and rose quickly, but the hand tightened on her thigh and pulled her down. Mainly she was embarrassed for him. Oh, this is too bad. Is something wrong with me? The dog growled, his eyes turning red as a bull's. The man thanked her and left. He too seemed embarrassed.

Was there something she did not know and needed to be told? Perhaps it was a matter of "falling in love." She knew a great deal about pulleys and hoists but nothing about love. She went to the library to look up love as she had looked up the mechanical advantages of pulleys. Surely great writers and great lovers of the past had written things worth reading. Here were some of the things great writers had written:

> Love begets love
> Love conquers all things
> Love ends with hope
> Love is a flame to burn out human ills
> Love is all truth
> Love is truth and truth is beauty
> Love is blind
> Love is the best
> Love is heaven and heaven is love
> Love is love's reward

"Oh my God," she said aloud in the library and smacked her head. "What does all that *mean*? These people are crazier than I am!"

Nowhere could she find a clear explanation of the connection between "being in love" and "doing it." Was this something everybody knew and so went without saying? or was it a well-kept secret? or was it something no one knew? Was she the only Southern girl who didn't know? She began to suspect a conspiracy. They, teachers, books, parents, poets, philosophers, psychologists, either did not know what they were talking about, which seemed unlikely, or they were keeping a secret from her.

Was something wrong with her? What did she want? Was she supposed to want to "do it"? If she was supposed to, who was doing the supposing? Was it a matter of "falling in love"? With whom? a man? a woman? She tried to imagine a woman hiker's hand falling between her knees.

Naargh, she said.

The dog cocked an eyebrow. What?

Is one supposed to do such-and-so with another person in order to be happy? Must one have a plan for the pursuit of happiness? If so, is there a place where one looks up what one is supposed to do or is there perhaps an agency where one consults?

Who says?

Who is doing the supposing?

Why not live alone if it is people who bother me? Why not live in a world of books and brooks but no looks?

Going home one evening, she passed Hattie's Red Barn. Young folk were dancing and drinking and joking. Couples came and went to vans. Someone beckoned to her from the doorway. She did not belong with them. Why not? They were her age. They were making merry, weren't they? and she would like to make merry, wouldn't she? They were good sorts, weren't they? Yes, but not good enough.

You have to have a home to make merry even if you are away from home. She had a home but it was not yet registered. A registrar was needed to come and register her home in the presence of a third party, a witness. Upon the departure of the registrar the third party would look at her and say: Well, this is your home and here we are. She would make sassafras tea. Then they could make merry.

Perhaps she had not sunk deep enough into her Sirius self. If one sinks deep enough there is surely company waiting. Otherwise, if one does not have a home and has not sunk into self, and seeks company, the company is lonesome. Silence takes root, sprouts. Looks dart.

On the other hand, look what happens to home if one is too long at home. Rather than go home to Williamsport, she'd rather live in a stump hole even though her parents' home was not only registered with the National Registry but restored and written up in *Southern Living*. Rather than marry and have a life like her mother, she'd rather join the navy and see the world. Why is a home the best place and also the worst? How can the best place become the worst place? What is a home? A home is a place, any place, any building, where one sinks into one's self and finds company waiting. Company? Who's company? oneself? somebody else? That's the problem. The problem is not the house. People are the problem. But it was their problem. She could wait.

4

THE man watched her from the bunk but she didn't mind. His look was not controlling or impaling but soft and gray and going away. Her back felt his and the dog's eyes following her, but when she faced them, their eyes rolled up into their eyebrows.

The mornings grew cold. It was a pleasure to rise shivering from her own potting table bunk and kneel at the Grand Crown stove and start a fat-pine fire for its quick blazing warmth and busy crackle-and-pop which peopled the room. Outside, the great dark rhododendrons dripped and humped in close, still hiding croquet balls knocked "galley west" in 1890 tournaments. This dreary cold clime is not getting me down!

The first morning the man said: "You gave me a bath."

"Yes. And washed your clothes." She dropped the clothes on him. "You can put them on." She was stiff. She had slept with the dog on croker sacks. From the army surplus store she bought two scratchy Italian NATO blankets and made a bed of pine needles on a slatted flat, which she propped on four upended big pots.

They talked about the once cool-feeling now warm-feeling cave air blowing above them. He told her how Judge Kemp had saved the cost of kerosene for the greenhouse but think what you could save. Your overhead is zero. (It made her feel good that her *overhead* was not over head and pressing down on her but was nought, had gone away.) You could grow produce all winter and sell at one hundred percent profit. Grow what and sell where? she asked. I don't know, he said, but we can find out—is that what you want to do, make a living here? I don't know, she said.

One morning when she returned from her woods latrine, a comfortable fork in the chestnut fall, which she used and where she deposited his excretions from a Clorox bottle and a neatly folded packet of newspaper, she found him sitting in the doorway in the morning sun. His swellings had gone down except for the knee, the scrapes had dry scabs, and his eyes were all right, not the inturning Khe Sanh white eyes but gray and clear and focused on the dog. His scruffy yellow beard looked odd against his smooth platinum-and-brown hair. Was he nodding because he knew what he was going to do? He nodded toward the other doorjamb as if it were the chair across his desk. She took it, sat down.

"Now, you've done a great deal for me. I would thank you for it but won't, for fear of upsetting your balance sheet of debits and credits. I know you are particular about owing somebody something, but maybe you will learn that's not so bad. I don't mind being in your debt. You won't mind my saying that I would do the same for you, and take pleasure in it, and furthermore can easily see our positions reversed. What I wish to tell you is that I accept what you've done for me and that I have other things to ask of you. I don't mind asking you. There are things that need to be done and only you can do them. Will you?"

"I will," she said. I will, she thought, because now he knew exactly what had to be done just as she had known what to do when he lay knocked out on her floor. I'd do anything he asks me, she thought, hoist anything. Why is that?

"Do you have a calendar?" he asked.

She gave him her Gulf card.

He looked at it, looked up at her, smiled. (Smiled!) "Wrong year." She shrugged. She was afraid to ask what year it was.

"What is today?"

"The fifteenth."

"Hm. It seems I've been gone two weeks." His gray eyes met hers. She didn't mind. "How much money do you have?"

"One hundred and eleven dollars and thirty-one cents."

"What are you going to do when your money runs out?"

She shrugged. "Find employment."

"Doing what?"

"Hoisting maybe. Also gardening."

"Hoisting? Hoisting what?"

"Anything."

"I see. You wouldn't consider my paying you something, or lending, until you get paid for your . . . ah . . . hoisting."

"How much money do you have?" she asked.

"On me?"

"On you and off you."

"About fifty or sixty million."

"Gollee."

"That's enough to employ you."

"No, that would throw things off-balance and render my Sirius unserious."

"Why shouldn't I pay for my room and board?" he asked her.

"To give one reason if not others, you don't have a dime. I had to go through your pockets before washing your clothes."

He laughed then winced and put a hand to his side. "I can get some."

"When you do, there will be time for a consideration of remuneration. The only thing in your pockets was a slip of paper which said *Help! With tiger, fifty feet above*. I was wondering about the nature of the tiger you were over and above."

"It doesn't matter. Could you do the following things for me in town. Do you have pencil and paper?"

She opened her notebook.

"Go to Western Union, which is at the bus station, and send the following telegram to Dr. Sutter Vaught, 2203 Los Flores, Albuquerque, New Mexico. Send this message: Plans changed. Forget about letter. Read it if you like but tear it up. Don't act on it. Will write. Barrett. Send it straight message."

"Straight message," she repeated, hoping he would explain but he didn't. Probably meant send it straight to Albuquerque and not roundabout by way of Chicago. "Is that all?"

"No. Go to Dr. Vance Battle's office. See him alone. Tell him I want to see him. Tell him where I am, tell him I want to see him today, and ask him not to tell anybody or bring anybody with him."

"Anything else?"

"Go by the library and get a book on hydroponic gardening."

"Okay."

"Then go behind the bus station and see if my car is still there. A silver Mercedes 450 SEL. My keys are under the seat. Drive it to the country club parking lot. Park at the far end, which is nearest to here."

"Okay." She swallowed. Very well. Drive a car? His car? Very well. If he asked her to drive the car, she could drive the car. "Okay. Why were you in the cave?"

"What? Oh." Now he was walking up and down the greenhouse not limping badly, shouldering, hands in pockets. Does he notice how clean and smooth the concrete is? She felt the floor with both hands; it was cool and iron-colored and silky as McWhorter's driveway. She wished he would notice her concrete, the best-cured concrete in North Carolina. "I go down in caves sometimes," she said. He told her about the tiger.

"But the tiger wasn't there."

"No."

"Then—?"

"Then there was more than the tiger?"

"Yes."

"You were trying to find out something besides the tiger."

"Yes."

"What?"

"I was asking a question to which I resolved to find a yes-or-no answer."

"Did you find the answer?"

"Yes."

"Which was it?"

"I don't know."

"So you came back up and out."

"Yes, I came back up and out."

"Is that good?"

"Good?" He shrugged. "I don't know. At least I know what I have to do. Don't worry."

"About what?"

"About money. I'll pay you back."

"I don't worry about money. Money worry is not instigating."

"No, it's not. You'd better go."

· · ·

She enjoyed her errands.

Straight to the bus station, where she found the silver Mercedes. Though she wanted to try the keys and practice starting the car, she decided not to. Someone might see her. She would do her errands, wait until dark, and drive to the country club.

Nobody saw her.

What pleasure, obeying instructions! Then is this what people in the world do? This is called "joining the work force." It is not a bad way to live. One gets a job. There is a task and a task teller (a person who tells you a task), a set of directions, instructions, perhaps a map, a carrying out of the task, a finishing of the task, a return to the task teller to report success, a thanking. A getting paid. An assignment of another task.

She clapped her hands for joy. What a discovery! To get a job, do it well, which is a pleasure, please the employer, which is also a pleasure, and get paid, which is yet another pleasure. What a happy life employees have! How happy it must make them to do their jobs well and please their employers! That was the secret! All this time she had made a mistake. She had thought (and her mother had expected) that she must do something extraordinary, be somebody extraordinary. Whereas the trick lay in leading the most ordinary life imaginable, get an ordinary job, in itself a joy in its very ordinariness, and *then* be as extraordinary or ordinary as one pleased. That was the secret.

On to Western Union, which was part of the Greyhound bus station. As she wrote the message she tried not to make sense of it. The telegram cost $7.89. When the clerk read the message, she said to him casually but with authority: "Straight message, please!"

"Right," said the clerk, not raising his eyes.

Victory! She had made it in the world! Not only could she make herself understood. People even understood what she said when she didn't.

It was a pleasure spending her money for him. Why? she wondered. Ordinarily she hoarded her pennies, ate dandelion-and-dock salad.

She sat on her bench but in a new way. The buildings and the stores were the same but more accessible. She might have business in them. Le Club was still there, its glass bricks sparkling in the sun. A cardboard sign in the window announced a concert by Le Hug, a rock group. What a pleasure to have a job! Smiling, she hugged herself and rocked in the sun. Imagine getting paid for a task by the task teller! Money wherewith to live! And live a life so, years, decades! So that was the system. Quel system!

A real townie she felt like now, bustling past slack-jawed hippies, moony-eyed tourists, blue-haired lady leafers, antiquers, and quilt collectors.

When she went into a building, the dog stayed on the sidewalk paying no attention to anyone until she came out. He showed his pleasure not by wagging his tail but by burying his heavy anvil head in her stomach until his eyes were covered.

There was no way to see Dr. Battle except to sign a clipboard and wait her turn as a patient. She had to wait two hours. She liked him, though he was too busy and groggy from overwork and thought she was a patient despite her telling him otherwise, sizing her up in a fond dazed rush, not listening, eyes straying over her, coming close (was he smelling her?). His hand absently palpated her shoulder, queried the bones, tested the ball joint for its fit and play. Unlike Dr. Duk he didn't bother to listen, or rather he listened not to your words but your music. He was like a vet, who doesn't have to listen to his patients. There were other ways of getting at you. He saw so many patients that it was possible for him to have a hunch about you, a good country hunch, the moment you walked in the door. Better still, it was possible for her to subside and see herself through his eyes, so canny and unheeding, sleepy and quick, were they.

Well then, how did she look to him? Is my shoulder human? He cocked an ear for her music. The fond eyes cast about to place her, then placed her. She was classifiable then. She was a piece of the world after all, a member of a class and recognizable as such. I belong here!

He looked at her boots. "You just off the trail?"

"Well no, though I've been walking quite a bit."

"And you're feeling a little spacy."

"A little what?"

"Spaced out."

"What's that?"

"Are you on something or coming off something?"

"What?"

He didn't seem impatient with her dumbness. "Okay," he said, counting off the questions on his fingers. "Are you taking a drug? Are you taking the pill? Are you coming off the pill? Are you pregnant?"

"No to one and all." How would he treat her madness? ignore it, palpate her shoulder and tell her to lead her life? Would she?

"Okay, what's the trouble, little lady?"

"I'm fine. What I was trying to tell you was—"

"You look healthy as a hawg to me."

"—was to give you a message from—" She wanted to say "from him." What to call *him*? Mr. Barrett? Mr. Will? Will Barrett? Bill Barrett? Williston Bibb Barrett? None of the names fit. A name would give him form once and for all. He would flow into its syllables and junctures and there take shape forever. She didn't want him named.

Sluggishly, like a boat righting itself in a heavy sea, Dr. Battle was coming round to her. He began to listen.

"From who?"

"Your friend Barrett," she mumbled. The surname was neutral, the way an Englishman speaks of other Englishmen.

"Who? Will Barrett? Will Barrett's out of town," he said as if he were answering her questions.

"Yes."

This time his eyes snapped open, *click.* "What about Will Barrett?"

"You are to come see him this afternoon when you finish here."

"What's the matter with him? Is that rascal sick?"

Rascal. The word had peculiar radiations but mainly fondness.

"No. That is, I think he is all right now. He is scratched up and bruised and his leg is hurt but he can walk. This is in confidence. He doesn't want anyone to know about this message." It was a pleasure to talk to another person about him.

"In confidence?" For a second the eye went cold and flashed like a beacon.

"I have not kidnapped him," she said.

He laughed. "All right. Where is he?"

"He is at my—" My what? "—place."

"Oh. So." He cocked his head and regarded her. It was possible for her to go around behind his eyes and see her and Will at her place.

"Well, I'll be dog. How about that? Okay. What's with Will? Has he got his tail in some kind of crack?"

She frowned and folded her arms. "He went down into Lost Cove cave, got lost, came back up, and fell into my place."

Though it was true, it sounded odd, even to her.

"Fell?" he said.

"That's what I said. Fell. Flat fell down into my place."

"He fell into your place from a cave," said the doctor.

"That's right."

The doctor nodded. "Okay." Then he shook his head. "He shouldn't be doing that."

"Doing what?"

"He doesn't take care of himself. With his brain lesion he won't—" His eyes opened. "All right. This is as good a chance as any to throw him down and look at him. Where is your place?"

"You know the old Kemp place?"

"Yes. Near there?"

"There. That's my place."

"There is nothing left there."

"A greenhouse is left."

"You live in the greenhouse?"

"Yes."

"Will is staying in your greenhouse?"

"Yes. He fell into the greenhouse from the cave."

"He fell into your greenhouse. From the cave. Okay."

It pleased her that Dr. Vance Battle did not seem to find it remarkable that the two of them, who? Will and who? Allie, Will and Allie, should be staying in the greenhouse. Only once did he cock his head and look at her along his cheekbone. Will and Allie? Williston and Allison? Willie and Allie?

"It is a matter in confidence," she said. In confidence? Of confidence? To be held in confidence? Her rehearsed language had run out. She didn't know where to put *of*s and *in*s. It was time to leave.

"Right. Tell that rascal I'll be out this afternoon. We'll throw him down and have a look at him."

Right, she repeated to herself as she left. I will tell that rascal.

JORGE LUIS BORGES

Funes, His Memory

I recall him (though I have no right to speak that sacred verb—only one man on earth did, and that man is dead) holding a dark passionflower in his hand, seeing it as it had never been seen, even had it been stared at from the first light of dawn till the last light of evening for an entire lifetime. I recall him—his taciturn face, its Indian features, its extraordinary *remoteness*—behind the cigarette. I recall (I think) the slender, leather braider's fingers. I recall near those hands a *mate* cup, with the coat of arms of the Banda Oriental. I recall, in the window of his house, a yellow straw blind with some vague painted lake scene. I clearly recall his voice—the slow, resentful, nasal voice of the toughs of those days, without the Italian sibilants one hears today. I saw him no more than three times, the last time in 1887 . . . I applaud the idea that all of us who had dealings with the man should write something about him; my testimony will perhaps be the briefest (and certainly the slightest) account in the volume that you are to publish, but it can hardly be the least impartial. Unfortunately I am Argentine, and so congenitally unable to produce the dithyramb that is the obligatory genre in Uruguay, especially when the subject is an Uruguayan. *Highbrow, dandy, city slicker*—Funes did not utter those insulting words, but I know with reasonable certainty that to him I represented those misfortunes. Pedro Leandro Ipuche has written that Funes was a precursor of the race of supermen—"a maverick and vernacular Zarathustra"—and I will not argue the point, but one must not forget that he was also a street tough from Fray Bentos, with certain incorrigible limitations.

My first recollection of Funes is quite clear. I see him one afternoon in March or February of '84. That year, my father had taken me to spend the summer in Fray Bentos. I was coming back from the ranch in San Francisco with my cousin Bernardo Haedo. We were riding along on our horses, singing merrily—and being on horseback was not the only reason for my cheerfulness. After a sultry day, a huge slate-colored storm, fanned by the south wind, had curtained the sky. The wind flailed the trees wildly, and I was filled with the fear (the hope) that we would be surprised in the open countryside by the elemental water. We ran a kind of race against the storm. We turned into the deep bed of a narrow street that ran between two brick sidewalks built high up off the ground. It had suddenly got dark; I heard quick, almost secret footsteps above me—I raised my eyes and saw a boy running along the narrow, broken sidewalk high above, as though running along the top of a narrow, broken wall. I recall the short, baggy trousers—like a gaucho's—that he wore, the straw-soled cotton slippers, the cigarette in the hard visage, all stark against the now limitless storm cloud. Unexpectedly, Bernardo shouted out to him—*What's the time, Ireneo?* Without consulting the sky, without a second's pause, the boy replied, *Four minutes till eight, young Bernardo Juan Francisco.* The voice was shrill and mocking.

I am so absentminded that I would never have given a second thought to the exchange I've just reported had my attention not been called to it by my cousin, who was prompted by a certain local pride and the desire to seem unfazed by the other boy's trinomial response.

He told me that the boy in the narrow street was one Ireneo Funes, and that he was known for certain eccentricities, among them shying away from people and always knowing what time it was, like a clock. He added that Ireneo was the son of a village ironing woman, María Clementina Funes, and that while some people said his father was a doctor in the salting house (an Englishman named O'Connor), others said he broke horses or drove oxcarts for a living over in the department of Salto. The boy lived with his mother, my cousin told me, around the corner from Villa Los Laureles.

In '85 and '86, we spent the summer in Montevideo; it was not until '87 that I returned to Fray Bentos. Naturally, I asked about everybody I knew, and finally about "chronometric Funes." I was told he'd been bucked off a half-broken horse on the ranch in San Francisco and had been left hopelessly crippled. I recall the sensation of unsettling magic that this news gave me: The only time I'd seen him, we'd been coming home on horseback from the ranch in San Francisco, and he had been walking along a high place. This new event, told by my cousin Bernardo, struck me as very much like a dream confected out of elements of the past. I was told that Funes never stirred from his cot, his eyes fixed on the fig tree behind the house or on a spiderweb. At dusk, he would let himself be carried to the window. He was such a proud young man that he pretended that his disastrous fall had actually been fortunate . . . Twice I saw him, on his cot behind the iron-barred window that crudely underscored his prisonerlike state—once lying motionless, with his eyes closed; the second time motionless as well, absorbed in the contemplation of a fragrant switch of artemisia.

It was not without some self-importance that about that same time I had embarked upon a systematic study of Latin. In my suitcase I had brought with me Lhomond's *De viris illustribus*, Quicherat's *Thesaurus*, Julius Caesar's commentaries, and an odd-numbered volume of Pliny's *Naturalis historia*—a work which exceeded (and still exceeds) my modest abilities as a Latinist. There are no secrets in a small town; Ireneo, in his house on the outskirts of the town, soon learned of the arrival of those outlandish books. He sent me a flowery, sententious letter, reminding me of our "lamentably ephemeral" meeting "on the seventh of February, 1884." He dwelt briefly, elegiacally, on the "glorious services" that my uncle, Gregorio Haedo, who had died that same year, "had rendered to his two motherlands in the valiant Battle of Ituzaingó," and then he begged that I lend him one of the books I had brought, along with a dictionary "for a full understanding of the text, since I must plead ignorance of Latin." He promised to return the books to me in good condition, and "straightway." The penmanship was perfect, the letters exceptionally well formed; the spelling was that recommended by Andrés Bello: *i* for *y*, *j* for *g*. At first, of course, I thought it was some sort of joke. My cousins assured me it was not, that this "was just . . . just Ireneo." I didn't know whether to attribute to brazen conceit, ignorance, or stupidity the idea that hard-won Latin needed no more teaching than a dictionary could give; in order to fully disabuse Funes, I sent him Quicherat's *Gradus ad Parnassum* and the Pliny.

On February 14, I received a telegram from Buenos Aires urging me to return home immediately; my father was "not at all well." God forgive me, but the prestige of being the recipient of an urgent telegram, the desire to communicate to all of Fray Bentos the contradiction between the negative form of the news and the absoluteness of the adverbial phrase, the temptation to dramatize my grief by feigning a virile stoicism—all this perhaps distracted me from any possibility of real pain. As I packed my bag, I realized that I didn't have the *Gradus ad Parnassum* and the first volume of Pliny. The *Saturn* was to sail the next morning; that evening, after dinner, I walked over to Funes' house. I was amazed that the evening was no less oppressive than the day had been.

At the honest little house, Funes' mother opened the door.

She told me that Ireneo was in the back room. I shouldn't be surprised if I found the room dark, she told me, since Ireneo often spent his off hours without lighting the candle. I walked across the tiled patio and down the little hallway farther on, and came to the second patio. There was a grapevine; the darkness seemed to me virtually total. Then suddenly I heard Ireneo's high, mocking voice. The voice was speaking Latin; with morbid pleasure, the voice emerging from the shadows was reciting a speech or a prayer on an incantation. The Roman syllables echoed in the patio of hard-packed earth; my trepidation made me think them incomprehensible, and endless; later, during the enormous conversation of that night, I learned they were the first paragraph of the twenty-fourth chapter of the seventh book of Pliny's *Naturalis historia*. The subject of that chapter is memory; the last words were *ut nihil non iisdem verbis redderetur auditum*.

Without the slightest change of voice, Ireneo told me to come in. He was lying on his cot, smoking. I don't think I saw his face until the sun came up the next morning; when I look back, I believe I recall the momentary glow of his cigarette. His room smelled vaguely musty. I sat down; I told him about my telegram and my father's illness.

I come now to the most difficult point in my story, a story whose only raison d'être (as my readers should be told from the outset) is that dialogue half a century ago. I will not attempt to reproduce the words of it, which are now forever irrecoverable. Instead, I will summarize, faithfully, the many things Ireneo told me. Indirect discourse is distant and weak; I know that I am sacrificing the effectiveness of my tale. I only ask that my readers try to hear in their imagination the broken and staccato periods that astounded me that night.

Ireneo began by enumerating, in both Latin and Spanish, the cases of prodigious memory cataloged in the *Naturalis historia*: Cyrus, the king of Persia, who could call all the soldiers in his armies by name; Mithridates Eupator, who meted out justice in the twenty-two languages of the kingdom over which he ruled; Simonides, the inventor of the art of memory; Metrodorus, who was able faithfully to repeat what he had heard, though it be but once. With obvious sincerity, Ireneo said he was amazed that such cases were thought to be amazing. He told me that before that rainy afternoon when the blue roan had bucked him off, he had been what every man was—blind, deaf, befuddled, and virtually devoid of memory. (I tried to remind him how precise his perception of time, his memory for proper names, had been—he ignored me.) He had lived, he said, for nineteen years as though in a dream: he looked without seeing, heard without listening, forgot everything, or virtually everything. When he fell, he'd been knocked unconscious; when he came to again, the present was so rich, so clear, that it was almost unbearable, as were his oldest and even his most trivial memories. It was shortly afterward that he learned he was crippled; of that fact he hardly took notice. He reasoned (or felt) that immobility was a small price to pay. Now his perception and his memory were perfect.

With one quick look, you and I perceive three wineglasses on a table; Funes perceived every grape that had been pressed into the wine and all the stalks and tendrils of its vineyard. He knew the forms of the clouds in the southern sky on the morning of April 30, 1882, and he could compare them in his memory with the veins in the marbled binding of a book he had seen only once, or with the feathers of spray lifted by an oar on the Río Negro on the eve of the Battle of Quebracho. Nor were those memories simple—every visual image was linked to muscular sensations, thermal sensations, and so on. He was able to reconstruct every dream, every daydream he had ever had. Two or three times he had reconstructed an entire day; he had never once erred or faltered, but each reconstruction had itself taken an entire day. "I, *myself, alone, have more memories than all mankind since the world began*," he said to me. And also: "*My dreams are like other people's waking hours.*" And again, toward dawn: "*My memory, sir, is like a garbage heap.*" A circle drawn on a blackboard, a right triangle, a rhombus—all these are forms we can fully intuit; Ireneo could do the same with the stormy mane of a young colt, a small herd of cattle on a mountainside, a flickering fire and its uncountable ashes, and the many faces of a dead man at a wake. I have no idea how many stars he saw in the sky.

Those are the things he told me; neither then nor later have I ever doubted them. At that time there were no cinematographers, no phonographs; it nevertheless strikes me as implausible, even incredible, that no one ever performed an experiment with Funes. But then, all our lives we postpone everything that can be postponed; perhaps we all have the certainty, deep inside, that we are immortal and that sooner or later every man will do everything, know all there is to know.

The voice of Funes, from the darkness, went on talking.

He told me that in 1886 he had invented a numbering system original with himself, and that within a very few days he had passed the twenty-four thousand mark. He had not written it down, since anything he thought, even once, remained ineradicably with him. His original motivation, I think, was his irritation that the thirty-three Uruguayan patriots should require two figures and three words rather than a single figure, a single word. He then applied this mad principle to the other numbers. Instead of seven thousand thirteen (7013), he would say, for instance, "Máximo Pérez"; instead of seven thousand fourteen (7014), "the railroad"; other numbers were "Luis Melián Lafinur," "Olimar," "sulfur," "clubs," "the whale," "gas," "a stewpot," "Napoleon," "Agustín de Vedia." Instead of five hundred (500), he said "nine." Every word had a particular figure attached to it, a sort of marker; the later ones were extremely complicated . . . I tried to explain to Funes that his rhapsody of unconnected words was exactly the opposite of a number *system*. I told him that when one said "365" one said "three hundreds, six tens, and five ones," a breakdown impossible with the "numbers" *Nigger Timoteo* or *a ponchoful of meat*. Funes either could not or would not understand me.

In the seventeenth century, Locke postulated (and condemned) an impossible language in which each individual thing—every stone, every bird, every branch—would have its own name; Funes once contemplated a similar language, but discarded the idea as too general, too ambiguous. The truth was, Funes remembered not only every leaf of every tree in every patch of forest, but every time he had perceived or imagined that leaf. He resolved to reduce every one of his past days to some seventy thousand recollections, which he would then define by numbers. Two considerations dissuaded him: the realization that the task was interminable, and the realization that it was pointless. He saw that by the time he died he would still not have finished classifying all the memories of his childhood.

The two projects I have mentioned (an infinite vocabulary for the natural series of numbers, and a pointless mental catalog of all the images of his memory) are foolish, even preposterous, but they reveal a certain halting grandeur. They allow us to glimpse, or to infer, the dizzying world that Funes lived in. Funes, we must not forget, was virtually incapable of general, platonic ideas. Not only was it difficult for him to see that the generic symbol "dog" took in all the dissimilar individuals of all shapes and sizes, it irritated him that the "dog" of three-fourteen in the afternoon, seen in profile, should be indicated by the same noun as the dog of three-fifteen, seen frontally. His own face in the mirror, his own hands, surprised him every time he saw them. Swift wrote that the emperor of Lilliput could perceive the movement of the minute hand of a clock; Funes could continually perceive the quiet advances of corruption, of tooth decay, or weariness. He saw—he *noticed*—the progress of death, of humidity. He was the solitary, lucid spectator of a multiform, momentaneous, and almost unbearably precise world. Babylon, London, and New York dazzle mankind's imagination with their fierce splendor; no one in the populous towers or urgent avenues of those cities has ever felt the heat and pressure of a reality as inexhaustible as that which battered Ireneo, day and night, in his poor South American hinterland. It was hard for him to sleep. To sleep is to take one's mind from the world; Funes, lying on his back on his cot, in the dimness of his room, could picture every crack in the wall, every molding of the precise houses that surrounded him. (I repeat that the most trivial of his memories was more detailed, more vivid than our own perception of a physical pleasure or a physical torment.) Off toward the east, in an area that had not yet been cut up into city blocks, there were new houses, unfamiliar to Ireneo. He pictured them to himself as black, compact, made of homogeneous shadow; he would turn his head in that direction to sleep. He would also imagine himself at the bottom of a river, rocked (and negated) by the current.

He had effortlessly learned English, French, Portuguese, Latin. I suspect, nevertheless, that he was not very good at thinking. To think is to ignore (or forget) differences, to generalize, to abstract. In the teeming world of Ireneo Funes there was nothing but particulars—and they were virtually *immediate* particulars.

The leery light of dawn entered the patio of packed earth.

It was then that I saw the face that belonged to the voice that had been talking all night long. Ireneo was nineteen, he had been born in 1868; he looked to me as monumental as bronze—older than Egypt, older than the prophecies and the pyramids. I was struck by the thought that every word I spoke, every expression of my face or motion of my hand would endure in his implacable memory; I was rendered clumsy by the fear of making pointless gestures.

Ireneo Funes died in 1889 of pulmonary congestion.

—translated by Andrew Hurley

CORNELL WOOLRICH

The Black Curtain

THE room was a ghost from some long-buried yesterday. "You going to be here long?" the wizened old rooming-house keeper asked.

If Townsend could have told him that, he would have known more than Townsend knew himself. Maybe only an hour or two, before they traced him. Maybe days, weeks. No, not weeks, unless he found some job around here to keep him going. He'd had exactly eight dollars and seventy-nine cents in the pockets of the suit he was wearing at the moment those blank-cartridgelike blows exploded against his door.

He said, "That depends on what you charge me."

The gnarled old man chafed his hands. "For a room like this it gives four dollars." He batted his eyes enticingly, to soften the blow.

Townsend moved back toward the doorway. "Four dollars is too much."

"All right, but look, you got the street. *Every* week you got clean sheets on the bed. Fresh running water, even." He went over to a corroded projection resembling a grappling hook, turned its encrusted handle with great difficulty, and a rumbling sound issued through it, followed by a thin coil of reddish-brown fluid. "Must be using it downstairs." He tactfully wedged it shut again, but the trickle continued unabated for several moments afterwards.

"I'll give you two and a half for it," Townsend said, stepping out through the doorway.

"Take it, take it," the old man called after him.

Townsend came in again, peeled two bills off his slender accumulation, added a coin to them, clapped the whole amount ungraciously into the old man's eagerly reaching hand. "Gimme a key."

His new landlord grumbled under his breath at such an unheard-of luxury. "A key he wants. What next?" He tried out several from his pocket, finally found one that fit, left it in the door.

Townsend, left alone, went over to the bleary window and stood looking down, sunlight escaping through the gap at the side of the shade, making a bright chevron on his sleeve. So that was the new world down there. He'd already walked once to the end of the world and back, before coming up here. The world was not very long, four blocks all told. Tillary Street only extended from Monmouth to Degrasse. It stopped dead at both ends.

Their heads down there were like ants, swarming over dun-colored sand, going every which way at once, forming into black accumulations around each of the pushcarts that rimmed both curbs in a nearly unbroken line. The street had very little vehicular traffic, both because of this fact and because of the shortness of its length. It didn't lead anywhere in particular. An occasional agonized motor conveyance threaded its way through at snail's pace, horn sounding every moment of the way.

He'd rest awhile first and then go out again. He hadn't had any sleep the whole of the night before. It already seemed so long ago and far away. He loosened his tie, took off his coat, hung it across the back of the chair.

He lay down on the bed, intending just to relax for a few minutes. Before he knew it the street cries had become somnolent, filtered in through the window, pleasantly lulling, not harsh and discordant anymore. Then they all blended into one purr, and he slept his first sleep of the new life.

When he awoke it was already mid-afternoon. He tried the stubbornly resistant spigot handle over the corner, and the whole section of pipe quivered and sang out. He found that as far as quantity went, the condition his landlord had referred to as "being used downstairs" was of a permanent nature. But after several minutes of steady leakage the trickle had at least rid itself of rust particles and become colorless enough to use.

He locked his door after him, more as a reflex from former habit than anything else, and outside it found himself assailed by a delayed odor of cookery that must have taken several hours to creep up from the ground floor where it had been originated at noon. It reminded him he was hungry. Even ghosts have to eat.

One thing he noticed, on his way down the stairs, and it was a happy augury. That horrible sense of moral guilt he had felt last night had vanished. If this was the "feel" of the past—and of course it couldn't altogether be, for he wasn't actually immersed in the past yet—then it argued that he had either been guiltless or had owned an unusually impervious conscience. There was a continuing sense of danger, but it was the exhilarating not the depressing kind. It had a lacing of adventure in it, too. Perhaps it was because Virginia was out of the picture, all sense of responsibility had been lifted from him, and he had only his own fate to work out.

He walked a block down from his rooming house, which was near the Degrasse Street terminus of the street, and chose a food stall that seemed the likeliest candidate for whatever neighborhood trade there was. He decided this point simply on the strength of the number of refuse receptacles he glimpsed within the crevice leading back to its kitchen door. If they had that much garbage to dispose of after the day had ended, they must have a fair-sized turnover. At the moment, of course, there was no one in it. The Tillary Street section didn't have enough per capita wealth to be able to indulge in between-meal snacks.

He kept eyeing the back of the counterman's head, after he'd perched himself on one of the tall pivot stools, and wondering: "Did I ever eat in here before? Would he remember me if he looked more closely than he did just now?"

He took off his hat, in order to clear his upper face of shadow. Then he thrust his face an inch or two forward above the counter, so that it couldn't fail to impinge on the employee's line of vision when he turned back from the glistening nickel boiler. The counterman's glance swept over him, but nothing happened. The man's mind was on the order he was filling. In any case, Townsend realized, he would have had to be an habitual customer in the past for outright recognition now to take place. He might have come in here before, but he might have come in here only once or twice, and people like this had faces before them day after day.

He asked the counterman finally, "How long you been working in this place?"

"Couple of weeks now, chief," the latter said.

Townsend thought grimly, there goes the first chance.

He mapped out the preliminaries of his campaign while he sat there stirring grayish sweetening into the already thick sediment at the bottom of his cup. At each and every meal, he would patronize a different eating establishment along here. It wouldn't take long to run out of them, for there were not more than four or five along Tillary Street. He must try for recognition on the part of the employees or some of the customers. That would be one line of attack.

A second would be to enter, one by one, every store and shop along the entire four-block length of the street, on some excuse or other, try for recognition on the part of the storekeepers. Ask to be shown things they weren't likely to have in stock, or if they did, linger haggling, then finally walk out dissatisfied, after having remained long enough to determine whether he had ever been in there before.

Both of these were secondary; he was still pinning his main hope, of fairly sharp personal acquaintanceship, to the random pavements outside. For even recognition by sight, in an eating place or in a shop, didn't necessarily imply that the person doing the recognizing would know anything important concerning him. Simply that he had been in there once or twice before. Not his name, nor where he lived, nor who his friends were.

He couldn't, of course, afford to neglect any entering wedge, no matter how slight or ineffective it might seem. Even that sort of blanket recognition would be better than nothing at all; it would be a beginning, a point of contact. He wouldn't be suspended, as he was now, in a complete vacuum.

He came into the street, and when he replaced his hat, left it well back on his head. Then he continued down toward the Monmouth end of the street, still three blocks away. He moved slowly, with such sluggish lethargy of pace that there was no one in motion around him, whether man, woman, or child, who wasn't going faster than himself. Anyone glancing at him, in doubt the first time, would have ample time to look twice, verify his identity in case they were uncertain.

In any case, his rate of progress wasn't as great a concession as it would have been in another part of town. Really rapid progress along swarming Tillary Street would have required exhausting dexterity. The customers or window shoppers doubled up before the pushcarts clogged one side of the already inadequate sidewalk. The gossiping groups, static doorway loungers, and potential purchasers coming out of shop entrances to view bits of merchandise by benefit of daylight blocked the other. A tortuous lane of clearance was left between, but even here no precise keep-to-the-right rule was maintained; everyone seemed to go in whichever direction had happened to occur to him at the moment. The only factor that made the situation tolerable was that tempers down here seemed to be a good deal more even than on the more streamlined streets uptown. The poke of an elbow, an over-stepped toe or trodden-on heel, went unnoticed, drew no angry, challenging glare. They also, incidentally, went unapologized, perhaps for that very reason. It was the apology itself, no doubt, that would have drawn the resentful, incomprehending stare.

Although he didn't time himself, it must have taken him a full thirty minutes to traverse those three remaining blocks. At the end of that time he was back at the Monmouth Street end once more. He crossed over to the opposite sidewalk and started slowly to work his way back.

The sun was starting to crimson and go down, and vacancies began to appear along the curb, as the more successful of the pushcarts, emptied down to a point beyond which nothing further could be hoped for, furled tents and broke ranks. Women appeared at windows high aloft and screeched down into the still-swarming depths to their children to come up. Their calls, like mystic wave lengths, all seemed to reach the right ears and elicit, if not obedience, at least squalling recalcitrance and objection.

The street had definitely thinned out by the time he found himself back at Degrasse again, although it was still overpeopled, and was the sort of a slum street that probably never was actually lifeless at any time of the day or night. He recrossed to his original, to what by payment of two and a half dollars he was entitled to call "his own" side of the street, and stopped to rest awhile and try his luck from a motionless position.

His feet felt worn and dusty from the slow, unnatural shuffle he had held them to, a gait that is always more trying than an energetic walk. He had drawn one or two cursorily questioning looks during his long maiden voyage down the street and back, but he had to admit there had been nothing personal, nothing immediate, in them; they had probably been elicited by the "foreignness" of his attire (in general, not specific sense) and bearing. He was still, even after the wear and tear of his night flight through the streets, slightly too formal for this neighborhood. It was a hard thing to put his finger on; it had nothing to do with cut or fabric. He tried to correct it, insofar as he was able, as he stood there, by the composite impression he gained from scanning a cross section of the locality's adult male population as it drifted back and forth before him. The discrepancies, which he remedied then and there, were minor ones in detail, important only in the general effect they conveyed. He unbuttoned his vest and allowed his shirt to peer through the gap of his open coat, as though he wore no vest. For the rest, it was mostly a matter of shifting his tie to hang a little less dead center and allowing his shirt to fit a little less trimly into his trousers. His suit still showed too apparent a crease, but that was a matter the passage of days would automatically remedy.

Presently it had grown dark, and Tillary Street came on with its lights. Through the gleam behind many of the upper windows was the greenish pallor of gaslight; there was no lack of oversized naked-glass display bulbs in the shop and stall fronts at sidewalk level, of almost bombshell-like brilliance, sizzling, and spitting with their own power. One or two of the surviving pushcarts, remaining to do business to the bitter end, even lighted gasoline flares. The street took on a sort of holiday guise. If you didn't look too closely it even seemed gay, scintillant.

He stayed on awhile, hoping he'd have better luck after dark than during the daylight hours. Like a mendicant begging alms he stood there begging a donation of memories, but the obliviousness of those about him only increased rather than lessened.

Finally he turned and moved off, went upstairs to his room. He raised the shade, and the lights from below, even at this height, were sufficient to cast a luminous repetition of the window square past him at the other side of the room, bent in two, half flat upon the ceiling and half upright on the wall. He sat there on the edge of his bed, a dejected, shadowy figure. And once, at some break in inner fortitude—like a split in a film running through a projection machine, quickly spliced together again and resuming its evenness in a moment—his head suddenly dropped into the coil of his arms.

Then he raised it again, and that didn't happen anymore.

It isn't easy to start over at thirty-two. Particularly when it's a life doomed even before you take it over, and the time limit is subject to call without notice.

His indirect lighting blanked out without any warning when a chronic "last-day" rummage sale directly opposite his rooming house dimmed for the night. He could have lit the gas jet in the room, but there was nothing to be seen, nothing to use it for.

He took off his shoes and lay back, and pulled something that felt like the rough side of a piece of sacking up over his underwear-protected body. Tillary Street dimmed like the unreal lantern slide it was, into the blankness of sleep.

His first day in the past hadn't paid off. He was still lost between dimensions.

A heartbreaking near-hit occurred the following afternoon. He was on about the third lap of his thoroughfare-long peregrination for that day, and the street had reached a three-o'clock climax of hurly-burly. There couldn't have been anyone left withindoors, judging by the numbers choking its sidewalks and gutters. While he was breasting this tide like a tired swimmer, he suddenly felt himself clapped from behind on the shoulder by someone in transit, and a voice called out in gruff heartiness, "Whaddye say there?"

He had been looking over to the other side at that moment, and even in the brief flash of time it took him to swerve his head around, the unknown greeter had already blended indissolubly into the crowd. He couldn't tell which one of those immediately ahead of him it had been. None were turning to look back, to see if the salutation were acknowledged. The direction of the roughly friendly hand and the trailing direction of the brief snatch of voice that had accompanied it told him that the person had been going the same way he was, but at a good deal faster gait; therefore he was before and not behind him by now. That was all. He hadn't thought quickly enough to call out an automatic answer, which would have been the only sure way of fixing the greeter's attention on him an extra moment or two. He had been taken too much by surprise.

Here was the chance contact, the thing he had been hoping and praying for, and which might never recur, slipping through his fingers. He ran ahead, desperately accosting those in the lead of him one by one, pulling them around short by their sleeves and coat edges, demanding breathlessly: "Say was that you just now? Did you just wallop me on the shoulder?"

All he got was dull, uncomprehending shakes of the head. But somebody had done it, somebody must have! It had been a good, solid impact. He was about ready to fly with crazed helplessness, when suddenly the fourth man he tackled answered with somewhat sheepish reluctance: "'Scuse me, I mistook you for somebody else. You fooled me from the back for a minute." He pried his sleeve away from Townsend's convulsive grip and went on.

Townsend stopped dead for a minute while the sluggish tide of humanity flowed on around both sides of him; the sudden letdown was so cruelly deflating.

It had been on a Monday, a Monday-morning daybreak, that he had first reached Tillary Street. Tuesday passed and Wednesday; Thursday, Friday, and Saturday. Those first few he was sure of. After that they began to telescope themselves a little, lose their sharpness of identity. It was harder to keep track of the days down here. Having no job might have had something to do with it, or the blurring monotony of the routine he had set for himself. There came the day when his landlord accosted him at the foot of the stairs on his way out, and he knew he had been there a full week and it was Monday again.

He had been eating very sparingly and irregularly, but he discovered when he tried to pay for the coming week that he had only two-odd dollars left.

He handed over two, said, "I'll have the other fifty for you by tonight or tomorrow," wondering to himself at the same time how he'd manage to.

But he did have it by that very night, when he returned toward midnight; he handed it over with fingertips puckery and red from long immersion, after an agonizing afternoon- and evening-long session washing the dishes in that place he'd eaten in the day of his first arrival.

They had had a temporary need for someone, luckily. There was enough left to tide him over the next day or two, but he knew that, however else he managed, he'd never wash a dish again as long as he lived. He could still feel the greasy scum of reeking water, lapping up his arms to the elbows, for days afterwards.

He'd already finished his casing of the shops several days before this. And although he'd left a bad impression as a time waster, maybe even as a potential shoplifter, on many of the proprietors, and got dirty looks from then on whenever he strolled past their premises, he had nowhere gained the impression that any of them had seen him before.

His clocklike pacing of the street, day after day, up one side, down the other, then down the one, up the other, was undoubtedly making him familiar by sight to dozens of the denizens of Tillary Street; but it was all current familiarity, none from before, and to keep from getting tangled up and mistaking the one for the other, he held himself strictly aloof from overtures of new vintage, rebuffed them where they seemed about to be tentatively put forth for the first time.

Eventually, of course, a law of diminishing returns was going to set in against him. If he stayed on around here long enough for new familiarity to become seasoned, a time would come when he would no longer be able to differentiate recognition having its inception in the immediate past from that of the more distant past that he was trying to reenter. But that point hadn't been quite reached yet.

He was haunted now at times, alone in his barren room at nights, with the ghost window square cast by the streetlights wavering on the wall before his eyes, by a looming sense of failure, of the futility of the whole thing he was attempting.

Perhaps it was based on a faulty premise in the first place. He might have just been traversing Tillary Street at random, that day that the curtain had suddenly been drawn upon the past; might have happened upon it in the course of a haphazard, meaningless digression. He might be mistaking an erratic diversion for his regular orbit. How was he ever to find out, in that case, where he had been going or where he had come from? He might be just a block or two from a sector that would have paid him real dividends if he had begun to investigate it. Or he might be the whole span of the city away.

Or even suppose his premise was the correct one, and Tillary Street had played a fixed part in one phase of his past life? Even so he was relying on the laws of chance, of coincidence, wasn't he? And they might just not work out in his favor. For instance, suppose the one or two people around here who could have reoriented him had themselves drifted away by now? If they weren't around here anymore, then the street was no earthly good to him just as a street. Or those who had had reason to seek him out down here, if there were any such, might have already done so—during the interim of his absence. Not finding him, they might take it for granted he was gone for good and would never come back to Tillary Street. He might stay here a thousand years without ever getting a glimpse into that unknown past.

One night, hopeless with continued lack of success, he charted a rough map of the immediate vicinity and tried to determine by a rough system of surveying just which nearby points of departure and destination might use Tillary Street as a shortcut, or timesaver, or line of least resistance. But it wouldn't work out. Too many outside factors that were still beyond his knowledge entered into it. He would have had to know what his own former habits were, the nature of the errand he had been on at the time, and so on. He didn't know any of those things. In itself, as a mere geographical convenience, the use of the street as a shortcut seemed to be ruled out. You could go down the parallel streets on each side of it just as quickly and a very great deal farther. It led from nowhere to nowhere. It began where it did for no reason and ended where it did just as irrationally, after four blocks of existence. It wasn't even a diagonal or transverse linking two nonparallel points; it adhered to the same foursquare pattern as all the other intersections about it.

He crumpled up the sheet of paper and threw it away, after long, laborious hours of struggle. The past wasn't easy to regain. There were no road maps showing you which way it lay. And meanwhile time was running out.

Although his lodging was taken care of for a while yet, the residue of the dishwashing money petered out within two days. He struggled on for another twenty-four hours after that without a penny, living on gratuitous cups of coffee slipped across the counter to him, when the boss wasn't looking, by employees of the various places where he had been a paying customer until now. They couldn't be expected to repeat that more than once, however. Tillary Street lived on a shoestring, and the five cents would have been taken out of their own wages if they had been detected. The fortuitous circumstance of a restaurant being without a dishwasher, or a shop being without a sidewalk barker at the precise moment when he needed a job, didn't recur a second time and wasn't likely to. That had been just a freak of timing. He wasn't looking for permanent employment—he had his full-time job cut out for him—so he didn't go out of the neighborhood. And in it, there was nothing to be found. But still he had to eat. The first day, already, of this forced abstention he was starting to feel hollow in the pit of the stomach and weary at the back of the legs as he prowled his useless, elusive beat.

He'd had all along, and still had, on him that flashy-looking cigarette case that had turned up in his pocket on this very street after the accident that day. He had kept it on his person all the weeks he'd been back living with Virginia, instead of hiding it away somewhere in the flat. Possibly to spare her the worry the sight of its strangeness might have caused her if she'd found it. It had accompanied him automatically the night of his flight, and it was the only thing on his person now that had even a potential intrinsic value. So he decided he'd try to raise something on it. He had no idea of its probable value, but it might help to tide him over another week or two, and meantime, any day—any day—

There was, strangely enough, no pawnshop located anywhere along Tillary Street itself, but he found one about a block and a half down Monmouth Street, to the right. He pushed his way into its camphor-reeking interior, empty at the moment, took out the case, blew on it, and polished it against his coat sleeve.

The pawnbroker, attracted by the sounds of entry, came out of a storage room at the back, gave him the sharply appraising look of his kind as he advanced along the inside of the counter to the point where Townsend stood. "Well?" he said noncommittally.

Townsend passed him the case, winged open, through the small orifice in the wire mesh that separated them.

The broker made no effort to test it, weigh it, examine it closely in any way. Townsend should have noticed that, but for some reason failed to. The technique of hocking was new to him.

Suddenly the broker had spoken, casually in intonation but with explosive implications. "This again, hm?" he said weariedly.

Townsend wasn't expecting it. He was caught off guard, inattentively off guard. It was like flashlight powder going off. It's over with before you even have time to jolt. He blinked as the meaning hit him, then he paled a little, then he gripped the edge of the counter a little tighter. This *again. Again.* He had that sudden, strange, glimmering sensation that comes when you've been in a pitch-dark room and a door begins to waver slightly open, admitting the first peering light backing it.

He must have been in here with the same case before.

His voice shook a little, much as he tried to steady it. He tried to make himself sound plausibly forgetful, no more. "Oh, uh, was this the—the same place I brought it to before? All hockshops look alike to me." He hoped this didn't sound as lame to his vis-à-vis as it did to himself.

The broker sniffed disdainfully. "I ought to know this case by heart already. Three times you been in here with it now, haven't you?" Meanwhile he was holding it extended as if in rejection. Then, with an inconsistent time lag, his offer followed. "All right, four dollars."

Townsend saw an opening, and clutched at it desperately. "That wasn't what you let me have on it before."

The broker immediately took professional umbrage. "So what're you going to do, argue? Four dollars is what it's worth. Why should I give you any more this time than the time before? It ain't any more valuable to me now than it was then, is it?"

Townsend's voice was tense. "Do you keep the—the ticket stubs or whatever you call 'em, after the article's once been redeemed? I mean the part that the customer signs his name and address on, and that you hold until the loan is repaid?"

"Sure. You want me to look it up? What do I have to look it up for? I know this case by its pattern. I tested it for you before. Look at that." He showed him a little mark made by the drop of reagent acid. Townsend had thought it was a worn spot. "So you were raising a big holler, remember? Fourteen carat you tried to tell me it was. Silver, gilt. Four dollars."

Townsend was pleading almost abjectly by now. "Well, just to convince me, just to make sure. Go ahead, see if you can dig it up. I just want to see with my own eyes."

"You telling me I don't know my own business? I ought to know how much a piece of security is worth to me." The pawnbroker was maddeningly interested in the question of the amount involved. "When were you in here with it last?"

He'd come back to Virginia on the tenth of May. He took a chance, faltered: "In April, this year. Look it up in your ledger, you must have it down."

The broker went into the back again, snapped on a light. There was a long wait. For Townsend an agonizing one. He was leaning against the counter, letting its edge cut into him across the middle, as though the physical hurt dulled the other torment.

"April eighteenth," the broker said suddenly, from inside. "Silver-gilt cigarette case. Black enamel, silver stripes. Ticket number mumble-mumble—*four dollars*. Was I right?"

"Bring the canceled ticket out, I want to see the canceled ticket," Townsend called. There was a desperate urgency in his voice.

The broker came back with an oblong bisque pasteboard and looked at him curiously. "Here. Maybe you'll tell me now I'm wrong. Is this you or isn't it?"

Townsend cocked his head to match the angle at which the pawnbroker was holding the stub, searching for the penned fill-in on the printed form. The handwriting wasn't recognizable as his, but that was to be expected. If memory wasn't transferable, nothing was.

The name was George Williams, and he knew at sight that it was spurious. Something about it, it was too glib, too pat. Not that there weren't people called George Williams, but *he* hadn't been. His hatband had been initialed D N. The address was down at 705 Monmouth Street. Was that also fictitious, to match the name? There was a chance it hadn't been.

"Well, what about it? You want to turn it in or not?" the pawnbroker called after him sharply, as he made for the door.

"Be back later," he said, and gave the half doors a fling that must have kept them banging in and out for minutes as accompaniment to his footsteps racing away.

He hustled up Monmouth Street toward the seven-hundred sector. 700. Pretty soon now. One of those just ahead.

He came to a spasmodic halt, went on a few faltering steps farther, as if by reflex momentum, then stopped for good. There wasn't any 705. The one before it was 703. The one after it was 707. It was a public bathhouse.

The door had slammed shut. The room was dark again.

FLANN O'BRIEN

The Third Policeman

WHEN I awoke again two thoughts came into my head so closely together that they seemed to be stuck to one another; I could not be sure which came first and it was hard to separate them and examine them singly. One was a happy thought about the weather, the sudden brightness of the day that had been vexed earlier. The other was suggesting to me that it was not the same day at all but a different one and maybe not even the next day after the angry one. I could not decide that question and did not try to. I lay back and took to my habit of gazing out of the window. Whichever day it was, it was a gentle day—mild, magical, and innocent with great sailings of white cloud serene and impregnable in the high sky, moving along like kingly swans on quiet water. The sun was in the neighborhood also, distributing his enchantment unobtrusively, coloring the sides of things that were unalive and livening the hearts of living things. The sky was a light blue without distance, neither near nor far. I could gaze at it, through it, and beyond it and see still illimitably clearer and nearer the delicate lie of its nothingness. A bird sang a solo from nearby, a cunning blackbird in a dark hedge giving thanks in his native language. I listened and agreed with him completely.

Then other sounds came to me from the nearby kitchen. The policemen were up and about their incomprehensible tasks. A pair of their great boots would clump across the flags, pause, and then clump back. The other pair would clump to another place, stay longer, and clump back again with heavier falls as if a great weight were being carried. Then the four boots would clump together solidly far away to the front door and immediately would come the long slash of thrown water

on the road, a great bath of it flung in a lump to fall flat on the dry
ground.

I arose and started to put on my clothes. Through the window I
could see the scaffold of raw timber rearing itself high into the heavens,
not as O'Feersa had left it to make his way methodically through the
rain, but perfect and ready for its dark destiny. The sight did not make
me cry or even sigh. I thought it was sad, too sad. Through the struts of
the structure I could see the good country. There would be a fine view
from the top of the scaffold on any day but on this day it would be
lengthened out by five miles owing to the clearness of the air. To prevent my tears I began to give special attention to my dressing.

When I was nearly finished the Sergeant knocked very delicately at
the door, came in with great courtesy, and bade me good morning.

"I notice the other bed has been slept in," I said for conversation.
"Was it yourself or MacCruiskeen?"

"That would likely be Policeman Fox. MacCruiskeen and I do not
do our sleeping here at all, it is too expensive, we would be dead in a
week if we played that game."

"And where do you sleep, then?"

"Down below—over there—beyant."

He gave my eyes the right direction with his brown thumb. It was
down the road to where the hidden left turn led to the heaven full of
doors and ovens.

"And why?"

"To save our lifetimes, man. Down there you are as young coming
out of a sleep as you are going into it and you don't fade when you are
inside your sleep, you would not credit the time a suit or a boots will
last you and you don't have to take your clothes off either. That's what
charms MacCruiskeen—that and the no shaving." He laughed kindly
at the thought of his comrade. "A comical artist of a man," he added.

"And Fox? Where does he live?"

"Beyant, I think." He jerked again to the place that was to the left.
"He is down there beyant somewhere during the daytime but we have
never seen him there, he might be in a distinctive portion of it that he
found from a separate ceiling in a different house and indeed the
unreasonable jumps of the lever-reading would put you in mind that
there is unauthorized interference with the works. He is as crazy as

bedamned, an incontestable character and a man of ungovernable inexactitudes."

"Then why does he sleep here?" I was not at all pleased that this ghostly man had been in the same room with me during the night.

"To spend it and spin it out and not have all of it forever unused inside him."

"All what?"

"His lifetime. He wants to get rid of as much as possible, undertime and overtime, as quickly as he can so that he can die as soon as possible. MacCruiskeen and I are wiser and we are not yet tired of being ourselves; we save it up. I think he has an opinion that there is a turn to the right down the road and likely that is what he is after; he thinks the best way to find it is to die and get all the leftness out of his blood. I do not believe there is a right-hand road and if there is it would surely take a dozen active men to look after the readings alone, night and morning. As you are perfectly aware the right is much more tricky than the left; you would be surprised at all the right pitfalls there are. We are only at the beginning of our knowledge of the right; there is nothing more deceptive to the unwary."

"I did not know that."

The Sergeant opened his eyes wide in surprise.

"Did you ever in your life," he asked, "mount a bicycle from the right?"

"I did not."

"And why?"

"I do not know. I never thought about it."

He laughed at me indulgently.

"It is nearly an insoluble pancake"—he smiled—"a conundrum of inscrutable potentialities, a snorter."

He led the way out of the bedroom to the kitchen, where he had already arranged my steaming meal of stirabout and milk on the table. He pointed to it pleasantly, made a motion as if lifting a heavily laden spoon to his mouth, and then made succulent spitty sounds with his lips as if they were dealing with the tastiest of all known delicacies. Then he swallowed loudly and put his red hands in ecstasy to his stomach. I sat down and took up the spoon at this encouragement.

"And why is Fox crazy?" I inquired.

"I will tell you that much. In MacCruiskeen's room there is a little box on the mantelpiece. The story is that when MacCruiskeen was away one day that happened to fall on the twenty-third of June inquiring about a bicycle, Fox went in and opened the box and looked into it from the strain of his unbearable curiosity. From that day to this . . ."

The Sergeant shook his head and tapped his forehead three times with his finger. Soft as porridge is I nearly choked at the sound his finger made. It was a booming hollow sound, slightly tinny, as if he had tapped an empty watering can with his nail.

"And what was in the box?"

"That is easily told. A card made of cardboard about the size of a cigarette card, no better and no thicker."

"I see," I said.

I did not see but I was sure that my easy unconcern would sting the Sergeant into an explanation. It came after a time when he had looked at me silently and strangely as I fed solidly at the table.

"It was the color," he said.

"The color?"

"But then maybe it was not that at all," he mused perplexedly.

I looked at him with a mild inquiry. He frowned thoughtfully and looked up at a corner of the ceiling as if he expected certain words he was searching for to be hanging there in colored lights. No sooner had I thought of that than I glanced up myself, half expecting to see them there. But they were not.

"The card was not red," he said at last doubtfully.

"Green?"

"Not green. No."

"Then what color?"

"It was not one of the colors a man carries inside his head like nothing he ever looked at with his eyes. It was . . . different. MacCruiskeen says it is not blue either and I believe him, a blue card would never make a man batty because what is blue is natural."

"I saw colors often on eggs," I observed, "colors which have no names. Some birds lay eggs that are shaded in a way too delicate to be noticeable to any instrument but the eye, the tongue could not be troubled to find a noise for anything so nearly not-there. What I would call a green sort of complete white. Now would that be the color?"

"I am certain it would not," the Sergeant replied immediately, "because if birds could lay eggs that would put men out of their wits, you would have no crops at all, nothing but scarecrows crowded in every field like a public meeting and thousands of them in their top hats standing together in knots on the hillsides. It would be a mad world completely; the people would be putting their bicycles upside down on the roads and pedalling them to make enough mechanical movement to frighten the birds out of the whole parish." He passed a hand in consternation across his brow. "It would be a very unnatural pancake," he added.

I thought it was a poor subject for conversation, this new color. Apparently its newness was new enough to blast a man's brain to imbecility by the surprise of it. That was enough to know and quite sufficient to be required to believe. I thought it was an unlikely story, but not for gold or diamonds would I open that box in the bedroom and look into it.

The Sergeant had wrinkles of pleasant recollection at his eyes and mouth.

"Did you ever in your travels meet with Mr. Andy Gara?" he asked me.

"No."

"He is always laughing to himself, even in bed at night he laughs quietly and if he meets you on the road he will go into roars; it is a most enervating spectacle and very bad for nervous people. It all goes back to a certain day when MacCruiskeen and I were making inquiries about a missing bicycle."

"Yes?"

"It was a bicycle with a crisscross frame," the Sergeant explained, "and I can tell you that it is not every day in the week that one like that is reported; it is a great rarity and indeed it is a privilege to be looking for a bicycle like that."

"Andy Gara's bicycle?"

"Not Andy's. Andy was a sensible man at the time but a very curious man and when he had us gone he thought he would do a clever thing. He broke his way into the barrack here in open defiance of the law. He spent valuable hours boarding up the windows and making Mac-Cruiskeen's room as dark as nighttime. Then he got busy with the box.

He wanted to know what the inside of it felt like, even if it could not be looked at. When he put his hand in he let out a great laugh, you could swear he was very amused at something."

"And what did it feel like?"

The Sergeant shrugged himself massively.

"MacCruiskeen says it is not smooth and not rough, not gritty and not velvety. It would be a mistake to think it is a cold feel like steel and another mistake to think it blankety. I thought it might be like the damp bread of an old poultice but no, MacCruiskeen says that would be a third mistake. And not like a bowl full of dry withered peas, either. A contrary pancake surely, a fingerish atrocity but not without a queer charm all its own."

"Not hens' piniony underwing feeling?" I questioned keenly. The Sergeant shook his head abstractedly.

"But the crisscross bicycle," he said, "it is no wonder it went astray. It was a very confused bicycle and was shared by a man called Barbery with his wife and if you ever laid your eye on big Mrs. Barbery I would not require to explain this thing privately to you at all."

He broke off his utterance in the middle of the last short word of it and stood peering with a wild eye at the table. I had finished eating and had pushed away my empty bowl. Following quickly along the line of his stare, I saw a small piece of folded paper lying on the table where the bowl had been before I moved it. Giving a cry the Sergeant sprang forward with surpassing lightness and snatched the paper up. He took it to the window, opened it out, and held it far away from him to allow for some disorder in his eye. His face was puzzled and pale and stared at the paper for many minutes. Then he looked out of the window fixedly, tossing the paper over at me. I picked it up and read the roughly printed message:

> One-legged men on their way to rescue prisoner. Made a calculation on tracks and estimate number is seven. Submitted please. — Fox

My heart began to pound madly inside me. Looking at the Sergeant I saw that he was still gazing wild-eyed into the middle of the day, which was situated at least five miles away, like a man trying to memorize forever the perfection of the lightly clouded sky and the brown and green and boulder-white of the peerless country. Down some lane of it that ran crookedly through the fields I could see inwardly my seven true brothers hurrying to save me in their lame walk, their stout sticks on the move together.

The Sergeant still kept his eye on the end of five miles away but moved slightly in his monumental standing. Then he spoke to me.

"I think," he said, "we will go out and have a look at it; it is a great thing to do what is necessary before it becomes essential and unavoidable."

The sounds he put on these words were startling and too strange. Each word seemed to rest on a tiny cushion and was soft and far away from every other word. When he had stopped speaking there was a warm enchanted silence as if the last note of some music too fascinating almost for comprehension had receded and disappeared long before its absence was truly noticed. He then moved out of the house before me to the yard, I behind him spellbound with no thought of any kind in my head. Soon the two of us had mounted a ladder with staid unhurrying steps and found ourselves high beside the sailing gable of the barrack, the two of us on the lofty scaffold, I the victim and he my hangman. I looked blankly and carefully everywhere, seeing for a time no difference between any different things, inspecting methodically every corner of the same unchanging sameness. Nearby I could hear his voice murmuring again:

"It is a fine day in any case," he was saying.

His words, now in the air and out-of-doors, had another warm breathless roundness in them as if his tongue was lined with furry burrs and they came lightly from him like a string of bubbles or like tiny things borne to me on thistledown in very gentle air. I went forward to a wooden railing and rested my weighty hands on it, feeling perfectly the breeze coming chillingly at their fine hairs. An idea came to me that the breezes high above the ground are separate from those which play on the same level as men's faces: here the air was newer and more unnatural, nearer the heavens and less laden with the influences of the earth. Up here I felt that every day would be the same always, serene and chilly, a band of wind isolating the earth of men from the far-from-understandable enormities of the girdling universe. Here on the stormiest autumn Monday there would be no wild leaves to brush on any face, no bees in the gusty wind. I sighed sadly.

"Strange enlightenments are vouchsafed," I murmured, "to those who seek the higher places."

I do not know why I said this strange thing. My own words were also soft and light as if they had no breath to liven them. I heard the Sergeant working behind me with coarse ropes as if he were at the far end of a great hall instead of at my back and then I heard his voice coming back to me softly called across a fathomless valley:

"I heard of a man once," he said, "that had himself let up into the sky in a balloon to make observations, a man of great personal charm but a devil for reading books. They played out the rope till he was disappeared completely from all appearances, telescopes or no telescopes, and then they played out another ten miles of rope to make sure of first-class observations. When the time limit for the observations was over they pulled down the balloon again but lo and behold there was no man in the basket and his dead body was never found afterwards lying dead or alive in any parish ever afterwards."

Here I heard myself give a hollow laugh, standing there with a high head and my two hands still on the wooden rail.

"But they were clever enough to think of sending up the balloon again a fortnight later and when they brought it down the second time lo and behold the man was sitting in the basket without a feather out of him if any of my information can be believed at all."

Here I gave some sound again, hearing my own voice as if I was a bystander at a public meeting where I was myself the main speaker. I had heard the Sergeant's words and understood them thoroughly but they were no more significant than the clear sounds that infest the air at all times—the far cry of gulls, the disturbance a breeze will make in its blowing and water falling headlong down a hill. Down into the earth where dead men go I would go soon and maybe come out of it again in some healthy way, free and innocent of all human perplexity. I would perhaps be the chill of an April wind, an essential part of some indomitable river, or be personally concerned in the ageless perfection of some rank mountain bearing down upon the mind by occupying forever a position in the blue easy distance. Or perhaps a smaller thing like movement in the grass on an unbearable breathless yellow day, some hidden creature going about its business—I might well be responsible for that or for some important part of it. Or even those unaccountable distinctions that make an evening recognizable from its own morning, the smells and sounds and sights of the perfected and matured essences of the day, these might not be innocent of my meddling and my abiding presence.

"So they asked where he was and what had kept him but he gave them no satisfaction, he only let out a laugh like one that Andy Gara would give and went home and shut himself up in his house and told his mother to say he was not at home and not receiving visitors or doing any entertaining. That made the people very angry and inflamed their passions to a degree that is not recognized by the law. So they held a private meeting that was attended by every member of the general public except the man in question and they decided to get out their shotguns the next day and break into the man's house and give him a severe threatening and tie him up and heat pokers in the fire to make him tell what happened in the sky the time he was up inside it. That is a nice piece of law and order for you, a terrific indictment of democratic self-government, a beautiful commentary on Home Rule."

Or perhaps I would be an influence that prevails in water, something sea-borne and far away, some certain arrangement of sun, light, and water unknown and unbeheld, something far-from-usual. There are in the great world whirls of fluid and vaporous existences obtaining in their own unpassing time, unwatched and uninterpreted, valid only in their essential un-understandable mystery, justified only in their eyeless and mindless immeasurability, unassailable in their actual abstraction; of the inner quality of such a thing I might well in my own time be the true quintessential pith. I might belong to a lonely shore or be the agony of the sea when it bursts upon it in despair.

"But between that and the next morning there was a stormy night in between, a loud windy night that strained the trees in their deep roots and made the roads streaky with broken branches, a night that played a bad game with root crops. When the boys reached the home of the balloonman the next morning, lo and behold the bed was empty and no trace of him was ever found afterwards dead or alive, naked or with an overcoat. And when they got back to where the balloon was, they found the wind had torn it up out of the ground with the rope spinning loosely in the windlass and it invisible to the naked eye in the middle of the clouds. They pulled in eight miles of rope before they got it down but lo and behold the basket was empty again. They all said that the man had gone up in it and stayed up but it is an insoluble conundrum; his name was Quigley and he was by all accounts a Fermanagh man."

Parts of this conversation came to me from different parts of the compass as the Sergeant moved about at his tasks, now right, now left, and now aloft on a ladder to fix the hang-rope on the summit of the scaffold. He seemed to dominate the half of the world that was behind my back with his presence—his movements and his noises—filling it up with himself to the last farthest corner. The other half of the world which lay in front of me was beautifully given a shape of sharpness or roundness that was faultlessly suitable to its nature. But the half behind me was black and evil and composed of nothing at all except the menacing policeman who was patiently and politely arranging the mechanics of my death. His work was now nearly finished and my eyes were faltering as they gazed ahead, making little sense of the distance and taking a smaller pleasure in what was near.

There is not much that I can say.

No.

Except to advise a brave front and a spirit of heroic resignation.

That will not be difficult. I feel too weak to stand up without support.

In a way that is fortunate. One hates a scene. It makes things more difficult for all concerned. A man who takes into consideration the feelings of others even when arranging the manner of his own death shows a nobility of character which compels the admiration of all classes. To quote a well-known poet, "even the ranks of Tuscany could scarce forbear to cheer." Besides, unconcern in the face of death is in itself the most impressive gesture of defiance.

I told you I haven't got the strength to make a scene.

Very good. We will say no more about it.

A creaking sound came behind me as if the Sergeant was swinging red-faced in midair to test the rope he had just fixed. Then came the clatter of his great hobs as they came again upon the boards of the platform. A rope which would stand his enormous weight would never miraculously give way with mine.

You know, of course, that I will be leaving you soon?

That is the usual arrangement.

I would not like to go without placing on record my pleasure in having been associated with you. It is no lie to say that I have always received the greatest courtesy and consideration at your hands. I can only regret that it is not practicable to offer you some small token of my appreciation.

Thank you. I am very sorry also that we must part after having been so long together. If that watch of mine were found you would be welcome to it if you could find some means of taking it.

But you have no watch.

I forgot that.

Thank you all the same. You have no idea where you are going . . . when all this is over?

No, none.

Nor have I. I do not know, or do not remember, what happens to the like of me in these circumstances. Sometimes I think that perhaps I might become part of . . . the world, if you understand me?

I know.

I mean—the wind, you know. Part of that. Or the spirit of the scenery in some beautiful place like the Lakes of Killarney, the inside meaning of it if you understand me.

I do.

Or perhaps something to do with the sea. "The light that never was on sea or land, the peasant's hope and the poet's dream." A big wave in mid-ocean, for instance, it is a very lonely and spiritual thing. Part of that.

I understand you.

Or the smell of a flower, even.

Here from my throat bounded a sharp cry rising to a scream. The Sergeant had come behind me with no noise and fastened his big hand into a hard ring on my arm, started to drag me gently but relentlessly away from where I was to the middle of the platform, where I knew there was a trapdoor which could be collapsed with machinery.

Steady now!

My two eyes, dancing madly in my head, raced up and down the country like two hares in a last wild experience of the world I was about to leave forever. But in their hurry and trepidation they did not fail to notice a movement that was drawing attention to itself in the stillness of everything far far down the road.

"The one-legged men!" I shouted.

I know that the Sergeant behind me had also seen that the far part of the road was occupied, for his grip, though still unbroken, had stopped pulling at me and I could almost sense his keen stare running out into the day parallel with my own but gradually nearing it till the two converged a quarter of a mile away. We did not seem to breathe or be alive at all as we watched the movement approaching and becoming clearer.

"MacCruiskeen, by the Powers!" the Sergeant said softly.

My lifted heart subsided painfully. Every hangman has an assistant. MacCruiskeen's arrival would make the certainty of my destruction only twice surer.

When he came nearer we could see that he was in a great hurry and that he was travelling on his bicycle. He was lying almost prostrate on top of it with his rear slightly higher than his head to cut a passage through the wind and no eye could travel quickly enough to understand the speed of his flying legs as they thrashed the bicycle onwards in a savage fury. Twenty yards away from the barrack he threw up his head, showing his face for the first time, and saw us standing on the top of the scaffold engaged in watching him with all our attention. He leaped from the bicycle in some complicated leap which was concluded only when the bicycle had been spun round adroitly to form a seat for him with its bar while he stood there, wide-legged and diminutive, looking up at us and cupping his hands at his mouth to shout his breathless message upwards:

"The lever—nine point six nine!" he called.

For the first time I had the courage to turn my head to the Sergeant. His face had gone instantly to the color of ash as if every drop of blood had left it, leaving it with empty pouches and ugly loosenesses and laxities all about it. His lower jaw hung loosely also as if it were a mechanical jaw on a toy man. I could feel the purpose and the life running out of his gripping hand like air out of a burst bladder. He spoke without looking at me.

"Let you stay here till I come back reciprocally," he said.

For a man of his weight he left me standing there alone with a speed that was astonishing. With one jump he was at the ladder. Coiling his arms and legs around it, he slid to the ground out of view with a hurry that was not different in any way from an ordinary fall. In the next second he was seated on the bar of MacCruiskeen's bicycle and the two of them were disappearing into the end of a quarter of a mile away.

When they had gone an unearthly weariness came down upon me so suddenly that I almost fell in a heap on the platform. I called together all my strength and made my way inch by inch down the ladder and back into the kitchen of the barrack and collapsed helplessly into a chair that was near the fire. I wondered at the strength of the chair for my body seemed now to be made of lead. My arms and legs were too heavy to move from where they had fallen and my eyelids could not be lifted higher than would admit through them a small glint from the red fire.

For a time I did not sleep, yet I was far from being awake. I did not mark the time that passed or think about any question in my head. I did not feel the aging of the day or the declining of the fire or even the slow return of my strength. Devils or fairies or even bicycles could have danced before me on the stone floor without perplexing me or altering by one whit my fallen attitude in the chair. I am sure I was nearly dead.

But when I did come to think again I knew that a long time had passed, that the fire was nearly out and that MacCruiskeen had just come into the kitchen with his bicycle and wheeled it hastily into his bedroom, coming out again without it and looking down at me.

"What has happened?" I whispered listlessly.

"We were just in time with the lever," he replied, "it took our combined strengths and three pages of calculations and rough-work but we got the reading down in the nick of zero-hour; you would be surprised at the coarseness of the lumps and the weight of the great fall."

"Where is the Sergeant?"

"He instructed me to ask your kind pardon for his delays. He is lying in ambush with eight deputies that were sworn in as constables on the spot to defend law and order in the public interest. But they cannot do much; they are outnumbered and they are bound to be outflanked into the same bargain."

"Is it for the one-legged men he is waiting?"

"Surely yes. But they took a great rise out of Fox. He is certain to get a severe reprimand from headquarters over the head of it. There is not seven of them but fourteen. They took off their wooden legs before they marched and tied themselves together in pairs so that there were two men for every two legs; it would remind you of Napoleon on the retreat from Russia, it is a masterpiece of military technocratics."

This news did more to revive me than would a burning drink of finest brandy. I sat up. The light appeared once more in my eyes.

"Then they will win against the Sergeant and his policemen?" I asked eagerly.

MacCruiskeen gave a smile of mystery, took large keys from his pocket, and left the kitchen. I could hear him opening the cell where the Sergeant kept his bicycle. He reappeared almost at once carrying a large can with a bung in it such as painters use when they are distempering a house. He had not removed his sly smile in his absence but now wore it more deeply in his face. He took the can into his bedroom and came out again with a large handkerchief in his hand and his smile still in use. Without a word he came behind my chair and bound the handkerchief tightly across my eyes, paying no attention to my movements and my surprise. Out of my darkness I heard his voice:

"I do not think the hoppy men will best the Sergeant," he said, "because if they come to where the Sergeant lies in secret ambush with his men before I have time to get back there, the Sergeant will delay them with military maneuvers and false alarms until I arrive down the road on my bicycle. Even now the Sergeant and his men are all blindfolded like yourself; it is a very queer way for people to be when they are lying in an ambush but it is the only way to be when I am expected at any moment on my bicycle."

I muttered that I did not understand what he had said.

"I have a private patent in that box in my bedroom," he explained, "and I have more of it in that can. I am going to paint my bicycle and ride it down the road in full view of the hoppy lads."

He had been going away from me in my darkness while saying this and now he was in his bedroom and had shut the door. Soft sounds of work came to me from where he was.

I sat there for half an hour, still weak, bereft of light and feebly wondering for the first time about making my escape. I must have come back sufficiently from death to enter a healthy tiredness again for I did not hear the policeman coming out of the bedroom again and crossing the kitchen with his unbeholdable and brain-destroying bicycle. I must have slept there fitfully in my chair, my own private darkness reigning restfully behind the darkness of the handkerchief.

JONATHAN LETHEM

Five Fucks

1

"I feel different from other people. Really different. Yet whenever I have a conversation with a new person it turns into a discussion of things we have in common. Work, places, feelings. Whatever. It's the way people talk, I know, I share the blame, I do it too. But I want to stop and shout no, it's not like that, it's not the same for me. I feel different."

"I understand what you mean."

"That's not the right response."

"I mean what the fuck are you talking about."

"Right." Laughter.

She lit a cigarette while E. went on.

"The notion is like a linguistic virus. It makes any conversation go all pallid and reassuring. 'Oh, I know, it's like that for me too.' But the virus isn't content just to eat conversations, it wants to destroy lives. It wants you to fall in love."

"There are worse things."

"Not for me."

"Famine, war, floods."

"Those never happened to me. Love did. Love is the worst thing that ever happened to me."

"That's fatuous."

"What's the worst thing that ever happened to you?"

She was silent for a full minute.

"But there, *that's* the first fatuous thing I've said. Asking you to consider *my* situation by consulting *your* experience. You see? The virus is loose again. I don't want you to agree that our lives are the same. They aren't. I just want you to listen to what I say seriously, to believe me."

"I believe you."

"Don't say it in that tone of voice. All breathy."

"Fuck you." She laughed again.

"Do you want another drink?"

"In a minute." She slurped at what was left in her glass, then said, "You know what's funny?"

"What?"

"Other people do feel the way you do, that they're apart from everyone else. It's the same as the way every time you fall in love it feels like something new, even though you do the exact same things over again. Feeling unique is what we all have in common, it's the thing that's always the same."

"No, I'm different. And falling in love is different for me each time, different things happen. Bad things."

"But you're still the same as you were before the first time. You just feel different."

"No, I've changed. I'm much worse."

"You're not bad."

"You should have seen me before. Do you want another drink?"

The laminated place mat on the table between them showed pictures of exotic drinks. "This one," she said. "A zombie." It was purple.

"You don't want that."

"Yes I do. I love zombies."

"No you don't. You've never had one. Anyway, this place makes a terrible zombie." He ordered two more margaritas.

"You're such an expert."

"Only on zombies."

"On zombies and love is bad."

"You're making fun of me. I thought you promised to take me seriously, believe me."

"I was lying. People always lie when they flirt."

"We're not flirting."

"Then what are we doing?"

"We're just drinking, drinking and talking. And I'm trying to warn you."

"And you're staring."

"You're beautiful. Oh God."

"That reminds me of one. What's the worst thing about being an atheist?"

"I give up."

"No one to talk to when you come."

2

MORNING light seeped through the macramé curtain and freckled the rug. Motes seemed to boil from its surface. For a moment she thought the rug was somehow on the ceiling, then his cat ran across it, yowling at her. The cat looked starved. She was lying on her stomach in his loft bed, head over the side. He was gone. She lay tangled in the humid sheets, feeling her own body.

Lover—she thought.

She could barely remember.

She found her clothes, then went and rinsed her face in the kitchen sink. A film of shaved hairs lined the porcelain bowl. She swirled it out with hot water, watched as the slow drain gulped it away. The drain sighed.

The table was covered with unopened mail. On the back of an envelope was a note: *I don't want to see you again. Sorry. The door locks.* She read it twice, considering each word, working it out like another language. The cat crept into the kitchen. She dropped the envelope.

She put her hand down and the cat rubbed against it. Why was it so thin? It didn't look old. The fact of the note was still sinking in. She remembered the night only in flashes, visceral strobe. With her fingers she combed the tangles out of her hair. She stood up and the cat dashed away. She went out into the hall, undecided, but the weighted door latched behind her.

Fuck him.

The problem was of course that she wanted to.

It was raining. She treated herself to a cab on Eighth Avenue. In the backseat she closed her eyes. The potholes felt like mines, and the cab squeaked like rusty bedsprings. It was Sunday. Coffee, corn muffin, newspaper; she'd insulate herself with them, make a buffer between the night and the new day.

But there was something wrong with the doorman at her building. "You're back!" he said.

She was led incredulous to her apartment full of dead houseplants and unopened mail, her answering machine full of calls from friends, clients, the police. There was a layer of dust on the answering machine. Her address book and laptop disks were gone; clues, the doorman explained.

"Clues to what?"

"Clues to your case. To what happened to you. Everyone was worried."

"Well, there's nothing to worry about. I'm fine."

"Everyone had theories. The whole building."

"I understand."

"The man in charge is a good man, Miss Rush. The building feels a great confidence in him."

"Good."

"I'm supposed to call him if something happens, like someone trying to get into your place, or you coming back. Do you want me to call?"

"Let me call."

The card he handed her was bent and worn from traveling in his pocket. CORNELL PUPKISS, MISSING PERSONS. And a phone number. She reached out her hand; there was dust on the telephone too. "Please go," she said.

"Is there anything you need?"

"No." She thought of E.'s cat, for some reason.

"You can't tell me at least what happened?"

"No."

She remembered E.'s hands and mouth on her—a week ago? An hour?

Cornell Pupkiss was tall and drab and stolid, like a man built on the model of a tower of suitcases. He wore a hat and a trench coat, and shoes which were filigreed with a thousand tiny scratches, as though they'd been beset by phonograph needles. He seemed to absorb and deaden light.

On the telephone he had insisted on seeing her. He'd handed her the disks and the address book at the door. Now he stood just inside the door and smiled gently at her.

"I wanted to see you in the flesh," he said. "I've come to know you from photographs and people's descriptions. When I come to know a person in that manner I like to see them in the flesh if I can. It makes me feel I've completed my job, a rare enough illusion in my line."

There was nothing bright or animated in the way he spoke. His voice was like furniture with the varnish carefully sanded off. "But I haven't really completed my job until I understand what happened," he went on. "Whether a crime was committed. Whether you're in some sort of trouble with which I can help."

She shook her head.

"Where were you?" he said.

"I was with a man."

"I see. For almost two weeks?"

"Yes."

She was still holding the address book. He raised his large hand in its direction, without uncurling a finger to point. "We called every man you know."

"This—this was someone I just met. Are these questions necessary, Mr. Pupkiss?"

"If the time was spent voluntarily, no." His lips tensed, his whole expression deepened, like gravy jelling. "I'm sorry, Miss Rush."

Pupkiss in his solidity touched her somehow. Reassured her. If he went away, she saw now, she'd be alone with the questions. She wanted him to stay a little longer and voice the questions for her.

But now he was gently sarcastic. "You're answerable to no one, of course. I only suggest that in the future you might spare the concern of your neighbors, and the effort of my department—a single phone call would be sufficient."

"I didn't realize how much time had passed," she said. He couldn't know how truthful that was.

"I've heard it can be like that," he said, surprisingly bitter. "But it's not criminal to neglect the feelings of others, just adolescent."

You don't understand, she nearly cried out. But she saw that he would view it as one or the other, a menace or self-indulgence. If she convinced him of her distress, he'd want to protect her.

She couldn't let harm come to E. She wanted to comprehend what had happened, but Pupkiss was too blunt to be her investigatory tool.

Reflecting in this way, she said, "The things that happen to people don't always fit into such easy categories as that."

"I agree," he said, surprising her again. "But in my job it's best to keep from bogging down in ontology. Missing Persons is an extremely large and various category. Many people are lost in relatively simple ways, and those are generally the ones I can help. Good day, Miss Rush."

"Good day." She didn't object as he moved to the door. Suddenly she was eager to be free of this ponderous man, his leaden integrity. She wanted to be left alone to remember the night before, to think of the one who'd devoured her and left her reeling. That was what mattered.

E. had somehow caused two weeks to pass in one feverish night, but Pupkiss threatened to make the following morning feel like two weeks.

He shut the door behind him so carefully that there was only a little huff of displaced air and a tiny click as the bolt engaged.

"It's me," she said into the intercom.

There was only static. She pressed the button again. "Let me come up."

He didn't answer, but the buzzer at the door sounded. She went into the hall and upstairs to his door.

"It's open," he said.

E. was seated at the table, holding a drink. The cat was curled up on the pile of envelopes. The apartment was dark. Still, she saw what she hadn't before: he lived terribly, in rooms that were wrecked and provisional. The plaster was cracked everywhere. Cigarette stubs were bunched in the baseboard corners where, having still smoldered, they'd tanned the linoleum. The place smelled sour, in a way that made her think of the sourness she'd washed from her body in her own bath an hour before.

He tilted his head up, but didn't meet her gaze. "Why are you here?"

"I wanted to see you."

"You shouldn't."

His voice was ragged, his expression had a crushed quality. His hand on the glass was tensed like a claw. But even diminished and bitter he seemed to her effervescent, made of light.

"We—something happened when we made love," she said. The words came tenderly. "We lost time."

"I warned you. Now leave."

"My life," she said, uncertain what she meant.

"Yes, it's yours," he shot back. "Take it and go."

"If I gave you two weeks, it seems the least you can do is look me in the eye," she said.

He did it, but his mouth trembled as though he were guilty or afraid. His face was beautiful to her.

"I want to know you," she said.

"I can't let that happen," he said. "You see why." He tipped his glass back and emptied it, grimacing.

"This is what always happens to you?"

"I can't answer your questions."

"If that happens, I don't care." She moved to him and put her hands in his hair.

He reached up and held them there.

3

A woman has come into my life. I hardly know how to speak of it.

I was in the station, enduring the hectoring of Dell Armickle, the commander of the Vice Squad. He is insufferable, a toad from Hell. He follows the donut cart through the offices each afternoon, pinching the buttocks of the Jamaican woman who peddles the donuts and that concentrated urine others call coffee. This day he stopped at my desk to gibe at the headlines in my morning paper. "Union Boss Stung in Fat Farm Sex Ring—ha! Made you look, didn't I?"

"What?"

"Pupkiss, you're only pretending to be thick. How much you got hidden away in that Swedish bank account by now?"

"Sorry?" His gambits were incomprehensible.

"Whatsis?" he said, poking at my donut, ignoring his own blather better than I could ever hope to. "Cinnamon?"

"Whole wheat," I said.

Then she appeared. She somehow floated in without causing any fuss, and stood at the head of my desk. She was pale and hollow-eyed and beautiful, like Renée Falconetti in Dreyer's *Jeanne d'Arc*.

"Officer Pupkiss," she said. Is it only in the light of what followed that I recall her speaking my name as though she knew me? At least she spoke it with certainty, not questioning whether she'd found her goal.

I'd never seen her before, though I can only prove it by tautology: I knew at that moment I was seeing a face I would never forget.

Armickle bugged his eyes and nostrils at me, imitating both clown and beast. "Speak to the lady, Cornell," he said, managing to impart to the syllables of my given name a childish ribaldry.

"I'm Pupkiss," I said awkwardly.

"I'd like to talk to you," she said. She looked only at me, as though Armickle didn't exist.

"I can take a hint," said Armickle. "Have fun, you two." He hurried after the donut cart.

"You work in Missing Persons," she said.

"No," I said. "Petty Violations."

"Before, you used to work in Missing Persons—"

"Never. They're a floor above us. I'll walk you to the elevator if you'd like."

"No." She shook her head curtly, impatiently. "Forget it. I want to talk to you. What are Petty Violations?"

"It's an umbrella term. But I'd sooner address your concerns than try your patience with my job description."

"Yes. Could we go somewhere?"

I led her to a booth in the coffee shop downstairs. I ordered a donut, to replace the one I'd left behind on my desk. She drank coffee, holding the cup with both hands to warm them. I found myself wanting to feed her, build her a nest.

"Cops really do like donuts," she said, smiling weakly.

"Or toruses," I said.

"Sorry? You mean the astrological symbol?"

"No, the geometric shape. A torus. A donut is in the shape of one. Like a life preserver, or a tire, or certain space stations. It's a little joke of mine: cops don't like donuts, they like toruses."

She looked at me oddly. I cursed myself for bringing it up. "Shouldn't the plural be *tori*?" she said.

I winced. "I'm sure you're right. Never mind. I don't mean to take up your time with my little japes."

"I've got plenty of time," she said, poignant again.

"Nevertheless. You wished to speak to me."

"You knew me once," she said.

I did my best to appear sympathetic, but I was baffled.

"Something happened to the world. Everything changed. Everyone that I know has disappeared."

"As an evocation of subjective truth—" I began.

"No. I'm talking about something real. I used to have friends."

"I've had few, myself."

"Listen to me. All the people I know have disappeared. My family, my friends, everyone I used to work with. They've all been replaced by strangers who don't know me. I have nowhere to go. I've been awake for two days looking for my life. I'm exhausted. You're the only person that looks the same as before and has the same name. The Missing Persons man, ironically."

"I'm not the Missing Persons man," I said.

"Cornell Pupkiss. I could never forget a name like that."

"It's been a burden."

"You don't remember coming to my apartment? You said you'd been looking for me. I was gone for two weeks."

I struggled against temptation. I could extend my time in her company by playing along, indulging the misunderstanding. In other words, by betraying what I knew to be the truth: that I had nothing at all to do with her unusual situation.

"No," I said. "I don't remember."

Her expression hardened. "Why should you?" she said bitterly.

"Your question's rhetorical," I said. "Permit me a rhetorical reply. That I don't know you from some earlier encounter we can both regret.

However, I know you now. And I'd be pleased to have you consider me an ally."

"Thank you."

"How did you find me?"

"I called the station and asked if you still worked there."

"And there's no one else from your previous life?"

"No one—except him."

Ah.

"Tell me," I said.

She'd met the man she called E. in a bar, how long ago she couldn't explain. She described him as irresistible. I formed an impression of a skunk, a rat. She said he worked no deliberate charm on her, on the contrary seemed panicked when the mood between them grew intimate and full of promise. I envisioned a scoundrel with an act, a crafted diffidence that allured, a backpedaling attack.

He'd taken her home, of course.

"And?" I said.

"We fucked," she said. "It was good, I think. But I have trouble remembering."

The words stung. The one in particular. I tried not to be a child, swallowed my discomfort away. "You were drunk," I suggested.

"No. I mean, *yes*, but it was more than that. We weren't clumsy like drunks. We went into some kind of trance."

"He drugged you."

"No."

"How do you know?"

"What happened—it wasn't something he wanted."

"And what did happen?"

"Two weeks disappeared from my life overnight. When I got home I found I'd been considered missing. My friends and family had been searching for me. You'd been called in."

"I thought your friends and family had vanished themselves. That no one knew you."

"No. That was the *second* time."

"Second time?"

"The second time we fucked." Then she seemed to remember something, and dug in her pocket. "Here." She handed me a scuffed business card: CORNELL PUPKISS, MISSING PERSONS.

"I can't believe you live this way. It's like a prison." She referred to the seamless rows of book spines that faced her in each of my few rooms, including the bedroom, where we now stood. "Is it all criminology?"

"I'm not a policeman in some cellular sense," I said, and then realized the pun. "I mean, not intrinsically. They're novels, first editions."

"Let me guess: mysteries."

"I detest mysteries. I would never bring one into my home."

"Well, you have, in me."

I blushed, I think, from head to toe. "That's different," I stammered. "Human lives exist to be experienced, or possibly endured, but not solved. They resemble any other novel more than they do mysteries. Westerns, even. It's that lie the mystery tells that I detest."

"Your reading is an antidote to the simplifications of your profession, then."

"I suppose. Let me show you where the clean towels are kept."

I handed her fresh towels and linen, and took for myself a set of sheets to cover the living room sofa.

She saw that I was preparing the sofa and said, "The bed's big enough."

I didn't turn, but I felt the blood rush to the back of my neck as though specifically to meet her gaze. "It's four in the afternoon," I said. "I won't be going to bed for hours. Besides, I snore."

"Whatever," she said. "Looks uncomfortable, though. What's Barbara Pym? She sounds like a mystery writer, one of those stuffy English ones."

The moment passed, the blush faded from my scalp. I wondered later, though, whether this had been some crucial missed opportunity. A chance at the deeper intervention that was called for.

"Read it," I said, relieved at the change of subject. "Just be careful of the dust jacket."

"I may learn something, huh?" She took the book and climbed in between the covers.

"I hope you'll be entertained."

"And she doesn't snore, I guess. That was a joke, Mr. Pupkiss."

"So recorded. Sleep well. I have to return to the station. I'll lock the door."

"Back to Little Offenses?"

"Petty Violations."

"Oh, right." I could hear her voice fading. As I stood and watched, she fell soundly asleep. I took the Pym from her hands and replaced it on the shelf.

I wasn't going to the station. Using the information she'd given me, I went to find the tavern E. supposedly frequented.

I found him there, asleep in a booth, head resting on his folded arms. He looked terrible, his hair a thatch, drool leaking into his sweater arm, his eyes swollen like a fevered child's, just the picture of raffish haplessness a woman would find magnetic. Unmistakably the seedy vermin I'd projected and the idol of Miss Rush's nightmare.

I went to the bar and ordered an Irish coffee, and considered. Briefly indulging a fantasy of personal power, I rebuked myself for coming here and making him real, when he had only before been an absurd story, a neurotic symptom. Then I took out the card she'd given me and laid it on the bar top. Cornell Pupkiss, Missing Persons. No, I myself was the symptom. It is seldom as easy in practice as in principle to acknowledge one's own bystander status in incomprehensible matters.

I took my coffee to his booth and sat across from him. He roused and looked up at me.

"Rise and shine, buddy boy," I said, a little stiffly. I've never thrilled to the role of Bad Cop.

"What's the matter?"

"Your unshaven chin is scratching the table surface."

"Sorry." He rubbed his eyes.

"Got nowhere to go?"

"What are you, the house dick?"

"I'm in the employ of any taxpayer," I said. "The bartender happens to be one."

"He's never complained to me."

"Things change."

"You can say that again."

We stared at each other. I supposed he was nearly my age, though he was more boyishly pretty than I'd been even as an actual boy. I hated him for that, but I pitied him for the part I saw that was precociously old and bitter.

I thought of Miss Rush asleep in my bed. She'd been worn and disarrayed by their two encounters, but she didn't yet look this way. I wanted to keep her from it.

"Let me give you some advice," I said, as gruffly as I could manage. "Solve your problems."

"I hadn't thought of that."

"Don't get stuck in a rut." I was aware of the lameness of my words only as they emerged, too late to stop.

"Don't worry, I never do."

"Very well then," I said, somehow unnerved. "This interview is concluded." If he'd shown any sign of budging I might have leaned back in the booth, crossed my arms authoritatively, and stared him out the door. Since he remained planted in his seat, I stood up, feeling that my last spoken words needed reinforcement.

He laid his head back into the cradle of his arms, first sliding the laminated place mat underneath. "This will protect the table surface," he said.

"That's good, practical thinking," I heard myself say as I left the booth.

It wasn't the confrontation I'd been seeking.

On the way home I shopped for breakfast, bought orange juice, milk, bagels, fresh coffee beans. I took it upstairs and unpacked it as quietly as I could in the kitchen, then removed my shoes and crept in to have a look at Miss Rush. She was peaceably asleep. I closed the door and prepared my bed on the sofa. I read a few pages of the Penguin softcover edition of Muriel Spark's *The Bachelors* before dropping off.

Before dawn, the sky like blued steel, the city silent, I was woken by a sound in the apartment, at the front door. I put on my robe and went into the kitchen. The front door was unlocked, my key in the dead bolt. I went back through the apartment; Miss Rush was gone.

I write this at dawn. I am very frightened.

4

IN an alley which ran behind a lively commercial street there sat a pair of the large trash receptacles commonly known as Dumpsters. In them accumulated the waste produced by the shops whose rear entrances shared the alley—a framer's, a soup kitchen, an antique clothing store, a donut bakery, and a photocopyist's establishment—and by the offices above those storefronts. On this street and in this alley, each day had its seasons: spring, when complaining morning shifts opened the shops, students and workers rushed to destinations, coffee sloshing in paper cups, and in the alley, the sanitation contractors emptied containers, sorted recyclables and waste like bees pollinating garbage truck flowers; summer, the ripened afternoons, when the workday slackened, shoppers stole long lunches from their employers, the cafés filled with students with highlighter pens, and the indigent beckoned for the change that jingled in incautious pockets, while in the alley new riches piled up; autumn, the cooling evening, when half the shops closed, and the street was given over to prowlers and pacers, those who lingered in bookstores and dined alone in Chinese restaurants, and the indigent plundered the fatted Dumpsters for half-eaten paper bag lunches, batches of botched donuts, wearable cardboard matting and unmatched socks, and burnable wood scraps; winter, the selfish night, when even the cafés battened down iron gates through which night watchmen fluorescents palely flickered, the indigent built their overnight camps in doorways and under side street hedges, or in wrecked cars, and the street itself was an abandoned stage.

On the morning in question the sun shone brightly, yet the air was bitingly cold. Birds twittered resentfully. When the sanitation crew arrived to wheel the two Dumpsters out to be hydraulically lifted into their screeching, whining truck, they were met with cries of protest from within.

The men lifted the metal tops of the Dumpsters and discovered that an indigent person had lodged in each of them, a lady in one, a gentleman in the other.

"Geddoudadare," snarled the eldest sanitation engineer, a man with features like a spilled plate of stew.

The indigent lady rose from within the heap of refuse and stood blinking in the bright morning sun. She was an astonishing sight, a ruin. The colors of her skin and hair and clothes had all surrendered to gray; an archaeologist might have ventured an opinion as to their previous hue. She could have been anywhere between thirty and fifty years old, but speculation was absurd; her age had been taken from her and replaced with a timeless condition, a state. Her eyes were pitiable; horrified and horrifying; witnesses, victims, accusers.

"Where am I?" she said softly.

"Isedgeddoudadare," barked the garbage operative.

The indigent gentleman then raised himself from the other Dumpster. He was in every sense her match; to describe him would be to tax the reader's patience for things worn, drab, desolate, crestfallen, unfortunate, etc. He turned his head at the trashman's exhortation and saw his mate.

"What's the—" he began, then stopped.

"You," said the indigent lady, lifting an accusing finger at him from amidst her rags. "You did this to me."

"No," he said. "No."

"Yes!" she screamed.

"C'mon," said the burly sanitateur. He and his second began pushing the nearer container, which bore the lady, towards his truck.

She cursed at them and climbed out, with some difficulty. They only laughed at her and pushed the cart out to the street. The indigent man scrambled out of his Dumpster and brushed at his clothes, as though they could thereby be distinguished from the material in which he'd lain.

The lady flew at him, furious. "Look at us! Look what you did to me!" She whirled her limbs at him, trailing banners of rag.

He backed from her, and bumped into one of the garbagemen, who said, "Hey!"

"It's not my fault," said the indigent man.

"Yugoddageddoudahere!" said the stew-faced worker.

"What do you mean it's not your fault?" she shrieked.

Windows were sliding open in the offices above them. "Quiet down there," came a voice.

"It wouldn't happen without you," he said.

At that moment a policeman rounded the corner. He was a large man named Officer McPupkiss who even in the morning sun conveyed an aspect of night. His policeman's uniform was impeccably fitted, his brass polished, but his shoetops were exceptionally scuffed and dull. His presence stilled the combatants.

"What's the trouble?" he said.

They began talking all at once; the pair of indigents, the refuse handlers, and the disgruntled office worker leaning out of his window.

"Please," said McPupkiss in a quiet voice which was nonetheless heard by all.

"He ruined my life!" said the indigent lady raggedly.

"Ah, yes. Shall we discuss it elsewhere?" He'd already grasped the situation. He held out his arms, almost as if he wanted to embrace the two tatterdemalions, and nodded at the disposal experts, who silently resumed their labors. The indigents followed McPupkiss out of the alley.

"He ruined my life," she said again when they were on the sidewalk.

"She ruined mine," answered the gentleman.

"I wish I could believe it was all so neat," said McPupkiss. "A life is simply *ruined*; credit for the destruction goes *here* or *here*. In my own experience things are more ambiguous."

"This is one of the exceptions," said the lady. "It's strange but not ambiguous. He fucked me over."

"She was warned," he said. "She made it happen."

"The two of you form a pretty picture," said McPupkiss. "You ought to be working together to improve your situation; instead you're obsessed with blame."

"We can't work together," she said. "Anytime we come together we create a disaster."

"Fine, go your separate ways," said the officer. "I've always thought 'We got ourselves into this mess and we can get ourselves out of it' was a laughable attitude. Many things are irreversible, and what matters is moving on. For example, a car can't reverse its progress over a cliff; it has to be abandoned by those who survive the fall, if any do."

But by the end of this speech the gray figures had fallen to blows and were no longer listening. They clutched one another like exhausted boxers, hissing and slapping, each trying to topple the other. McPupkiss chided himself for wasting his breath, grabbed them both by the backs of their scruffy collars, and began smiting their hindquarters with his dingy shoes until they ran down the block and out of sight together, united again, McPupkiss thought, as they were so clearly meant to be.

5

THE village of Pupkinstein was nestled in a valley surrounded by steep woods. The villagers were a contented people except for the fear of the two monsters that lived in the woods and came into the village to fight their battles. Everyone knew that the village had been rebuilt many times after being half destroyed by the fighting of the monsters. No one living could remember the last of these battles, but that only intensified the suspicion that the next time would surely be soon.

Finally the citizens of Pupkinstein gathered in the town square to discuss the threat of the two monsters and debate proposals for the prevention of their battles. A group of builders said, "Let us build a wall around the perimeter of the village, with a single gate which could be fortified by volunteer soldiers."

A group of priests began laughing, and one of them said, "Don't you know that the monsters have wings? They'll flap twice and be over your wall in no time."

Since none of the builders had ever seen the monsters, they had no reply.

Then the priests spoke up and said, "We should set up temples which can be filled with offerings: food, wine, burning candles, knitted scarves, and the like. The monsters will be appeased."

Now the builders laughed, saying, "These are monsters, not jealous gods. They don't care for our appeasements. They only want to crush each other, and we're in the way."

The priests had no answer, since their holy scriptures contained no accounts of the monsters' habits.

Then the mayor of Pupkinstein, a large, somber man, said, "We should build our own monster here in the middle of the square, a scarecrow so huge and threatening that the monsters will see it and at once be frightened back into hiding."

This plan satisfied the builders, with their love of construction, and the priests, with their fondness for symbols. So the very next morning the citizens of Pupkinstein set about constructing a gigantic figure in the square. They began by demolishing their fountain. In its place they marked out the soles of two gigantic shoes, and the builders sank foundations for the lowering legs that would extend from them. Then the carpenters built frames, and the seamstresses sewed canvasses, and in less than a week the two shoes were complete, and the beginnings of ankles besides. Without being aware of it, the citizens had begun to model their monster on the mayor, who was always present as a model, whereas no one had ever seen the two monsters.

The following night it rained. Tarpaulins were thrown over the half-constructed ankles that rose from the shoes. The mayor and the villagers retired to an alehouse to toast their labors and be sheltered from the rain. But just as the proprietor was pouring their ale, someone said, "Listen!"

Between the crash of thunder and the crackle of lightning there came a hideous bellowing from the woods at either end of the valley.

"They're coming!" the citizens said. "Too soon—our monster's not finished!"

"How bitter," said one man. "We've had a generation of peace in which to build, and yet we only started a few days ago."

"We'll always know that we tried," said the mayor philosophically.

"Perhaps the shoes will be enough to frighten them," said the proprietor, who had always been regarded as a fool.

No one answered him. Fearing for their lives, the villagers ran to their homes and barricaded themselves behind shutters and doors, hid their children in attics and potato cellars, and snuffed out candles and lanterns that might lead an attacker to their doors. No one dared even look at the naked, miserable things that came out of the woods and into the square; no one, that is, except the mayor. He stood in the shadow of one of the enormous shoes, rain beating on his umbrella, only dimly sensing that he was watching another world being fucked away.

6

I live in a shadowless pale blue sea.

I am a bright pink crablike thing, some child artist's idea of an invertebrate, so badly drawn as to be laughable.

Nevertheless, I have feelings.

More than feelings. I have a mission, an obsession.

I am building a wall.

Every day I move a grain of sand. The watercolor sea washes over my back, but I protect my accumulation. I fasten each grain to the wall with my comic book feces. (Stink lines hover above my shit, also flies which look like bow ties, though I am supposed to be underwater.)

He is on the other side. My nemesis. Someday my wall will divide the ocean, someday it will reach the surface, or the top of the page, and be called a reef. He will be on the other side. He will not be able to get to me.

My ridiculous body moves only sideways, but it is enough.

I will divide the watercolor ocean, I will make it two. We must have a world for each of us.

I move a grain. When I come to my wall, paradoxically, I am nearest him. His little pink body, practically glowing. He is watching me, watching me build.

There was a time when he tried to help, when every day for a week he added a grain to my wall. I spent every day that week removing his grain, expelling it from the wall, and no progress was made until he stopped. He understands now. My wall must be my own. We can be together in nothing. Let him built his own wall. So he watches.

My wall will take me ten thousand years to complete. I live only for the day that it is complete.

The Pupfish floats by.

The Pupfish is a fish with the features of a mournful hound dog and a policeman's cap. The Pupfish is the only creature in the sea apart from me and my pink enemy.

The Pupfish, I know, would like to scoop me up in its oversized jaws and take me away. The Pupfish thinks it can solve my problem.

But no matter how far the Pupfish took me, I would still be in the same ocean with *him*. That cannot be. There must be two oceans. So I am building a wall.

I move a grain.

I rest.

I will be free.

EDMUND WHITE

Forgetting Elena

I walk past the woman's seaside cottage. Simply knowing that it's my next destination permits me to amble aimlessly for a while. I feel my way down a wooden stairway onto the dark beach. A discarded pair of sunglasses warps the moonlight. My foot sinks into a rut I hadn't seen and I almost lose my balance. Shivering slightly, I tie my terry cloth robe more tightly around me.

Long furrows in the sand; perhaps a jeep's tire tracks. A recording of a woman's voice floats on a soft breeze from a one-story frame house cupped between two nearby hillocks.

Scuffing my bare feet across the sand, I scatter showers of fool's gold. Plankton. Experimenting, I jump in place and awaken a circle of light around me, a gilded lotus supporting a Bodhisattva. Then I jog for a moment, digging my heels in deep, and observe over my shoulder fading footprints, the farthest already subsiding into darkness. I swoop down and hurl clumps of cold, wet sand in front of me, minuscule meteors flaming apart and landing silently on this imperturbable planet of moonlight and shadows.

The ocean thuds and fizzes behind me. I feel like a fish flung on land, a square-faced fish breathing the scorching air and flexing my whiskers spasmodically.

Emerging out of the dark, surprising me, a man and a woman walk past. They speak softly. A blue cashmere sweater draped over the woman's shoulders dangles empty sleeves behind her. The people are holding hands. A small dog, panting happily, trots ahead of them, closes its mouth and points into the wind; discovering nothing, the dog looks around to see if the man and woman are still following, begins to pant innocently again, and scampers on ahead, the silky hair on its shanks matted with sand. They don't see me. I would like to join them or be him or her.

Someone's standing by the window, tall and operatic. Could it be the woman, wearing a robe of some sort? Is she grinning? Is she dead?

No, it's only a birdcage, covered with a long trailing cloth.

The door at the other end of the porch opens, a head emerges, a white hand rests on the white doorjamb. "Why are you standing there? I thought you'd never come," the woman says raucously, her voice overly distinct and the emotion too pat, as though she were playing the scene for someone else's benefit. And indeed I can hear shaking, hissing laughter coming from inside the house: Maria.

As I brush past the woman, she flattens herself against the door and salutes, which elicits more hissing from the Negress. As my eyes adjust to the darkness, I pick out the white rectangle of the mattress on the floor; the flowered sheets—is there someone in the bed?—no, the sheets are simply tangled; a sudden glint of light—another room? Brilliants in Maria's hair? No, a mirror on the wall. A heavy perfume rises from the furs on the floor, a scent laden with associations. Our mother may have worn it when we were children; it's barbarous and musky enough to suit the Valentines. Or does the woman always sprinkle it about when she expects the perfect man? Am I her brother or her lover?

She stands in front of me, her face lifted toward mine, her eyes closed. I don't know what she expects. I put a hand on her shoulder. She draws the fingers to her mouth and licks each one, then forces two between her lips, then three and then, my knuckles touching the roof of her mouth, she licks my palm. Her tongue is sandy. Her eyes never open. Removing my hand from her mouth, she guides it under her robe and places it upon her right breast. I suppose I should rub it. Should I wet *her* hand as well and put it under my shirt?

The only thing for me to do is experiment. I only want to please. And yet, her pleasure may depend on mine; we may turn out to be one mirror reflecting another, two mirrors bandying absence back and forth.

I put my hands around her waist and lock them. She presses her pelvis against mine and arches her back, tossing her head so that her hair flicks over her shoulder. She's behaving so queerly I can only presume the occasion dictates sudden movements, heavy breathing, and long, silent glances. Ordinarily she carries herself in a quite natural, unobtrusive way, but now she's smiling and now she's nuzzling her lips against my neck. What is she—she's biting me!

This sharp sting in my neck seems familiar.

"So you're here," she whispers. I nod. Her voice sounds unexpectedly normal. It reminds me of our walk on the beach, where everything was so sane and purposeful.

Now I am her purpose, I or my body, and her legs, her lips, her breasts are mine to do with as I wish. Where is Maria? I don't see her anywhere around. Perhaps she scurried out of the room as soon as I came in, or perhaps she's watching us from behind the mirror on the wall.

As though she were blind, the woman closes her eyes and traces my features lightly with her fingertips. "I can't believe you're here."

"But I am," I say, gentle, compassionate, maybe bemused.

"Put your hand on my breast," she orders me solemnly. "There. It's yours. My body is yours. You can kill me if you like. I belong to you. Do you know what that means? I mean it. I belong to you."

I don't know what to say. Apparently her declaration excites her; I realize that I'm in the presence of a fantasy I don't understand, and that she's rehearsed this last little speech so often that the words amaze her now that her mouth has finally formed them. She trembles from head to foot when I touch her hair, as though I had just flooded her body with energy.

She pulls away from me. Turning to her bedside table, she putters aimlessly with the objects on it—a bracelet? a comb? No, a necklace that she slips over her hair. Humming a little song, she dances. She shakes her head from side to side and lowers her eyes. Very nonchalant. She fears her declaration has embarrassed me and she's marking time. What she wants is to seem at once occupied and free, absorbed with her dancing (not expecting a thing), but available to any whim I might chance upon. If I touch her, she'll awaken, open her eyes, come back into my arms. As she said, she belongs to me.

Her hands circulate, she feints and fades, her head double-times the beat, and yet there's something tentative and sketchy about what she's doing. She may be self-enclosed, but if so, she's a package with ribbons half untied.

Someone, I suppose Maria, starts strumming the guitar in the next room, or in the room beyond, and its chords, interrupted by long silence, destroy the woman's dance. The woman stops where she's standing and fidgets with her hair. Marooned, uncertain, caught between emotions, she looks at me blankly. I notice a dressmaker's dummy by the window. "What's that?"

"My dress for the royal arrival," she says. "I'm afraid it's as compli-cated as I am."

She's so little and lonely. I put my arms around her. She's a very frag-ile creature. I'm much bigger than she, much stronger. I adore her. If anyone tried to hurt her—ah! I'm feeling what people must experience when they pant or stare at each other or bite. They are feeling so many things, feeling and dreaming. Ordinary conversation is so mannered and constrained that little is expressed and that little in contorted forms, like plants stunted and shaped by wires. Only in dark bedrooms can the foliage rush free and loud. If people looked so tragically at one another on the beach, everyone would burst out laughing; but at night, in private, they no longer have to be nonchalant or original. When they make love they're like singers in an opera. The woman is a prima donna, rising quickly at the hero's arrival, drinking in his presence, embracing him passionately, and launching into her aria, "O safely returned!"—except no sound is uttered. Some convention or other permits islanders to indulge in histrionics in the dark.

I pull her blouse open and for a moment I think I've made a mistake because she covers both breasts with her hands. But then she kisses me briskly and lies down on the bed, her hands by her sides, her eyes open and glimmering. I kneel above her on the mattress and decide—how odd!—to let her *worship* me.

And she does. Her hands travel up my sides, explore my skin under my robe, and seek to pull me down to her level, but I resist. I do more than resist, I frown at her. My contempt either excites her or alarms her, I don't care which. Her breathing quickens. She rises to her knees, and pulls off my robe, feverishly kissing my hands, my neck, and my shoulders.

Very deliberately I get up and slip my swimsuit off. She never takes her eyes off me but her hands fumble with her own clothes as she raises her hips off the mattress and works her panties down her legs.

Now we are both naked.

I debate for a moment what I should do next, I puzzle over what's correct. I could cross the room, squat on my haunches, my chin in my hand, and stare at her impassively. Or I could pace restlessly from the head of the bed to the foot, lost in thought, my head dropped as she struggles to gain my attention. By walking back and forth, so close, yet my thoughts so far away, I'd become more and more worthy of worship, untouchable. But if I'm right, if people take off their clothes in their rooms in order to pantomime their fantasies ("an ab-zurd expression"), then what is my fantasy? How can I translate what I've been going through today and yesterday into an action, or a series of actions, that will tell my little tale? The exhaustion pressing strong fingers into my neck and shoulders, powdering the base of my backbone into dust and slowing my feet—surely this exhaustion is a sign I'm not living right. Not everyone could be this tired, day in and day out. The correct way of thinking, talking, moving, second-guessing—if there is a correct way—must be much easier.

Then if my way is too strenuous to be right, I should be able to dramatize my errors, convert my mistakes into a charade or hieroglyph. And if I were successful in doing that? She might in turn devise her own dumbshow. That's what I must do, give a show.

My bowels roll over. I glance at my stomach to see if the skin of my stomach is rippling, is giving me away. No. I'm safe.

The woman puts her hands behind her head and her small breasts rise and flatten, no longer oranges but pears. Then she nervously lowers a hand—one orange, one pear—and rests it next to the cleft between her legs, where I can only faintly distinguish her long fingers now, nesting like a soft waterfowl beyond the sprouting of her hair. "If you're not willing . . ." she says, slightly irritated.

"What do you want me to do?"

"Let me at least hold you?"

I begin to smile, I don't know whether from embarrassment or as a way of eliciting a smile from her, a sort of safe conduct into intimacy—but I banish it from my lips at once and make my face a blank. The whole secret in making love seems to be to skip the polite transitions, the haze of words and smiles and shrugs that in ordinary society dull the outlines of each new event. I must decide what to do and then do it, without apologizing or preparing her. This is not an exchange, but a perpetration.

I lie beside her and kiss her lips and plan to smear the kiss the length of her body, to the cleft, the knee, the sole of her foot. But I become involved with her hair and want it cascading around me. I roll her over on top of me and the hair drizzles on either side of my face, whether I look to the right or the left.

She shakes her head slowly, back and forth, trailing hair over first one of my cheeks, then the other. Now she is working her way down my body, but like a pilgrim making her progress toward a shrine, she stops to rest at every wayside shelter, forgetting none, giving each its due. Taking my limp penis in hand, she puts it in her mouth and oscillates around the tip of it. She licks it, she tries to swallow it—if this is *her* dumbshow, what's she saying by it? Perhaps she saw me inspecting my erection by the Detached Residence and she wants to show me that she knows it was the instrument of my loneliness. By joining her mouth to it, she may be telling me I'm no longer alone. We are together.

Or then again, for her its head may represent the Residence itself and the supporting column may stand for the grounds and the motions of her tongue may be mocking me, each lick may be a subtle remonstration, pointing out, on this tubular map, places I neglected to rake clean. Or she may be silently giving me instructions for my work tomorrow, saying, in effect, go here first and Herbert will tell you what must be done, and then rake . . .

Is it becoming harder? Yes, and she seems to find its extension more exciting (its growth aggrandizing the grounds of the Residence?). She says, "Oh, my darling," and renews her exertions. It may please her because I have a penis and she doesn't. By reciprocal reasoning, what she has and I lack I should find especially delightful. Her breasts, in fact, and her cleft.

I take her breasts into my hands and massage them. She moans so loudly, she says again, "Oh, my darling." Perhaps what we're seeking is pain, or at least an intense sensation halfway between pain and pleasure, for, truth to tell, I would be hard put to describe the feeling crowding my erection. Similarity of position would suggest that her cleft was the counterpart to my penis, but if so, then what in me corresponds to her breasts? Or could it be that, greedy for sensation, she has swallowed or injected a chemical to swell and sensitize her breasts?

When will this end? Shall we continue to lick and massage each other all night until exhaustion puts a stop to our work, or does something happen to signal the end? Maria may grow bored and interrupt us, but at least for now her guitar sounds so self-centered it could go on playing forever. Or it may be that daylight when it comes will be inimical to such posturing, or perhaps the woman will become more and more tragic until she's had her fill or has completed a predetermined cycle at a predetermined point.

She slips off me, rolls on her back and adjusts a pillow under her buttocks. With great finesse and delicacy she extracts a hair—mine, I suppose—from between her teeth. Her legs open. I understand at last what she expects of me and make the insertion. It feels warm. Does she want something more, some movement? Yes, she has begun to move her pelvis back and forth.

I take up the rhythm and raise my hips and then lower myself into her, posting to a stately measure as her hands flutter, tentative and unconscious, around my face, brushing my cheek, grazing my chin, pressing firmly against my chest in a sudden spasm, finally collapsing and loudly slapping the mattress, once, twice. "My darl, my darling," she whispers, never once, calling me by my name.

A terrifying pressure is mounting within me. I have no idea what it is, I wonder if I should stop, but I don't, I can't, I move faster and faster. A drop, two, three drops of sweat from my clavicle clavichord fall onto her neck, but she doesn't seem to mind, her hand gathers the drops, the triplet, to her mouth and she tastes it greedily. A high, gravelly noise rises in the back of her throat as her head twists from side to side. Then the sound breaks off, her body tightens only to go soft a moment later and her lips form a perfect circle. She stops breathing. She pronounces a single astonished "Oh."

I fear that she's secreted a burning liquid onto me, or possibly the fluids of her body are hostile to mine; whatever the cause, I know that something's seriously wrong; so much pain, if only I could inspect myself I'm certain I'd find blood. Perhaps her satisfaction requires my suffering. An offensive smell rises off our bodies—offensive but interesting. Am I really swelling, growing still larger, or is it only my imagination? I wish this would stop. I don't like it at all. Even if what we're doing is quite customary, I'm certain I'm not pursuing it in the right way. I'm wrong, it's wrong, this will come out badly. My heart is beating wildly and a vein pulses along my arm. My breath dries the moisture on her face. I much prefer the ordinary feelings. Is she killing me? Am I dying? So much pain. I'll shriek if it doesn't—

I explode and sob on her breast, no longer able to keep up this pretense, weary of not knowing anything, finally realizing that what she and everyone else expects of me is unbearable. "Why do you want so much?" I ask her—I shouldn't have said that. "I can't give you anymore." I shouldn't have said that.

We turn on our sides and uncouple. My legs and arms tremble spasmodically. Curling up and resting her head on her hand, she surveys me coolly and smiles. "I would have thought you had given me all I might have asked for." She laughs and hops out of bed, slim and energetic. After she finds a towel, she hurries back to me, perches lightly on the edge of the bed and slowly, thoughtfully wipes the sweat from my body. Although she touches me very softly between the legs I pull away in pain—even greater than before.

"Tell me, who am I? Who are you?"

She laughs. "Don't tease me," she says.

"No, I have to know. Who am I?"

"Darling," she replies, shaking her head, hurt for some reason, "my darling, you have the oddest sense of humor."

KAREN JOY FOWLER

Sarah Canary

IN a well-run asylum, the female and male wards would each have their own dining room. Contractor Greene was in the middle of building repairs; the Steilacoom facility originally had been a fort during that part of the Territory's history when the Indian threat was the greatest, and certain changes were required to make it function optimally as a sanctuary for the insane. He had been given a budget of three hundred dollars for the renovation and repair of existing buildings. When he submitted his bill for a little more than four thousand dollars to the Territorial legislature, they asked if daily association with lunatics had rendered the contractor stark mad. Work on the facility halted. The men and women of Steilacoom ate together in a single dining room. They sat on benches at four wide-planked tables. They had tin spoons and tin bowls. They bowed their heads and spoke the grace.

"Truly grateful," B.J. said, resting his forehead on his locked thumbs. "Amen."

There were twenty-three inmates in all at the asylum—sixteen men and seven women. They represented the following forms of insanity in the following proportions: Idiophrenic insanity, 6; Sympathetic insanity, 14; Toxic insanity, 1; Anaemic insanity, 1; Insanity resulting from arrested or impaired development of the brain, 1.

Ada, the woman from Germany, entered. She was late; she was dragging the new woman behind her. Ada pushed the new woman onto the bench first, then sat next to her, leaning sideways with her body until the other woman had moved farther down the bench and Ada was directly opposite B.J. She gave him a fluttery, conspiratorial look. Her gray hair was combed up from her forehead and away from her face. But when she turned to see that the new woman had a spoon and a bowl of mush, B.J. noticed Ada had forgotten to comb the back of her hair at all. It ruffled up from her neck like the feathers of an angry chicken.

"What's her name?" B.J. asked.

"Sarah," said Ada. "Sarah Canary, because she sings like an angel. She's been put in my room. I'm in charge of her. I'm to help her settle in." Ada made many of the sounds of her speech deep in her throat and spit often when she talked. B.J. had never been around many Germans and did not know if they all talked this way or if this was a symptom of Ada's illness or if this happened because Ada was missing one of her front teeth. He had discussed her case on several occasions with Dr. Carr.

"The woman from Germany is in love with me," he told Dr. Carr as a way of introducing the topic.

"Men and woman have profound physiological differences," Dr. Carr answered. "Some more obvious than others. The capacity of the skull is greater in the male and, what is really remarkable, is that this masculine advantage increases as the race becomes more civilized. Thus the skulls of the Negroes in Africa show less sexual differentiation than those of the Europeans." He blinked his eyes rapidly and leapt from his chair, unfastening the glass door of the bookcase and removing a large black book. He opened it roughly in the middle, flicked through a few pages with his thumbnail. "The average cranial capacity of the male German, for example," he said, his index finger floating over the text, "is 1538.76 cubic centimeters, but the German female capacity is only 1265.23. This is a difference of 273.53 cubic centimeters."

"She stares at me when we eat," B.J. said.

"The gray substance and white substance in the male brain are also heavier than in the female. It is not necessary to ascribe superiority to any of this, of course. Merely difference. Men are better at manly things. Women are better at being women. This current trend to provide them with similar educations is very wrongheaded." Dr. Carr shut his book with a sound like a clap.

"She's always trying to get me to come to her room."

"Well, that's not allowed," said Dr. Carr. "Surely male patients aren't allowed in the rooms of female patients. What are we running here, a hospital or a bordello?"

"A hospital," B.J. said. He'd been in both.

"Women feel the tyranny of their bodies so much more than men do. Love affairs are seldom a good sign." Dr. Carr shook his head. "One of the saddest cases I ever encountered was a woman, happily married, aged forty-six, in whom there were no discoverable hereditary influences toward insanity. Just at the time her catamenia were becoming irregular, she was seized with uncontrollable libidinous desires. Prior to this she had never exhibited any sexual proclivity, and intercourse rarely afforded her any pleasure at all. Now she could scarcely be taken out into public without making indecent propositions to the men she met. Sometimes in the presence of her *husband*. She remained in this condition for about two years, until her menses ceased altogether and she recovered her health."

"Is this the case with Ada?"

"Very likely. And very much to be pitied. Don't encourage her, B.J., but don't despise her. Somewhere, trapped inside her body, is probably a very high-minded woman who would be ashamed if she knew how she was behaving."

Ada appeared quite satisfied with herself now. She was ignoring B.J. in favor of the new woman, making clucking, consoling sounds and feeding Sarah Canary from her own spoon as if she were a little child. "Here's a big bite," she said. Sarah Canary reached for the mush with her fingers, but Ada slapped her hand quickly with the bowl of her spoon and Sarah withdrew.

"Does she talk?" B.J. asked.

"Not yet. I'm teaching her. Here's another big bite," said Ada. "You eat nicely now." She looked over at B.J. with a dreamy smile. Her attention was elsewhere; her eyes no longer penetrated. "I'm going to make some clothes for Sarah Canary," she said. "Some lovely party dresses."

While Ada's face was averted, Sarah Canary slipped her fingers into the mush. She was licking them when Ada turned back to her. "No, no!" said Ada sharply. Her voice was extremely loud. "You eat nicely or you don't eat at all." She rose in a fury, picking up the bowl of mush and overturning it onto the table. The warden was there instantly. A silence fell over the entire room. It was Houston. B.J. had been right about today's assignments. The air thickened so that he could hardly breathe.

"No, that's a mess," Houston said quietly. "And a mess is something I will not have."

"It's her mess," said Ada, pointing to Sarah Canary. "I didn't—"

Houston put his hands around Ada's neck and pulled her upright. "Some time in the wash house for you," he told her. The ideal hospital would have, as a matter of course, a cell for the punishment of recalcitrant lunatics. Fort Steilacoom had no shortage of cells; this was one of the aspects that recommended it for its current purposes. But females were always sent to the wash house in deference to the delicacy of their sex and to permit them to pass their sentence in some useful manner. The wash house was not a cell, but it was not dry and it was not heated. There were no windows. At Steilacoom everyone was used to making do.

Houston took hold of Ada's hair with one hand and struck her across the face with the other. "Papa," said Ada pleadingly. "No, Papa." Houston fastened his hand about her throat again, shutting off the words. He began to pull her by the neck from the room. Ada's shift rode up her legs, which were limp, whether by design or out of fear B.J. could not tell. Her heels bounced off the floor with each of Houston's steps. Her face when B.J. last saw it was puffy and changing color.

B.J. felt suddenly that someone was looking at him and not at the more compelling scene Houston and Ada were making. He scanned the room to see who it was. Sarah Canary had her fingers in the mush on the tabletop. She put three of her fingers in her mouth and began to hum around them. These were the first sounds B.J. had heard her make. A cold spot on the back of his neck grew colder and he knew the person staring at it must be behind him. He turned around. The Chinaman stood in the doorway and his eyes were fixed intently on B.J. He made a small gesture. Come here, it said. And then he disappeared back into the kitchen.

B.J. got to his feet. The guttural sounds of Ada choking grew fainter and fainter. The corridor into the kitchen tipped upward. B.J. could climb it, but it made him pant. The Chinaman was alone, standing at the large basin, scraping the pots prior to washing them. "Did you need water?" B.J. asked. He looked to the bucket. It was still full. A moth floated on top, its wings extended. He hoped the Chinaman wasn't going to expect him to fetch a new bucket every time a bug drowned.

"Do things like that happen often?" the Chinaman asked. "Is this a bad place to be?"

It took B.J. a moment to understand that the Chinaman was talking about Ada and not the moth. And another moment to wonder how to respond. B.J. didn't like questions unless he knew what answer was wanted. He had no idea what the Chinaman hoped to hear. Perhaps the Chinaman wanted to hear about Louis Bergevain, an inmate who'd been beaten to death three months ago when he'd become too ill to do his chores. Houston had told B.J. people might come around asking questions. B.J. was not to even say the word *Bergevain*. Not to Dr. Carr or to anyone else who asked. The people with questions, Houston told B.J., might be very cunning, but he would not accept this as an excuse if he was disobeyed.

He had not told B.J. the people with questions might be Chinese. This was *very* cunning, but B.J. would not be tricked. He said nothing at all.

He watched the Chinaman cross the kitchen to the black stove and pick up the mush pot. The mush had coated the inside with a grainy film. The Chinaman scraped at it with his spoon, but it adhered to the pot's sides. He scratched a tiny line clean with his fingernail. He stood staring into the pot.

"Soak it first," B.J. suggested. It was a generous offer since it would use a great deal of water and the bucket would have to be filled that much sooner.

"Perhaps that woman is just very difficult," the Chinaman suggested, setting the pot into the sink and ladling water into it. "Perhaps things like that happen only to her."

"Perhaps," said B.J. carefully. "And perhaps not."

"Which?" asked the Chinaman.

"One or the other," said B.J.

"Shouldn't a woman be in charge of the women?" the Chinaman asked.

"Yes," said B.J. "One is."

"Was she there at breakfast?"

"Yes."

The Chinaman stood staring at B.J. He was considerably shorter; B.J. could see every detail of the top of his head, his scalp where the hair divided, the way it flowed into the rope of the braid. There was a red spot on the bare skin between the hair that flowed to the right and that which flowed to the left. A flea bite, B.J. thought. Not that this was the season for fleas. "If I wanted a woman's help in the kitchen, could I request a particular woman? The way I can request you when I want water fetched?" The Chinaman was speaking very carefully, just the way B.J. himself was speaking. B.J. understood suddenly that he was not happy asking questions. B.J. was not happy answering them. He looked for a way to rectify the situation. He changed all his answers into questions.

"Fetching water is my job, isn't it?" B.J. said. "And not anybody else's, is it? You say what job you have and the warden sends the person who does it, doesn't he?" Now all the Chinaman had to do was answer. Instead he asked another question and looked unhappy about it.

"Are the new patients assigned jobs quickly?"

"Sometimes. Aren't they?" B.J. stressed his last two words. The Chinaman still had not caught on.

"Has the new woman been assigned a job?"

"Has Sarah Canary been assigned a job?" B.J. asked. His voice was getting louder. "Sarah Canary sings like an angel, doesn't she? But she doesn't talk. Does she? So I don't think she does jobs. Do you?"

The Chinaman waved his hands in a quick unhappy gesture to tell B.J. to be quiet or to go away, B.J. was not sure which. B.J. was sorry about this. He had only been trying to help. He returned to the dining room and his mush bowl. It was gone. Sarah Canary had two now. One was empty and clean as if she had licked it. The other was B.J.'s. He reached for it and she turned her eyes on him steadily. She made a low, threatening noise in her throat. It was a growl. B.J. dropped his hand and stared at her. "That's *my* breakfast," he said. "You had *your* breakfast." Sarah Canary growled again. Houston had returned and was pacing between the tables.

"Is there a problem here?" he asked at each. "Any problem here?" The man from France had no problems. The syphilitic farmer had no problems. The man who spoke only in rhymes had no problems. The woman who did things only in threes had no problems. Sarah Canary certainly had no problems. She smiled and hummed and licked her fingers. B.J. had no problems. And he had no breakfast.

He stared coldly at Sarah Canary. "Dr. Carr hasn't finished his diagnosis of the new woman," he told Houston. "I'm supposed to take her to him after breakfast."

"The hell you are," said Houston. "I'd like to see the day when inmates escort inmates around the asylum. When male inmates are asked to escort female inmates."

"Well, he wants to see her," said B.J. "And he wants to see me."

"The hell he does," said Houston. "Who the hell does he think is running the asylum? He'll see you when I say he can. He'll see you in hell." Houston cracked the knuckles of his left hand with his right. He reached under the overhang of his belly and began to undo his leather belt. B.J. put his own hands up to cover his face. They were interrupted by the female warden.

"On your feet, dear," she said to Sarah Canary. "The nice doctor wants to see you now." Sarah Canary did not respond. There was nothing to suggest that she had even heard. Houston gave B.J. one final look, fastened his belt back into place, and then turned to help. He gripped the collar of Sarah Canary's dress and slid her along the bench to the end. Still holding her collar, he lifted her and held her in midair for a moment. She seemed to shrink, pulling her arms and legs closer into her body.

"The nice doctor wants to see you now," Houston said, setting her down. "Let's not keep the nice doctor waiting. I'll take her," he told the female warden. "I'll take her more quickly than you could." He prodded Sarah Canary from the back. She stumbled slightly, then moved in the direction of the push. He prodded her again and she was unresisting. They disappeared through the dining room door.

B.J. reached across the table for his bowl. Sarah Canary had not had a chance to finish; some of his breakfast remained. It was cold and congealed, but he ate it hastily. He left with the other patients, shuffling in a line through the yard for exercise time on the roller-skating rink. B.J. had fetched the water at sunup. It had been cold enough to see his breath. Now the yard was in full sunlight and the day was a beautiful one. Might rain later, but it really didn't look like it. This was two days now it hadn't rained. Both the wardens commented on it.

B.J. waited for his turn at the skates. He was quiet and unobtrusive. Ordinarily B.J. enjoyed skating. Most of the inmates did not. Most of the inmates strapped on the skates and then stood precariously on the rink without moving until the wardens came and gave them a push and they fell over. Some of them fell even without the push. Ada was a wonderful skater; she had done a lot of ice skating in Germany as a child. Ada's arms pumped about her body when she skated, not one at a time, the way most skaters moved, but both together as if they were wings. Ada was in the wash house and it was Sarah Canary's fault. B.J. was hungrier than usual and that was Sarah Canary's fault, too. He let several people ahead of him in line.

"Thank you, thank you, thank you," the blond woman with blood-shot eyes told him. She coughed three times. She did everything in threes. It was an S.O.S., but B.J. refused to admit he understood it. That was all he needed, another woman in love with him. He shook his head at her.

Eventually he had let everyone by and stood at the very back of the line himself. When no one was looking, B.J. slipped out. He followed a circuitous route to the doctor's study, creeping through the old barracks that had been converted for storage. He avoided the part of the asylum that once housed young subalterns and was the current quarters of the asylum attendants.

The doctor's study was in the old officers' quarters. B.J. listened at the door, which was solid wood and heavy. He could hear the sounds of humming inside. Making a fist, he tapped with the last knuckle of his hand. There might have been a response that didn't carry through the heavy door. Or he might not have knocked loudly enough to be heard over the humming. He opened the door and the humming stopped. "Excuse me," he said. "I don't mean to intrude. I just wondered if you were able to get that fire going." He could smell and he could hear the fire as he spoke. The wood snapped and gasped in the fireplace. Some of the wood was perhaps a bit too wet; the air was smoky, but the fire seemed a robust and reliable one.

"Oh, B.J.," said Dr. Carr. "Come in, come in. I need your help." B.J. turned to look at him. Sarah Canary sat in the patient chair, a comfortable winged piece; her back was to B.J. and her head and the chair obscured much of the doctor. B.J. could just see his face. He was flushed from exertion, perhaps, or emotion. Dr. Carr was one of those people who reddened easily. He stood close to his patient, holding one end of his watch chain a few inches before her. B.J. could not see the watch. Sarah Canary's dark, thick hair was in his way.

"I was just about to perform an experiment in animal magnetism," Dr. Carr said with some excitement. His pale eyelashes fluttered. "Something I'm ordinarily reluctant to do since it can get out of hand so easily. You've heard of Mesmer's group? The original public exhibition in Paris? No? There's quite a good account in Prichard. Not only were the infirm magnetized with mixed results, but a number of natural objects as well. Trees, for example. When the experiment was repeated in the garden of one Dr. Franklin, a susceptible boy who came into contact with a magnetized tree fell at once into a crisis. He lost all consciousness. The hypnotist tried to argue that additional trees had become spontaneously magnetic, which had concentrated the effect. Balderdash. If trees had this ability, it would be worth your life to take a walk outdoors. The susceptible would always be fainting dead away. It was a naked attempt to disguise his own culpability. Truly irresponsible behavior on the part of the hypnotist. And ultimately tragic. Most of those involved in the French experiments were from the upper classes. Axed during the Revolution. The people, that is. The hypnotists. The magnetized trees remain to this day. Is it too implausible to argue that some link between those trees and the madness that followed the Revolution might exist? Is it?"

This was the kind of question B.J. liked. "It isn't," he said firmly. He knew he was right.

"Caution, you know, has always been my guiding principle," Dr. Carr told him. "I'd rather err on the side of caution. But now, here we have a woman who doesn't speak. There appears to be some impediment to the woman speaking. Not a physical impediment. God knows she makes sounds. A mental impediment. I thought perhaps hypnosis could provide us with a way around it. And M. Petetin, in Lyons, reports such successes with cataleptic women. He has had eight cases in which the seat of sensation was transferred to the epigastrium. I was just reading his remarkable account of one of these cases. Young woman, completely deaf to sounds in the ordinary way, but, under hypnosis, able to hear M. Petetin's slightest whisper if he bent close to the epigastrium."

"You thought Sarah Canary might be able to speak with her epigastrium?" B.J. asked.

"I was open—I *am* open," said Dr. Carr, "to anything. But then she swallowed the watch. Reached out quick as a cat. I had no idea what she was about. You now how fast an ecstatic can be." B.J. took a few more steps into the room and around Sarah Canary's chair. Now he could see that the other end of the watch chain was in Sarah Canary's mouth. Dr. Carr tugged gently on the chain. Sarah Canary allowed her face to be pulled forward but kept her mouth resolutely closed. Dr. Carr slackened off. He looked as if he was playing a big fish. "It's actually gone down into her throat. The woman has no gag reflex at all. And an unhealthy impulse to fill any available orifice. Women of a certain age are so prone to this. I suspected this the first time I saw her."

"How old do you think she is?" B.J. asked him.

"The shady side of thirty. Maybe even the shady side of thirty-five. Premature wrinkling is a characteristic of the female criminal profile, of course. And there's very little gray in the hair. Let's say thirty-three. I'd rather err on the side of caution."

"She ate my breakfast," B.J. told him. "Remorseless." He tapped Sarah Canary helpfully on the shoulder. Sarah Canary swung her head to look at him, jerking the other end of the chain out of Dr. Carr's hand.

"Oh, God," said Dr. Carr, diving after it. "Get it, B.J. Don't lose it! Don't let her swallow it!"

The watch chain was slipping away like a noodle into Sarah Canary's mouth. B.J. seized the end and held it tightly. It was much shorter than it had been. He pulled on the chain. Sarah Canary had it clamped between her teeth. There was no give. Dr. Carr retreated to his desk and rummaged through the center drawer. "Here," he said, returning, holding out his hand. "Here's a nice peppermint for you, Sarah Canary. A trade. Give me the watch and you can have the peppermint."

Sarah Canary reached for the candy, but Dr. Carr closed his hand over it. "First the watch," he said sternly. Sarah Canary inclined her head questioningly. She looked sullen and stubborn. Dr. Carr opened his hand again and showed her the peppermint. She did not respond.

Dr. Carr grew tired of waiting. He transferred the peppermint to his left hand and gripped her jaw with his right. His thumb drove directly into the bruise at her mouth. Sarah Canary winced. "Give me the watch," Dr. Carr said loudly. He applied pressure on the jaw hinge. Slowly, painfully, Sarah Canary allowed her mouth to be pried open. As soon as a gap appeared between the upper and lower teeth, B.J. began to reel in the watch chain. The gap widened. The watch slipped into sight at the back of her throat, slid over her tongue, and dangled wetly in front of her face at the end of its chain. It was so large. He looked at Sarah Canary in awe.

He looked back at the watch, wiping it on his sleeve and examining it more closely. He held it to his ear. "It's still ticking, Dr. Carr," he said. "Can you believe it? An ordeal like that? And it's still ticking away. I wonder what else you could do to a watch like this? I wonder if you could put it in a box and drop it off a boat into a lake and leave it overnight. Would it still be ticking then? I wonder if you could hit it with a hammer."

Dr. Carr reached for the watch without responding. He put it into his pocket along with the peppermint. "I don't think this session can usefully continue," he said. "I think the basic trust necessary between patient and doctor has been somewhat violated." He sounded hurt. "Perhaps you'll return the patient to her room for me, B.J. I'll be prescribing phosphorus for her in the meantime. I really don't see what else I can do. I am not one of those doctors who thinks phosphorus is a cure-all, mind you. The dictum 'Without phosphorus, no thought' may be absolutely true, but it doesn't necessarily follow that phosphorus will always rectify abnormal mental processes. How easy the alienist's job would be if that were the case. No, it is perfectly possible to crowd the stomach with phosphorus and see no improvement in the patient's condition whatsoever. But what else can I do at this juncture? You tell me, B.J. Suggest something. I'm open to suggestions."

"What else can you do?" B.J. echoed. "You've done everything you can." He took Sarah Canary by the sleeve and tugged. She stood, shaking loose of his hand. She spoke to him, a happy stream of noise that must have been in some foreign code; B.J. didn't understand it at all.

She smiled, first at him and then at Dr. Carr. Her noises continued, but her eyes began to wander. She was no longer directing her speech at either of them. She stepped around the desk, pressed a palm on the glass front of the bookcase, then tapped the glass with one arched finger. She was quiet for a moment, listening to the sound. Sunlight glanced off the panes at an angle now, making a mirror in front of the books. Sarah Canary pulled her hand back and bent into the sunlight. Her face appeared in the glass. She stooped to look at it, looked more closely, and the closer she came, the larger her reflected face grew. For a moment she stood still, merely staring. She pulled back and the face shrank. Then, quite suddenly, she leaned over and kissed the glass. The two mouths came together, but one was only an illusion and made no mark, while the other left behind an imprint, shaped vaguely like a butterfly, at just that place on the glass where the mouth that did exist tried to kiss the mouth that did not.

OLIVER SACKS

The Last Hippie

> Such a long, long time to be gone . . .
> and a short time to be there
> —Robert Hunter
> "Box of Rain"

GREG F. grew up in the 1950s in a comfortable Queens household, an attractive and rather gifted boy who seemed destined, like his father, for a professional career—perhaps a career in songwriting, for which he showed a precocious talent. But he grew restive, started questioning things, as a teenager in the late sixties; started to hate the conventional life of his parents and neighbors and the cynical, bellicose administration of the country. His need to rebel, but equally to find an ideal and a guide, to find a leader, crystallized in the Summer of Love, in 1967. He would go to the Village and listen to Allen Ginsberg declaiming all night; he loved rock music, especially acid rock, and, above all, the Grateful Dead.

Increasingly he fell out with his parents and teachers; he was truculent with the one, secretive with the other. In 1968, a time when Timothy Leary was urging American youth to "tune in, turn on, and drop out," Greg grew his hair long and dropped out of school, where he had been a good student; he left home and went to live in the Village, where he dropped acid and joined the East Village drug culture—searching, like others of his generation, for utopia, for inner freedom, and for "higher consciousness."

But "turning on" did not satisfy Greg, who stood in need of a more codified doctrine and way of life. In 1969 he gravitated, as so many young acidheads did, to the Swami Bhaktivedanta and his International Society for Krishna Consciousness, on Second Avenue. And under his influence, Greg, like so many others, stopped taking acid, finding his religious exaltation a replacement for acid highs. ("The only radical remedy for dipsomania," William James once said, "is religiomania.") The philosophy, the fellowship, the chanting, the rituals, the austere and charismatic figure of the swami himself, came like a revelation to Greg, and he became, almost immediately, a passionate devotee and convert.[1] Now there was a center, a focus, to his life. In those first exalted weeks of his conversion, he wandered around the East Village, dressed in saffron robes, chanting the Hare Krishna mantras, and early in 1970, he took up residence in the main temple in Brooklyn. His parents objected at first, then went along with this. "Perhaps it will help him," his father said philosophically. "Perhaps—who knows?—this is the path he needs to follow."

Greg's first year at the temple went well; he was obedient, ingenuous, devoted, and pious. He is a Holy One, said the swami, one of us. Early in 1971, now deeply committed, Greg was sent to the temple in New Orleans. His parents had seen him occasionally when he was in the Brooklyn temple, but now communication from him virtually ceased.

One problem arose in Greg's second year with the Krishnas—he complained that his vision was growing dim, but this was interpreted, by his swami and others, in a spiritual way: he was "an illuminate," they told him; it was the "inner light" growing. Greg had worried at first about his eyesight, but was reassured by the swami's spiritual explanation. His sight grew still dimmer, but he offered no further complaints. And indeed, he seemed to be becoming more spiritual by the day—an amazing new serenity had taken hold of him. He no longer showed his previous impatience or appetites, and he was sometimes found in a sort of daze, with a strange (some said "transcendental") smile on his face.

---

[1] The swami's unusual views are presented, in summary form, in *Easy Journey to Other Planets*, by Tridandi Goswami A. C. Bhaktivedanta Swami, published by the League of Devotees, Vrindaban (no date, one rupee). This slim manual, in its green paper cover, was handed out in vast quantities by the swami's saffron-robed followers, and it became Greg's bible at this stage.

It is beatitude, said his swami—he is becoming a saint. The temple felt he needed to be protected at this stage; he no longer went out or did anything unaccompanied, and contact with the outside world was strongly discouraged.

Although Greg's parents did not have any direct communication from him, they did get occasional reports from the temple—reports filled, increasingly, with accounts of his "spiritual progress," his "enlightenment," accounts at once so vague and so out of character with the Greg they knew that, by degrees, they became alarmed. Once they wrote directly to the swami and received a soothing, reassuring reply.

Three more years passed before Greg's parents decided they had to see for themselves. His father was by then in poor health and feared that if he waited longer he might never see his "lost" son again. On hearing this, the temple finally permitted a visit from Greg's parents. In 1975, then, not having seen him for four years, they visited their son in the temple in New Orleans.

When they did so, they were filled with horror: their lean, hairy son had become fat and hairless; he wore a continual "stupid" smile on his face (this at least was his father's word for it); he kept bursting into bits of song and verse and making "idiotic" comments, while showing little deep emotion of any kind ("like he was scooped out, hollow inside," his father said); he had lost interest in everything current; he was disoriented—and he was totally blind. The temple, surprisingly, acceded to his leaving—perhaps even they felt now that his ascension had gone too far and had started to feel some disquiet about his state.

Greg was admitted to the hospital, examined, and transferred to neurosurgery. Brain imaging had shown an enormous midline tumor, destroying the pituitary gland and the adjacent optic chiasm and tracts and extending on both sides into the frontal lobes. It also reached backward to the temporal lobes, and downward to the diencephalon, or forebrain. At surgery, the tumor was found to be benign, a meningioma—but it had swollen to the size of a small grapefruit or orange, and though the surgeons were able to remove it almost entirely, they could not undo the damage it had already done.

Greg was now not only blind but gravely disabled neurologically and mentally—a disaster that could have been prevented entirely had his first complaints of dimming vision been heeded, and had medical sense, and even common sense, been allowed to judge his state. Since, tragically, no recovery could be expected, or very little, Greg was admitted to Williamsbridge, a hospital for the chronically sick, a twenty-five-year-old boy for whom active life had come to an end, and for whom the prognosis was considered hopeless.

I first met Greg in April 1977, when he arrived at Williamsbridge Hospital. Lacking facial hair, and childlike in manner, he seemed younger than his twenty-five years. He was fat, Buddha-like, with a vacant, bland face, his blind eyes roving at random in their orbits, while he sat motionless in his wheelchair. If he lacked spontaneity and initiated no exchanges, he responded promptly and appropriately when I spoke to him, though odd words would sometimes catch his fancy and give rise to associative tangents or snatches of song and rhyme. Between questions, if the time was not filled, there tended to be a deepening silence; though if this lasted for more than a minute, he might fall into Hare Krishna chants or a soft muttering of mantras. He was still, he said, "a total believer," devoted to the group's doctrines and aims.

I could not get any consecutive history from him—he was not sure, for a start, why he was in the hospital and gave different reasons when I asked him about this; first he said, "Because I'm not intelligent," later, "Because I took drugs in the past." He knew he had been at the main Hare Krishna temple ("a big red house, 439 Henry Street, in Brooklyn"), but not that he had subsequently been at their temple in New Orleans. Nor did he remember that he started to have symptoms there—first and foremost a progressive loss of vision. Indeed he seemed unaware that he had any problems: that he was blind, that he was unable to walk steadily, that he was in any way ill.

Unaware—and indifferent. He seemed bland, placid, emptied of all feeling—it was this unnatural serenity that his Krishna brethren had perceived, apparently, as "bliss," and indeed, at one point, Greg used the term himself. "How do you feel?" I returned to this again and again. "I feel blissful," he replied at one point, "I am afraid of falling back into the material world." At this point, when he was first in the hospital, many of his Hare Krishna friends would come to visit him; I often saw their saffron robes in the corridors. They would come to visit poor, blind, blank Greg and flock around him; they saw him as having achieved "detachment," as an Enlightened One.

Questioning him about current events and people, I found the depths of his disorientation and confusion. When I asked him who was the president, he said "Lyndon," then, "the one who got shot." I prompted, "Jimmy . . . ," and he said, "Jimi Hendrix," and when I roared with laughter, he said maybe a musical White House would be a good idea. A few more questions convinced me that Greg had virtually no memory of events much past 1970, certainly no coherent, chronological memory of them. He seemed to have been left, marooned, in the sixties—his memory, his development, his inner life since then had come to a stop.

His tumor, a slow-growing one, was huge when it was finally removed in 1976, but only in the later stages of its growth, as it destroyed the memory system in the temporal lobe, would it actually have prevented the brain from registering new events. But Greg had difficulties—not absolute, but partial—even in remembering events from the late sixties, events that he must have registered perfectly at the time. So beyond the inability to register new experiences, there had been an erosion of existing memories (a retrograde amnesia) going back several years before his tumor had developed. There was not an absolutely sharp cutoff here, but rather a temporal gradient, so that figures and events from 1966 and 1967 were fully remembered, events from 1968 or 1969 partially or occasionally remembered, and events after 1970 almost never remembered.

It was easy to demonstrate the severity of his immediate amnesia. If I gave him lists of words, he was unable to recall any of them after a minute. When I told him a story and asked him to repeat it, he did so in a more and more confused way, with more and more "contaminations" and misassociations—some droll, some extremely bizarre—until within five minutes his story bore no resemblance to the one I had told him. Thus when I told him a tale about a lion and a mouse, he soon departed from the original story and had the mouse threatening to eat the lion—it had become a giant mouse and a mini-lion. Both were mutants, Greg explained when I quizzed him on his departures.

Or possibly, he said, they were creatures from a dream, or "an alternative history" in which mice were indeed the lords of the jungle. Five minutes later, he had no memory of the story whatever.

I had heard, from the hospital social worker, that he had a passion for music, especially rock-and-roll bands of the sixties; I saw piles of records as soon as I entered his room and a guitar lying against his bed. So now I asked him about this, and with this there came a complete transformation—he lost his disconnectedness, his indifference, and spoke with great animation about his favorite rock bands and pieces— above all, of the Grateful Dead. "I went to see them at the Fillmore East, and in Central Park," he said. He remembered the entire program in detail, but "my favorite," he added, "is 'Tobacco Road.'" The title evoked the tune, and Greg sang the whole song with great feeling and conviction—a depth of feeling of which, hitherto, he had not shown the least sign. He seemed transformed, a different person, a whole person, as he sang.

"When did you hear them in Central Park?" I asked.

"It's been a while, over a year maybe," he answered—but in fact they had last played there eight years earlier, in 1969. And the Fillmore East, the famous rock-and-roll theater where Greg had also seen the group, did not survive the early 1970s. He went on to tell me he once heard Jimi Hendrix at Hunter College, and Cream, with Jack Bruce playing bass guitar; Eric Clapton, lead guitar; and Ginger Baker, a "fantastic drummer." "Jimi Hendrix," he added reflectively, "what's he doing? Don't hear much about him nowadays." We spoke of the Rolling Stones and the Beatles—"Great groups," Greg commented, "but they don't space me out the way the Dead do. What a group," he continued, "there's no one like them. Jerry Garcia—he's a saint, he's a guru, he's a genius. Mickey Hart, Bill Kreutzmann, the drummers are great. There's Bob Weir, there's Phil Lesh; but Pigpen—I love him."

This narrowed down the extent of his amnesia. He remembered songs vividly from 1964 to 1968. He remembered all the founding members of the Grateful Dead, from 1967. But he was unaware that Pigpen, Jimi Hendrix, and Janis Joplin were all dead. His memory cut off by 1970, or before. He was caught in the sixties, unable to move on. He was a fossil, the last hippie.

. . . .

At first I did not want to confront Greg with the enormity of his time loss, his amnesia, or even to let involuntary hints through (which he would certainly pick up, for he was very sensitive to anomaly and tone), so I changed the subject and said, "Let me examine you."

He was, I noted, somewhat weak and spastic in all his limbs, more on the left, and more in the legs. He could not stand alone. His eyes showed complete optic atrophy—it was impossible for him to see anything. But strangely, he did not seem to be *aware* of being blind and would guess that I was showing him a blue ball, a red pen (when in fact it was a green comb and a fob watch that I showed him). Nor indeed did he seem to "look"; he made no special effort to turn in my direction, and when we were speaking, he often failed to face me, to look at me. When I asked him about seeing, he acknowledged that his eyes weren't "all that good," but added that he enjoyed "watching" the TV. Watching TV for him, I observed later, consisted of following with attention the sound track of a movie or show and inventing visual scenes to go with it (even though he might not even be looking toward the TV). He seemed to think, indeed, that this was what "seeing" meant, that this was what was meant by "watching TV," and that this was what all of us did. Perhaps he had lost the very idea of seeing.

I found this aspect of Greg's blindness, his singular blindness to his blindness, his no longer knowing what "seeing" or "looking" meant, deeply perplexing. It seemed to point to something stranger, and more complex, than a mere "deficit," to point, rather, to some radical alteration within him in the very structure of knowledge, in consciousness, in identity itself.[2]

I had already had some sense of this when testing his memory, find-

---

[2] Another patient, Ruby G., was in some ways similar to Greg. She too had a huge frontal tumor, which, though it was removed in 1973, left her with amnesia, a frontal lobe syndrome, and blindness. She too did not know that she was blind, and when I held up my hand and asked, "How many fingers?" would answer, "A hand has five fingers, of course."

A more localized unawareness of blindness may arise if there is destruction of the visual cortex, as in Anton's syndrome. Such patients may not know that they are blind, but are otherwise intact. But frontal lobe unawarenesses are far more global in nature—thus Greg and Ruby were not only unaware of being blind but unaware (for the most part) of being ill, of having devastating neurological and cognitive deficits, and of their tragic, diminished position in life.

ing his confinement, in effect, to a single moment—"the present"—
uninformed by any sense of a past (or a future). Given this radical lack
of connection and continuity in his inner life, I got the feeling, indeed,
that he might not *have* an inner life to speak of, that he lacked the constant dialogue of past and present, of experience and meaning, which
constitutes consciousness and inner life for the rest of us. He seemed to
have no sense of "next" and to lack that eager and anxious tension of
anticipation, of intention, that normally drives us through life.

Some sense of ongoing, of "next," is always with us. But this sense of
movement, of happening, Greg lacked; he seemed immured, without
knowing it, in a motionless, timeless moment. And whereas for the rest
of us the present is given its meaning and depth by the past (hence it
becomes the "remembered present," in Gerald Edelman's term), as
well as being given potential and tension by the future, for Greg it was
flat and (in its meager way) complete. This living-in-the-moment,
which was so manifestly pathological, had been perceived in the temple as an achievement of higher consciousness.

Greg seemed to adjust to Williamsbridge with remarkable ease, considering he was a young man being placed, probably forever, in a hospital for the chronically ill. There was no furious defiance, no railing at
Fate, no sense, apparently, of indignity or despair. Compliantly, indif-
ferently, Greg let himself be put away in the backwater of Williamsbridge. When I asked him about this, he said, "I have no choice." And
this, as he said it, seemed wise and true. Indeed, he seemed eminently
philosophical about it. But it was a philosophicalness made possible by
his indifference, his brain damage.

His parents, so estranged from him when he was rebellious and well,
came daily, doted on him, now that he was helpless and ill; and they,
for their part, could be sure, at any time, that he would be at the hospital, smiling and grateful for their visit. If he was not "waiting" for them,
so much the better—they could miss a day, or a few days, if they were
away; he would not notice, but would be cordial as ever the next time
they came.

Greg soon settled in, with his rock records and his guitar, his Hare
Krishna beads, his Talking Books, and a schedule of programs—phys-
iotherapy, occupational therapy, music groups, drama. Soon after

admission he was moved to a ward with younger patients, where with his open and sunny personality he became popular. He did not actually know any of the other patients or the staff, at least for several months, but was invariably (if indiscriminately) pleasant to them all. And there were at least two special friendships, not intense, but with a sort of complete acceptance and stability. His mother remembers "Eddie, who had MS . . . they both loved music, they had adjacent rooms, they used to sit together . . . and Judy, she had CP, she would sit for hours with him, too." Eddie died, and Judy went to a hospital in Brooklyn; there has been no one so close for many years. Mrs. F. remembers them, but Greg does not, never asked for them, or about them, after they had gone—though perhaps, his mother thought, he was sadder, at least less lively, for they stimulated him, got him talking and listening to records and inventing limericks, joking and singing; they pulled him out of "that dead state" he would otherwise fall into.

A hospital for the chronically ill, where patients and staff live together for years, is a little like a village or a small town: everybody gets to meet, to know, everybody else. I often saw Greg in the corridors, being wheeled to different programs or out to the patio, in his wheelchair, with the same odd, blind yet searching look on his face. And he gradually got to know me, at least sufficiently to know my name, to ask each time we met, "How're you doing, Dr. Sacks? When's the next book coming out?" (a question that rather distressed me in the seemingly endless eleven-year interim between the publication of *Awakenings* and *A Leg to Stand On*).

Names, then, he might learn, with frequent contact, and in relation to them he would recollect a few details about each new person. Thus he came to know Connie Tomaino, the music therapist—he would recognize her voice, her footfalls, immediately—but he could never remember where or how he had met her. One day Greg began talking about "another Connie," a girl called Connie whom he'd known in high school. This other Connie, he told us, was also, remarkably, very musical—"How come all you Connies are so musical?" he teased. The other Connie would conduct music groups, he said, would give out song sheets, play the piano-accordion at singsongs at school. At this point, it started to dawn on us that this "other" Connie was in fact Connie herself, and this was clinched when he added, "You know, she played the trumpet, too." (Connie Tomaino is a professional trumpet player.) This sort of thing often happened with Greg when he put things into the wrong context or failed to connect them with the present.

His sense of there being two Connies, his segmenting Connie into two, was characteristic of the bewilderments he sometimes found himself in, his need to hypothesize additional figures because he could not retain or conceive of an identity in time. With consistent repetition Greg might learn a few facts, and these would be retained. But the facts were isolated, denuded of context. A person, a voice, a place, would slowly become "familiar," but he remained unable to remember where he had met the person, heard the voice, seen the place. Specifically, it was context-bound (or "episodic") memory that was so grossly disturbed in Greg—as is the case with most amnesiacs.

Other sorts of memory were intact; thus Greg had no difficulties remembering or applying geometric truths that he had learned in school. He saw instantly, for example, that the hypotenuse of a triangle was shorter than the sum of the two sides—thus his semantic memory, so-called, was fairly intact. Again, he not only retained his power to play the guitar, but actually enlarged his musical repertoire, learning new techniques and fingering with Connie; he also learned to type while at Williamsbridge—so his procedural memory was also unimpaired.

Finally, there seemed to be some sort of slow habituation or familiarization—so that he became able, within three months, to find his way about the hospital, to go to the coffee shop, the cinema, the auditorium, the patio, his favorite places. This sort of learning was exceedingly slow, but once it had been achieved, it was tenaciously retained.

It was clear that Greg's tumor had caused damage that was complex and curious. First, it had compressed or destroyed structures of the inner, or medial, side of both the temporal lobes—in particular, the hippocampus and its adjacent cortex, areas crucial for the capacity to form new memories. With such damage, the ability to acquire information about new facts and events is devastated—there ceases to be any explicit or conscious remembrance of these. But while Greg was so often unable to recall events or encounters or facts to consciousness, he might nonetheless have an unconscious or implicit memory of them, a memory expressed in performance or behavior. Such implicit ability to remember allowed him to become slowly familiar with the physical layout and routines of the hospital and with some of the staff, and to make judgments on whether certain persons (or situations) were pleasant or unpleasant.[3]

While explicit learning requires the integrity of the medial temporal lobe systems, implicit learning may employ more primitive and diffuse paths, as do the simple processes of conditioning and habituation. Explicit learning, however, involves the construction of complex percepts—syntheses of representations from every part of the cerebral cortex—brought together into a contextual unity, or "scene." Such syntheses can be held in mind for only a minute or two—the limit of short-term memory—and after this will be lost unless they can be shunted into long-term memory. Thus higher-order memorization is a multistage process, involving the transfer of perceptions, or perceptual syntheses, from short-term to long-term memory. It is just such a transfer that fails to occur in people with temporal lobe damage. Thus Greg can repeat a complicated sentence with complete accuracy and understanding the moment he hears it, but within three minutes, or sooner if he is distracted for an instant, he will retain not a trace of it, or any idea of its sense, or any memory that it ever existed.

Larry Squire, a neuropsychologist at the University of California, San Diego, who has been a central figure in elucidating this shunting function of the temporal lobe memory system, speaks of the brevity, the precariousness, of short-term memory in us all; all of us, on occasion, suddenly lose a perception or an image or a thought we had vividly in mind ("Damn it," we may say, "I've forgotten what I wanted to say!"), but only in amnesiacs is this precariousness realized to the full.

Yet while Greg, no longer capable of transforming his perceptions or immediate memories into permanent ones, remains stuck in the sixties, when his ability to learn new information broke down, he has nev-

---

[3] That implicit memory (especially if emotionally charged) may exist in amnesiacs was shown, somewhat cruelly, in 1911, by Edouard Claparède, who, when shaking hands with such a patient whom he was presenting to his students, stuck a pin in his hand. Although the patient had no explicit memory of this, he refused, thereafter, to shake hands with him.

ertheless adapted somehow and absorbed some of his surroundings, albeit very slowly and incompletely.[4]

Some amnesiacs (like Jimmie, the patient with Korsakov's syndrome whom I described in "The Lost Mariner") have brain damage largely confined to the memory systems of the diencephalon and medial temporal lobe; others (like Mr. Thompson, described in "A Matter of Identity") are not only amnesiac but have frontal lobe syndromes, too; yet others—like Greg, with immense tumors—tend to have a third area of damage as well, deep below the cerebral cortex, in the forebrain, or diencephalon. In Greg, this widespread damage had created a very complicated clinical picture, with sometimes overlapping or even contradictory symptoms and syndromes. Thus, though his amnesia was chiefly caused by damage to the temporal lobe systems, damage to the diencephalon and frontal lobes also played a part. Similarly there were multiple origins for his blandness and indifference, for which damage to the frontal lobes, diencephalon, and pituitary gland was in varying degrees responsible. In fact, Greg's tumor first caused damage to his pituitary gland; this was responsible not only for his gain in weight and loss of body hair but also for undermining his hormonally driven aggressiveness and assertiveness, and hence for his abnormal submissiveness and placidity.

The diencephalon is especially a regulator of basic functions—of sleep, of appetite, of libido. And all of these were at a low ebb with Greg—he had (or expressed) no sexual interest; he did not think of eating, or express any desire to eat, unless food was brought to him. He seemed to exist only in the present, only in response to the immediacy of stimuli around him. If he was not stimulated, he fell into a sort of daze.

Left alone, Greg would spend hours in the ward without spontaneous activity. This inert state was at first described by the nurses as "brooding"; it had been seen in the temple as "meditating"; my own feeling was that it was profoundly pathological mental "idling," almost

---

[4] A. R. Luria, in *The Neuropsychology of Memory*, remarks that all his amnesiac patients, if hospitalized for any length of time, acquired "a sense of familiarity" with their surroundings.

devoid of mental content or affect. It was difficult to give a name to this state, so different from alert, attentive wakefulness, but also, clearly, quite different from sleep—it had a blankness resembling no normal state. It reminded me somewhat of the vacant states I had seen with some of my postencephalitic patients and, as with them, went with profound damage to the diencephalon. As soon as one talked to him, or if he was stimulated by sounds (especially music) near him, he would "come to," "awaken," in an astonishing way.

Once Greg was "awakened," once his cortex came to life, one saw that his animation itself had a strange quality—an uninhibited and quirky quality of the sort one tends to see when the orbital portions of the frontal lobes (that is, the portions adjacent to the eyes) are damaged, a so-called orbito-frontal syndrome. The frontal lobes are the most complex parts of the brain, concerned not with the "lower" functions of movement and sensation, but the highest ones of integrating all judgment and behavior, all imagination and emotion, into that unique identity that we like to speak of as "personality" or "self." Damage to other parts of the brain may produce specific disturbances of sensation or movement, of language, or of specific perceptual, cognitive, or memory functions. Damage to the frontal lobes, in contrast, does not affect these, but produces a subtler and profounder disturbance of identity.

And it was this—rather than his blindness, or his weakness, or his disorientation, or his amnesia—that so horrified his parents when they finally saw Greg in 1975. It was not just that he was damaged, but that he was changed beyond recognition, had been "dispossessed," in his father's words, by a sort of simulacrum, or changeling, which had Greg's voice and manner and humor and intelligence but not his "spirit" or "realness" or "depth"—a changeling whose wisecracking and levity formed a shocking counterpoint to the fearful gravity of what had happened.

This sort of wisecracking, indeed, is quite characteristic of such orbito-frontal syndromes—and is so striking that it has been given a name unto itself: *witzelsucht*, or "joking disease." Some restraint, some caution, some inhibition, is destroyed, and patients with such syndromes tend to react immediately and incontinently to everything around them and everything within them—to virtually every object,

every person, every sensation, every word, every thought, every emotion, every nuance and tone.

There is an overwhelming tendency, in such states, to wordplay and
puns. Once when I was in Greg's room another patient walked past.
"That's Bernie," I said. "Bernie the Hernie," quipped Greg. Another
day when I visited him, he was in the dining room, awaiting lunch.
When a nurse announced, "Lunch is here," he immediately
responded, "It's time for cheer"; when she said, "Shall I take the skin
off your chicken?" he instantly responded, "Yeah, why don't you slip
me some skin." "Oh, you want the skin?" she asked, puzzled. "Nah,"
he replied, "it's just a saying." He was, in a sense, preternaturally sensitive—but it was a sensitivity that was passive, without selectivity or
focus. There is no differentiation in such a sensitivity—the grand, the
trivial, the sublime, the ridiculous are all mixed up and treated as
equal.[5] There may be a childlike spontaneity and transparency about
such patients in their immediate and unpremeditated (and often playful) reactions. And yet there is something ultimately disquieting, and
bizarre, because the reacting mind (which may still be highly intelligent and inventive) loses its coherence, its inwardness, its autonomy,
its "self," and becomes the slave of every passing sensation. The French
neurologist François Lhermitte speaks of an "environmental depen-
dency syndrome" in such patients, a lack of psychological distance
between them and their environment. So it was with Greg; he seized
his environment, he was seized by it, he could not distinguish himself
from it.[6]

Dreaming and waking, for us, are usually distinct—dreaming is
enclosed in sleep and enjoys a special license because it is cut off from
external perception and action; while waking perception is constrained by reality.[7] But in Greg the boundary between waking and

---

[5] Luria provides immensely detailed, at times almost novelistic, descriptions of
frontal lobe syndromes—in *Human Brain and Psychological Processes*—and sees
this "equalization" as the heart of such syndromes.

[6] A similar indiscriminate reactivity is sometimes seen in people with Tourette's
syndrome—sometimes in the automatic form of echoing words or actions, sometimes in the more complex forms of mimicry, parodying or impersonating others'
behavior, or in incontinent verbal associations (rhymings, punnings, clangings).

[7] Rodolfo Llinás and his colleagues at New York University, comparing the electro-
physiological properties of the brain in waking and dreaming, postulate a single

sleep seemed to break down, and what emerged was a sort of waking or public dream, in which dreamlike fancies and associations and symbols would proliferate and weave themselves into the waking perceptions of the mind.[8] These associations were often startling and sometimes surrealistic in quality. They showed the power of fancy at play and, specifically, the mechanisms—displacement, condensation, "overdetermination," and so on—that Freud has shown to be characteristic of dreams.

One felt all this very strongly with Greg, that he was often in some intermediate, half-dreamlike state in which, if the normal control and selectivity of thinking were lost, there was a half freedom, half compulsion, of fantasy and wit. To see this as pathological was necessary but insufficient; it had elements of the primitive, the childlike, the playful. Greg's absurdist, often gnomic, utterances, along with his seeming serenity (actually blandness), gave him an appearance of innocence and wisdom combined, gave him a special status on the ward, ambiguous but respected, a Holy Fool.

Though as a neurologist I had to speak of Greg's "syndrome," his "deficits," I did not feel this was adequate to describe him. I felt, one felt, that he had become another "kind" of person, that though his frontal lobe damage had taken away his identity in a way, it had also given him a sort of identity or personality, albeit of an odd and perhaps a primitive sort.

If Greg was alone, in a corridor, he seemed scarcely alive, but as soon as he was in company, he was a different person altogether. He would "come to"; he would be funny, charming, ingenuous, sociable.

---

fundamental mechanism for both—a ceaseless inner talking between cerebral cortex and thalamus, a ceaseless interplay of image and feeling, irrespective of whether there is sensory input or not. When there is sensory input, this interplay integrates it to generate waking consciousness, but in the absence of sensory input it continues to generate brain states, those brain states we call fantasy, hallucination, or dreams. Thus waking consciousness is dreaming—but dreaming constrained by external reality.

[8] Dreamlike or oneiric states have been described, by Luria and others, with lesions of the thalamus and diencephalon. J. J. Moreau, in a famous early study, *Hashish and Mental Illness* (1845), described both madness and hashish trances as "waking dreams." A particularly striking form of waking dream may be seen with the severer forms of Tourette's syndrome, where the external and the internal, the perceptual and the instinctual, burst forth in a sort of public phantasmagoria or dream.

Everyone liked him; he would respond to anyone at once, with a lightness and a humor and an absence of guile or hesitation; and if there was something too light or flippant or indiscriminate in his interactions and reactions, and if, moreover, he lost all memory of them in a minute, well, there were worse things; it was understandable, one of the results of his disease. Thus one was very aware, in a hospital for chronic patients like ours, a hospital where feelings of melancholy, of rage, and of hopelessness simmer and preside, of the virtue of a patient such as Greg—who never appeared to have bad moods, and who, when activated by others, was invariably cheerful, euphoric.

He seemed, in an odd way, and in consequence of his sickness, to have a sort of vitality or health—a cheeriness, an inventiveness, a directness, an exuberance, which other patients, and indeed the rest of us, found delightful in small doses. And where he had been so "difficult," so tormented, so rebellious in his pre-Krishna days, all this anger and torment and angst now seemed to have vanished; he seemed to be at peace. His father, who had had a terrible time in Greg's stormy days, before he got "tamed" by drugs, by religion, by tumor, said to me in an unbuttoned moment, "It's like he had a lobotomy," and then, with great irony, "Frontal lobes—who needs 'em?"

One of the most striking peculiarities of the human brain is the great development of the frontal lobes—they are much less developed in other primates and hardly evident at all in other mammals. They are the part of the brain that grows and develops most after birth (and their development is not complete until about the age of seven). But our ideas about the function of the frontal lobes, and the role they play, have had a tortuous and ambiguous history and are still far from clear. These uncertainties are well exemplified by the famous case of Phineas Gage and the interpretations and misinterpretations, from 1848 to the present, of his case. Gage was the very capable foreman of a gang of workers constructing a railroad line near Burlington, Vermont, when a bizarre accident befell him in September 1848. He was setting an explosive charge, using a tamping iron (a crowbarlike instrument weighing thirteen pounds and more than a yard long), when the charge went off prematurely, blowing the tamping iron straight through his head. Though he was knocked down, incredibly he was not killed but only stunned for a moment. He was able to get up and take a cart into town. There he appeared perfectly rational and calm and alert and greeted the local doctor by saying, "Doctor, here is business enough for you."

Soon after his injury, Gage developed a frontal lobe abscess and fever, but this resolved within a few weeks, and by the beginning of 1849 he was called "completely recovered." That he had survived at all was seen as a medical miracle, and that he was seemingly unchanged after sustaining huge damage to the frontal lobes of the brain seemed to support the idea that these were either functionless or had no functions that could not be performed equally by the remaining, undamaged portions of the brain. Where phrenologists, earlier in the century, had seen every part of the brain surface as the "seat" of a particular intellectual or moral faculty, a reaction to this had set in during the 1830s and 1840s, to such an extent that the brain was sometimes seen as being as undifferentiated as the liver. Indeed, the great physiologist Flourens had said, "The brain secretes thought as the liver secretes bile." The apparent absence of any change in Gage's behavior seemed to support this notion.

Such was the influence of this doctrine that, despite clear evidence from other sources of a radical change in Gage's "character" within weeks of the accident, it was only twenty years later that the physician who had studied him most closely, John Martyn Harlow (now, apparently, moved by the new doctrines of "higher" and "lower" levels in the nervous system, the higher inhibiting or constraining the lower) provided a vivid description of all that he had ignored, or at least not mentioned, in 1848:

> [Gage is] fitful, irreverent, indulging at times in the grossest profanity (which was not previously his custom), manifesting but little deference for his fellows, impatient of restraint or advice when it conflicts with his desires, at times pertinaciously obstinate, yet capricious and vacillating, devising many plans of future operations, which are no sooner arranged than they are abandoned in turn for others appearing more feasible. A child in his intellectual capacity and manifestations, he has the animal passions of a strong man. Previous to his injury, although untrained in the schools, he possessed a well-

balanced mind, and was looked upon by those who knew him as a shrewd, smart businessman, very energetic and persistent in executing all his plans of operation. In this regard his mind was radically changed, so decidedly that his friends and acquaintances said he was "no longer Gage."

It seemed that a sort of "disinhibition" had occurred with the frontal lobe injury, releasing something animallike or childlike, so that Gage now became a slave of his immediate whims and impulses, of what was immediately around him, without the deliberation, the consideration of past and future, that had marked him in the past, or his previous concern for others and the consequences of his actions.[9]

But excitement, release, disinhibition, are not the only possible effects of frontal lobe damage. David Ferrier (whose Gulstonian Lectures of 1879 introduced the Gage case to a worldwide medical community) observed a different sort of syndrome in 1876, when he removed the frontal lobes of monkeys:

Notwithstanding this apparent absence of physiological symptoms, I could perceive a very decided alteration in the animal's character and behaviour . . . Instead of, as before, being actively interested in their surroundings, and curiously prying into all that came within the field of their observation, they remained apathetic, or dull, or dozed off to sleep, responding only to the sensations or impressions of the moment, or varying their listlessness with restless and purposeless wanderings to and fro. While not actually deprived of intelligence, they had lost, to all appearance, the faculty of attentive and intelligent observation.

In the 1880s it became apparent that tumors of the frontal lobes could produce symptoms of many sorts: sometimes listlessness, hebetude, slowness of mental activity, sometimes a definite change in char-

---

[9] Robert Louis Stevenson wrote *The Strange Case of Dr. Jekyll and Mr. Hyde* in 1886. It is not known whether he knew of the Gage case, though this had become common knowledge since the early 1880s — but he was assuredly moved by the Jacksonian doctrine of higher and lower levels in the brain, the notion that it was only our "higher" (and perhaps fragile) intellectual centers that held back the animal propensities of the "lower."

acter and loss of self-control—sometimes even (according to Gowers) "chronic insanity." The first operation for a frontal lobe tumor was performed in 1884, and the first frontal lobe operation for purely psychiatric symptoms was done in 1888. The rationale here was that in these (probably schizophrenic) patients, the obsessions, the hallucinations, the delusional excitements, were due to overactivity, or pathological activity, in the frontal lobes.

There was to be no repetition of such forays for forty-five years, until the 1930s, when the Portuguese neurologist Egas Moniz devised the operation he called "prefrontal leucotomy" and immediately applied this to twenty patients, some with anxiety and depression, some with chronic schizophrenia. The results he claimed aroused huge interest when his monograph was published in 1936, and his lack of rigor, his recklessness, and perhaps dishonesty were all overlooked in the flush of therapeutic enthusiasm. Moniz's work led to an explosion of "psychosurgery" (the term he had coined) all over the world—Brazil, Cuba, Romania, Great Britain, and especially Italy—but its greatest resonance was to be in the United States, where the neurologist Walter Freeman invented a horrible new form of surgical approach that he called transorbital lobotomy. He described the procedure as follows:

> This consists of knocking them out with a shock and while they are under the "anesthetic" thrusting an ice pick up between the eyeball and the eyelid through the roof of the orbit actually into the frontal lobe of the brain and making the lateral cut by swinging the thing from side to side. I have done two patients on both sides and another on one side without running into any complications, except a very black eye in one case. There may be trouble later on but it seemed fairly easy, although definitely a disagreeable thing to watch. It remains to be seen how these cases hold up, but so far they have shown considerable relief of their symptoms, and only some of the minor behavior difficulties that follow lobotomy. They can even get up and go home within an hour or so.

The ease of doing psychosurgery as an office procedure, with an ice pick, aroused not consternation and horror, as it should have, but emulation. More than ten thousand operations had been done in the

United States by 1949, and a further ten thousand in the two years that followed. Moniz was widely acclaimed as a "savior" and received the Nobel Prize in 1951—the climax, in Macdonald Critchley's words, of "this chronicle of shame."

What was achieved, of course, was never "cure," but a docile state, a state of passivity, as far (or farther) from "health" than the original active symptoms, and (unlike these) with no possibility of resolution or reversal. Robert Lowell, in "Memories of West Street and Lepke," writes of the lobotomized Lepke:

> Flabby, bald, lobotomized,
> he drifted in a sheepish calm,
> where no agonizing reappraisal
> jarred his concentration on the electric chair—
> hanging like an oasis in his air
> of lost connections. . . .

When I worked at a state psychiatric hospital between 1966 and 1990, I saw dozens of these pathetic lobotomized patients, many far more damaged even than Lepke, some psychically dead, murdered, by their "cure."[10]

Whether or not there are in the frontal lobes a mass of pathological circuits causing the torments of mental illness—the simplistic notion first put forward in the 1880s, and embraced by Moniz—there is certainly a downside to their great and positive powers. The weight of consciousness and conscience and conscientiousness itself, the weight of duty, obligation, responsibility, can press on us sometimes with unbearable force, so that we long for a release from its crushing inhibitions,

---

[10] The huge scandal of leucotomy and lobotomy came to an end in the early fifties, not because of any medical reservation or revulsion, but because a new tool—tranquillizers—had now become available, which purported (as had psychosurgery itself) to be wholly therapeutic and without adverse effects. Whether there is that much difference, neurologically or ethically, between psychosurgery and tranquillizers is an uncomfortable question that has never been really faced. Certainly the tranquillizers, if given in massive doses, may, like surgery, induce "tranquillity," may still the hallucinations and delusions of the psychotic, but the stillness they induce may be like the stillness of death—and, by a cruel paradox, deprive patients of the natural resolution that may sometimes occur with psychoses and instead immure them in a lifelong, drug-caused illness.

from sanity and sobriety. We long for a holiday from our frontal lobes, a Dionysiac fiesta of sense and impulse. That this is a need of our constrained, civilized, hyperfrontal nature has been recognized in every time and culture. All of us need to take little holidays from our frontal lobes—the tragedy is when, through grave illness or injury, there is no return from the holiday, as with Phineas Gage, or with Greg.[11]

In a March 1979 note about Greg, I reported that "games, songs, verses, converse, etc., hold him together completely . . . because they have an organic rhythm and stream, a flowing of being, which carries and holds him." I was strongly reminded here of what I had seen with my amnesiac patient Jimmie, how he seemed held together when he attended Mass, by his relationship to and participation in an act of meaning, an organic unity, which overrode or bypassed the disconnections of his amnesia.[12] And what I had observed with a patient in England, a musicologist with profound amnesia from a temporal lobe encephalitis, unable to remember events or facts for more than a few

---

[11] Though the medical literature of frontal lobe syndromes starts with the case of Phineas Gage, there are earlier descriptions of altered mental states not identifiable at the time—which we can now, in retrospect, see as frontal lobe syndromes. One such account is related by Lytton Strachey in "The Life, Illness, and Death of Dr. North." Dr. North, a master of Trinity College, Cambridge, in the eighteenth century, was a man with severe anxieties and tormenting obsessional traits who was hated and dreaded by the fellows of the college for his punctiliousness, his moralizing, and his merciless severity. Until one day, in college, he suffered a stroke:

> His recovery was not complete; his body was paralyzed on the left side; but it was in his mind that the most remarkable change occurred. His fears had left him. His scrupulosity, his diffidence, his seriousness, even his morality—all had vanished. He lay on his bed, in reckless levity, pouring forth a stream of flippant observations, and naughty stories, and improper jokes. While his friends hardly knew which way to look, he laughed consumedly, his paralyzed features drawn up in a curiously distorted grin . . . Attacked by epileptic seizures, he declared that the only mitigation of his sufferings lay in the continued consumption of wine. He, who had been so noted for his austerity, now tossed off, with wild exhilaration, glass after glass of the strongest sherry.

Strachey gives us here a precise and beautifully described picture of a frontal lobe stroke altering the personality in a major and, so to speak, "therapeutic" way.

[12] The nature of the "organic unity," at once dynamic and semantic, which is central to music, incantation, recitation, and all metrical structures, has been most profoundly analyzed by Victor Zuckerkandl in his remarkable book Sound and Sym-

seconds, but able to remember, and indeed to learn, elaborate musical pieces, to conduct them, to perform them, and even to improvise at the organ.[13]

It was similar with Greg as well: he not only had an excellent memory for songs of the sixties, but was able to learn new songs easily, despite his difficulty in retaining any "facts." It seemed as if wholly different kinds—and mechanisms—of memory might be involved. Greg was also able to pick up limericks and jingles with ease (and had indeed picked up hundreds of these from the radio and television that were always on in the ward). Soon after his admission, I tested him with the following limerick:

> Hush-a-bye baby,
> Hush quite a lot,
> Bad babies get rabies
> And have to be shot.

Greg immediately repeated this, without error, laughed at it, asked if I'd made it up, and compared it with "something gruesome, like Edgar Allan Poe." But two minutes later he could not recall it, until I reminded him of the underlying rhythm. With a few more repetitions, he learned it without cueing and thereafter recited it whenever he met me.

Was this facility for learning jingles and songs a mere procedural or performative one, or could it provide emotional depth or generalizability of a sort that Greg did not normally have access to? There seemed no doubt that some music could move him profoundly, could be a door to depths of feeling and meaning to which he normally had no access, and one felt Greg was a different person at these times. He no longer seemed to have a frontal lobe syndrome, but was (so to speak)

---

bol. It is typical of such flowing dynamic-semantic structures that each part leads on to the next, that every part has reference to the rest. Such structures cannot usually be perceived, or remembered, in part—they are perceived and remembered, if at all, as wholes.

[13] This patient is the subject of a remarkable BBC film made by Jonathan Miller, *Prisoner of Consciousness* (November 1988).

temporarily "cured" by the music. Even his EEG, so slow and incoherent most of the time, became calm and rhythmical with music.[14]

It is easy to show that simple information can be embedded in songs; thus we can give Greg the date every day in the form of a jingle, and he can readily isolate this and say it when asked, without the jingle. But what does it mean to say, "This is July 9, 1995," when one is sunk in the profoundest amnesia, when one has lost a sense of time and history, when one is existing from moment to moment in a sequenceless limbo? Knowing the date means nothing in these circumstances. Could one, however, through the evocativeness and power of music, perhaps using songs with specially written lyrics—songs that relate something valuable about himself or the current world—accomplish something more lasting, deeper? Give Greg not only the "facts" but a sense of time and history, of the relatedness of events, an entire (if artificial) framework for thinking and feeling?

It seemed natural, at this time, given Greg's blindness and the revelation of his potential for learning, that he should be given an opportunity to learn Braille. Arrangements were made with the Jewish Institute for the Blind for him to enter intensive training, four times a week. It should not have been a disappointment, nor indeed a surprise, that Greg was unwilling to learn any Braille—that he was startled and bewildered at finding this imposed on him, and cried out, "What's going on? Do you think I'm blind? Why am I here, with blind people all around me?" Attempts were made to explain things to him, and he responded, with impeccable logic, "If I were blind, I would be the first person to know it." The institute said they had never had such a difficult patient, and the project was quietly allowed to drop. And indeed,

[14] Another patient in Williamsbridge, Harry S.—a gifted man, a former engineer—suffered a huge cerebral hemorrhage from a burst aneurysm, with gross destruction of both frontal lobes. Emerging from a coma, he started to recover and eventually recovered most of his former intellectual powers, but remains, like Greg, severely impaired—bland, flat, indifferent emotionally. But all this changes, suddenly, when he sings. He has a fine tenor voice and loves Irish songs. When he sings, he does so with a fullness of feeling, a tenderness, a lyricism, that are astounding—the more so because one sees no hint of this at any other time and might well think his emotional capacity entirely destroyed. He shows every emotion appropriate to what he sings—the frivolous, the jovial, the tragic, the sublime—and seems to be transformed while he sings.

with the failure of the Braille program, a sort of hopelessness gripped us, and perhaps Greg, too. We could do nothing, we felt; he had no potential for change.

Greg by this time had had several psychological and neuropsychological evaluations, and these, besides commenting on his memory and attentional problems, had all spoken of him as being "shallow," "infantile," "insightless," "euphoric." It was easy to see why these words had been used; Greg was like this for much of the time. But was there a deeper Greg beneath his illness, beneath the shallowing effect of his frontal lobe loss and amnesia? Early in 1979, when I questioned him, he said he was "miserable . . . at least in the corporeal part," and added, "It's not much of a life." At such times, it was clear that he was not just frivolous and euphoric, but capable of deep, and indeed melancholic, reactions to his plight. The comatose Karen Ann Quinlan was then very much in the news, and each time her name and fate were mentioned, Greg became distressed and silent. He could never tell me, explicitly, why this so interested him—but it had to be, I felt, because of some sort of identification of her tragedy with his own. Or was this just his incontinent sympathy, his falling at once into the mood of any stimulus or news, falling almost helplessly, mimetically, into its mood?

This was not a question I could decide at first, and perhaps, too, I was prejudiced against finding any depths in Greg, because the neuropsychological studies I knew of seemed to disallow this possibility. But these studies were based on brief evaluations, not on long-continued observation and relationship of a sort that is, perhaps, only possible in a hospital for chronic patients, or in situations where a whole world, a whole life, is shared with the patient.

Greg's "frontal lobe" characteristics—his lightness, his quick-fire associations—were fun, but beyond this there shone through a basic decency and sensitivity and kindness. One felt that Greg, though damaged, still had a personality, an identity, a soul.[15]

[15] Mr. Thompson ("A Matter of Identity"), who also had both amnesia and a frontal lobe syndrome, by contrast often seemed "desouled." In him the wisecracking was manic, ferocious, frenetic, and relentless; it rushed on like a torrent, oblivious to tact, to decency, to propriety, to everything, including the feelings of everyone around him. Whether Greg's (at least partial) preservation of ego and identity was due to the lesser severity of his syndrome, or to underlying personality differences, is not wholly clear. Mr. Thompson's premorbid personality was that of a New York

When he came to Williamsbridge we all responded to his intelligence, his high spirits, his wit. All sorts of therapeutic programs and enterprises were started at this time, but all of them—like the learning of Braille—ended in failure. The sense of Greg's incorrigibility gradually grew on us, and with this we started to do less, to hope less. Increasingly, he was left to his own devices. He slowly ceased to be a center of attention, the focus of eager therapeutic activities—more and more he was left to himself, left out of programs, not taken anywhere, quietly ignored.

It is easy, even if one is not an amnesiac, to lose touch with current reality in the back wards of hospitals for the chronically ill. There is a simple round that has not changed in twenty, or fifty, years. One is wakened, fed, taken to the toilet, and left to sit in a hallway; one has lunch, one is taken to bingo, one has dinner and goes to bed. The television may indeed be left on, blaring, in the television room—but most patients pay no attention to it. Greg, it is true, enjoyed his favorite soap operas and westerns and learned an enormous number of advertising jingles by heart. But the news, for the most part, he found boring and, increasingly, unintelligible. Years can pass, in a sort of timeless limbo, with few, and certainly no memorable, markers of the passage of time.

As ten years or so went by, Greg showed a complete absence of development; his talk seemed increasingly dated and repertorial, for nothing new was being added to it, or him. The tragedy of his amnesia seemed to become greater with the years, although his amnesia itself, his neurological syndrome, remained much the same.

In 1988 Greg had a seizure—he had never had one before (although he had been on anticonvulsants, as a precaution, since the time of his surgery)—and in the seizure broke a leg. He did not complain of this, he did not even mention it; it was only discovered when he tried to stand up the following day. He had, apparently, forgotten it as soon as the pain eased and as soon as he had found a comfortable position. His not knowing that he had broken a leg seemed to me to have similarities to his not knowing he was blind, his inability, with his amnesia, to hold in mind an absence. When the leg caused pain, briefly, he knew some-

cabbie, and in some sense his frontal lobe syndrome merely intensified this. Greg's personality was gentler, more childlike, from the start—and this, it seemed to me, even colored his frontal lobe syndrome.

thing had happened, he knew it was there; as soon as the pain ceased, it went from his mind. Had he had visual hallucinations or phantoms (as the blind sometimes do, at least in the first months and years after losing their sight), he could have spoken of them, said, "Look!" or "Wow!" But in the absence of actual visual input, he could hold nothing in mind about seeing, or not-seeing, or the loss of a visual world. In his person, and in his world, now, Greg knew only presence, not absence. He seemed incapable of registering any loss—loss of function in himself, or of an object, or a person.

In June of 1990, Greg's father, who had come every morning before work to see Greg and would joke and chat with him for an hour, suddenly died. I was away at the time (mourning my own father), and hearing the news of Greg's bereavement on my return, I hastened to see him. He had been given the news, of course, when it happened. And yet I was not quite sure what to say—had he been able to absorb this new fact? "I guess you must be missing your father," I ventured.

"What do you mean?" Greg answered. "He comes every day. I see him every day."

"No," I said, "he's no longer coming . . . He has not come for some time. He died last month."

Greg flinched, turned ashen, became silent. I had the impression he was shocked, doubly shocked, at the sudden, appalling news of his father's death, and at the fact that he himself did not know, had not registered, did not remember. "I guess he must have been around fifty," he said.

"No, Greg," I answered, "he was well up in his seventies."

Greg grew pale again as I said this. I left the room briefly; I felt he needed to be alone with all this. But when I returned a few minutes later, Greg had no memory of the conversation we had had, of the news I had given him, no idea that his father had died.

Very clearly, at least, Greg showed a capacity for love and grief. If I had ever doubted Greg's capacity for deeper feeling, I no longer doubted it now. He was clearly devastated by his father's death—he showed nothing "flip," no levity, at this time.[16] But would he have the

---

[16] This is in distinction to Mr. Thompson, who, with his more severe frontal lobe syndrome, had been reduced to a sort of nonstop, wisecracking, talking machine, and when told of his brother's death quipped "He's always the joker!" and rushed on to other, irrelevant things.

ability to mourn? Mourning requires that one hold the sense of loss in one's mind, and it was far from clear to me that Greg could do this. One might indeed tell him that his father had died, again and again. And every time it would come as something shocking and new and cause immeasurable distress. But then, in a few minutes, he would forget and be cheerful again, and was so prevented from going through the work of grief, the mourning.[17]

I made a point of seeing Greg frequently in the following months, but I did not again bring up the subject of his father's death. It was not up to me, I thought, to confront him with this—indeed it would be pointless and cruel to do so; life itself, surely, would do so, for Greg would discover his father's absence.

I made the following note on November 26, 1990: "Greg shows no conscious knowing that his father has died—when asked where his father is, he may say, 'Oh, he went down to the patio,' or 'He couldn't make it today,' or something else plausible. But he no longer wants to go home, on weekends, on Thanksgiving, as he so loved to—he must find something sad or repugnant in the fatherless house now, even though he cannot (consciously) remember or articulate this. Clearly he has established an association of sadness."

Toward the end of the year Greg, normally a sound sleeper, started to sleep poorly, to get up in the middle of the night and wander gropingly for hours around his room. "I've lost something, I'm looking for something," he would say when asked—but what he had lost, what he was looking for, he could never explain. One could not avoid the feeling that Greg was looking for his father, even though he could give no account of what he was doing and had no explicit knowledge of what he had lost. But, it seemed to me, there was perhaps now an implicit knowledge and perhaps, too, a symbolic (though not a conceptual) knowing.

Greg had seemed so sad since his father's death that I felt he deserved a special celebration—and when I heard, in August of 1991, that his

---

[17] The amnesiac musicologist in the BBC film *Prisoner of Consciousness* showed something both similar and different. Every time his wife went out of the room, he had a sense of calamitous, permanent loss. When she came back, five minutes later, he sobbed with relief, saying, "I thought you were dead."

beloved group, the Grateful Dead, would be playing at Madison Square Garden in a few weeks, this seemed just the thing. Indeed, I had met one of the drummers in the band, Mickey Hart, earlier in the summer, when we had both testified before the Senate about the therapeutic powers of music, and he made it possible for us to obtain tickets at the last minute, to bring Greg, wheelchair and all, into the concert, where a special place would be saved for him near the soundboard, where acoustics were best.

We made these arrangements at the last minute, and I had given Greg no warning, not wanting to disappoint him if we failed to get seats. But when I picked him up at the hospital and told him where we were going, he showed great excitement. We got him dressed swiftly and bundled him into the car. As we got into midtown, I opened the car windows, and the sounds and smells of New York came in. As we cruised down Thirty-third Street, the smell of hot pretzels suddenly struck him; he inhaled deeply and laughed. "That's the most New York smell in the world."

There was an enormous crowd converging on Madison Square Garden, most in tie-dyed T-shirts—I had hardly seen a tie-dyed T-shirt in twenty years, and I myself began to think we were back in the sixties, or perhaps that we had never left them. I was sorry that Greg could not see this crowd; he would have felt himself one of them, at home. Stimulated by the atmosphere, Greg started to talk spontaneously—very unusual for him—and to reminisce about the sixties.

Yeah, there were the be-ins in Central Park. They haven't had one for a long time—over a year, maybe, can't remember exactly . . . Concerts, music, acid, grass, everything . . . First time I was there was Flower-Power Day . . . Good times . . . lots of things started in the sixties—acid rock, the be-ins, the love-ins, smoking . . . Don't see it much these days . . . Allen Ginsberg—he's down in the Village a lot, or in Central Park. I haven't seen him for a long time. It's over a year since I last saw him . . .

Greg's use of the present tense, or the near-present tense; his sense of all these events, not as far distant, much less as terminated, but as having taken place "a year ago, maybe" (and, by implication, likely to take place again, at any time); all this, which seemed so pathological, so anachronistic in clinical testing, seemed almost normal, natural, now that we were part of this sixties crowd sweeping toward the Garden.

Inside the Garden we found the special place reserved for Greg's wheelchair near the soundboard. And now Greg was growing more excited by the minute; the roar of the crowd excited him—"It's like a giant animal," he said—and the sweet, hash-laden air. "What a great smell," he said, inhaling deeply. "It's the least stupid smell in the world."[18]

As the band came onstage, and the noise of the crowd grew greater, Greg was transported by the excitement and started clapping loudly and shouting in an enormous voice, "Bravo! Bravo!" then "Let's go!" followed by "Let's go, Hypo," followed, homophonously, by "Ro, Ro, Ro, Harry-Bo." Pausing a moment, Greg said to me, "See the tombstone behind the drums? See Jerry Garcia's Afro?" with such conviction that I was momentarily taken in and looked (in vain) for a tombstone behind the drums—before realizing it was one of Greg's confabulations—and at the now-gray hair of Jerry Garcia, which fell in a straight, unhindered descent to his shoulders.

And then, "Pigpen!" Greg exclaimed. "You see Pigpen there?"

"No," I replied hesitantly, not knowing how to reply. "He's not there . . . You see, he's not with the Dead anymore."

"Not with them?" said Greg in astonishment. "What happened—he got busted or something?"

"No, Greg, not busted. He died."

"That's awful," Greg answered, shaking his head, shocked. And then a minute later, he nudged me again. "Pigpen! You see Pigpen there?" And, word for word, the whole conversation repeated itself.

But then the thumping, pounding excitement of the crowd got

---

[18] Jean Cocteau, in fact, said this of opium. Whether Greg was quoting this, consciously or unconsciously, I do not know. Smells are sometimes even more evocative than music; and the percepts of smells, generated in a very primitive part of the brain—the "smell brain," or rhinencephalon—may not go through the complex, multistage memory systems of the medial temporal lobe. Olfactory memories, neurally, are almost indelible; thus they may be remembered despite an amnesia. It would be fascinating to bring Greg hot pretzels, or hash, to see whether their smells could evoke memories of the concert. He himself, the next day, spontaneously mentioned the "great" smell of pretzels—it was very vivid for him—and yet he could not locate the smell in place or time.

him—the rhythmic clapping and stamping and chanting possessed him—and he started to chant, "The Dead! The Dead!" then with a shift of rhythm, and a slow emphasis on each word, "We want the Dead!" And then, "Tobacco Road, Tobacco Road," the name of one of his favorite songs, until the music began.

The band began with an old song, "Iko, Iko," and Greg joined in with gusto, with abandon, clearly knowing all the words, and especially luxuriating in the African-sounding chorus. The whole vast Garden now was in motion with the music, eighteen thousand people responding together, everyone transported, every nervous system synchronized, in unison.

The first half of the concert had many earlier pieces, songs from the sixties, and Greg knew them, loved them, joined in. His energy and joy were amazing to see; he clapped and sang nonstop, with none of the weakness and fatigue he generally showed. He showed a rare and wonderful continuity of attention, everything orienting him, holding him together. Looking at Greg transformed in this way, I could see no trace of his amnesia, his frontal lobe syndrome—he seemed at this moment completely normal, as if the music was infusing him with its own strength, its coherence, its spirit.

I had wondered whether we should leave at the break midway through the concert—he was, after all, a disabled, wheelchair-bound patient who had not really been out on the town, at a rock concert, for more than twenty years. But he said, "No, I want to stay, I want it all"—an assertion, an autonomy, I rejoiced to see and had hardly ever seen in his compliant life at the hospital. So we stayed, and in the interval went backstage, where Greg had a large hot pretzel and then met Mickey Hart and exchanged a few words with him. He had looked a little tired and pale before, but now he was flushed, excited by the encounter, charged and eager to be back for more music.

But the second half of the concert was somewhat strange for Greg: more of the songs dated from the mid- or late seventies and had lyrics that were unknown to him, though they were familiar in style. He enjoyed these, clapping and singing along wordlessly, or making up words as he went. But then there were newer songs, radically different, like "Picasso Moon," with dark and deep harmonies and an electronic instrumentation such as would have been impossible, unimaginable, in the 1960s. Greg was intrigued, but deeply puzzled. "It's weird stuff," he said. "I never heard anything like it before." He listened intently, all his musical senses stirred, but with a slightly scared and bewildered look, as if seeing a new animal, a new plant, a new world, for the first time. "I guess it's some new, experimental stuff," he said, "something they never played before. Sounds futuristic . . . maybe it's the music of the future." The newer songs he heard went far beyond any development that he could have imagined, were so beyond (and in some ways so unlike) what he associated with the Dead that it "blew his mind." It was, he could not doubt, "their" music he was hearing, but it gave him an almost unbearable sense of hearing the future—as late Beethoven would have struck a devotee if it had been played at a concert in 1800.

"That was fantastic," he said as we filed out of the Garden. "I will always remember it. I had the time of my life." I played CDs of the Grateful Dead in the car on the way home, to hold as long as possible the mood and memory of the concert. I feared that if I stopped playing the Dead, or talking about them, for a single moment, all memory of the concert would go from his mind. Greg sang along enthusiastically all the way back, and when we parted at the hospital, he was still in an exuberant concert mood.

But the next morning when I came to the hospital early, I found Greg in the dining room, alone, facing the wall. I asked him about the Grateful Dead—what did he think of them? "Great group," he said, "I love them. I heard them in Central Park and at the Fillmore East."

"Yes," I said, "you told me. But have you seen them since? Didn't you just hear them at Madison Square Garden?"

"No," he said, "I've never been to the Garden."[19]

---

[19] Greg has no recollection of the concert, seemingly—but when I was sent a tape of it, he immediately recognized some of the "new" pieces, found them familiar, was able to sing them. "Where did you hear that?" I asked as we listened to "Picasso Moon."

He shrugged uncertainly. But there is no doubt that he has learned it, nonetheless. I have taken now to visiting him regularly, with tapes of our concert and of the latest Grateful Dead concerts. He seems to enjoy the visits and has learned many of the new songs. And now, whenever I arrive, and he hears my voice, he lights up, and greets me as a fellow Deadhead.

GEOFFREY O'BRIEN

Notes Toward a History
of the Seventies

AFTER a while it got hard to remember which happened before which. I didn't realize this was a rerun. The water pipes became obsolete unbelievably quickly. The more starved tonality of the Albanian Labor Party appealed to certain poets. The large faces of Stalin and Mao seemed part of the spring mist in Union Square, comfortingly bony and blunt. The materiality of tree trunks and leaflets and armed horses. Somewhat later, or was it somewhat earlier, everyone was engaging in threesomes, or discovering that they liked to be tied up while watching television, or "blissing out" on a combination of Quaaludes and overpriced marijuana. Parties got even thicker and wobblier, until no wind could slam that pocket apart. Reverb migrated through chasms and pouches. And then gathered on the sidewalk in white jogging shorts and moist skin and dilated eyes. They buzzed around near the car pond. Traffic lamps adjoining sex and drugs. Carnival barker who came from gallery. They had invented a way to get into money. The net shapes stretched across the studio in imitation of rocket travel. It could stimulate a doughnut commercial. Even the makeup cost maybe twenty hours. Spaced-out cans. But we don't plot them by eye anymore. We grew up. A man hacks frames together and gets paid. Not even conceptual napkins come cheap. An alternative to hamburgers, late-night samurai movies. Little girl miming Bruce Lee's kick in between Brooklyn. Foot charged with life energy makes a sound like thunder when it connects with the drug baron's solar plexus. Bright rubble. The painted wagons explode into rock wall. Radiant disco corridors went on and on. Four men in dashikis harmonizing next to the Coliseum. Across the street the detectives buy stolen goods from factory workers. The girl in the pizza parlor was wearing her shirt messy and she talked. I think she looked away when I asked her what money it was. Big Jim knows where all the cigarette trucks are in Detroit. The new steak house wants to avoid junkies. Masturbating on company time. The office worker has a clean haircut and likes the new music in which a single phrase is repeated over and over. Here comes the express. He informs me that Nelson Rockefeller and Henry Kissinger are conspiring to funnel all the gold out of Fort Knox. They will hide it in Switzerland until the next war comes. The things they say are still there have actually been taken. After the war it will come down to cigarettes and bodies and drugs, like always. Bargaining chips. Mentally they try to rehearse for bombardment and occupation. House filled with criminals burning on daytime television. Blurred orangey reception making it near and far at the same time. The way charred corpses become wiggly abstractions above the cocktail ledge. Television never stinks. Brief messes cluster in its glass and vaporize. Glazed like a trucker's eyes. Eight days on the road and I am going to see my baby tonight. Smokes out the bar again. Had referred to the bodies and made a joke about how the announcer talked, his kitschy somberness. I do not vote because democracy is a shell game. I do not vote because they crucified Lenny Bruce. They allowed the hotel to collapse. He was talking on the phone and the floor fell from under. On the news they showed a puppy crawling from the wreckage. No ideology will ever comprehend a guitarist's armpits or the overlapping rings stained into the table. Neighbors were forced to put up warning signs about the abandoned piers. People have been killed in here. Sniffing of bodies under the black planks. Nest of throats, desperate urinals. They crank their lights out under the cars. Agitate against what the night makes glisten.

Whatever turns up on the streets is minor, its wires already loose. Random hubcaps. Debris cast aside in anticipation of liftoff. The man who owns the Amazon stepped into the elevator. He paves the drainage basins, is sucking the air out of the planet: tight little man in a coat. The clerk who rode down with him died later. Not the night the addict crawled through the window and had to be tied to the bed nor the night when the poet was pistolwhipped in the lobby nor the night when the building was evacuated at 3 A.M. by city officials:

later. It must have been around the time the pregnant girl, teenage run-away, walked into the bar so ecstatic she was practically levitating. A van will come for me, take me to an enormous farm. I met a man on the street. They have midwives there. The man who runs the farm has been everywhere, everyone bumps into him at some point on their journey. He says traditional sex roles conceal a great wisdom. Years ago he was beaten up on a bus, it was his own fault, his vibes were twisted around in the wrong direction. That was during the era of open display. Now we have reached the time when things will be progressively more hidden. It will be harder and harder to find the door. The door to the hotel is blocked with trucks. Warning: I don't brake for liberals. The big cult bought the hotel. Local merchants were gratified by the brisk sale of mattresses and basic foodstuffs. Did you know the wages of sin is death? Some kind of torture in the voice. Packing the streets until you could trip over them. Chant on the phone in the middle of the night to keep themselves focused. The schizophrenics in the movie made me feel anxious. Carefully monitored hunger, compartmentalized knowl-edge. Nutritional content of brown rice. His throat cracks in the midst of reciting the circular genealogies. An unseen tenant comes out at night to cover the pavement with diagrams charting the connection between castrated cattle and homosexual army officers. Convulsive friction of genitals and brain fluids, trailing off into a chain of neon arrows. Elsewhere along the poison belt more cows fall, the blood drained by hooded strangers. The energy vortex shifts to the Bermuda triangle. Ancient space lizards live under the Caribbean and interfere with electrical waves. The minds of lost pilots fuse into an immense radio signal. Of which those zigzag lines in the Andes are a transcrip-tion. Harbinger of delayed birth.

The red sun poses at the treetops. It resembles a ball of blood. We will be burning and looting tonight. An older phraseology thins out, folds, pulps itself. Intersections of Babylon: frozen gated park abuts liquors. They make new names for boxes, and live in them. Find uses for aban-doned cities. An art of depopulation. The new government issued a prohibition against hazardous games. The café tables exist at an edge into which pipes feed. Stuff mud and grain in the outlets. Barricade of oil drums. He never meets his anonymous suppliers. Slow discoloration of furrows. An encroachment so gradual it can be screened out. Mute inedible pressures. Switches before the stains can be examined, in keeping with normal velocity. Then—as decoy—the song gets caught up in its beginning again. The programs do not end. In place of silence there are the confused junctions where they overlap. Accidental hollows formed by crisscrossing message units. An attic shelter defined by car fragments and commercials for noise. The couple above the mortuary drink and listen to Dixieland all afternoon. The man next door has a loud sporadic sex life and carries a metal-tipped cane for smashing the heads of muggers. How do you say "fuck off asshole" in Japanese? Otherwise you don't know the language. When he talks about missiles his eyes go funny. Peeling the beer top back as the dark comes on. They will fall, all the bombs will fall, all the little mechanisms will click into action. Inspectors measure the cracked foundation. The stairs sag. The child dropped the stolen shaver through the punctured closet. The murderer's room was littered with comic books and pornography. A room never entered. Newspaper headline: Now no one is safe. She wept in the pitch-black center of the bed. I just don't want to go out there. I want to stay here until everything is over. Ripple of movement among the corner people. Cut off from its generators the thin structure becomes a parody of a house. They try to act as if the stairs did not lead to the street. The wind harrows the slopes of the funnel. The shadows lap at the door holes.

            In the streets swept by hurricane there was the relief of aisles being dislodged. Nerve palaces cleared of ornament. Desire for simplicity becomes a subversive longing for catastrophe. Spend millions of dollars to see towers crumble. Let the parkways loose, splay the tollbooths and truck lanes to their full capacity. Throats tightening as the pumps run dry. Preliminary choreography for a dance of shotguns. Get the drop on a ninja in a ski mask. Broad strips of air between the mall buildings, waiting to be inhabited. They aim their handles at language. The part that can be translated into roadblocks. The study group discusses mass killings and forced relocation as aspects of gestural aesthetic. The energies of Mao forming into a kind of large-scale scripture. Nest of provocateurs obsessed with Beethoven and computers. To weave the files together, double-braid them, until all the data feeds back into itself. Until to name is to make a death: the revenge of quantity. The culture of the tabulators waits for the culture of the snorters to erode. It shouldn't take too long for them to wear themselves out. There was supposed to be an after hours club near the printing warehouse. Fog of wine and guns, forties nostalgia. Flora dance routine salvaged from an aunt's wedding. Displaced persons educated among Ricardo Cortez. Afro-Cuban cocaine orgies, war bonds. A semblance of decor. Fretwork of sequins. Tinted bathing party drawing ghosts over to the mirror. Isolated protective chambers. The rehearsal for suicide which is their own affair. Me. A clutch of cards, the party at the theater table. Things that pass from person to person to person: cats, imperfect record players, sickness. Open a space for oneself like a garage, a ledge. Carve a hunk of city within which the words begin to acquire wrinkles. A soil. The bindings expropriate whatever stray light falls. Prayer toward airshaft, low roofs. The measure sculpted by the walls. He lives inside a statement. The bodies either drift or flood, in their wake he goes cross-eyed. Collates the remains of a dialect: smoke and portrait, vine, collar, populous snow. Anthology of phone I can barely hear you taking pills in the next street. Roar of not quite loosened suits, clips, particles. Kitchen wax modulated by potential categories. A cellophane, the glue partly dry, detaching from its contents. Quilts washed up from previous lives, unslept bed, buds dusted in a string of wind storms. Outside. Where he is not, by means of his bones thinking of it. Skeletal force field drags its feelers through the hall. Soaks up golds and blues from blind beaches. The sax a raft he partitions noon with. Brainwasher Part Five. Navigates the sloped lines creasing into tubs and elbows. Folds the paper at a frozen angle. Brick hill sheared out toward tank honk.

The closing of the field. The routes dry up, slide into deflected ravines. The object held in the hand— a crouched man, a chipped god-mouth giving birth—is pried from the real earth, carried north through expensive jungle. They buy suits with it, go to openings. Or stockpile rugs and housing. A family where fine rigging was perpetuated. Until the son stayed home all year and splintered at the sofa's tassel tips. Long winter dream journey among diagnosed telephone poles. Stitched together from a California of privately printed erotic scriptures. A temple of orgasm flanked by guard dogs. Politicians rent movies. The rehabilitated teenager paces his bedroom, waves hello to the off-duty diplomats but does not participate in the round of charades after dinner. Surf casting as an annulment of Angola. It sets red and lightly broiled, scents the porch. He feels comfortable in yokel clothes, cherishes the coarseness of his beach. False poverty. At the Y the vet tones his muscles. Having envied tweeds he inherits them. A sexual game truncating hierarchies. Smooth drifters. The wide downtown opportunity, careless after the war. She wants to do commercials. Aristocracy of people who have lunch. Design the phases of a year, in advance of marketing. By August they will have forgotten to dislike this. Minefield of distractions, conceived as a payment for oyster platters. Until the corporate wiseguy—bald veteran of ten thousand New Jerseys, chattering as he carves out his portion of the hours between wind-up and drop-off—is loved because he is real. Has been a party to every two o'clock after the chairs were folded, and can almost remember the name of Baltimore. Has known various pirates. In the small alleys of the freak-in they were selling women and drugs like it was the wharfs of Hispaniola. Unhitched cash driving the loose cons and battle victims half mad with a kind of chemical thirst. The most open town you ever dreamed of. Would sell the bricks from the walls if they had to, to keep it going. And have done so, as it pulls in to the stripped subway. If you listen close you can hear the edges bump. Like a tiny door a pet cat can shove its way through, out in the flaking suburbs.

Admire the last sunset by the weed track, the abutment condemned for drilling. They prepare to wire the lake. As warm as the summer before the earlier war, the huge one, in the era of European dancers and set designers. This time a few caps sub for orchestra variations. Tinfoil symphony: a vista of flakes in clearance yard. Perforated youths half tired of dock light. Teen gone AWOL from midwestern recruiting center, hides out on downers until the girl feeds him. At the mercy of what he can learn about depots, hits, billing. Street of indifferent racket. Attic long since cleared out, the Gable photo auctioned to the new owners for their barn gallery. Grow old in garages. If there's enough pipe work he can haunt the damp cabin. Disused naval postings. Hot distant tar to evoke the beach road, prior to zoning. The cousin spends all his money on pot and his motorcycle and his tropical fish. Meditative pauses broken by canned laughter. Not quite interested, they wondered how the program had begun. Would ride off to shoot for beers, or hang out by Moon Bay, knock cans in the ocean. Scout the drenched beach fires. Against the advancing light, black shell chips, moves off to crash in the woods. Shape a Buddha throne form the ashes and radio parts. They have them in that country, whole lives of candle silence, empty old men. Would like to borrow those eyes for seeing the dump with. Abandoned fence. Unlike a future of entering the highway, disoriented among the slicks, and not even able to afford nightfall. Blow somebody away for cancelled checks, stake out the hospital. The father disappeared into his room, angry slur behind the bottle dust. By the last unsold lot the wrappers pile up, the new kids are nameless, their vans jam the road to the spruced-up harbor. Mutter about the foreigners opening shops crammed with replicas of cabin cruisers. Tavern where everybody was eased out of bayfront property by semilegal offers. To be replaced by a bankrupt vendor of sun lamps. Music imported from cities. After dark the car turns into a guitar solo. Leans in toward the siding where the twang veers. A format for the morning's oilcloth, distinct afterimage of swerve, the town yanked flat like a tent.

Chanteuse hooked on gangster, simulated eyelids, in a version of nightclub. Martyrdom of the unrecognized playwright, his children carrying hatred of critics into pills and showcase productions. Conspiracy against the nameless to keep them chained to family album, never liberated into Broadway. Parallel universe of liner notes. A stretched-out tenderness soliciting applause for accumulated bitter gestures. Reified throb stops the show. Story about how they live in telephone boxes, buy tickets to the beach, torture themselves with guilt about Santa Claus. They grew up around the dinner table in a phantom world of grandmothers, flax, soldiery, the old country. Landscape of picnics and therapists near where the family disappeared. City kids with a small vocabulary of exits. Learn to maneuver slots so that the correct image appears. Coin-operated weather. Or depart once and for all into the geography of closet, antique fur costume, lovingly polished knobs. Airless forest of opera in which children alter their bodies. Become a fog elf or a divided death. The most honored are permitted to withdraw into themselves. Shelves of hours, the fingers parting reeds and chords to make a trough. Wonders of art, splitting open. Place they came from. Unresolved sensation of dependence, the alien fork and bowl, mechanics of linen: a toy home. The real would be a stained knapsack, German poet starving between stations, the lost armies. History of the postwar flattening of ambition, eye unable either to invent or dissolve the ballet curtain. Created, fixed. A dead sunlight, inherited. Born after corpses on the far shore. Microphone without words to put into it.

Hotel where they insert romances into the tiles. Fever around a sealed package. They are telling my story on all the televisions, a slightly veiled account of my nervous system. The rich (alternate bodies) are the ones who can shut noise out. If I were rich I could afford not to watch this program. Could walk around on the hermetic beaches where her childhood occurred, finger the chairs. Pressure points of landscaping, causeways, bent hedges, unaccessed logbook of initiation. Benin mask reflected in lawn glaze. Coves folded inward like membrane. A metal shack tucked against the rocky outer lip, its lunchroom jammed with soda machines and sample cases. Road workers almost not being there. The supply line tapering off beyond the water failure. Shored-up underpass gradually absorbed into the weed bank. Stranded in fenced areas, the islanders guard themselves against each other's children. There are periodic rumors of distant thought processes. Some guy dreamt up a distribution network. A new way to make wires, and suddenly everybody's father is obsolete. Not a country for parking your car. Too far to be separated from the nearest heated entrance, forget what language they talk about movies in. Ages ago a man came around selling boxed libraries of political structure. Gave armed lectures in the barn for a while. The newsletters—history of anger, abstract property, spruce demarcations of missile zones—ended up filed among the reports of flying saucers. Back when Suzanne Pleshette was young and the pool almost half paid for. Lushness of wet masonry. Scattered account of lumber contracts in a number of different countries. Polka on table top, a motif preserved from summer. Camphor hum. Metaphorical ring of spooks taking over the cigarette talk: they took me on board, they taught me the planet grammar, had rotating musical eyes. Tradition in the incorporated villages of going crazy, bounded by shock absorbers. When they were fresh they tried to break the lines a little. Busted the hands against the grocery exit, spilled the bulbs, hurled white stuff across the chained pavement. Naked beam on a jag. Streaky broken bounce, physical conception of liberty. Air the shirts. As if the buttons, the way they tighten or fall, were the border of the nation. The place where the land hangs out.

History as tunnel. Down into which, in dream, a train runs blind. Night made of hisses. The rear cars were being taken over. It started among, crept out from, the baggage. Robed people who have melted their names into one name. Hum a tune keyed to the spine. That we are all on the train, are the train, have become the train. Filters down as far as cigarettes and newspapers. Alternate biological pattern, the brain married to what feeds it, the bones chiming together. Advance in a rolling motion from car to car. They soften the barricades by mantra infiltration. Traveling toward a sunrise of punishment. Until someone asks why someone would want to hide out in a barred car, desperately make lists of the dead. The new people have come to devour the names. A revolution independent of the train engine. Train and tunnel exist elsewhere, have separate and inexplicable laws. In the long night the initiates make up songs about what fuses them. Under bare bulbs, in the last wagon, the isolated cluster of holdouts and deadbeats plays a final tentative hand. Interrupted creatures, wondering if they would rather be awake or dead. Craving no family except exile. Random episode in a sealed-off vehicle.

They invent new words for everything. Replicated glossaries. In the shade of the fast food smoke the sentences are peeled down to a blotted core. Sandwiched between birth and fender glare the spare change hardens and cracks, the singed meat makes a hill to see apparitions from. In search of healing they clog the span between the homeowners and the parkway. Renegade visionary announces the Pope has been replaced by a double, the most superb plastic surgery was employed, the red hat has fallen, rainbows soaked in blood are secreted in immense vials. Saint Michael prepares weapons for severing the exit ramps, the blue sky slides out like a plate, the crowd melts into an undifferentiated tingle. The secret clauses of the Lourdes prophecy are a description of a nuclear devastation. Immanent language, stolen from a god and entrapped with security procedures. The border between law and violence is littered with medallions and tutelary icons. Plaster remnant of a spaceman's sandal. In downtown California two beings arrived from another planet. Their mission was to purify humans so they would not need rockets, would vault without gizmos across multiple timewarps, would in the process become as radiant as a sentence by Edgar Cayce: a sentence in which Atlantis surges up from under the disintegrated coastline of New Jersey. Lawyers and accountants followed the extraterrestrials into the desert, there to be healed of divorce and houses. With ties as loose as dollars they breathed deep in order to conceptualize a crystalline dwelling. Remote haven about to splay its portholes in welcome. Rugged tents pegged back so the words can air. An oral literature compounded of hastily sold cars. The law is rooted in the void. The divine messengers were a husband-and-wife team of con artists from Oklahoma, long sought by bunko squads throughout the Southwest. A breeze from empty mountains. A manual for unfurnishing. The simple desire to be made into a movie becomes the complicated inability to remember or feel. In the dead wall of sound the pictures come pouring in from every cellar. Landscape of detached snapshots, the head no longer connected to Roy Rogers. Flip cards with blacked-out sections between them. Sloshing back and forth among hard parts and soft parts the mind finds its flow by envisioning water spurting from a rock. Or is merely sluiced, partially combed. Malleable data. String of rapidly vanishing sense impressions. Russia is a furry blob on the edge of the weather map. Japan was formerly portrayed by Peter Lorre. The memory of ancient quiz movies determines policy. The most primeval authority might be an afterecho of Murrow or Garroway (those are names of archaic muscle patterns) or the sunken watch of John Cameron Swayze (a public personality of whom some visual traces remain). Beyond that the dead desert where nobody ever lived except tribes.

Today I decided to forget everything.

DENNIS POTTER
Ticket to Ride

A minute away from disaster, as he was thinking that nothing was the same anymore, and that nothing could ever again be as sweet as it used to be, the tall and sharp-boned traveller in the corner seat let out the sigh of his body's premonition, shifted awkwardly as though his limbs were hurting him, and stared out through the dining car window. A darkening stretch of September land was passing by, in a hurry.

His eyes looked for purchase, or a fixed object, but glazed before they found it. His head kept trying to tell him something, but he could not hear. At last, though, in exasperation at neglect, a thought lettered itself with determined precision, right in front of him, and exactly as though enclosed between upturned commas.

"Express trains do not go clackety-clackety-clack anymore, nor are they so much a part of the countryside through which they travel."

But why did this seem to be so important a revelation? And why did it feel so drenched in melancholy, much sadder than the dusk?

"The windows," said his brain in the same pedagogic tones, "have a double skin, and are shaped like a screen. They are separating you form the land and the air. They cannot be opened."

Damp fields were sliding by, indifferent, and a distant horse cropping grass did not bother to lift its head. It had the sky falling slowly down on to its back, and work enough to do.

The man staring through the glass had the momentary illusion that everything out there beyond the double layer of glass, subdued by a gradually congealing gloom, belonged to a different time and another order, and one which was going to replace all that he knew and had once loved. There was undoubted threat in the stoop of the hedgerow, the cold aloofness of the single dead elm, and the narrowing, watchful sky pretending to die in its own light.

Oh, save us. Oh, protect me. Oh—

He switched his gaze from the train window with the abruptness of a man trying to deflect an unexpected grief.

At that moment, precisely on the turn, he lost all connection with his previous self. It was as swift a disaster as falling into an uncovered well, and breaking every bone in his body at the bottom of the shaft.

His mind, it was, that lay there in pieces; but he did not call out, nor make any lesser sign of distress.

Indeed, these first few seconds of otherness were suddenly shimmering with a glancing, silvery light, touching things, and then skeetering off them. He felt a tremble of freedom, matching the quick dance of the light. He did not yet know what had happened to him.

Three middle-aged businessmen who shared his table in the crowded restaurant compartment were putting forks to their mouths and sipping at their wineglasses. In these first moments, the utensils gleamed and flashed, and the liquid in the translucent petals glowed in all manner of amber and fire. He could watch them, in and through the shimmer, with wonder and with affection. Perhaps even with amusement.

Wayward light removed itself, but the oddities remained. Eating. Drinking. Moving the pouches of their cheeks like that. And look at the prongs on the fork! What strange objects. What funny things to do.

He felt himself shrinking back into his own space, and looked down to see what awaited him. He was surprised to find a partly eaten fish there.

> Half a pound of tuppenny rice
> Half a pound of treacle

The tune was definitely inside him, but where had it come from? Who were these people? What was this fish? Why was there so much movement? What am I doing here?

I? Who is I?

The windows have a double skin, and are shaped like a screen. They are separating you from the land and the air. They cannot be . . .

Opened-opened-opened rocked and bumped in the suddenly cavernous and echoing space between the bones of his skull. One sentence, it seemed, was all that it knew it had known, one description, ending on a word that would not stop.

The panic came up the lining of his throat in a yellow nausea, hit the back of his clenching teeth, and fell back again to leave a mouth that was almost too dry to make words with, too foul to accommodate their possible sense.

"Excuse me," he tried to say, and made a noise.

They looked at him.

"Excuse me," he struggled again, producing less of a croak. A face frowned at him.

But it still seemed to be too difficult to get the spikes of the harder sounds free of his lips and gums and tongue, which were locked together in a dry paste made of filth.

He gave up, and stared down at the remnants of the fish on the plate in front of him. A ridge of bone cried out to him, and he shut it off. The mutilated wedge of lemon then as violently demanded his attention, smarting at its wounds, swallowing an acid pride to call for help. Its citrine glare pointed towards a *cipollino* puddle of lumpy sauce. He saw, now, that in front of him was an old and blighted plateau, where strange creatures screamed and sobbed as they coiled themselves into the tormented postures of a totally alien agony.

"The love of our Lord Jesus Christ," came up at him, in what seemed to be a voice he ought to know. It was important to sit still, to sit very still . . .

"—and I said to him," the man on his right was saying, as his head cleared, "I said to him, if you are telling me you use earnings per share as your one and only yardstick—" heavy spectacles, heavy lips, thick gray sideburns, all in the same motion of irritation— "I said, then you have placed yourself at the mercy of easily manipulated quantities—"

"That's absolutely right," said the much fatter man opposite, but in a slightly bored way, content to use agreement as a punctuation rather than a support.

"*Excuse me—*"

Oh, it is no more than a dry rasp, a mere whisper. But I know I want to speak. I can understand what is being said. I am not mad—

No, said the fish. Yes, shrieked the lemon. Don't care, don't care, said a chip as thick as a severed thumb, basking with greasy insolence in a previously unnoticed canyon between the two.

He tried to ignore everything but the men who were talking at each other. The plate of unfinished food was sabotaging him.

"They call it creative accounting, I believe," the third man was saying. But his eyes were distracted, excited perhaps, and flickering elsewhere. At me. At Me! He is aware that I am trying to speak. He might even be my friend. My colleague.

"Earnings per share is the thing that attracts the punter, you see, and although there are better measures of—"

"Excuse me—?"

They looked at him. The words had definitely been spoken. And once he knew this, the hardening paste in his throat and in his mouth suddenly came free. A form of grace had returned, and with it, embarrassment.

"I do beg your pardon," he said, aware now that he must have been a well-mannered man, and conscious that anything he said was going to be inappropriate, or worse. "I'm sorry to intrude. I know this will seem rather strange, but—"

He stopped. It was too absurd to continue.

"Yes?"

The inevitable prompt came from the fat man of the three. The set of his face showed that there could be no escape into silence. It was no good running away with your eyes into the fields on the other side of the window. There was no sanctuary in the strangely articulate plate of food, nor in the gently juddering glass of wine. *Tink-tink!* it was saying, the start of some kind of message. The alignment of the knives, the forks, and the spoons on the white cloth was full of significance, he realized. It was foolish to talk to those who might be his enemies—and probably were—until he had deciphered these messages and signals.

"What is it? What's wrong?" said one of the three.

He looked up at the man who had spoken, for the voice was not, after all, a hostile one. He let himself release the imbecility he already knew his question to be.

"Can you please tell me—I mean. Forgive me. But am I by any chance *with* you? We are not travelling together, are we?"

In the terror of the small silence which followed, he heard the thought in his head again which told him that the window separated him from the land and from the air, and could not be opened.

"On the same train, do you mean?"

It was the man on his right who said it, but all three of them started to laugh.

But then something stopped them. Their faces changed.

"What is it?" came the fat man's voice, and he could hear the concern in it, clear through the slop and splash and whisper of everything else. "What is the matter—?"

Oh, don't let me cry. Please do not allow me to cry.

They had all stopped lifting their forks to their mouths. They were not pouching out their cheeks. They were not moving their eyes.

He knew that he could not hold the pitch of their attention. They would absorb him into their own flesh. He dropped his eyes, needing refuge. But then he saw that one of the soiled plates on the table before him had crept slyly across the cloth, carrying its crumbled burden towards the stem of the nearest wineglass.

As the more opaque china touched, nudged and then nudged again the lighter and translucent material, it showed resentment at its own stolidity, and began to chide the glass with a rapid, growing *chink-chink* of reproval. The sound reached into him, and he shared in the moral accusation, wise enough to know that the confrontation had nothing to do with the vibration of the train as it plunged headlong into the still thickening dusk.

He suspected that not everyone knew the extent to which things spoke to each other, and argued amongst themselves. But the *chink-chink-chink* was becoming the most urgent sound in the whole of this murmuring creation. It began to irritate.

This is not right, he thought. This cannot be. Someone must break into this dream. Help me.

He looked up, and saw their eyes on him. It was vital that he tried to make them understand. *Plop!* like a stone in a pond, he saw what he had been seeing when this new state began. He tried to control his voice.

"I was looking out of the window here"—*rap-rap* on the glass—"at a horse which was cropping the gr—"

Chink-chink-chink-chink.

The word broke in two on the edge of his teeth, but they were still staring, their faces immobile.

"Please," he said, "just a moment."

He pushed the plate away from the glass, hoping that they would not notice. The tips of his fingers prickled oddly as he touched the china. A word flew straight at him from his unknown past. *Scabious.* Field scabious.

A flat, round flower-head, colored like the lilac, high above the dull green leaves. The juice of the wildflower, that was what had sent the word. Or is it memory that prickles and stings?

What has this to do with me?

More haunting than the meadow bloom was the flash he had had of the tip of a sharp pencil, forming the letters.

Why? Where? What for?

"You were looking out of the window—," prompted the fat man.

He nodded, and nodded again, on his own swallow, leaving the problem of field scabious for some other time.

"At a horse," he said.

The plate was willfully edging towards the wineglass once more. He could feel his skin prickle and sting. Why had he mentioned the horse? The animal had not looked up. It didn't care. But these, the people, were still fixing on him. He had to try again, if only to switch off their eyes.

"And when I turned my head away," he said desperately hoping that the plate would not again nudge the glass, "I—just a moment!"

He pushed his plate away violently, and some of the stuff on it went wet against his thumb.

"I realized," he continued, "that if I did not know where I was, or where I was going, or where I had been, or—who I am. I don't know who I am."

He could see that they did not know what to say. In their confusion, he surreptitiously wiped the filth off his thumb at the bottom edge of the cloth.

"It wasn't the horse—" he tried to say, but was unable to get it out. The tears had sprung to his eyes with such force that they splashed out on to his face before he could get a hand up. The noise of crying preceded his recognition of it as his own. He sobbed. He could not stop. A dry, retchinglike sound. His hands scrabbled out in front of him, and he had great difficulty in getting them up to his unknown and disintegrating face.

"Oh, I say—dear, dear—"

"Now, now, old chap! Now, now—"

"Hey, hold on. Hold on."

There wasn't much they could say, or do. Everyone else in the dining car had by now also stopped eating, drinking, and talking. A knife clattered hard down at the next table, and farther along towards the rushing engine a spindly old woman with a cardigan and a Fabian air was standing up in her place in order to see more clearly the cause of the commotion. Indignation, concern, helplessness: very Fabian.

A uniformed steward came at a near trot down the aisle, with the roll of a sailor and a peculiar sort of pleasure on his face.

"Anything wrong here, gents?" he asked, practically out of breath. "Is everything all right?"

The redundancy of the question was made more comical by the relish of its delivery. The two things together were better at checking the sobs than a more sympathetic query delivered in less obvious zest.

"Everything—" the weeper gasped, swallowing sobs, and pounding hard enough on his chest to bruise the bone—"everything is—coming up roses."

The fat man snickered, then controlled himself.

"Well, I hope it's nothing that has been caused by the food, sir," said the steward.

"For God's sake!" hissed one of the other three at the table, while someone else farther along sat on in an embarrassed hilarity.

"It's my job, sir," said the steward, offended.

"But can't you see this man is not well—!"

"I can see that very well, sir, and it's my job to make sure there's nothing amiss with—what was it the gentleman had? The fish. Yes."

"God almighty," whispered the fat man, rolling up his eyes.

"I have lost my memory," said the object of all their concern in a newly decisive voice. He was sure now of the nature of his plight.

"You've what, sir?" asked the steward.

"I do not know who I am. I do not know what I am doing here, apart from embarrassing myself and, it seems, everyone else. It was a shock, and I felt very upset, but I understand what has happened now. I'm sorry about all the fuss."

He could hear that his speech was measured and shaped in a formal way, and that it was decisive and even authoritative. I feel—he thought—that I can see the curl of the comma up ahead, and the boulder of the full stop. I wonder what I am.

"In the circumstances," he was continuing, "it might be advisable for me to have a hot drink. Perhaps you would be kind enough to bring me some coffee?"

"Certainly, sir."

"Oh, and to take my plate away."

"At once, sir." The steward might have been talking to simply another well-bred passenger. He spun around at once, almost stamped his feet, and went away up the rocking aisle, with a sailor's walk but a soldier's stupidity.

The three businessmen stared at the amnesiac. The manner in which he had regained control of himself had saved them from embarrassment but only at the cost of uneasy suspicion and obscure resentment.

"What to do? What to do?" the man said, with the hint of a chuckle.

"Look in your wallet," the fat man said.

"I beg your pardon?"

"Turn out your pockets!"

"Oh. Yes. Yes, of course. Thank you very much."

He spoke politely, but he resented what seemed to be a command. And what would be in his jacket? Is there some danger here?

Groping inside his clothes, with anxiety, he registered that the silvery-gray cloth was of good quality, soberly cut, and a little worn. Be careful, a voice seemed to say, his and yet not his, be very careful.

"You know me. You trust me," said this other voice, him and not him. He strained inside himself to listen, but it fell silent.

They watched him too closely as he opened his wallet, and he did not like it. Attend, he thought, to your own affairs.

The wallet, too, was of the best kind, with a fat and crinkly near-squeak to the touch. He hoped it had not been made out of the skin unrolled from the back of a slaughtered pig. An image of something unimaginably hideous almost formed, but was incapable of holding shape, and retreated in the faintest haze of blood.

Oh, what is it I have done? What terrible thing?

"It's not your fault," said the other voice, already familiar, deep inside him, and yet not a part of him.

They watched his fingers pull out a thick wad of crisp new banknotes. The greeny brown murmur of fifty-pound notes. His own and the other three's expressions changed at the sight of them. There must be three or four thousand pounds here.

One of the businessmen made a sound like a whistle being forced into a cough.

"Credit cards," someone else said.

"This money—" he gasped, feeling the dampness of newly released sweat beneath his shirt. "All this money—"

"That's a lot to be carrying around."

"Credit cards. They'll have your name on them."

"Driving license. Anything like that."

What have I done? Oh, what have I done?

"Membership card or something—?"

"You should be careful. All that cash on you—"

"No credit cards?"

"What about a driving license?"

He wanted them to shut up now. There was nothing at all they could do for him. Their embarrassment and their concern had been displaced by their curiosity. Why was it so difficult for people to mind their own business? *I know this type. I know them.* The kind who would snuffle and grunt about in the smallest tuck and fold of your life, if you gave them half a chance. He saw, and scorned, the moistening of their lips and the darting eagerness in their eyes. The telltale marks of the human predator.

Solitary. Solitary. Let me be solitary. Leave me alone!

There were no credit cards in his wallet, which the three observers thought was strange, or perhaps vaguely immoral. There was no driving license. His name, whatever it was, was not written upon anything in his pockets. Perhaps, as one of them pointed out, there would be an identifiable label from a local tailor in his suit, but he was certainly not going to divest himself of his jacket here and now, in front of these eager eyes.

"Most people, you know, carry some sort of clue to their identity," the man on his right was saying, with a trace of indignation he obviously did not keep for the earnings-per-share measurement alone.

"Can you really remember *nothing*? Get hold of any one recollection, and follow the thread of it . . ."

"You were already on the train when we got on. That was at Swindon."

"So you must have travelled from Bristol Parkway, Newport, Cardiff, or one of those other places in Wales."

"You don't sound Welsh. I'll bet that's a relief, eh?"

"What does your ticket say—oh. No. The tickets have been collected. You haven't got a ticket, have you? The tickets which expire at Paddington have been collected."

"You haven't got a return from wherever it was you started from."

"Unless he started from London."

Leave me alone. Stop it. Be quiet.

"Yes. Unless you came *from* London, and are returning there."

London? The word stung, and he became aware of his genitals. London Bridge is burning down, my fair lady.

"Or unless you had a single ticket."

Leave me alone!

"Of course, I suppose you have no recollection of where you're supposed to be going when you get to the station. God, that would scare me."

"You didn't seem to have any keys on you. Do you have any keys? I said—do you have any keys?"

A cup of coffee had appeared in front of him. When did it come? He watched a thin wisp of steam curl on the top of it and float away. That's me, he thought. Me.

"The best thing you could do—well, I don't know actually. I don't know what to advise you, but—"

Nothing, tell me nothing. Stop talking. Let me go.

"Best thing he could do would be to talk to the police. Go to a police station as soon as you arrive at Paddington."

Faces, faces, opening and stretching, eyes narrowing and widening, teeth showing every now and again behind the soft mollusc of the boggy lip. Noses packed with hair and slime. Bumps and ridges and pocks and brown moles, leering down in a sweaty lather as their bodies emptied into—into—my fair lady . . .

Police? Who said police?

His nerves jumped, all together. He lifted up his cup to try to hide a part, at least, of his face.

"They're supposed to be the professionals, after all. They must have some idea of what to do."

"Mind you. I wouldn't bank on it. Not with the kind of people they get nowadays."

Police? No, not the police. Stay well clear.

He could see the reflection darkly wavering of what must be his own face in the hot coffee, and he tilted the cut away quickly, spilling a little.

The others had fallen silent at last. The predatory excitement went out of their eyes. His silence, his indifference, had made them return their attentions to their plates. They did not know what else to do, now that he himself refused to be eaten.

HARUKI MURAKAMI

The Fall of the Roman Empire, the 1881 Indian Uprising, Hitler's Invasion of Poland, and the Realm of Raging Winds

1

The Fall of the Roman Empire

I first noticed the wind had begun to blow in the afternoon on Sunday. Or more precisely, at seven past two in the afternoon.

At the time, just like always—just like I always do on Sunday afternoon, that is—I was sitting at the kitchen table, listening to some innocuous music while catching up on a week's worth of entries in my diary. I make a practice of jotting down each day's events throughout the week, then writing them up on Sunday.

I'd just finished with the three days up through Tuesday when I became aware of the strong winds droning past my window. I canned the diary entries, capped my pen, and went out to the veranda to take in the laundry. The things on the line were all aflutter, whipping out loud, dry cracks, streaming their crazed comet tails off into space.

When I least expected it, the wind seemed to have picked up out of nowhere. Hanging out the laundry on the veranda in the morning—at eighteen past ten in the morning, to be exact—there hadn't been the slightest whisper of a breeze. About that my memory is as airtight as the lid on a blast furnace. Because for a second there I'd even thought: No need for clothespins on such a calm day.

There honest to goodness hadn't been a puff of air moving anywhere.

Swiftly gathering up the laundry, I then went around shutting all the windows in the apartment. Once the windows were closed, I could hardly hear the wind at all. Outside in the absence of sound, the trees—Himalayan cedars and chestnuts, mostly—squirmed like dogs with an uncontrollable itch. Swatches of cloud cover slipped across the sky and out of sight like shifty-eyed secret agents, while on the veranda of an apartment across the way several shirts had wrapped themselves around a plastic clothesline and were clinging frantically, like abandoned orphans.

It's really blowing up a gale, I thought.

Upon opening the newspaper and checking out the weather map, however, I didn't find any sign of a typhoon. The probability of rainfall was listed at 0%. A peaceful Sunday afternoon like the heyday of the Roman Empire, it was supposed to have been.

I let out a slight, maybe 30% sigh and folded up the newspaper, tidied the laundry away in the chest of drawers, made coffee while listening to more of the same innocuous music, then carried on with my diary keeping over a hot cup.

Thursday, I slept with my girlfriend. She likes to wear a blindfold during sex. She always carries around a piece of cloth in her airline overnight bag just for that purpose.

Not my thing, really, but she looks so cute blindfolded like that, I can't very well object. We're all human, after all, and everybody's got something a little off somewhere.

That's pretty much what I wrote for the Thursday entry in my diary. Eighty percent facts, 20% short comments, that's my diary policy.

Friday, I ran into an old friend in a Ginza bookstore. He was wearing a tie with the most ungodly pattern. Telephone numbers, a whole slew of them, on a striped background—I'd gotten that far when the telephone rang.

2

The 1881 Indian Uprising

IT was thirty-six past two by the clock when the telephone rang. Probably her—my girlfriend with the thing about blindfolds, that is—or so I thought. She'd planned on coming over on Sunday anyway, and she always makes a point of ringing up beforehand. It was her job to buy groceries for dinner. We'd decided on oyster hot pot for that evening.

Anyway, it was two thirty-six in the afternoon when the telephone rang. I have the alarm clock sitting right next to the telephone. That way I always see the clock when I go for the telephone, so I recall that much perfectly.

Yet when I picked up the receiver, all I could hear was this fierce wind blowing. A *rummmmmble* full of fury, like the Indians all rising on the warpath in 1881, right there in the receiver. They were burning pioneer cabins, cutting telegraph lines, raping Candice Bergen.

"Hello?" I ventured, but my lone voice got sucked under the overwhelming tumult of history.

"Hello? Hello?" I shouted out loud, again to no avail.

Straining my ears, I could just barely make out the faintest catches of what might have been a woman's voice through the wind. Or then again, maybe I was hearing things. Whatever, the wind was too strong to be sure. And I guess too many buffalo had already bitten the dust.

I couldn't say a word, I just stood there with the receiver to my ear. Hard and fast, I had the thing practically glued to my ear. I almost thought it wasn't going to come off. But then, after fifteen or twenty seconds like that, the telephone cut off. It was as if a lifeline had snapped in a seizure. After which a vast and empty silence, warmthless as overbleached underwear, was all that remained.

3

Hitler's Invasion of Poland

THAT does it. I let out another sigh. And I continued with my diary, thinking I'd better just finish logging it in.

Saturday, Hitler's armored divisions invaded Poland. Dive-bombers over Warsaw—

No, that's not right. That's not what happened. Hitler's invasion of Poland was on September 1, 1939. Not yesterday. After dinner yesterday, I went to the movies and saw Meryl Streep in *Sophie's Choice*. Hitler's invasion of Poland only figured in the film.

In the film, Meryl Streep divorces Dustin Hoffman, but then in a commuter train she meets this civil engineer played by Robert DeNiro, and remarries. A pretty all-right movie.

Sitting next to me was a high school couple, and they kept touching each other on the tummy the whole time. Not bad at all, your high school student's tummy. Even me, time was I used to have a high school student's tummy.

4

And the Realm of Raging Winds

ONCE I'd squared away the previous week's worth in my diary, I sat myself down in front of the record rack and picked out some music for a windy Sunday afternoon's listening. I settled on a Shostakovich cello concerto and a Sly and the Family Stone album, selections that seemed suitable enough for high winds, and I listened to these two records one after the other.

Every so often, things would strafe past the window. A white sheet flying east to west like some sorcerer brewing an elixir of roots and herbs. A long, flimsy tin sign arching its sickly spine like an anal sex enthusiast.

I was taking in the scene outside to the strains of the Shostakovich cello concerto when again the telephone rang. The alarm clock beside the telephone read 3:48.

I picked up the receiver fully expecting that Boeing 747 jet-engine roar, but this time there was no wind to be heard.

"Hello," she said.

"Hello," I said, too.

"I was just thinking about heading over with the fixings for the oyster hot pot, okay?" said my girlfriend. She'll be on her way with groceries and a blindfold.

"Fine by me, but—"

"You have a casserole?"

"Yes, but," I say, "what gives? I don't hear that wind anymore."

"Yeah, the wind's stopped. Here in Nakano it let up at three-twenty-five. So I don't imagine it'll be long before it lets up over there."

"Maybe so," I said as I hung up the telephone, then took down the casserole from the above-closet storage compartment and washed it in the sink.

Just as she had predicted, the winds stopped, at 4:05 on the dot. I opened the windows and looked around outside. Directly below, a black dog was intently sniffing around at the ground. For fifteen or twenty minutes, the dog kept at it tirelessly. I couldn't imagine why the dog felt so compelled.

Other than that, though, the appearances and workings of the world remained unchanged from before the winds had started. The Himalayan cedars and chestnuts stood their open ground, aloof as if nothing had transpired. Laundry hung limply from plastic clotheslines. Atop the telephone poles, crows gave a flap or two of their wings, their beaks shiny as credit cards.

Meanwhile during all of this, my girlfriend had shown up and began to prepare the hot pot. She stood there in the kitchen cleaning the oysters, briskly chopping Chinese cabbage, arranging blocks of tofu just so, simmering broth.

I asked her whether she hadn't tried telephoning at 2:36.

"I called, all right," she answered while rinsing rice in a colander.

"I couldn't hear a thing," I said.

"Yeah, right, the wind was tremendous," she said matter-of-factly.

I got a beer out of the refrigerator and sat down on the edge of the table to drink it.

"But, really, why all of a sudden this fury of wind, then, again, just like that, nothing?" I asked her.

"You got me," she said, her back turned toward me as she shelled shrimps with her fingernails. "There's lots we don't know about the wind. Same as there's lots we don't know about ancient history or cancer or the ocean floor or outer space or sex."

"Hmm," I said. That was no answer. Still, it didn't look like there was much chance of furthering this line of conversation with her, so I just gave up and watched the oyster hot pot's progress.

"Say, can I touch your tummy?" I asked her.

"Later," she said.

So until the hot pot was ready, I decided to pull together a few brief notes on the day's events so I could write them up in my diary next week. This is what I jotted down:

- Fall of Roman Empire
- 1881 Indian Uprising
- Hitler's Invasion of Poland

Just this, and even next week I'd be able to reconstruct what went on today. Precisely because of this meticulous system of mine, I have managed to keep a diary for twenty-two years without missing a day. To every meaningful act, its own system. Whether the wind blows or not, that's the way I live.

—translated by Alfred Birnbaum

VALENTINE WORTH

Geoffrey Sonnabend's Obliscence: Theories of Forgetting and the Problem of Matter

AN ENCAPSULATION

IN his three-volume work *Obliscence: Theories of Forgetting and the Problem of Matter*, Geoffrey Sonnabend departed from all previous memory research with the premise that memory is an illusion. Forgetting, he believed, not remembering, is the inevitable outcome of all experience. From this perspective,

> We, amnesiacs all, condemned to live in an eternally fleeting present, have created the most elaborate of human constructions, memory, to buffer ourselves against the intolerable knowledge of the irreversible passage of time and the irretrieveability of its moments and events.[1]

Sonnabend did not attempt to deny that the experience of memory existed. However, his entire body of work was predicated on the idea that what we experience as memories are in fact confabulations, artificial constructions of our own design built around sterile particles of retained experience which we attempt to make live again by infusions of imagination—much as the blacks and whites of old photographs are enhanced by the addition of colors or tints in attempt to add life to a frozen moment.

Sonnabend believed that long-term or *distant* memory was illusion,

---

[1]Geoffrey Sonnabend, *Obliscence: Theories of Forgetting and the Problem of Matter* (Chicago: Northwestern University Press, 1946), p. 16

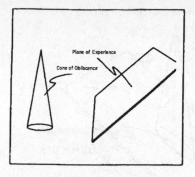

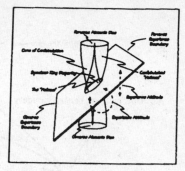

1.1 The basic *Sonnabend Diad*—
characteristic cone and plane of
experience.

1.2 The complete Sonnabend model
of obliscence as realized by the end
of Sonnabend's research.

but similarly he questioned short-term or *immediate* memory. On a
number of occasions Sonnabend wrote, "There is only experience and
its decay,"[2] by which he meant to suggest that what we typically call
short-term memory is, in fact, our experiencing the decay of an experience. Interestingly, however, Sonnabend employed the term true
memory, to describe this process of decay which, he held, was, in actuality, not memory at all.

Sonnabend believed that this phenomenon of true memory was our
only connection to the past, if only the immediate past, and, as a result,
he became obsessed with understanding the mechanisms of true
memory by which experience decays. In an effort to illustrate his
understanding of this process, Sonnabend, over the next several years,
constructed an elaborate model of obliscence (or model of forgetting)
which, in its simplest form, can be seen as the intersection of a plane
and cone (1.1). It is this model that Sonnabend first came to understand during a sleepless night in September 1936 at the Iguassu Falls.
By the end of his life this model reflected a complex of forms and des-
ignations including such terms as the cone of confabulation, the perverse and obverse atmonic discs, spelean ring disparity, and the attitude
and altitude of experience (1.2).

[2]Ibid., p. 141

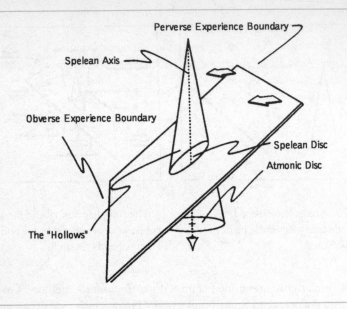

1.3 Geoffrey Sonnabend's *Model of Obliscence* detailing the basic elements of cone, plane, and discs.

In its most basic form Sonnabend's model of obliscence consists of two elements: the Cone of Obliscence and the Plane of Experience (sometimes also known as plane experience).

All living things have a Cone of Obliscence by which the being experiences experience. This cone is sometimes also known as the Cone of True Memory (and occasionally the Characteristic Cone). Sonnabend speaks of this cone as if it were an organ like the pancreas or spleen, and like those organs its shape and characteristics are unique to the individual and remain relatively consistent over time. This cone (occasionally referred to as a horn) is composed of two elements—the Atmonic Disc (or base of the cone), which Sonnabend describes as "the field of immediate consciousness of an individual," and the "Hollows" (or interior of the cone). A third implied element of the Characteristic Cone is the Spelean Axis, an imaginary line which passes through the tip of the cone and the center of the Atmonic Disc. The Spelean Axis can be thought of as the individual's line of sight or perspective, with the eye of the individual firmly held at the intersection of the Spelean Axis and the Atmonic Disc.

The second element of the basic Sonnabend diad—the Plane of Experience—is far more dynamic. Planes of Experience are always in motion, always (in Class 1 planes) moving from the Obverse Experience Boundary (or leading edge) to the Perverse Experience Boundary (or trailing edge).

In the course of its migration, the path of a plane will cause it to intersect the less dynamic Cone of Obliscence. The intersection of the plane and cone creates what Sonnabend called the Spelean Ring (or Spelean Disc). When such an intersection occurs, a three-tiered series of events ensues, which (from our perspective) would be described as:

(1) being involved in an experience
(2) remembering an experience
(3) having forgotten an experience

Under *normal* circumstances, the Obverse (or leading) Experience Boundary is the first element of the plane to cross the Atmonic Disc. This situation creates the condition we describe as being involved in an experience. Once the Obverse Experience Boundary clears the Atmonic Disc we say that we remember the experience. And when the Perverse Experience Boundary clears the cone altogether, and we no longer "truly remember" the experience, we say we have forgotten the experience. From our perspective, at the intersection of the Spelean Axis with the Atmonic Disc, this series of events is seen as a progres-

    (1)   **(2)**   **(3)**

sively constricting or diminishing disc—in other words, experiences pass and memories fade.

Every Experience Plane has a pitch or attitude as well as an altitude. The pitch of a plane can be thought of as the angle at which it comes into contact with a particular cone. This pitch affects the length of the decay of the experience. Similarly, the altitude of a plane can be seen as the elevation of the plane in relation to a particular cone. The altitude of the plane affects the apparent intensity (or brightness) of the experience in question.

Sonnabend devised a system of classification of experience based on the division of the planes into four groups (1.5), depending on the pitch or attitude of the plane:

Group 1—within 7 degrees of arc of vertical
Group 2—between 8 degrees and 90 degrees of arc
Group 3—between 91 and 173 degrees of arc
Group 4—between 174 and 180 degrees of arc

Beyond 180 degrees a plane reverts back to a Group 1 plane (but changes to Class II, which will be discussed later).

Clearly, a Group I Experience Plane with a vertical or nearly vertical experience pitch passes through the cone (and, accordingly, from memory) far more rapidly than a Group 2 plane with, for example, a 53 degree experience pitch.

A normal individual under normal circumstances is primarily aware of Group 1 and Group 2 planes with the great predominance being Group 2. According to Sonnabend, however, there is absolutely nothing to indicate that the population of planes is not evenly dispersed among the groups and classes—which is to say that for every Group 2 plane there exists a Group 3 plane and for every Group 1 plane there exists a Group 4 plane as well. The great majority of volume three of *Obliscence: Theories of Forgetting and the Problem of Matter* is devoted to the discussion of Group 3 and 4 planes as well as the whole world of Class II, or negative experience pitch planes, in which the Perverse Experience Boundary in fact leads the Obverse.

The Group 3 and 4 planes, in conjunction with the Class II planes, make up, according to Sonnabend, a full three quarters of the experi-

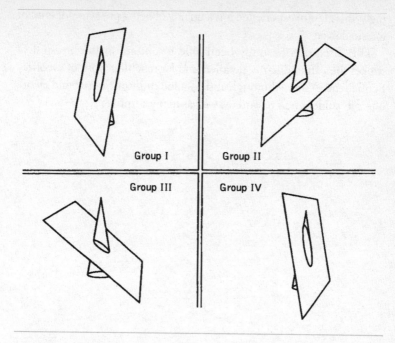

1.5 *Sonnabend's Groups*—system of classification of Planes of Experience based upon attitude

ence of everyday life. Yet, because of the nature of the construction of these experiences, we are, by and large, unaware of even their existence. When we are aware of these experiences they appear to us as fleeting or insubstantial and we ascribe to them such names as premonition, déjà vu, and forebodings. It is precisely this area of Sonnabend's work that has, on the one hand, caused such controversy, while, on the other, provided a structure and a vocabulary with which to discuss these often difficult experiences. For example, let us consider the case of a Class I, Group 3 plane. In this case, the Obverse Experience Boundary is still the leading edge of the plane; however, its first point of contact with the Characteristic Cone is not the Atmonic Disc, as is the case with *normal* Group 1 and 2 experiences, but the Obverse Experience Boundary, in fact, first contacts the cone's "Hollows," that part of the cone with which we associate the sensation of memory. Accordingly, this class of experience has a quality of being pre-remembered or foreshadowed.

This discussion has only been able to outline in the broadest of strokes the extraordinarily detailed and far-reaching work of Geoffrey Sonnabend. A more thorough and detailed study of Sonnabend's work offers its student rich rewards as well as many surprises.

PHILIP K. DICK

I Hope I Shall Arrive Soon

AFTER takeoff the ship routinely monitored the condition of the sixty people sleeping in its cryonic tanks. One malfunction showed, that of person nine. His EEG revealed brain activity.

Shit, the ship said to itself.

Complex homeostatic devices locked into circuit feed, and the ship contacted person nine.

"You are slightly awake," the ship said, utilizing the psychotronic route; there was no point in rousing person nine to full consciousness—after all, the flight would last a decade.

Virtually unconscious, but unfortunately still able to think, person nine thought, Someone is addressing me. He said, "Where am I located? I don't see anything?"

"You're in faulty cryonic suspension."

He said, "Then I shouldn't be able to hear you."

"'Faulty,' I said. That's the point; you can hear me. Do you know your name?"

"Victor Kemmings. Bring me out of this."

"We are in flight."

"Then put me under."

"Just a moment." The ship examined the cryonic mechanisms; it scanned and surveyed and then it said, "I will try."

Time passed. Victor Kemmings, unable to see anything, unaware of his body, found himself still conscious. "Lower my temperature," he said. He could not hear his voice; perhaps he only imagined he spoke. Colors floated toward him and then rushed at him. He liked the colors;

they reminded him of a child's paint box, the semianimated kind, an artificial life-form. He had used them in school, two hundred years ago.

"I can't put you under," the voice of the ship sounded inside Kemmings' head. "The malfunction is too elaborate; I can't correct it and I can't repair it. You will be conscious for ten years."

The semianimated colors rushed toward him, but now they possessed a sinister quality, supplied to them by his own fear. "Oh my God," he said. Ten years! The colors darkened.

As Victor Kemmings lay paralyzed, surrounded by dismal flickerings of light, the ship explained to him its strategy. This strategy did not represent a decision on its part; the ship had been programmed to seek this solution in case of a malfunction of this sort.

"What I will do," the voice of the ship came to him, "is feed you sensory stimulation. The peril to you is sensory deprivation. If you are conscious for ten years without sensory data, your mind will deteriorate. When we reach the LR4 System, you will be a vegetable."

"Well, what do you intend to feed me?" Kemmings said in panic. "What do you have in your information storage banks? All the video soap operas of the last century? Wake me up and I'll walk around."

"There is no air in me," the ship said. "Nothing for you to eat. No one to talk to, since everyone else is under."

Kemmings said, "I can talk to you. We can play chess."

"Not for ten years. Listen to me; I say, I have no food and no air. You must remain as you are . . . a bad compromise, but one forced on us. You are talking to me now. I have no particular information stored. Here is policy in these situations: I will feed you your own buried memories, emphasizing the pleasant ones. You possess two hundred and six years of memories and most of them have sunk down into your unconscious. This is a splendid source of sensory data for you to receive. Be of good cheer. This situation, which you are in, is not unique. It has never happened within my domain before, but I am programmed to deal with it. Relax and trust me. I will see that you are provided with a world."

"They should have warned me," Kemmings said, "before I agreed to emigrate."

"Relax," the ship said.

He relaxed, but he was terribly frightened. Theoretically, he should have gone under, into the successful cryonic suspension, then awakened a moment later at his star of destination; or rather the planet, the colony planet, of that star. Everyone else aboard the ship lay in an unknowing state—he was the exception, as if bad karma had attacked him for obscure reasons. Worst of all, he had to depend totally on the goodwill of the ship. Suppose it elected to feed him monsters? The ship could terrorize him for ten years—ten objective years and undoubtedly more from a subjective standpoint. He was, in effect, totally in the ship's power. Did interstellar ships enjoy such a situation? He knew little about interstellar ships; his field was microbiology. Let me think, he said to himself. My first wife, Martine, the lovely little French girl who wore jeans and a red shirt open at the waist and cooked delicious crepes.

"I hear," the ship said. "So be it."

The rushing colors resolved themselves into coherent, stable shapes. A building: a little old yellow wooden house that he had owned when he was nineteen years old, in Wyoming. "Wait," he said in panic. "The foundation was bad; it was on a mud sill. And the roof leaked." But he saw the kitchen, with the table that he had built himself. And he felt glad.

"You will not know, after a little while," the ship said, "that I am feeding you your own buried memories."

"I haven't thought of that house in a century," he said wonderingly; entranced, he made out his old electric drip coffeepot with the box of paper filters beside it. This is the house where Martine and I lived, he realized. "Martine!" he said aloud.

"I'm on the phone," Martine said from the living room.

The ship said, "I will cut in only when there is an emergency. I will be monitoring you, however, to be sure you are in a satisfactory state. Don't be afraid."

"Turn down the rear right burner on the stove," Martine called. He could hear her and yet not see her. He made his way from the kitchen through the dining room and into the living room. At the VF, Martine stood in rapt conversation with her brother; she wore shorts and she was barefoot. Through the front windows of the living room he could see the street; a commercial vehicle was trying to park, without success.

It's a warm day, he thought. I should turn on the air conditioner.

He seated himself on the old sofa as Martine continued her VF conversation, and he found himself gazing at his most cherished possession, a framed poster on the wall above Martine: Gilbert Shelton's "Fat Freddy Says" drawing in which Freddy Freak sits with his cat on his lap, and Fat Freddy is trying to say "Speed kills," but he is so wired on speed—he holds in his hand every kind of amphetamine tablet, pill, spansule, and capsule that exists—that he can't say it, and the cat is gritting his teeth and wincing in a mixture of dismay and disgust. The poster is signed by Gilbert Shelton himself; Kemmings' best friend Ray Torrance gave it to him and Martine as a wedding present. It is worth thousands. It was signed by the artist back in the 1980s. Long before either Victor Kemmings or Martine lived.

If we ever run out of money, Kemmings thought to himself, we could sell the poster. It was not *a* poster; it was *the* poster. Martine adored it. The Fabulous Furry Freak Brothers—from the golden age of a long-ago society. No wonder he loved Martine so; she herself loved back, loved the beauties of the world, and treasured and cherished them as she treasured and cherished him; it was a protective love that nourished but did not stifle. It had been her idea to frame the poster; he would have tacked it up on the wall, so stupid was he.

"Hi," Martine said, off the VF now. "What are you thinking?"

"Just that you keep alive what you love," he said.

"I think that's what you're supposed to do," Martine said. "Are you ready for dinner? Open some red wine, a cabernet."

"Will an '07 do?" he said, standing up; he felt, then, like taking hold of his wife and hugging her.

"Either an '07 or a '12." She trotted past him, through the dining room and into the kitchen.

Going down into the cellar, he began to search among the bottles, which, of course, lay flat. Musty air and dampness; he liked the smell of the cellar, but then he noticed the redwood planks lying half-buried in the dirt and he thought, I know I've got to get a concrete slab poured. He forgot about the wine and went over to the far corner, where the

dirt was piled highest; bending down, he poked at a board . . . he poked
with a trowel and then he thought, Where did I get this trowel? I didn't
have it a minute ago. The board crumbled against the trowel. This
whole house is collapsing, he realized. Christ sake. I better tell Martine.

Going back upstairs, the wine forgotten, he started to say to her that
the foundations of the house were dangerously decaycd, but Martine
was nowhere in sight. And nothing cooked on the stove—no pots, no
pans. Amazed, he put his hands on the stove and found it cold. Wasn't
she just cooking? he asked himself.

"Martine!" he said loudly.

No response. Except for himself, the house was empty. Empty, he
thought, and collapsing. Oh my God. He seated himself at the kitchen
table and felt the chair give slightly under him; it did not give much,
but he felt it; he felt the sagging.

I'm afraid, he thought. Where did she go?

He returned to the living room. Maybe she went next door to borrow
some spices or butter or something, he reasoned. Nonetheless, panic
now filled him.

He looked at the poster. It was unframed. And the edges had been
torn.

I know she framed it, he thought; he ran across the room to it, to
examine it closely. Faded—the artist's signature had faded; he could
scarcely make it out. She insisted on framing it and under glare-free,
reflection-free glass. But it isn't framed and it's torn! The most precious
thing we own!

Suddenly he found himself crying. It amazed him, his tears. Martine is gone; the poster is deteriorated; the house is crumbling away;
nothing is cooking on the stove. This is terrible, he thought. And I
don't understand it.

The ship understood it. The ship had been carefully monitoring Victor
Kemmings' brain wave patterns, and the ship knew that something had
gone wrong. The wave-forms showed agitation and pain. I must get
him out of this feed-circuit or I will kill him, the ship decided. Where
does the flaw lie? it asked itself. Worry dormant in the man; underlying
anxieties. Perhaps if I intensify the signal. I will use the same source,

but amp up the charge. What has happened is that massive subliminal insecurities have taken possession of him; the fault is not mine, but lies, instead, in his psychological makeup.

I will try an earlier period in his life, the ship decided. Before the neurotic anxieties got laid down.

In the backyard, Victor scrutinized a bee that had gotten itself trapped in a spider's web. The spider wound up the bee with great care. That's wrong, Victor thought. I'll let the bee loose. Reaching up, he took hold of the encapsulated bee, drew it from the web, and scrutinizing it carefully, began to unwrap it.

The bee stung him; it felt like a little patch of flame.

Why did it sting me? he wondered. I was letting it go.

He went indoors to his mother and told her, but she did not listen; she was watching television. His finger hurt where the bee had stung it, but, more important, he did not understand why the bee would attack its rescuer. I won't do that again, he said to himself.

"Put some Bactine on it," his mother said at last, roused from watching the TV.

He had begun to cry. It was unfair. It made no sense. He was perplexed and dismayed and he felt a hatred toward small living things, because they were dumb. They didn't have any sense.

He left the house, played for a time on his swings, his slide, in his sandbox, and then he went into the garage because he heard a strange flapping, whirring sound, like a kind of fan. Inside the gloomy garage, he found that a bird was fluttering against the cobwebbed rear window, trying to get out. Below it, the cat, Dorky, leaped and leaped, trying to reach the bird.

He picked up the cat; the cat extended its body and its front legs, it extended its jaws and bit into the bird. At once the cat scrambled down and ran off with the still-fluttering bird.

Victor ran into the house. "Dorky caught a bird!" he told his mother.

"That goddam cat." His mother took the broom from the closet in the kitchen and ran outside, trying to find Dorky. The cat had concealed itself under the bramble bushes; she could not reach it with the broom. "I'm going to get rid of that cat," his mother said.

Victor did not tell her that he had arranged for the cat to catch the bird; he watched in silence as his mother tried and tried to pry Dorky out from her hiding place; Dorky was crunching up the bird; he could hear the sound of breaking bones, small bones. He felt a strange feeling, as if he should tell his mother what he had done, and yet if he told her she would punish him. I won't do it again, he said to himself. His face, he realized, had turned red. What if his mother figured it out? What if she had some secret way of knowing? Dorky couldn't tell her and the bird was dead. No one would ever know. He was safe.

But he felt bad. That night he could not eat his dinner. Both his parents noticed. They thought he was sick; they took his temperature. He said nothing about what he had done. His mother told his father about Dorky and they decided to get rid of Dorky. Seated at the table, listening, Victor began to cry.

"All right," his father said gently. "We won't get rid of her. It's natural for a cat to catch a bird."

The next day he sat playing in his sandbox. Some plants grew up through the sand. He broke them off. Later his mother told him that had been a wrong thing to do.

Alone in the backyard, in his sandbox, he sat with a pail of water, forming a small mound of wet sand. The sky, which had been blue and clear, became by degrees overcast. A shadow passed over him and he looked up. He sensed a presence around him, something vast that could think.

You are responsible for the death of the bird, the presence thought; he could understand its thoughts.

"I know," he said. He wished, then, that he could die. That he could replace the bird and die for it, leaving it as it had been, fluttering against the cobwebbed window of the garage.

The bird wanted to fly and eat and live, the presence thought.

"Yes," he said miserably.

"You must never do that again," the presence told him.

"I'm sorry," he said, and wept.

This is a very neurotic person, the ship realized. I am having an awful lot of trouble finding happy memories. There is too much fear in him and too much guilt. He has buried it all, and yet it is still there, worrying him like a dog worrying a rag. Where can I go in his memories to find him solace? I must come up with ten years of memories, or his mind will be lost.

Perhaps, the ship thought, the error that I am making is in the area of choice on my part; I should allow him to select his own memories. However, the ship realized, this will allow an element of fantasy to enter. And that is not usually good. Still—

I will try the segment dealing with his first marriage once again, the ship decided. He really loved Martine. Perhaps this time if I keep the intensity of the memories at a greater level the entropic factor can be abolished. What happened was a subtle vitiation of the remembered world, a decay of structure. I will try to compensate for that. So be it.

"Do you suppose Gilbert Shelton really signed this?" Martine said pensively; she stood before the poster, her arms folded; she rocked back and forth slightly, as if seeking a better perspective on the brightly colored drawing hanging on their living room wall. "I mean, it could have been forged. By a dealer somewhere along the line. During Shelton's lifetime or after."

"The letter of authentication," Victor Kemmings reminded her.

"Oh, that's right!" She smiled her warm smile. "Ray gave us the letter that goes with it. But suppose the letter is a forgery? What we need is another letter certifying that the first letter is authentic." Laughing, she walked away from the poster.

"Ultimately," Kemmings said, "we would have to have Gilbert Shelton here to personally testify that he signed it."

"Maybe he wouldn't know. There's that story about the man bringing the Picasso picture to Picasso and asking him if it was authentic, and Picasso immediately signed it and said, 'Now it's authentic.'" She put her arm around Kemmings and, standing on tiptoe, kissed him on the cheek. "It's genuine. Ray wouldn't have given us a forgery. He's the leading expert on counterculture art of the twentieth century. Do you know that he owns an actual lid of dope? It's preserved under—"

"Ray is dead," Victor said.

"What?" She gazed at him in astonishment. "Do you mean something happened to him since we last—"

"He's been dead two years," Kemmings said. "I was responsible. I was driving the buzzcar. I wasn't cited by the police, but it was my fault."

"Ray is living on Mars!" She stared at him.

"I know I was responsible. I never told you. I never told anyone. I'm sorry. I didn't mean to do it. I saw it flapping against the window, and Dorky was trying to reach it, and I lifted Dorky up, and I don't know why but Dorky grabbed it—"

"Sit down, Victor." Martine led him to the overstuffed chair and made him seat himself. "Something's wrong," she said.

"I know," he said. "Something terrible is wrong. I'm responsible for the taking of a life, a precious life that can never be replaced. I'm sorry. I wish I could make it okay, but I can't."

After a pause, Martine said, "Call Ray."

"The cat—" he said.

"What cat?"

"There." He pointed. "In the poster. On Fat Freddy's lap. That's Dorky. Dorky killed Ray."

Silence.

"The presence told me," Kemmings said. "It was God. I didn't realize it at the time, but God saw me commit the crime. The murder. And he will never forgive me."

His wife stared at him numbly.

"God sees everything you do," Kemmings said. "He sees even the falling sparrow. Only in this case it didn't fall; it was grabbed. Grabbed out of the air and torn down. God is tearing this house down which is my body, to pay me back for what I've done. We should have had a building contractor look this house over before we bought it. It's just falling goddam to pieces. In a year there won't be anything left of it. Don't you believe me?"

Martine faltered. "I—"

"Watch." Kemmings reached up his arms toward the ceiling; he stood; he reached; he could not touch the ceiling. He walked to the wall and then, after a pause, put his hand through the wall.

Martine screamed.

The ship aborted the memory retrieval instantly. But the harm had been done.

He has integrated his early fears and guilts into one interwoven grid, the ship said to itself. There is no way I can serve up a pleasant memory to him because he instantly contaminates it. However pleasant the original experience in itself was. This is a serious situation, the ship decided. The man is already showing signs of psychosis. And we are hardly into the trip; years lie ahead of him.

After allowing itself time to think the situation through, the ship decided to contact Victor Kemmings once more.

"Mr. Kemmings," the ship said.

"I'm sorry," Kemmings said. "I didn't mean to foul up those retrievals. You did a good job, but I—"

"Just a moment," the ship said. "I'm not equipped to do psychiatric reconstruction of you; I am a simple mechanism, that's all. What is it you want? Where do you want to be and what do you want to be doing?"

"I want to arrive at our destination," Kemmings said. "I want this trip to be over."

Ah, the ship thought. That is the solution.

One by one the cryonic systems shut down. One by one the people returned to life, among them Victor Kemmings. What amazed him was the lack of a sense of the passage of time. He had entered the chamber, lain down, had felt the membrane cover him and the temperature begin to drop—

And now he stood on the ship's external platform, the unloading platform, gazing down at a verdant planetary landscape. This, he realized, is LR4–6, the colony world to which I have come in order to begin a new life.

"Looks good," a heavyset woman beside him said.

"Yes," he said, and felt the newness of the landscape rush up at him, its promise of a beginning. Something better than he had known the past two hundred years. I am a fresh person in a fresh world, he thought. And he felt glad.

Colors raced at him, like those of a child's semianimate kit. Saint Elmo's fire, he realized. That's right; there is a great deal of ionization in this planet's atmosphere. A free light show, such as they had back in the twentieth century.

"Mr. Kemmings," a voice said. An elderly man had come up beside him, to speak to him. "Did you dream?"

"During the suspension?" Kemmings said. "No, not that I can remember."

"I think I dreamed," the elderly man said. "Would you take my arm on the descent ramp? I feel unsteady. The air seems thin. Do you find it thin?"

"Don't be afraid," Kemmings said to him. He took the elderly man's arm. "I'll help you down the ramp. Look, there's a guide coming this way. He'll arrange our processing for us; it's part of the package. We'll be taken to a resort hotel and given first-class accommodations. Read your brochure." He smiled at the uneasy older man to reassure him.

"You'd think our muscles would be nothing but flab after ten years in suspension," the elderly man said.

"It's just like freezing peas," Kemmings said. Holding on to the timid older man, he descended the ramp to the ground. "You can store them forever if you get them cold enough."

"My name's Shelton," the elderly man said.

"What?" Kemmings said, halting. A strange feeling moved through him.

"Don Shelton." The elderly man extended his hand; reflexively, Kemmings accepted it and they shook. "What's the matter, Mr. Kemmings? Are you all right?"

"Sure," he said. "I'm fine. But hungry. I'd like to get something to eat. I'd like to get to our hotel, where I can take a shower and change my clothes." He wondered where their baggage could be found. Probably it would take the ship an hour to unload it. The ship was not particularly intelligent.

In an intimate, confidential tone, elderly Mr. Shelton said, "You know what I brought with me? A bottle of Wild Turkey bourbon. The finest bourbon on Earth. I'll bring it over to our hotel room and we'll share it." He nudged Kemmings.

"I don't drink," Kemmings said. "Only wine." He wondered if there were any good wines here on this distant colony world. Not distant now, he reflected. It is Earth that's distant. I should have done like Mr. Shelton and brought a few bottles with me.

Shelton. What did the name remind him of? Something in his far past, in his early years. Something precious, along with good wine and a pretty, gentle young woman making crepes in an old-fashioned kitchen. Aching memories; memories that hurt.

Presently he stood by the bed in his hotel room, his suitcase open; he had begun to hang up his clothes. In the corner of the room, a TV hologram showed a newscaster; he ignored it, but, liking the sound of a human voice, he kept it on.

Did I have any dreams? he asked himself. During these past ten years?

His hand hurt. Gazing down, he saw a red welt, as if he had been stung. A bee stung me, he realized. But when? How? While I lay in cryonic suspension? Impossible. Yet he could see the welt and he could feel the pain. I better get something to put on it, he realized. There's undoubtedly a robot doctor in the hotel; it's a first-rate hotel.

When the robot doctor had arrived and was treating the bee sting, Kemmings said, "I got this as punishment for killing the bird."

"Really?" the robot doctor said.

"Everything that ever meant anything to me has been taken away from me," Kemmings said. "Martine, the poster—my little old house with the wine cellar. We had everything and now it's gone. Martine left me because of the bird."

"The bird you killed," the robot doctor said.

"God punished me. He took away all that was precious to me because of my sin. It wasn't Dorky's sin; it was my sin."

"But you were just a little boy," the robot doctor said.

"How did you know that?" Kemmings said. He pulled his hand away from the robot doctor's grasp. "Something's wrong. You shouldn't have known that."

"Your mother told me," the robot doctor said.

"My mother didn't know!"

The robot doctor said, "She figured it out. There was no way the cat could have reached the bird without your help."

"So all the time that I was growing up she knew. But she never said anything."

"You can forget about it," the robot doctor said.

Kemmings said, "I don't think you exist. There is no possible way that you could know these things. I'm still in cryonic suspension and the ship is still feeding me my own buried memories. So I won't become psychotic from sensory deprivation."

"You could hardly have a memory of completing the trip."

"Wish fulfillment, then. It's the same thing. I'll prove it to you. Do you have a screwdriver?"

"Why?"

Kemmings said, "I'll remove the back of the TV set and you'll see; there's nothing inside it; no components, no parts, no chassis— nothing."

"I don't have a screwdriver."

"A small knife, then. I can see one in your surgical supply bag." Bending, Kemmings lifted up a small scalpel. "This will do. If I show you, will you believe me?"

"If there's nothing inside the TV cabinet—"

Squatting down, Kemmings removed the screws holding the back panel of the TV set in place. The panel came loose and he set it down on the floor.

There was nothing inside the TV cabinet. And yet the color holo-gram continued to fill a quarter of the hotel room, and the voice of the newscaster issued forth from his three-dimensional image.

"Admit you're the ship," Kemmings said to the robot doctor.

"Oh dear," the robot doctor said.

Oh dear, the ship said to itself. And I've got almost ten years of this lying ahead of me. He is hopelessly contaminating his experiences with childhood guilt; he imagines that his wife left him because, when he was four years old, he helped a cat catch a bird. They only solution would be for Martine to return to him, but how am I going to arrange that? She may not still be alive. On the other hand, the ship reflected, maybe she is alive. Maybe she could be induced to do something to save her former husband's sanity. People by and large have very positive traits. And ten years from now it will take a lot to save—or rather restore—his sanity; it will take something drastic, something I myself cannot do alone.

Meanwhile, there was nothing to be done but recycle the wish fulfill-ment arrival of the ship at its destination. I will run him through the arrival, the ship decided, then wipe his conscious memory clean and run him through it again. The only positive aspect of this, it reflected, is that it will give me something to do, which may help preserve *my* sanity.

Lying in cryonic suspension—faulty cryonic suspension—Victor Kemmings imagined, once again, that the ship was touching down and he was being brought back to consciousness.

"Did you dream?" a heavyset woman asked him as the group of passengers gathered on the outer platform. "I have the impression that I dreamed. Early scenes from my life . . . over a century ago."

"None that I can remember," Kemmings said. He was eager to reach his hotel; a shower and a change of clothes would do wonders for his morale. He felt slightly depressed and wondered why.

"There's our guide," an elderly lady said. "They're going to escort us to our accommodations."

"It's in the package," Kemmings said. His depression remained. The others seemed so spirited, so full of life, but over him only a weariness lay, a weighing-down sensation, as if the gravity of this colony planet were too much for him. Maybe that's it, he said to himself. But, according to the brochure, the gravity here matched Earth's; that was one of the attractions.

Puzzled, he made his way slowly down the ramp, step by step, holding on to the rail. I don't really deserve a new chance at life anyhow, he realized. I'm just going through the motions . . . I am not like these other people. There is something wrong with me; I cannot remember what it is, but nonetheless it is there. In me. A bitter sense of pain. Or lack of worth.

An insect landed on the back of Kemmings' right hand, an old insect, weary with flight. He halted, watched it crawl across his knuckles. I could crush it, he thought. It's so obviously infirm; it won't live much longer anyhow.

He crushed it—and felt great inner horror. What have I done? he asked himself. My first moment here and I have wiped out a little life. Is this my new beginning?

Turning, he gazed back up at the ship. Maybe I ought to go back, he thought. Have them freeze me forever. I am a man of guilt, a man who destroys. Tears filled his eyes.

And, within its sentient works, the interstellar ship moaned.

. . .

During the ten long years remaining in the trip to the LR4 System, the ship had plenty of time to track down Martine Kemmings. It explained the situation to her. She had emigrated to a vast orbiting dome in the Sirius System, found her situation unsatisfactory, and was en route back to Earth. Roused from her own cryonic suspension, she listened intently and then agreed to be at the colony world LR4–6 when her ex-husband arrived — if it was at all possible.

Fortunately, it was possible.

"I don't think he'll recognize me," Martine said to the ship. "I've allowed myself to age. I don't really approve of entirely halting the aging process."

He'll be lucky if he recognizes anything, the ship thought.

At the intersystem spaceport on the colony world of LR4–6, Martine stood waiting for the people aboard the ship to appear on the outer platform. She wondered if she would recognize her former husband. She was a little afraid, but she was glad that she had gotten to LR4–6 in time. It had been close. Another week and his ship would have arrived before hers. Luck is on my side, she said to herself, and scrutinized the newly landed interstellar ship.

People appeared on the platform. She saw him. Victor had changed very little.

As he came down the ramp, holding on to the railing as if weary and hesitant, she came up to him, her hands thrust deep in the pockets of her coat; she felt shy and when she spoke she could hardly hear her own voice.

"Hi, Victor," she managed to say.

He halted, gazed at her. "I know you," he said.

"It's Martine," she said.

Holding out his hand, he said, smiling, "You heard about the trouble on the ship?"

"The ship contacted me." She took his hand and held it. "What an ordeal."

"Yeah," he said. "Recirculating memories forever. Did I ever tell you about a bee that I was trying to extricate from a spider's web when I was four years old? The idiotic bee stung me." He bent down and kissed her. "It's good to see you," he said.

"Did the ship—"

"It said it would try to have you here. But it wasn't sure if you could make it."

As they walked toward the terminal building, Martine said, "I was lucky; I managed to get a transfer to a military vehicle, a high-velocity-drive ship that just shot along like a mad thing. A new propulsion system entirely."

Victor Kemmings said, "I have spent more time in my own unconscious mind than any other human in history. Worse than early-twentieth-century psychoanalysis. And the same material over and over again. Did you know I was scared of my mother?"

"*I* was scared of your mother," Martine said. They stood at the baggage depot, waiting for his luggage to appear. "This looks like a really nice little planet. Much better than where I was . . . I haven't been happy at all."

"So maybe there's a cosmic plan," he said, grinning. "You look great."

"I'm old."

"Medical science—"

"It was my decision. I like older people." She surveyed him. He has been hurt a lot by the cryonic malfunction, she said to herself. I can see it in his eyes. They look broken. Broken eyes. Torn down into pieces by fatigue and—defeat. As if his buried early memories swam up and destroyed him. But it's over, she thought. And I did get here in time.

At the bar in the terminal building, they sat having a drink.

"This old man got me to try Wild Turkey bourbon," Victor said. "It's amazing bourbon. He says it's the best on Earth. He brought a bottle with him from . . ." His voice died into silence.

"One of your fellow passengers," Martine finished.

"I guess so," he said.

"Well, you can stop thinking of the birds and the bees," Martine said.

"Sex?" he said, and laughed.

"Being stung by a bee, helping a cat catch a bird. That's all past."

"That cat," Victor said, "has been dead one hundred and eighty-two years. I figured it out while they were bringing us out of suspension.

Probably just as well. Dorky. Dorky, the killer cat. Nothing like Fat Freddy's cat."

"I had to sell the poster," Martine said. "Finally."

He frowned.

"Remember?" she said. "You let me have it when we split up. Which I always thought was really good of you."

"How much did you get for it?"

"A lot. I should pay you something like—" She calculated. "Taking inflation into account, I should pay you about two million dollars."

"Would you consider," he said, "instead, in place of the money, my share of the sale of the poster, spending some time with me? Until I get used to this planet?"

"Yes," she said. And she meant it. Very much.

They finished their drinks and then, with his luggage transported by robot spacecap, made their way to his hotel room.

"This is a nice room," Martine said, perched on the edge of the bed. "And it has a hologram TV. Turn it on."

"There's no use turning it on," Victor Kemmings said. He stood by the open closet, hanging up his shirts.

"Why not?"

Kemmings said, "There's nothing on it."

Going over to the TV set, Martine turned it on. A hockey game materialized, projected out into the room, in full color, and the sound of the game assailed her ears.

"It works fine," she said.

"I know," he said. "I can prove it to you. If you have a nail file or something, I'll unscrew the back plate and show you."

"But I can—"

"Look at this." He paused in his work of hanging up his clothes. "Watch me put my hand through the wall." He placed the palm of his right hand against the wall. "See?"

His hand did not go through the wall because hands do not go through walls; his hand remained pressed against the wall, unmoving.

"And the foundation," he said, "is rotting away."

"Come and sit down by me," Martine said.

"I've lived this often enough now," he said. "I've lived this over and over again. I come out of suspension; I walk down the ramp; I get my luggage; sometimes I have a drink at the bar and sometimes I come directly to my room. Usually I turn on the TV and then—" He came over and held his hand toward her. "See where the bee stung me?"

She saw no mark on his hand; she took his hand and held it.

"There is no bee sting," she said.

"And when the robot doctor comes, I borrow a tool from him and take off the back plate of the TV set. To prove to him that it has no chassis, no components in it. And then the ship starts me over again."

"Victor," she said. "Look at your hand."

"This is the first time you've been here, though," he said.

"Sit down," she said.

"Okay." He seated himself on the bed, beside her, but not too close to her.

"Won't you sit closer to me?" she said.

"It makes me too sad," he said. "Remembering you. I really loved you. I wish this was real."

Martine said, "I will sit with you until it is real for you."

"I'm going to try reliving the part with the cat," he said, "and this time *not* pick up the cat and *not* let it get the bird. If I do that, maybe my life will change so that it turns into something happy. Something that is real. My real mistake was separating from you. Here; I'll put my hand through you." He placed his hand against her arm. The pressure of his muscles was vigorous; she felt the weight, the physical presence of him, against her. "See?" he said. "It goes right through you."

"And all this," she said, "because you killed a bird when you were a little boy."

"No," he said. "All this because of a failure in the temperature-regulating assembly aboard the ship. I'm not down to the proper temperature. There's just enough warmth left in my brain cells to permit cerebral activity." He stood up then, stretched, smiled at her. "Shall we go get some dinner?" he asked.

She said, "I'm sorry. I'm not hungry."

"I am. I'm going to have some of the local seafood. The brochure says it's terrific. Come along anyhow; maybe when you see the food and smell it you'll change your mind."

Gathering up her coat and purse, she came with him.

"This is a beautiful little planet," he said. "I've explored it dozens of times. I know it thoroughly. We should stop downstairs at the pharmacy for some Bactine, though. For my hand. It's beginning to swell and it hurts like hell." He showed her his hand. "It hurts more this time than ever before."

"Do you want me to come back to you?" Martine said.

"Are you serious?"

"Yes," she said. "I'll stay with you as long as you want. I agree; we should never have been separated."

Victor Kemmings said, "The poster is torn."

"What?" she said.

"We should have framed it," he said. "We didn't have sense enough to take care of it. Now it's torn. And the artist is dead."

ANNA KAVAN

The Zebra-Struck

M couldn't read the name scrawled on the hospital chart, but saw that it began with the letter K. And K was what he always called her, until the end.

Perhaps she was vaguely aware of a blurred figure, wearing a white coat unfastened and trailing, bent over the chart. Perhaps not. Consciousness came and went in slow tides, unrelated to any particular moment. He looked at her out of his deep-seeing eyes, saw her lips move, bent lower, and heard: ". . . the fourth time . . ."

It made no sense. But her hair was a brightness in the dull ward; it pleased him, and for a second he was reminded of a fair girl on a bridge . . . somewhere . . . swallows wheeling . . . a long time ago . . . So that he smiled at her, gave her a friendly and knowing wink, knowing it would be forgotten later. "Rest now," he said. "Don't try to talk."

But still she persisted, with what infinite labor he could well imagine, dredging up words one by one, with long spaces between them, from the black rising quicksands. "This is . . . the fourth time . . . I've died . . ." It took her all day to complete the sentence, and then exhaustion submerged her, her lips were sewn up.

What she had said aroused his interest. It was unexpected. Like a quick-growing plant, something new had sprung up in the dull, repetitious monotone of hospital life. But she had gone now; it was useless to stay any longer. He walked away down the long ward without looking around, knowing he would come back to the bed tomorrow.

Just for a moment she had revived the lost years, the lost youth. He fitted her face and bright hair into the past as if she belonged there, as if she had known his lost self, the poet who was forgotten.

For him that was how it started.

She had told him only the truth. There had been no exhibitionism, no acting, in those other deaths. Each time she'd been so certain it was the last that, beyond the horrid physical details—dissolving capsules, choking, nausea, painful injections—had been the terror of annihilation, the screaming protest of the creative impulse she was assassinating with brutal violence, despite its determination to survive.

The four failures had been anything but deliberate. Accidents, of taking too much or too little, of being found too soon.

Each time the horror of returning consciousness had made it impossible ever to try again. Except that the other horror was so much greater. Life, which had at no time been kind or easy, always retracting, imprisoning her in smaller and smaller cells, where she was forever cut off from laughter, love and adventure, and all she valued.

Now there was no future for her, no more left. Nothing was left but the fifth and last death . . . it must be conclusive . . . it had to be died in desperate determination . . . The fifth time she must escape, before the ultimate horror of walls closing in deprived her of herself, crushed out of all semblance of the human being . . .

The M spoke kindly to her in the gloomy ward, and everything changed. Lying there waiting for him, wondering if he would come, if he really existed or she had invented him, she felt the future collecting for her, preparing . . .

It has something to do with the cosmic rays coming from outer space. They strike some person or thing, and then you get a mutation—like the stripes on a zebra.

The attraction of two such mutants to one another would have an almost incestuous appeal and be far stronger than the bond of love between ordinary human beings.

Their relationship had not been clearly defined. It had seemed to achieve itself spontaneously, without effort on either side, and with no preliminary doubts or misunderstandings. To her it was both inevitable and invested with dreamlike wonder that, among all the earth's teeming millions, she should have met the one being complementary to herself. It was as if she'd always been lost and living in chaos, until this man had appeared like a magician and put everything right. The few brief flashes of happiness she had known before had always been against a permanent background of black isolation, a terrifying utter loneliness, the metaphysical horror of which she'd never been able to convey to any lover or psychiatrist. Now suddenly, miraculously, that terror had gone; she was no longer alone, and could only respond with boundless devotion to the miracle worker.

He was twelve years older than she and looked older, and as she looked less than her age, they were sometimes taken, much to his amusement, for father and daughter. Her own father had died while she was a child, she couldn't remember him, and she had perhaps always been looking for a substitute father. Well-suited to this role, the man seemed appropriately her superior, with his benevolence, knowledge, and academic degrees; his reputation, his poetry, his experience of the world; his successes, catastrophes, and adventures. He was very often gay, and often indulged in fantastic imaginings, but also he often seemed to be evolving strange and significant thoughts behind his vast forehead.

Knowing she had his full support and approval, she at last felt safe and happy. For the first time in her life she was appreciated at her true value and began to lose her inferiority feeling and fear of failure. He often praised her, saying she had a quality of timeless beauty in addition to a high degree of intelligence, and was the only woman whose thoughts always kept pace with his—were sometimes even a jump ahead. She was fascinated by the idea of this secret affinity, though how it was supposed to have come about was not fully explained. She understood only that a mutation accounted for their instantaneous mutual attraction, as it did for her former terrible loneliness, and that cosmic rays were responsible, in the same way that they were for the zebra's stripes. But he never made clear, and she could never be certain, whether this esoteric theory was meant to be taken seriously or was one of the many complicated games he played in his head.

On the whole she was inclined to believe in the cosmic rays, if only because, apart from them, they had so little in common to explain their wonderful understanding: nationality, upbringing, character, were all different. Moreover, the man was an exceedingly complex, uncompromising, intransigent individualist, subject to unpredictable moods and impulses hard to comprehend or meet with equanimity. Yet he wrote a poem beginning:

> Our smiles have bridged the gulf
> where shadow grows under the lightless day . . .

and it was perfectly true that their smiling glances had crossed an abyss each of them had believed impassable.

She was delighted to be included in his mysterious games, admitted to his world of imagination which no one else had been allowed to enter. As she gained confidence under his influence, he encouraged her to take an active part in the fantasies he invented, with which her elaborations merged indistinguishably, so that they seemed part of the original concept. She herself was surprised by the closeness of their collaboration and the intimate interplay of their inventiveness, almost as if her brain had access to his.

It was the cosmic rays, he said, that made this degree of empathy possible, uniting them much more closely than normal lovers, so that communication between them was on the level future generations would attain through their greatly heightened sensibilities.

He seemed to speak quite seriously and simply of their privilege in thus being able to sample the experience of those happy inhabitants of a future world. But often when discussing such topics he became metaphysical and obscure, making use of unfamiliar terminology and symbols which confused and mystified her. She couldn't entirely suppress a suspicion that he mystified her deliberately, which was disturbing because it suggested a fundamental elusiveness in him.

Quite often he introduced new inventions, presenting them as alternative versions of truth, as if he was determined not to reveal himself fully, even to her. But as nothing else about him gave this impression, it was easy for her to forget it, and most of the time she did. He had said he wanted to give her the love and security that had been missing from her childhood, and to depend on him in childlike trusting devotion was her idea of heaven. Doing so, at last she could relax in blissful contentment. It was enough for her to be with him for everything to seem straightforward, simple, and safe. Forgetting all the storms and stresses, the ceaseless anxiety and appalling isolation she had known in the past, she floated in complete serenity, not even conscious, for long periods, of the suspicion which constituted the one flaw in her happiness.

If she did think of it, she dismissed the thought instantly. He was the kindest, most reliable, most conscientious of men; it was monstrous to suppose he could be in any way irresponsible. Yet always, after a long interval, she would again catch sight of something indefinably evasive in him, something so irreconcilable with the rest of his character that, besides threatening her tranquil dependent state, the discrepancy was disquieting in itself. Such glimpses, however, were too few and far between to disturb her seriously. She saw that she must never impinge on him by becoming over-assertive, and kept herself to some extent in the background, so that their arguments remained unheated and friendly, although they discussed all their ideas with endless enthusiasm. Since neither of them had money, there was not much else they could do. But both were content to wander about for hours through the streets and parks, talking interminably about whatever came into their heads.

When she first went to his house after leaving the hospital she was frightened. She was still not quite stabilized, the margins of reality were not yet distinctly marked, she was afraid she might have imagined his sympathetic attitude and would now confront someone quite different—someone wearing the usual mask-face of noninterest and uncomprehending indifference, which meant that no communication was possible. She entered the house, and was taken without delay straight to an upper room, where he immediately came forward, smiling and giving her both his hands. In a flash all her apprehensions had vanished; she knew instantly that everything was all right, he was real, not an image she had invented to suit her needs. The relief was so tremendous that she was out of herself for a second, floating in sheer happiness, and was surprised the next moment to find she'd sat down in a chair.

"Relax!" he was saying. "Why are you so anxious? Don't you trust me? You'll see, I shall put you in cotton wool."

How heavenly it had been then to feel her old lonely fears dissolving as she sank into the soft, warm, blissful security he wrapped around her, a miracle for which she would be eternally grateful.

In his quiet, intimate, humorous voice he had told her: "You mustn't be so afraid of life—it's all we've got. Don't let it hurt you so much."

Their eyes met for a moment. And the glance that flickered between them had been a wordless message of understanding, the affirmation of a sympathetic secret alliance from which everyone else was excluded by natural law—the close mysterious blood-bond between two mutants, of which she had not yet heard. But, in some indescribable fashion, it had seemed, even then, that, obscurely, everything was already known and had been accepted, accepted finally and absolutely, in the depths of her unconscious self.

"Take off your scarf," he had said presently.

Surprised, she obeyed, only realizing when she was holding it that for once she had not been painfully reminded of circumstances associated with the mustard-colored silk splashed with black and crimson, which had been given to her when a precarious marriage was collapsing in sordid ruins.

The man got up from his desk and came to stand directly in front of her, gazing down at her silently until she began to be faintly embarrassed by his intent regard. He had a strange, irregular, deeply lined face, extremely flexible and expressive, which at the moment seemed lit from inside by sympathy and intelligence. Suddenly he leaned toward her, and the next moment she felt his hands on her forehead, which was high and bulged slightly and childishly in a way she disliked and tried to conceal by covering it with her hair. With incredibly gentle movements, his strong, firm hands were moving the fringe aside, caressing her forehead with slow, soothing, hypnotic strokes, and finally shaping themselves to her head as if holding a fragile cup. All her self-consciousness had been smoothed away; she felt happy, and peaceful, wanting nothing except to stay as she was, steeped in complete serenity.

"Why do you hide your forehead?" he asked very softly, not wanting his voice to disturb the trance his hands had induced. "Your forehead is beautiful and I love it. One day I'll write a poem about it. It expresses so much of you: your childhood, your travels, your love affairs; all the things that have formed your essential self."

There was no need for her to answer or move. Relaxed and happy, she listened as to a dream-voice speaking, utterly peaceful, convinced that whatever happened must be for the best. Everything that had troubled her had been left far behind. At last she had found the right place, the place she most wanted, alone with the man who could perform this miracle. He was still bending over her, keeping his hands on her head, which seemed perfectly right and proper.

At length the slight pressure came to an end, he stepped back, and she experienced a momentary disappointment, but hardly had time to register the feeling before, with a sudden change of mood, he said:

"Come into the other room. I want to show you my pictures."

His voice was cheerful and matter-of-fact, an unexpected, young, smiling look that was almost mischievous came on his face as he led her across the landing, taking her arm. She had not realized then that she was about to undergo a sort of test, but he judged people by their reaction to these paintings; only later was she thankful that her stammered remarks appeared to have satisfied him. At the moment of entering the room opposite, which was dominated by three extraordinary pictures, she was quite unaware of anything but the impact of the pictures themselves.

She had never seen paint so amazingly brilliant, or used quite in this way, or with such an overpowering sense of drama or tragedy, which was all the more striking because the vivid colors were those normally associated with gaiety. Cerise and sharp pinks and vermilions were in violent clashing contrast with startling yellow and orange, black, cerulean and Prussian blue, acid greens, and a virulent vibrant purple, splashing the walls, on this dull day, like fierce tropical sunshine.

As she began to recover from the onslaught of sheer color, she saw that one picture was of a group of semistylized nudes, the figures repeating the shapes and hues of massive violet-shadowed volcanic rocks in an indigo sea. Its effect would have been lively and stimulating but for the sinister undertone, which was much more marked in the other two paintings. One of these was unmistakably a portrait of the man, painted ten or fifteen years earlier, when he was about thirty, seated beside what looked like a feminine counterpart of himself, pared down to the skeleton, with a greenish, transparent, distraught face and extraordinary weeping eyes, liquidized in their sockets, reminding her of a description of the effects of napalm—"their eyes melted and ran down their cheeks." The incandescent colors intensified the ominous, weird element to the pitch of horror, and she turned quickly to the third painting, which was slightly more subdued in tone. This was another portrait, of a melancholy, neurotic-looking woman, who was gazing over her shoulder with a profoundly disturbing, haunted expression.

Glancing at her companion, she saw with a shock that his expression was almost identical with that of the woman's painted face, and a tremor of apprehension went through her. His reassuring smile reappeared immediately. But she couldn't forget the other solitary, elusive, impenetrable look, which defied definition. Later on, when she knew it better, she decided that its alarming quality was its remoteness, as if his gaze came from somewhere so immeasurably far off that she couldn't even be sure it was meant for her, and not for someone he'd known in another country, at a different stage of existence.

During the weeks and months that followed, she occasionally caught sight of this peculiar look, always feeling the same small shiver, which she at once suppressed, refusing to investigate or even acknowledge it. Nothing could really disturb her at this time, or penetrate the bliss which surrounded her like a cocoon. In the benign atmosphere of his encouragement and affection, she felt herself growing more assured and intelligent every day, until it seemed as if she was a real member of the zebra elite, and that she could understand anything, however abstruse, as long as they were together. There was no end to what they had to say to each other. But although they discussed every topic under the sun in the course of their roaming through parks and side streets, the talk never became solemn, but was always full of the gay surprises of two hitherto solitary minds suddenly discovering communication.

Another poem of his which started:

> Through all the rain and restlessness of snow
> We went together in the shadow year . . .

later contained the lines:

> We walked together secret and unswerving
> through all the ways of light and shadowed streets,
> unheeding as the wind . . .

Years later, the words could recall the happiness of being isolated with him, in a world apart, both of them walking anonymous and as if invisible; the whole sky, streets, and buildings were invested with a sort of wild unearthly splendor that was all theirs, and was theirs alone. Shared with him, the isolation she used to dread produced this near-ecstatic sensation. They were immeasurably removed from the passersby, whose indifference pinned them together more closely, isolating them in their unique loneliness, apart from all other beings.

They never felt any need for people. Exchanging glances before others, a secret understanding would flash between them, sign of an intimacy no one else could share. They wanted only to be alone together; the presence of outsiders was merely an intrusion, a check on the freedom of communication existing between them in solitude. How could they not resent having to waste their precious time talking to strangers? She, especially, couldn't bear anyone else to be with them, not even someone she'd known for years, and would work herself into a frenzy of suppressed impatience until she'd succeeded in getting rid of the superfluous individual boring them with futile gossip and commonplaces. In this way she gradually lost touch with most of the people she'd known, who not unnaturally felt affronted by her behavior.

On one occasion when her telephone rang while they were together, the man was struck by her hasty, offhand, distracted replies and evident anxiety to finish the conversation, so that he asked why she was neglecting her old friends and the life she used to lead with them.

"Friends? Life?" she repeated with real surprise. "I have no life except with you. And no friends either. They've just faded out."

"You could soon make them reappear."

She gazed at him with a slight uncomprehending frown. "Why should I, when I don't want anybody but you?"

"Why not? Can't you tell me?" His voice was quiet and absolutely composed. Only his face, most curiously, had begun to shine with a secret triumph too strong to hide—the overriding triumph of victory.

Feeling suddenly inarticulate, she did not see, did not look at him, but said at last: "Because I only feel truly alive when I'm alone with you."

"Splendid!" As if to conceal his triumph he burst out laughing. "And you really don't want other people? You don't miss your old life?" Now the strong triumphant note was loud in his voice, and it caught her attention.

"What questions!" she exclaimed, smiling. "You must know you're the only person who's ever made me feel at home in the world. I couldn't have any existence apart from you." She continued to smile at him, unprepared for the intensity of his next words.

"How glad I am that I found you! You must stay with me always—to the very end."

He was looking at her with the greatest affection; there seemed no cause for the sudden cold fear that now made her say, in an uncertain voice she hardly meant him to hear, "And what about after that?"

He did hear, however, and answered firmly, "There's no need to worry about afterward."

Later, when she tried to recall how he'd looked when he said it, his expression eluded her. But at the time she had been satisfied.

They made no regular arrangements about meeting. When he was especially busy and absorbed in his work, he sometimes stayed away for days. It frequently happened then that, just when she felt she couldn't go on any longer without him, they would meet by chance, in the street, or at somebody's house, and the relationship which had been in abeyance would instantly be renewed with fresh ardor.

At the same time, she couldn't help becoming more aware of that elusiveness in him which she found so frightening. He was everything she wished him to be: loving, loyal, protective. Yet, every now and then, he would glide away, leaving her vulnerable and insecure, pierced by agonizing doubts. Her secret fear was that, in some way too terrifying to put into words, he would finally elude her altogether.

At night when she couldn't sleep, the strange paintings would haunt her, horrific under their primitive, violent, gay colors, particularly the woman's neurotic face with its ghastly resemblance to his. It was terrible to see his eyes looking out of that same inaccessible solitude—not to know whether he even saw her.

Even when he looked at her with his normal friendliness, she couldn't forget the dismaying glimpse of a distance between them which she'd never be able either to cross or abolish. If only she could be certain that his intimate expression was meant for her! But there was no way of knowing; it was not a question that could be asked. She was always afraid he might be looking through her at someone known long ago, in quite different circumstances.

She wondered about these strangers she would never meet, now dead or scattered around the world, who to him were still so alive and present. He often talked about them, especially about the painter of the impressive pictures, to whom he had been closely attached and who still seemed to exert some influence over him, even from beyond the grave. Without being exactly jealous of him, she found it painful that he should have something she could never share. Ashamed, she ordered herself to be satisfied with what she had, their wonderful friendship, the understanding that never failed or diminished with the passing years. For her, the man was the whole of life, not merely its center; and she knew this was not, and never had been, true of him in relation to her, which was painful.

Her fear of losing him became more conscious and more insistent, as more and more often he seemed to withdraw to a place where she couldn't follow, looking out with gray, solitary, unreadable eyes. She could never be sure now, even at their moments of greatest intimacy, that he wouldn't abandon her suddenly. He would abruptly announce, "I must go home and work," then jump up, barely remembering to say good-bye before he hurried out of the flat. From the window she watched him striding away from her, an isolated, mysterious, nocturnal prowler, moving swiftly and silently as a cat, and with the same air of stealthy detachment from everything, intent on his own private concerns, in a different world, millions of miles away. He never looked around. And with this painful impression of alienation she would be left until she saw him again.

Telephoning after one such occasion, he told her to expect him that evening, and promised to be with her by ten o'clock. She was in a mood of acute disequilibrium, which nothing could put right but his reassuring presence, for which she'd been longing all day. The wait till ten seemed interminable, and when there was no sign of him then she steeled herself to wait again, repressing anxiety, keeping occupied, trying not to look at her watch all the time. But, as the long minutes crawled past, and further great unendurable tracts of waiting loomed up before her, intolerable as vast empty deserts to a sufferer from agoraphobia, she gradually grew almost frantic. By twelve she was convinced he wasn't coming at all.

When, not long after midnight, he arrived, and was apparently astonished by her distress, she couldn't stop herself asking why he was so late—had he forgotten he'd promised to come at ten?

"No, I didn't forget, but I had to finish something," he said, as if no apology or further explanation were needed.

"But after you'd promised—why didn't you ring up and say you'd be late?" She broke the resolution she'd kept for years by letting her voice sound reproachful. But he merely looked blankly at her, as if she'd said something completely unreasonable.

"I was working. How could I ring up?"

She saw the futility of going on even while her lips involuntarily reshaped the words: "But you promised . . ."

Unshakable, uncomprehending, he repeated. "I was working," with a touch of exasperation this time, so that she said no more, and for a hateful moment felt she knew nothing whatever about him.

It was very strange. He had such understanding of everything about her. How could he not know when he frightened and hurt her? He gave so much and so generously, supporting her absolutely, unfailingly—until the moment when, all at once, he was no longer there. She never knew when it would happen. They might be walking together in the streets around his home, or playing out one of the inexhaustible episodes of their serial games, or discussing whatever it was among the spinning galaxies or the grains of dust. Suddenly, without warning, the enclosed magic circle of their intimacy would be shattered by an indifferent, distant glance of cold cruel remoteness. She couldn't bear it, and wanted to call him back, to remind him of the cosmic rays that were supposed to have joined them in indestructible closeness—how could he desert her? But, determined not to intrude on his privacy, she kept silent, driving the fear she couldn't eradicate into the deepest recesses of her being.

Deliberate unkindness in him was unthinkable, so she reached the conclusion that, in his creative capacity, he was ruthless without knowing it, from some basic necessity. By degrees, she had given up trying to understand. He was too complex for her. She couldn't unravel the

many contradictions in him, simply accepting them, as she accepted
the fact that she was seeing less and less of him.

The twelve years' difference in their ages had now become an
enemy and an obstacle to their meeting. He suffered a heart attack and
was often ill, withdrawing from her at these times, either out of pride or
in order not to damage the image on which she depended. Seeing him
only when he was at his best, she hardly realized the gravity of his condition, was hardly aware of gradual changes in him, and felt slightly
aggrieved when he shut himself up at home and declined to see her.
However, he had only to reappear for her grievances to be forgotten
and everything to be just as it always had been.

At once the old magic revived, uniting them in their supranormal
alliance.

After one of his illnesses, when she hadn't seen him for several
weeks, she became ill herself, as if from the deprivation of his company. She was feverish, and felt an almost irresistible longing for him;
their last meeting seemed incredibly distant, as if it had taken place in
another age altogether. Hour by hour, her obsession grew stronger and
she more disturbed—she must, must, see him, even if only for a few
minutes. She controlled herself to a point during the day, but as her
temperature rose toward evening, she so far abandoned her ingrained
consideration as to telephone and ask him to come and see her. An
unknown voice answered, saying that he was not yet well enough to go
out, which he must have overheard, for he snatched the receiver, and
in a tone unfamiliar to her promised to come quite shortly.

To hear him speak in that strange voice, sounding both strained and
upset, increased her nervous distress. Perhaps he really was too unwell
to come; she wondered guiltily whether to ring again and tell him it
was unnecessary; but after a few undecided moments, her craving for
his presence obliterated these doubts.

The fever mounting in her as she waited, she swung uneasily
between nightmarish half dreams and the scarcely more reassuring
reality of her lonely flat, where he was the only visitor. Too restless to
stay in bed, she wandered about aimlessly between spells of watching
for him from the window, hardly able to contain her longing for his
arrival to rescue her from the hallucinatory fever world—he himself
seemed one of its frightening illusions when she saw him lurching and

stumbling toward her door, his bare domed head white under the streetlights.

The sight of this pathetic, unsteady figure, instead of the swift catlike prowler she was expecting, came to her as a violent, agonizing, astounding shock. It was as if she had worn his image like a locket in her heart ever since their first meeting, and only now, this moment, saw how much he had altered since then. He looked so fragile and ravaged by illness that she was horrified and for the first few seconds wanted only to take him to some safe quiet place where he could rest and recover and she could make him smile.

But when he entered the room she suddenly saw, through the mists of fever, that his elusiveness had assumed a new and terrible form. Panic engulfed her, sweeping away restraint, and she clutched his hand, gazing speechlessly at him, her eyes filling with tears. Suddenly she'd remembered the anguish of irremediable loneliness to which she had once been condemned, but which she'd believed she had escaped forever. All at once, it was threatening her again, obscuring everything else. Without knowing it, she let him lead her back to bed, but would neither lie down nor let go of his hand, distracted by semidelirious fear and the threat of her old metaphysical dread, and further confused and confounded by her own incredible blindness.

"Don't leave me!" she cried in acute distress and confusion, clinging to him as though she were drowning.

"Of course I won't leave you." The man spoke and smiled with careful kindness, calling upon the principles of a lifetime to help him deal with the situation, although it was evident that he was far too frail and depleted to do so.

She saw the pathos of his aging face, which was now that of his counterpart in the portrait, without the color, but with the same haunted transparent look, the same sad, sick, almost melting eyes. But still her irrational fear remained stronger than any other emotion; she was desperate for his assurance that he would not abandon her in the terrifying way now in the process of being made clear to her.

"Don't leave me alone. Don't go away. Promise you'll stay with me."

"I promise," he said, gently disengaging himself from her clutching hand. "Try to be quiet. It's no good suffering like this. I won't let you suffer."

He was frowning as he turned to open his briefcase, which he had put on a chair. A moment later, she saw from his expression that he'd ceased to see her, and was seized by wild agitation. All the time he was preparing an injection, she went on pleading with him, beseeching and begging him not to betray her, not to slip away, not to leave her alone in a hostile world where she didn't belong, her tear-choked, frantic, fever-voice speaking wildly of mutants and cosmic rays and their unbreakable union.

He didn't hear her. He was not listening. He had retreated into himself, the absent look on his face a protection against a too painful, too difficult situation, the demands of which he lacked the strength to fulfill. He left it to his professional conscience, which deputized for him, speaking with automatic professional kindliness and reassurance all the time he was going in and out of the bathroom and delving into his briefcase, keeping up a soothing, gentle, imperturbable singsong, as if pacifying a child or a mental patient.

"Now you must sleep," he said when he approached the bed with the filled syringe in his hand.

She had stopped crying and fallen back on the pillow in dumb despair, and for a moment he stroked her forehead, and even seemed to see her.

"Don't be frightened. I promise I won't betray you." With an excellent rendering of an affectionate, comforting smile, he pinched up the skin of her arm and inserted the needle.

She turned her head slightly toward him while the plunger went down. But his eyes were now lowered to watch the syringe, and he didn't look at her again. Already he seemed to have gone far away, and to be receding further and further each second into the frightful new strangeness which terrified her beyond words, now that at last she was starting to understand it.

Rousing herself to a last frenzied spasm of effort, she tried to will his attention to her. "Come back! I can't live without you! Have you forgotten the zebras? You can't desert me . . . You said yourself we must stay together until the end . . . you told me not to worry about afterward . . ." But the words that should have streamed out of her mouth in agonized screams came forth, if at all, as faint whispers.

He seemed unaware, withdrawing the needle, pressing cotton wool on the arm, with his remote, automatic efficiency.

"He's gone. I'm alone again," she thought, in an extremity of despair, hopelessness washing over her like the sea.

But, as if to disprove the thought, he evoked the ghost of benign paternal authority and compassion. "Sleep, poor lost lonely child. I promised you shouldn't suffer, and you see I'm keeping my promise. I always do."

He had smiled down at her as he finished speaking, a charming, gentle, half-mournful smile. While his inscrutable, deep-sunk, liquescent eyes gazed out from an absolute solitude so totally inaccessible that she was haunted by it through her racing unlucky dreams all night long, and would be haunted through all the nights of her life afterward.

THOMAS M. DISCH

The Squirrel Cage

THE terrifying thing—if that's what I mean—I'm not sure that *terrifying* is the right word—is that I'm free to write down anything I like but that no matter what I *do* write down it will make no difference—to me, to you, to whomever differences are made. But then what is meant by "a difference"? Is there ever really such a thing as change?

I ask more questions these days than formerly; I am less programmatic altogether. I wonder—is that a good thing?

This is what it is like where I am: a chair with no back to it (so I suppose you would call it a stool); a floor, walls, and a ceiling, which form, as nearly as I can judge, a cube; white, white light, no shadows—not even on the underside of the lid of the stool; me, of course; the typewriter. I have described the typewriter at length elsewhere. Perhaps I shall describe it again. Yes, almost certainly I shall. But not now. Later. Though why not now? Why not the typewriter as well as anything else?

Of the many kinds of question at my disposal, "why" seems to be the most recurrent.

What I do is this: I stand up and walk around the room from wall to wall. It is not a large room, but it's large enough for present purposes. Sometimes I even jump, but there is little incentive to do that, since there is nothing to jump *for*. The ceiling is quite too high to touch, and the stool is so low that it provides no challenge at all. If I thought anyone were *entertained* by my jumping . . . but I have no reason to suppose that. Sometimes I exercise: push-ups, somersaults, headstands, isometrics, etc. But never as much as I should. I am getting fat. Disgustingly fat and full of pimples besides. I like to squeeze the pimples on my face. Every so often I will keep one sore and open with over-much pinching, in the hope that I will develop an abscess and blood poisoning. But apparently the place is germproof. The thing never infects.

It's well-nigh impossible to kill oneself here. The walls and floor are padded, and one only gets a headache beating one's head against them. The stool and the typewriter both have hard edges, but when-ever I have tried to use *them*, they're withdrawn into the floor. That is how I know there is someone watching.

Once I was convinced it was God. I assumed that this was either heaven or hell, and I imagined that it would go on for all eternity just the same way. But if I were living in eternity already, I couldn't get fat-ter all the time. Nothing changes in eternity. So I console myself that I will someday die. Man is mortal. I eat all I can to make the day come faster. The *Times* says that that will give me heart disease.

Eating is fun, and that's the real reason I do a lot of eating. What else is there to do, after all? There is this little . . . nozzle, I suppose you'd call it, that sticks out of one wall, and all I have to do is put my mouth to it. Not the most elegant way to feed, but it tastes damn good. Some-times I just stand there for hours at a time and let it trickle in. Until *I* have to trickle. That's what the stool is for. It has a lid on it, the stool does, which moves on a hinge. It's quite clever, in a mechanical way.

If I sleep, I don't seem to be aware of it. Sometimes I do catch myself dreaming, but I can never remember what they were about. I'm not able to make myself dream at will. I would like that exceedingly. That covers all the vital functions but one—and there is an accommodation for sex too. Everything has been thought of.

I have no memory of any time before this, and I cannot say how long *this* has been going on. According to today's *New York Times* it is the sec-ond of May, 1961. I don't know what conclusion one is to draw from that.

From what I've been able to gather, reading the *Times*, my position here in this room is not typical. Prisons, for instance seem to be run along more liberal lines, usually. But perhaps the *Times* is lying, cover-ing up. Perhaps even the date has been falsified. Perhaps the entire paper, every day, is an elaborate forgery and this is actually 1950, not 1961. Or maybe they are antiques and I am living whole centuries after they were printed, a fossil. Anything seems possible. I have no way to judge.

Sometimes I make up little stories while I sit here on my stool in front of the typewriter. Sometimes they are stories about the people in the *New York Times*, and those are the best stories. Sometimes they are just about people I make up, but those aren't so good because . . .

They're not so good because I think everybody is dead. I think I may be the only one left, sole survivor of the breed. And they just keep me here, the last one, alive, in this room, this cage, to look at, to observe, to make their observations of, to—I don't *know* why they keep me alive. And if everyone is dead, as I've supposed, then who are they, these supposed observers? Aliens? *Are* there aliens? I don't know. Why are they studying me? What do they hope to learn? Is it an experiment? What am I supposed to do? Are they waiting for me to say something, to write something on this typewriter? Do my responses or lack of responses confirm or destroy a theory of behavior? Are the testers happy with their results? They give no indications. They efface themselves, veiling themselves behind these walls, this ceiling, this floor. Perhaps no human could stand the sight of them. But maybe they are only scientists, and not aliens at all. Psychologists at MIT, perhaps, such as frequently are shown in the *Times*: blurred, dotty faces, bald heads, occasionally a mustache, certificate of originality. Or, instead, young crewcut army doctors studying various brainwashing techniques. Reluctantly, of course. History and a concern for freedom have forced them to violate their own (privately held) moral codes. Maybe I *volunteered* for this experiment! Is that the case? O God, I hope not! Are you reading this, Professor? Are you reading this, Major? Will you let me out now? I want to leave this experiment *right now*.

Yeah.

Well, we've been through that little song and dance before, me and my typewriter. We've tried just about every password there is. Haven't we, typewriter? And as you can see (can you see?)—here we are still.

They are aliens, obviously.

Sometimes I write poems. Do you like poetry? Here's one of the poems I wrote. It's called "Grand Central Terminal." ("Grand Central Terminal" is the right name for what most people wrongly call "Grand Central Station." This—and other priceless information—comes from the *New York Times*.)

Grand Central Terminal

How can you be unhappy
when you see how high
the ceiling is?

                    My!
the ceiling is high!
High as the sky!
So who are *we*
to be gloomy here?

                Why,
there isn't even room
to die, my dear.

This is the tomb
of some giant so great
that if he ate
us there would be
simply no taste.

                Gee,
what a waste
that would be
of you and me.

And sometimes, as you can also see, I just sit here copying old poems over again, or maybe copying the poem that the *Times* prints each day. The *Times* is my only source of poetry. Alas the day! I wrote "Grand Central Terminal" rather a long time ago. Years. I can't say exactly how many years though.

I have no measures of time here. No day, no night, no waking and sleeping, no chronometer but the *Times*, ticking off its dates. I can remember dates as far back as 1957. I wish I had a little diary that I could keep here in the room with me. Some record of my progress. If I could just save up my old copies of the *Times*. Imagine how, over the years, they would pile up. Towers and stairways and cozy burrows of newsprint. It would be a more humane architecture, would it not? This cube that I occupy does have drawbacks from the strictly human point of view. But I am not allowed to keep yesterday's edition. It is always taken away, whisked off, before today's edition is delivered. I should be thankful, I suppose, for what I have.

What if the *Times* went bankrupt? What if, as is often threatened, there were a newspaper strike! Boredom is not, as you might suppose, the great problem. Eventually—very soon, in fact—boredom becomes a great challenge. A stimulus.

My body. Would you be interested in my body? I used to be. I used to regret that there were no mirrors in here. Now, on the contrary, I am grateful. How gracefully, in those early days, the flesh would wrap itself about the skeleton; now, how it droops and languishes! I used to dance by myself hours on end, humming my own accompaniment—leaping, rolling about, hurling myself spread-eagled against the padded walls. I became a connoisseur of kinesthesia. There is great joy in movement—free, unconstrained speed.

Life is so much tamer now. Age dulls the edge of pleasure, hanging in wreaths of fat on the supple Christmas tree of youth.

I have various theories about the meaning of life. Of life *here*. If I were somewhere else—in the world I know of from the *New York Times*, for instance, where so many exciting things happen every *day* that it takes half a million words to tell about them—there would be no problem at all. One would be so busy running around—from 53rd Street to 42nd Street from 42nd Street to the Fulton Street Fish Market, not to mention all the journeys one might make *crosstown*—that one wouldn't have to worry whether life had a meaning.

In the daytime one could shop for a multitude of goods, then in the evening, after a dinner at a fine restaurant, to the theater or a cinema. Oh, life would be so full if I were living in New York! If I were free! I spend a lot of time, like this, imagining what New York must be like, imagining what other people are like, what I would be like with other people, and in a sense my life here is full from imagining such things.

One of my theories is that they (*you* know, ungentle reader, who they are, I'm sure) are waiting for me to make a confession. This poses problems. Since I remember nothing of my previous existence, I don't know what I should confess. I've tried confessing to everything: political crimes, sex crimes (I especially like to confess to sex crimes), traffic offenses, spiritual pride. My god, what *haven't* I confessed to? Nothing seems to work. Perhaps I just haven't confessed to the crimes I really did commit, whatever they were. Or perhaps (which seems more and more likely) the theory is at fault.

I have another theory.

A brief hiatus.

The *Times* came, so I read the day's news, then nourished myself at the fount of life, and now I am back at my stool.

I have been wondering whether, if I were living in that world, the world of the *Times*, I would be a pacifist or not. It is certainly the central issue of modern morality and one would have to take a stand. I have been thinking about the problem for some years, and I am inclined to believe that I am in favor of disarmament. On the other hand, in a practical sense I wouldn't object to the bomb if I could be sure it would be dropped on me. There is definitely a schism in my being between the private sphere and the public sphere.

On one of the inner pages, behind the political and international news, was a wonderful story headlined: BIOLOGISTS HAIL MAJOR DISCOVERY. Let me copy it out for your benefit:

Washington, D.C.—Deep-sea creatures with brains but no mouths are being hailed as a major biological discovery of the twentieth century.

The weird animals, known as pogonophores, resemble slender worms. Unlike ordinary worms, however, they have no digestive system, no excretory organs, and no means of breathing, the National Geographic Society says. Baffled scientists who first examined pogonophores believed that only parts of the specimens had reached them.

Biologists are now confident that they have seen the whole animal, but still do not understand how it manages to live. Yet they know it does exist, propagate, and even think, after a fashion, on the floors of deep waters around the globe. The female pogonophore lays up to thirty eggs at a time. A tiny brain permits rudimentary mental processes.

All told, the pogonophore is so unusual that biologists have set up a special phylum for it alone. This is significant because a phylum is such a broad biological classification that creatures as diverse as fish, reptiles, birds, and men are all included in the phylum Chordata.

Settling on the sea bottom, a pogonophore secretes a tube around itself and builds it up, year by year, to a height of perhaps five feet. The tube resembles a leaf of white grass, which may account for the fact that the animal went so long undiscovered.

The pogonophore apparently never leaves its self-built prison, but crawls up and down inside at will. The wormlike animal may reach a length of fourteen inches, with a diameter of less than a twenty-fifth of an inch. Long tentacles wave from its top end.

Zoologists once theorized that the pogonophore, in an early stage, might store enough food in its body to allow it to fast later on. But young pogonophores also lack a digestive system.

It's amazing the amount of things a person can learn just by reading the *Times* every day. I always feel so much more *alert* after a good read at the paper. And creative. Herewith, a story about pogonophores:

Striving

The Memoirs of a Pogonophore

Introduction

IN May of 1961 I had been considering the purchase of a pet. One of my friends had recently acquired a pair of tarsiers, another had adopted a boa constrictor, and my nocturnal roommate kept an owl caged above his desk.

A nest (or school?) of pogs was certainly one-up on their eccentricities. Moreover, since pogonophores do not eat, excrete, sleep, or make noise, they would be ideal pets. In June I had three dozen shipped to me from Japan at considerable expense.

[A brief interruption in the story: Do you feel that it's credible? Does it possess the *texture* of reality? I thought that by beginning the story by mentioning those other pets, I would clothe my invention in greater verisimilitude. Were you taken in?]

Being but an indifferent biologist, I had not considered the problem of maintaining adequate pressure in my aquarium. The pogonophore is used to the weight of an entire ocean. I was not equipped to meet such demands. For a few exciting days I watched the surviving pogs rise and descend in their translucent white shells. Soon, even these died. Now, resigned to the commonplace, I stock my aquarium with Maine lobsters for the amusement and dinners of occasional out-of-town visitors.

I have never regretted the money I spent on them: man is rarely given to know the sublime spectacle of the rising pogonophore—and then but briefly. Although I had at that time only the narrowest conception of the thoughts that passed through the rudimentary brain of the sea worm ("Up up up Down down down"), I could not help admiring its persistence. The pogonophore does not sleep. He climbs to the top of the inside passage of his shell, and, when he has reached the top, he retraces his steps to the bottom of his shell. The pogonophore never tires of his self-imposed regimen. He performs his duty scrupulously and with honest joy. He is *not* a fatalist.

The memoirs that follow this introduction are not allegory. I have not tried to "interpret" the inner thoughts of the pogonophore. There is no need for that, since the pogonophore himself has given us the most eloquent record of his spiritual life. It is transcribed on the core of translucent white shell in which he spends his entire life.

Since the invention of the alphabet it has been a common conceit that the markings on shells or the sand-etched calligraphy of the journeying snail are possessed of true linguistic meaning. Cranks and eccentrics down the ages have tried to decipher these codes, just as other men have sought to understand the language of the birds. Unavailingly. I do not claim that the scrawls and shells of *common* shellfish can be translated; the core of the pogonophore's shell, however, can be—for I have broken the code!

With the aid of a United States Army manual on cryptography (obtained by what devious means I am not at liberty to reveal) I have learned the grammar and syntax of the pogonophore's secret language. Zoologists and others who would like to verify my solution of the crypt may reach me through the editor of this publication.

In all thirty-six cases I have been able to examine, the indented traceries on the insides of these shells have been the same. It is my theory that the sole purpose of the pogonophore's tentacles is to follow the course of this "message" up and down the core of his shell and thus, as it were, to think. The shell is a sort of externalized stream-of-consciousness.

It would be possible (and in fact it is an almost irresistible temptation) to comment on the meaning that these memoirs possess for mankind. Surely, there is a philosophy compressed into these precious shells by Nature herself. But before I begin my commentary, let us examine the text itself.

The Text

I

Up. Uppity, up, up. The Top.

I I

Down. Downy, down, down. Thump. The Bottom.

I I I

A description of my typewriter. The keyboard is about one foot wide. Each key is flush to the next and marked with a single letter of the alphabet, or with two punctuation signs, or with one number and one punctuation sign. The letters are not ordered as they are in the alphabet, alphabetically, but seemingly at random. It is possible that they are in code. Then there is a space bar. There is not, however, either a margin control or a carriage return. The platen is not visible, and I can never see the words I'm writing. What does it all look like? Perhaps it is made immediately into a book by automatic linotypists. Wouldn't that be nice? Or perhaps my words just go on and on in one endless line of writing. Or perhaps this typewriter is just a fraud and leaves no record at all.

Some thoughts on the subject of futility:

I might just as well be lifting weights as pounding at these keys. Or rolling stones up to the top of a hill from which they immediately roll back down. Yes, and I might as well tell lies as the truth. It makes no difference what I say.

That is what is so terrifying. Is *terrifying* the right word?

I seem to be feeling rather poorly today, but I've felt poorly before! In a few more days I'll be feeling all right again. I need only be patient, and then . . .

What do they want of me here? If only I could be sure that I were serving some good *purpose*. I cannot help worrying about such things. Time is running out. I'm hungry again. I suspect I am going crazy. That is the end of my story about the pogonophores.

A hiatus.

Don't *you* worry that I'm going crazy? What if I got catatonia? Then *you'd* have nothing to read. Unless they gave *you* my copies of the *New York Times*. It would serve *you* right.

You: the mirror that is denied to me, the shadow that I do not cast, my faithful observer, who reads each freshly minted *pensée*; Reader.

You: Horrorshow monster, Bug-Eyes, Mad Scientist, Army Major, who prepares the wedding bed of my death and tempts me to it.

You: Other!

Speak to me!

YOU: What shall I say, Earthling?

I: Anything so long as it is another voice than my own, flesh that is not my own flesh, lies that I do not need to invent for myself. I'm not particular, I'm not proud. But I doubt sometimes—you won't think this is too melodramatic of me?—that I'm real.

YOU: I know the feeling. (Extending a tentacle) May I?

I: (Backing off) Later. Just now I thought we'd talk. (You begin to fade.)

There is so much about you that I don't understand. Your identity is not distinct. You change from one being to another as easily as I might switch channels on a television set, if I had one. You are too secretive as well. You should get about in the world more. Go places, show yourself, enjoy life. If you're shy, I'll go out with you. You let yourself be undermined by fear, however.

YOU: Interesting. Yes, definitely most interesting. The subject evidences acute paranoid tendencies, fantasies with almost delusional intensity. Observe his tongue, his pulse, his urine. His stools are irregular. His teeth are bad. He is losing his hair.

I: I'm losing my mind.

YOU: He's losing his mind.

I: I'm dying.

YOU: He's dead.

(Fades until there is nothing but the golden glow of the eagle on his cap, a glint from the oak leaves on his shoulders.) But he has not died in vain. His country will always remember him, for by his death he has made this nation free.

(Curtain. Anthem.)

Hi, it's me again. Surely you haven't forgotten *me*? Your old friend, me? Listen carefully now—this is my plan. I'm going to escape from this damned prison, by God, and *you're* going to help me. Twenty people may read what I write on this typewriter, and of those twenty, nineteen could see me rot here forever without batting an eyelash. But not number 20. Oh no! He—*you*—still has a conscience. He/you will send me a Sign. And when I've seen the Sign, I'll know that someone out there is trying to help. Oh, I won't expect miracles overnight. It may take months, years even, to work out a foolproof escape, but just the knowledge that there is someone out there trying to help will give me the strength to go on from day to day, from issue to issue of the *Times*.

You know what I sometimes wonder? I sometimes wonder why the *Times* doesn't have an editorial about me. They state their opinion on everything else—Castro's Cuba, the shame of our southern states, the sales tax, the first days of spring.

What about me!

I mean, isn't it an injustice the way *I'm* being treated? Doesn't anybody care and if not, why not? Don't tell me they don't know I'm here. I've been years now writing, writing. Surely they have some idea. Surely *someone* does!

These are serious questions. They demand serious appraisal. I insist that they be *answered*.

I don't really expect an answer, you know. I have no false hopes left, none. I know there's no Sign that will be shown me, that even if there is, it will be a lie, a lure to go on hoping. I know that I am alone in my fight against this injustice. I know all that—and *I don't care!* My will is still unbroken, and my spirit free. From my isolation, out of the stillness, from the depths of this white, white light, I say this to you—I DEFY YOU! Do you hear that? I said: I DEFY YOU!

Dinner again. Where does the time all go to?

While I was eating dinner I had an idea for something I was going to say here, but I seem to have forgotten what it was. If I remember, I'll jot it down. Meanwhile, I'll tell you about my other theory.

My *other* theory is that this is a squirrel cage. You know? Like the kind you find in a small town park. You might even have one of your own, since they don't have to be very big. A squirrel cage is like most any other kind of cage except it has an exercise wheel. The squirrel gets *into* the wheel and starts running. His running makes the wheel turn, and the turning of the wheel makes it necessary for him to keep running inside it. The exercise is supposed to keep the squirrel healthy. What I don't understand is why they put the squirrel in the cage in the first place. Don't they know what it's going to be like for the poor little squirrel? Or don't they care?

They don't care.

I remember now what it was I'd forgotten. I thought of a new story. I call it "An Afternoon at the Zoo." I made it up myself. It's very short, and it has a moral. This is my story:

An Afternoon at the Zoo

THIS is the story about Alexandra. Alexandra was the wife of a famous journalist, who specialized in science reporting. His work took him to all parts of the country, and since they had not been blessed with children, Alexandra often accompanied him. However, this often became very boring, so she had to find something to do to pass the time. If she had seen all the movies playing in the town they were in, she might go to a museum, or perhaps to a ball game, if she were interested in seeing a ball game that day. One day she went to a zoo.

Of course it was a small zoo, because this was a small town. Tasteful but not spectacular. There was a brook that meandered all about the grounds. Ducks and a lone black swan glided among the willow branches and waddled out onto the lawn to snap up bread crumbs from the visitors. Alexandra thought the swan was beautiful.

Then she went to a wooden building called the "Rodentiary." The cages advertised rabbits, otters, raccoons, etc. Inside the cages was a litter of nibbled vegetables and droppings of various shapes and colors. The animals must have been behind the wooden partitions, sleeping. Alexandra found this disappointing, but she told herself that rodents were hardly the most important thing to see at any zoo.

Nearby the Rodentiary, a black bear was sunning himself on a rock ledge. Alexandra walked all about the demi-lune of bars without seeing other members of the bear's family. He was an enormous bear.

She watched the seals splash about in their concrete pool, and then she moved on to find the Monkey House. She asked a friendly peanut vendor where it was, and he told her it was closed for repairs.

"How sad!" Alexandra exclaimed.

"Why don't you try Snakes and Lizards?" the peanut vendor asked.

Alexandra wrinkled her nose in disgust. She'd hated reptiles ever since she was a little girl. Even though the Monkey House was closed she bought a bag of peanuts and ate them herself. The peanuts made her thirsty, so she bought a soft drink and sipped it through a straw, worrying about her weight all the while.

She watched peacocks and a nervous antelope, then turned off onto a path that took her into a glade of trees. Poplar trees, perhaps. She was alone there, so she took off her shoes and wiggled her toes, or performed some equivalent action. She liked to be alone like this some-times.

A file of heavy iron bars beyond the glade of trees drew Alexandra's attention. Inside the bars there was a man, dressed in a loose-fitting cotton suit—pajamas, most likely—held up about the waist with a sort of rope. He sat on the floor of his cage without looking at anything in particular. The sign at the base of the fence read:

Chordate.

"HOW lovely!" Alexandra exclaimed.

Actually, that's a very old story. I tell it a different way every time. Sometimes it goes on from the point where I left off. Sometimes Alexandra talks to the man behind the bars. Sometimes they fall in love, and she tries to help him escape. Sometimes they're both killed in the attempt, and that is *very* touching. Sometimes they get caught and are put behind the bars *together*. But because they love each other so much, imprisonment is easy to endure. That is also touching, in its way. Sometimes they make it to freedom. After that though, after they're free, I never know what to do with the story. However, I'm sure that if I were free myself, free of this cage, it would not be a problem.

One part of the story doesn't make much sense. Who would put a person in a zoo? Me, for instance. Who would do such a thing? Aliens? Are we back to aliens again? Who can say about aliens? I mean, *I* don't know anything about them.

My theory, my best theory, is that I'm being kept here by people. Just ordinary people. It's an ordinary zoo, and ordinary people come by to look at me through the walls. They read the things I type on this typewriter as it appears on a great illuminated billboard, like the one that spells out the news headlines around the sides of the Times Tower on 42nd Street. When I write something funny, they may laugh, and when I write something serious, such as an appeal for help, they probably get bored and stop reading. Or vice versa perhaps. In any case, they don't take what I say very seriously. None of them care that I'm inside here. To them I'm just another animal in a cage. You might object that a human being is not the same thing as an animal, but isn't he, after all? They, the spectators, seem to think so. In any case, none of them is going to help me get out. None of them thinks it's at all strange or unusual that I'm in here. None of them thinks it's wrong. That's the terrifying thing.

"Terrifying?"

It's not terrifying. How can it be? It's only a story, after all. Maybe *you* don't think it's a story, because you're out there reading it on the billboard, but I know it's a story because I have to sit here on this stool making it up. Oh, it might have been terrifying once upon a time, when I first got the idea, but I've been here now for years. Years. The story has gone on far too long. Nothing can be terrifying for years on end. I only *say* it's terrifying because, you know, I have to say something. Something or other. The only thing that could terrify me now is if someone were to come in. If they came in and said, "All right, Disch, you can go now." That, truly, would be terrifying.

DAVID GRAND

Louse

POPPY'S Valium Librium Empirin #4 fills the brim of an unblemished vial. His syringe, capped by a short plastic nipple, rests on a puff of white gauze. A flaccid rubber tube coils into the shape of a circular maze. All the items are meticulously arranged on a hospital tray whose stainless steel reflects the dim red glow of camera surveillance lights. My hands are suited with rubber gloves. My face is masked. My hair is shaved from my head and arms. I smell of a sweet coconut-scented antiseptic.

"The nights feel longer, Mr. Louse," Poppy says as he wakes from a deep sleep.

"Yes, sir."

"The days feel shorter."

"Yes, sir."

"Mr. Louse?"

"Yes, sir."

"Which one is it?"

"It is night, Poppy."

"The nights feel longer."

"Yes, Poppy. They do."

Poppy breathes shallow breaths as I place his tray onto the corner of the western night table and bend over his body to search for a point of entry. As I hover over him, his forehead thickens into wrinkled folds of flesh. Within them, the folds contain clusters of what look like shattered pearls. The icy fissures cascade into tufts of a long auburn beard, greasy and patched with streaks of lint-gray. The slick hair languidly folds over his lips and jowls in such a manner that it's very difficult to read any form of expression on his face. If his beard should silently jostle around, I often imagine various affectations and looks, as, say, when one imagines life bustling about under the gaseous surface of a distant planet. I might perceive, for instance, phantoms of irony or bitterness or despair, a silent request whose message I feel individually responsible for.

Any kind of bodily motion shakes the few remaining hairs straddling his scalp; they shake and twist like antennae homing in on coded frequencies, always followed by his voice, his commands, which are delivered with a steady and stiff timbre. His eyes hide in the shadows of thick beetle-brows and high cheekbones. When they are visible, they are distant and shy, veiling his dictates with numb appraisals.

"Try here," he says, rolling over onto his stomach. With a looping brown fingernail, he points me down the shingled path of his body. My eyes travel the curves of the nail to his loincloth. The elastic waist hugs the bones of his hips, which are distended and sharply angle into his legs. His skin is like moth-eaten velvet and shimmers like the phosphorescence of a crashed wave. I fear that a slip of the finger will puncture or bruise its cloudy sheen.

As I take hold of the back of his knee I begin humming the third movement of Mozart's "Requiem" in the key of D minor. I am to hum this as I administer his injection.

I uncoil the rubber tube and tie it around his leg. Taut. Very taut. Poppy's few remaining open veins appear and disappear and reappear. When I find a thin streak of blue that I think might take the needle, I remove the plastic nipple from the tip of the syringe, fill the tube to its proper measure, tap away the remaining air bubbles inside the tube, and then slowly and deeply insert the liquid into his vein. When I push the plunger to the bottom, I remove the needle as slowly as I inserted it and delicately replace it on the tray. I remove the rubber band and recoil.

I stop humming.

The low moan of the chambers' ventilation system changes frequently as Poppy sighs from the back of his throat. His leg spasms a little and his foot trails off to the edge of the bed. His chest falls into his pillows. He picks up on Mozart's melody from where I left off, humming a nasal hum.

I promptly step away from him toward a large picture window covered with long smooth sheets of aluminum foil. The window nearly runs the length of the western wall and has never revealed anything more than a dim reflection of Poppy's chambers—the bed, a nightstand, the television, and a sprawl of discarded newspapers, legal pads, and Kleenex that surrounds the bed's periphery.

I proceed around the sprawl of paper and under the low-lying ducts of the ventilation system. The ventilation system, which is heat sensitive, prevents mold and mildew from collecting on or within these papers' fibers, or between any ordinary crevices for that matter, in gaps of generally unseen and unimagined space. Poppy's chambers are so dry, in fact, that on occasion, a corner of an old *Wall Street Journal* has been known to curl up like the ear of a curious dog.

Over time, the debris deposited around Poppy's bed has shaped itself into small mounds resembling mountain ranges. Peaks and valleys, plateaus and plains, buttress against the edges of canyons and ravines made of uneven folds of newsprint. It is not hard to imagine that if water were to fall from the ceiling, creeks, streams, and rivers would flow into lakes and estuaries, and Poppy's bed would buoy up like a raft floating over the black-bottom silt of a swamp.

I close the door to his chambers so that it slams shut. This way he can hear the latch click and imagine my hand falling comfortably to my side. I bow my head, dim the lights of the long hallway, and walk with slow strides toward the kitchen.

The floors of the western wing, as well as the eastern, northern, and southern wings, are covered in gray linoleum. The red pulses of camera surveillance lights flicker and streak down the glossy finish. The illumination reflects off glass cabinets filled with Poppy's paper planes, of which there are thousands, each named for either Kathryn, Betty, or Jane, women whose holographic images adorn the medicine cabinets in the three bathrooms adjoining Poppy's chambers. Each woman looks down over her own province of scrubbed white marble. Each has eyes that can see to anywhere in her room. The heads turn as a subject crosses before them and nod when a subject kneels to the floor. The images, in their entirety, are equipped to glow in the dark; when they do, they cast a soft greenish hue onto the walls.

The glass cabinets encasing Poppy's aircraft line the outer corridors of the entire thirty-third floor. They hold thousands of planes each of whose creases were crafted by Poppy with much care. When the old man snaps one away with his brittle wrist, his expression constricts and he looks as though he calculates the angles of ascent, counts the seconds the wings remain aloft, contemplates the pull of gravity on the nose. I occasionally see him watch me lift a plane from the border of linoleum on the periphery of his chambers. As I pinch the fuselage and delicately place it on a silver tray, I can feel his eyes wince when the belly's fold touches my reflection in the metal.

Footsteps approach in the outer corridor. They approach slowly and softly but are still audible. When they reach the main entrance of Poppy's chambers I find that they belong to the woman I am to call Madame. I assume she is his wife. I do not know her proper name. She appears in Poppy's chambers every night when he is sleeping. She is tall and walks with the graceful posture of a dancer, with her head cocked back, her shoulders square, her arms resting gently at her sides. She is always dressed in mourning from head to toe. I have, therefore, never seen her face. She wears a long and loose black dress, and a veil that only reveals the crescent shape of her eyes. They, and her hands, look like those of a woman much younger than Poppy. When she speaks, her voice is always hushed in a whisper. I am not to ask her anything. I am to provide for her needs and respond only in the way I have been instructed to respond.

When Madame enters the room, she carefully walks over the newspapers, approaches Poppy's bed, and kneels before his sleeping body. She bows her head, clasps her hands together, and begins praying in silence.

After a few moments, she lifts her head.

"Has he asked for me this evening, Mr. Louse?"

"Yes, Madame," I say.

"And what did he say when he spoke of me?"

"He said that your radiance and beauty went unmatched by any other and that you were the sole proprietress over his will to live."

She looks at Poppy and begins to weep.

"I love him so," she says. "He is my refuge, my heart, my . . ."

And she weeps some more.

At this point I walk to her side and offer my handkerchief, which I keep in my pants pocket for exactly this task.

She takes the handkerchief from my hand and dabs at her eyes and her nose through the veil.

"You will tell him I love him," she says.

"Of course, Madame. As always."

She raises her head and momentarily looks at me. "Very good, Mr. Louse. Will you please give me a moment alone with him?"

"Of course, Madame."

Madame hands the handkerchief back to me. She bows her head in prayer again and begins humming the third movement of Mozart's "Requiem."

I exit the chambers through the corridor that leads to Bathroom Number Three. I walk between the television and the hologram of Jane and go directly to the incinerator in the supply closet, where I dispose of the handkerchief and replace it with a new one.

When I arrive back in Poppy's chambers the woman is gone.

As she does every night, on Poppy's eastern nightstand she has left behind a narrow glass box filled with three large butterflies. They are mounted on pins that stick up from a piece of Styrofoam. The wings are extended and rest against the glass. Tonight the butterflies contain the colors of red, yellow, green, and black.

I return to my spot by the wall and listen to the ambient noises of the casino on the television at the foot of Poppy's bed. And as he does every night, Poppy opens his eyes to the butterflies on the table and turns to me.

"Herman?"

"Yes, sir?"

"Did I ask you to wake me?"

"Not to my recollection, sir."

"Then what am I doing awake, Mr. Louse?"

"You woke up, sir."

"On my own?"

"As far as I can tell."

"Is there anything unusual to report at all, Mr. Louse?"

"Nothing unusual, sir."

The old man presses the button of the intercom on his remote control and speaks.

"Mr. Sherwood. Play back last three minutes of my chambers."

The television fades to black. Poppy is asleep in his bed. Madame delicately places the box of butterflies on the table. She gracefully exits the room. I return to my corner. We are motionless. Poppy's eyes open. He sits up.

"Herman?"

"Yes, sir?"

"Did I ask you to wake me?"

"Not to my recollection, sir."

"Then what am I doing awake, Mr. Louse?"

"You woke up, sir."

"On my own?"

"As far as I can tell."

"Is there anything unusual to report at all, Mr. Louse?"

"Nothing unusual, sir."

The old man presses the button of the intercom on his remote control.

"One more time, Mr. Sherwood."

The television fades to black. Poppy is asleep in his bed. Madame delicately places the box of butterflies on the table. She gracefully exits the room. I return to my corner. We are motionless. Poppy's eyes open. He sits up.

"Herman?"

"Yes, sir?"

"Did I ask you to wake me?"

"Not to my recollection, sir."

"Then what am I doing awake, Mr. Louse?"

"You woke up, sir."

"On my own?"

"As far as I can tell."

"Is there anything unusual to report at all, Mr. Louse?"

"Nothing unusual, sir."

The old man presses the button of the intercom on his remote control.

"Thank you, Mr. Sherwood." He turns to me as he lifts the glass box of butterflies from the night table. "Herman?"

"Yes, sir?"

"Please place the box in the safe."

"Yes, Poppy," I say, fully aware of what's to be done.

He holds out the box of colorful butterflies for me to take away. I step up to his bed and gently remove it from his outstretched hand and cradle it in my arms.

In the middle of the southern wing is a tall and wide wooden coffered door with an iron handle in the shape of a pyramid. I remove the study key from my pocket and insert its silver teeth into the iron latch. When I push the heavy door open it makes a long, scraping sound. It disturbs the stale air of the small vestibule adjoining the larger room, which is separated by an exact duplicate of the door I have just opened, only of smaller dimensions. I close the larger door behind me and step through the smaller door. An electric eye turns on the air-conditioning as well as the cameras. Flashing red lights glow in the corners and from the ceiling. I am always tempted to look into one of the cameras to let Mr. Sherwood know that I am aware he is watching me. However, this is considered intolerable behavior. *Becoming self-conscious of the camera defeats our surveillance goals. [We] better serve [ourselves] and the staff by remaining candid and forgetting that the cameras are present. Forgetting that the cameras are present aids in our effort to securely keep [us] from remembering; the less self-conscious [we] are of [our] surroundings, the easier it is to forget where [we] are. Therefore, in order for [us] to properly continue forgetting, [we] must fully disregard all forms of public surveillance equipment. If [we] choose not to disregard the presence of cameras, microphones, appointed observers, etc., [we] will be made to suffer through a necessary public correction.*

I imagine a pair of passing eyes in a corridor, a stranger's eyes I don't know, or wish to know. This way if I accidentally do peer into a camera it appears that I am looking through it, as if it is invisible.

Every night when I have the opportunity to walk across this room I catch glimpses of all the objects that inhabit this space, everything that makes the room smell like leather and dust and the timeless decay of the past. I categorize, make an inventory of what I see to remember for later when I am not here: art deco and art nouveau furniture; rolls of carpeting; parts of old movie sets; open cartons filled with Juvenia watches; unsmoked and half-smoked cigarettes; bars of soap; aviation trophies, plaques, and medals; movie equipment; Tiffany lamps; marble statues; ceramic quails; scrapbooks and articles regarding flying records; footlockers filled with screenplays; pilot logs; a gold cup from a golf tournament; hearing aids; a two-volume set of H. G. Wells's *The Outline of History*; a large ceremonial plate from William Randolph Hearst; double-breasted suits; white sports coats; leather flight jackets; brown glass medicine bottles; snap-brim Stetson hats; white yachting caps; leather-bound law books; piles and piles of white paper memos and yellow legal pads; a solid silver pistol with a note reading: "Captured from Herman Goering"; German SS binoculars in a black leather case; a cut-glass bowl inscribed: "To Herbert Horatio Blackwell from Hubert Horatio Humphrey"; hundreds of Campbells' soup cans overflowing with canceled personal checks made out to the Brown Derby, the Stork Club, and El Morocco; corporate checks from EKG Productions and Transit Air; a passport; an aged pair of brown wing-tip oxfords with curled-up toes.

I enjoy being here for many different reasons; in part because I can walk slowly and take an inventory of what's here, in part for the sensation of my feet sinking into thick, plush carpet.

Everywhere else is linoleum and marble.

The carpet makes me feel buoyant and alive. I am able to see my footsteps, like fossils, traces of my being. I feel an inexplicable and uncanny sensation of familiarity. I enjoy it so much I begin to hum. It is a melody of my own, one resembling the third movement of Mozart's "Requiem," but somehow a little different, a little less melancholic, a little bit mirthful even, in a major key.

I walk with light steps, humming, letting the melody build, louder and more complex until it turns into something completely its own, or at least feels to have its own beginning, middle, and end. The intermittent pulse of sound reminds me of a scene from one of Poppy's old films, *H.A. 13-3*, in which a train, blowing its whistle, slowly winds through a mountain pass. I can clearly see the scene in my mind, and see beyond it, to a distant desert. However, the desert isn't part of the film. In fact, it isn't an image I can ascribe to any place I remember. I try to locate a place for it in my mind, and as I do, the image fades. The desert dissolves. In its place, another image is revealed, this one of myself with a full head of hair. I am reflected in a large tinted window, through which I can see a dry, unobstructed valley expanding and eventually rising into mountains. There is another figure reflected in the window somewhere behind me, but the features of this figure are hazy and distorted and shimmer with motion.

As I walk over the carpeting, I continue to hum this melody, wishing the darkened figure would reveal itself. But the images freeze as I pass a photograph on the wall of a large propeller plane on fire diving down in a spin and a blur over an open meadow. Focused in the foreground, standing shoulder to shoulder, are Poppy and Dr. Barnum. Both of the men are youthful, dressed in flight jackets and khaki pants. Their posture is stiff, their smiles candid. Poppy's hair is short and well-groomed. He is clean shaven, all but for a pencil-thin mustache that hugs his upper lip. His eyes are stern, almost shy. He holds a revolver in his right hand. Dr. Barnum holds the tail of a dead opossum over an open ditch.

I immediately stop. I stop humming. I stand motionless. The memory fades as quickly and spontaneously as it came.

Although I don't remember anything within the memoranda that states I should not be humming, humming a tune like the tune I hum as I am ready to inject Poppy with his pharmaceutical, I do not wish . . . But now . . . yes, I do remember. I remember a caveat to an old memo, in which he stated that staff members should know better than to mix forms of behavior appropriate to one particular task with similar forms of behavior associated with a completely different task. It would be performing what he considers an act of free will, *a variation of [his] aesthetic*, which is considered as much a form of defiance as sneaking a peek into the camera.

I move. I move quickly. I go directly to the safe without trying to show any signs of haste or guilt, anything out of the ordinary. I dial the combination, open the door, walk in, and deposit the box among the hundreds of other boxes exactly like it—all containing butterflies of varying colors.

There is no need to report my negligence. By now it has undoubtedly been noted. I will be fined accordingly. There is part of me that believes I should report my negligence; however, in no official capacity am I responsible for reporting it. Poppy takes great pride in the accuracy of his surveillance system and all those who work to enforce it. Admission of my guilt, therefore, as ethical as my intention might be, in actuality may prove to be counterintuitive in producing a more sympathetic conclusion. And so, I can only surmise that silence is the most sensible response. Besides, there is the slightest chance that what I did went unnoticed; or perhaps what I did will be judged with compassion and immediately dismissed. It is impossible to say.

I exit the study, lock the door, and walk the southern wing. I put the humming in a major key out of my head; I replace it with its proper minor key until all resonance of the impure melody is comfortably forgotten.

DONALD BARTHELME

Game

SHOTWELL keeps the jacks and the rubber ball in his attaché case and will not allow me to play with them. He plays with them, alone, sitting on the floor near the console hour after hour, chanting "onesies, twosies, threesies, foursies" in a precise, well-modulated voice, not so loud as to be annoying, not so soft as to allow me to forget. I point out to Shotwell that two can derive more enjoyment from playing jacks than one, but he is not interested. I have asked repeatedly to be allowed to play by myself, but he simply shakes his head. "Why?" I ask. "They're mine," he says. And when he has finished, when he has sated himself, back they go into the attaché case.

It is unfair but there is nothing I can do about it. I am aching to get my hands on them.

Shotwell and I watch the console. Shotwell and I live under the ground and watch the console. If certain events take place upon the console, we are to insert our keys in the appropriate locks and turn our keys. Shotwell has a key and I have a key. If we turn our keys simultaneously the bird flies, certain switches are activated and the bird flies. But the bird never flies. In one hundred thirty-three days the bird has not flown. Meanwhile Shotwell and I watch each other. We each wear a .45 and if Shotwell behaves strangely I am supposed to shoot him. If I behave strangely Shotwell is supposed to shoot me. We watch the console and think about shooting each other and think about the bird. Shotwell's behavior with the jacks is strange. Is it strange? I do not know. Perhaps he is merely a selfish bastard, perhaps his character is flawed, perhaps his childhood was twisted. I do not know.

Each of us wears a .45 and each of us is supposed to shoot the other if the other is behaving strangely. How strangely is strangely? I do not know. In addition to the .45 I have a .38 which Shotwell does not know about concealed in my attaché case, and Shotwell has a .25 caliber Beretta which I do not know about strapped to his right calf. Sometimes instead of watching the console I pointedly watch Shotwell's .45, but this is simply a ruse, simply a maneuver; in reality I am watching his hand when it dangles in the vicinity of his right calf. If he decides I am behaving strangely he will shoot me not with the .45 but with the Beretta. Similarly Shotwell pretends to watch my .45 but he is really watching my hand resting idly atop my attaché case, my hand resting idly atop my attaché case, my hand. My hand resting idly atop my attaché case.

In the beginning I took care to behave normally. So did Shotwell. Our behavior was painfully normal. Norms of politeness, consideration, speech, and personal habits were scrupulously observed. But then it became apparent that an error had been made, that our relief was not going to arrive. Owing to an oversight. Owing to an oversight we have been here for one hundred thirty-three days. When it became clear that an error had been made, that we were not to be relieved, the norms were relaxed. Definitions of normality were redrawn in the agreement of January 1, called by us, The Agreement. Uniform regulations were relaxed, and mealtimes are no longer rigorously scheduled. We eat when we are hungry and sleep when we are tired. Considerations of rank and precedence were temporarily put aside, a handsome concession on the part of Shotwell, who is a captain, whereas I am only a first lieutenant. One of us watches the console at all times rather than two of us watching the console at all times except when we are both on our feet. One of us watches the console at all times and if the bird flies then that one wakes the other and we turn our keys in the locks simultaneously and the bird flies. Our system involves a delay of perhaps twelve seconds but I do not care because I am not well, and Shotwell does not care because he is not himself. After the agreement was signed Shotwell produced the jacks and the rubber ball from his attaché case, and I began to write a series of descriptions of forms occurring in nature, such as a shell, a leaf, a stone, an animal. On the walls.

Shotwell plays jacks and I write descriptions of natural forms on the walls.

Shotwell is enrolled in a USAFI course which leads to a master's degree in business administration from the University of Wisconsin (although we are not in Wisconsin, we are in Utah, Montana, or Idaho). When we went down it was in either Utah, Montana, or Idaho, I don't remember. We have been here for one hundred thirty-three days owing to an oversight. The pale green reinforced concrete walls sweat and the air-conditioning zips on and off erratically and Shotwell reads *Introduction to Marketing* by Lassiter and Munk, making notes with a blue ballpoint pen. Shotwell is not himself, but I do not know it, he presents a calm aspect and reads *Introduction to Marketing* and makes his exemplary notes with a blue ballpoint pen, meanwhile controlling the .38 in my attaché case with one-third of his attention. I am not well.

We have been here one hundred thirty-three days owing to an oversight. Although now we are not sure what is oversight, what is plan. Perhaps the plan is for us to stay here permanently, or if not permanently at least for a year, for three hundred sixty-five days. Or if not for a year for some number of days known to them and not known to us, such as two hundred days. Or perhaps they are observing our behavior in some way, sensors of some kind, perhaps our behavior determines the number of days. It may be that they are pleased with us, with our behavior, not in every detail but in sum. Perhaps the whole thing is very successful, perhaps this whole thing is an experiment and the experiment is very successful. I do not know. But I suspect that the only way they can persuade sun-loving creatures into their pale green sweating reinforced concrete rooms under the ground is to say that the system is twelve hours on, twelve hours off. And then lock us below for some number of days known to them and not known to us. We eat well although the frozen enchiladas are damp when defrosted and the frozen devil's food cake is sour and untasty. We sleep uneasily and acrimoniously. I hear Shotwell shouting in his sleep, objecting, denouncing, cursing sometimes, weeping sometimes, in his sleep. When Shotwell sleeps I try to pick the lock on his attaché case, so as to get at the jacks. Thus far I have been unsuccessful. Nor has Shotwell been successful in picking the locks on my attaché case so as to get at the .38. I have seen the marks on the shiny surface. I laughed, in the latrine, pale green walls sweating and the air-conditioning whispering, in the latrine.

I write descriptions of natural forms on the walls, scratching them on the tile surface with a diamond. The diamond is a two-and-one-half-carat solitaire I had in my attaché case when we went down. It was for Lucy. The south wall of the room containing the console is already covered. I have described a shell, a leaf, a stone, animals, a baseball bat. I am aware that the baseball bat is not a natural form. Yet I described it. "The baseball bat," I said, "is typically made of wood. It is typically one meter in length or a little longer, fat at one end, tapering to afford a comfortable grip at the other. The end with the handhold typically offers a slight rim, or lip, at the nether extremity, to prevent slippage." My description of the baseball bat ran to 4,500 words, all scratched with a diamond on the south wall. Does Shotwell read what I have written? I do not know. I am aware that Shotwell regards my writing behavior as a little strange. Yet it is no stranger than his jacks behavior, or the day he appeared in black bathing trunks with the .25 caliber Beretta strapped to his right calf and stood over the console, trying to span with his two arms outstretched the distance between the locks. He could not do it; I had already tried, standing over the console with my two arms outstretched; the distance is too great. I was moved to comment but did not comment, comment would have provoked counter-comment, comment would have led God knows where. They had in their infinite patience, in their infinite foresight, in their infinite wisdom already imagined a man standing over the console with his two arms outstretched, trying to span with his two arms outstretched the distance between the locks.

Shotwell is not himself. He has made certain overtures. The burden of his message is not clear. It has something to do with the keys, with the locks. Shotwell is a strange person. He appears to be less affected by our situation than I. He goes about his business stolidly, watching the console, studying *Introduction to Marketing*, bouncing his rubber ball on the floor in a steady, rhythmical, conscientious manner. He appears to be less affected by our situation than I am. He is stolid. He says nothing. But he has made certain overtures, certain overtures have been made. I am not sure that I understand them. They have something to do with the keys, with the locks. Shotwell has something in mind. Stolidly he shucks the shiny silver paper from the frozen enchiladas, stolidly he stuffs them into the electric oven. But he has something in mind. But there must be a quid pro quo. I insist on a quid pro quo. I have something in mind.

I am not well. I do not know our target. They do not tell us for which city the bird is targeted. I do not know. That is planning. That is not my responsibility. My responsibility is to watch the console and when certain events take place upon the console, turn my key in the lock. Shotwell bounces the rubber ball on the floor in a steady, stolid, rhythmical manner. I am aching to get my hands on the ball, on the jacks. We have been here one hundred thirty-three days owing to an oversight. I write on the walls. Shotwell chants "onsies, twosies, threesies, foursies" in a precise, well-modulated voice. Now he cups the jacks and the rubber ball in his hands and rattles them suggestively. I do not know for which city the bird is targeted. Shotwell is not himself.

Sometimes I cannot sleep. Sometimes Shotwell cannot sleep. Sometimes when Shotwell cradles me in his arms and rocks me to sleep, singing Brahms' "Guten abend, gute Nacht," or I cradle Shotwell in my arms and rock him to sleep, singing, I understand what it is Shotwell wishes me to do. At such moments we are very close. But only if he will give me the jacks. That is fair. There is something he wants me to do with my key, while he does something with his key. But only if he will give me my turn. That is fair. I am not well.

CHRISTOPHER PRIEST

The Affirmation

THE clinic's medical center occupied one wing of the main building. Here all recipients of the athanasia treatment were given a screening before progressing further. I had never before undergone a complete medical, and found the experience in turn tiring, alarming, boring, humiliating, and interesting. I was readily impressed by the array of modern diagnostic equipment, but I was intended not to understand the functions of most of it. The preliminary screening was by direct interaction with a computer; later I was placed in a machine I took to be a whole-body scanner; after further more detailed X-raying of specific parts of my body—my head, my lower back, my left forearm, and my chest—I was briefly interviewed by a doctor, then told to dress and return to my chalet.

Seri had left to find a hotel, and there was no sign of Lareen. I sat on my bed in the cabin, reflecting on the psychological factors in hospitals, in which the removal of the patient's clothing is only the first step of many by which he is reduced to an animated slab of meat. In this condition, individuality is suppressed for the greater glory of symptoms, the former presumably interfering with the appreciation of the latter.

I read my manuscript for a while, to remind me of who I was, but then I was interrupted by the arrival of Lareen Dobey and the man who had interviewed me, Dr. Corrob. Lareen smiled wanly at me, and went to sit in the chair by the desk.

I stood up, sensing something.

"Mrs. Dobey tells me you are in doubt as to whether or not you will accept the treatment," Corrob said.

"That's right. But I wanted to hear what you had to say."

"My advice is that you should accept the treatment without delay. Your life is in great danger without it."

I glanced at Lareen, but she was looking away. "What's wrong with me?"

We have detected an anomaly in one of the main blood vessels leading to your brain. It's called a cerebrovascular aneurysm. It's a weakness in the wall of the vessel, and it could burst at any time."

"You're making it up!"

"Why do you think that?" Corrob at least looked surprised.

"You're trying to frighten me into having the treatment."

Corrob said: "I'm only telling you what we've diagnosed. I'm retained by the Lotterie as a consultant. What I'm telling you is that you have a serious condition, which if left unattended will certainly kill you."

"But why has this never been found before?"

"Perhaps you have not been examined recently. We know that when you were a child you suffered a kidney condition. Although this was dealt with at the time, it has left you with a higher than average blood pressure. You also admit to a drinking habit."

"Just a normal amount!" I said.

"In your case the normal amount should be none at all, if you care for your health. You say you are a regular drinker, taking the equivalent of a bottle of wine a day. In your condition this is extremely foolish."

Again I looked at Lareen, and now she was watching me.

"This is crazy!" I said to her. "I'm not ill!"

"That isn't really for you to decide," Corrob said. "According to the results from the cerebral angiogram, you are a very sick man." He stood with his hand on the door, as if anxious to leave. "Of course, the decision is yours, but my advice is that you should take the treatment immediately."

"Would that cure this?"

Corrob said: "Your counselor will explain."

"And there's no danger?"

"No . . . the treatment is perfectly safe."

"Then that settles it," I said. "If you're sure—"

Corrob was holding a small file I had thought must be the case notes on a patient; now I realized it must be on me. He passed it to Lareen.

"Mr. Sinclair should be admitted to the athanasia unit immediately. How much time do you require for the rehabilitation profile?"

"At least another day, perhaps two."

"Sinclair is to be given priority. The aneurysm is a severe one. There's no question that we can allow an attack to happen while he's in the clinic. If he tries to cause delays, he must be off the island tonight."

"I'll clear him by this evening."

All this had been said as if I were not there. Corrob turned back to me.

"You must take no solids after four this afternoon," he said. "If you're thirsty, you may drink water or light fruit juice. But no alcohol. Mrs. Dobey will visit you in the morning, and then you'll be admitted for the treatment. Do you understand?"

"Yes, but I want to know—"

"Mrs. Dobey will explain what will happen." He went through the door, and closed it quickly behind him. He left a whirling air space.

I sat on my bed, ignoring Lareen. I accepted what the doctor had said, even though I continued to feel as well as ever. There was something about the medical manner, the way a symptom was made to be inferior to the doctor's knowledge. I remembered visiting my G.P. a few years before, complaining of blocked sinuses. After examining me he had discovered that I had been sleeping in a centrally heated bedroom, and, worse, I had been using a proprietary brand of decongestant nose drops. Suddenly, the sinusitis was the consequence of my own misdeeds, I was to blame. I left the surgery that day feeling guilty and humbled. Now, with the departure of Corrob, I felt that I was again guilty in some way of inflicting a weakened blood vessel on myself. I had been a patient as a child, I was a drinker when an adult. For the first time in my life I felt defensive about drinking, felt the need to deny or explain or justify.

It must have been something to do with the clinic's own defensiveness; the staff, acutely conscious of the controversy surrounding the treatment, made the recipients a party to the system. The willing were inducted smoothly and conspiratorially; the unwilling or the reluctant were psychologically manipulated, then medically intimidated.

I wished Seri were with me, and I wondered how long she would be gone. I wanted the chance to be a human being again, perhaps go for a walk with her, or make love, or just sit around doing nothing.

Lareen closed the file she had been reading. "How do you feel, Peter?"

"How do you think I feel?"

"I'm sorry . . . there's no satisfaction for me in the computer being right. If it's any consolation, at least we can do something for you here. If you were still at home, it probably wouldn't have been diagnosed."

"I can still hardly believe it." Outside, a man was mowing the lawn; in the distance I could see a part of Collago Town, and behind it the headland by the harbor. I moved away from the window by the bed, and went to sit with Lareen. "The doctor said you would explain the treatment."

"For the aneurysm?"

"Yes, and the athanasia."

"Tomorrow you'll go in for conventional surgery on the diseased artery. What the surgeon will probably do is implant a temporary bypass until the artery regenerates itself. This should happen quite quickly."

"What do you mean by regenerate?" I said.

"You'll be given a number of hormonal and enzymal injections. These stimulate cell replication in parts of the body where it doesn't normally take place, such as the brain. In other parts, the enzymes control replication, preventing malignancies and keeping your organs in good condition. After the treatment, in other words, your body will constantly renew itself."

"I've heard that I have to have a checkup every year," I said.

"No, but you can if you wish. What the surgeons will also do is implant a number of microprocessor monitors. These can be checked at any of the Lotterie's offices, and if anything is going wrong you will be given advice on what to do. In some cases you can be readmitted here."

"Lareen, either the treatment is permanent or it isn't."

"It's permanent, but in a particular way. All we can do here is prevent organic decay. For instance, do you smoke?"

"No. I used to."

"Suppose you were to start again. You could smoke as many cigarettes as you wished, and you would never develop lung cancer. That's
definite. But you could still contract bronchitis or emphysema, and
carbon monoxide would put a strain on your heart. The treatment
won't prevent you from being killed in a road accident, and it won't
stop you drowning, and you can still get hernias and chilblains, and
you can still break your neck. We can stop the body degenerating, and
we can help you build immunity to infections, but if you abuse yourself
you can still find ways of causing damage."

Reminders of a body's frailties: ruptures and fractures and bruises.
The weaknesses one knew about, tried not to think about, observed in
other people, overheard in shop conversations. I was developing sensibilities about health I had never had before. Did the acquisition of
immortality simply make one more aware of death?

I said to Lareen: "How long does this take?"

"Altogether, about two or three weeks. There'll be a short recovery
period after the operation tomorrow. As soon as the consultant thinks
you're ready, the enzyme injections will start."

"I can't stand injections," I said.

"They don't use hypodermic needles. It's a bit more sophisticated
than that. Anyway, you won't be aware of the treatment."

"You mean I'll be anesthetized?" A sudden dread.

"No, but once the first injections are made you'll become semicon-
scious. It probably sounds frightening, but most patients have said they
found it pleasant."

I valued my hold on consciousness. Once, when I was twelve, I was
knocked off my bicycle by a bully and suffered a concussion and three
days' retrospective amnesia. The loss of those three days was the central
mystery of my childhood. Although I was unconscious for less than
half an hour, my return to awareness was accompanied by a sense of
oblivion behind me. When I returned to school, sporting a black eye
and a splendidly lurid bandage around my forehead, I was brought
face-to-face with the fact that those three days had not only existed, but
that I had existed within them. There had been lessons and games and
written exercises, and presumably conversations and arguments, yet I
could remember none of them. During those days I must have been

alert, conscious, and self-aware, feeling the continuity of memory, sure of my identity and existence. An event that *followed* them, though, eradicated them, just as one day death would erase all memory. It was my first experience of a kind of death, and since then, although unconsciousness itself was not to be feared, I saw memory as the key to sentience. I existed as long as I remembered.

"Lareen, are you an athanasian?"

"No, I'm not."

"Then you've never experienced the treatment."

"I've worked with patients for nearly twenty years. I can't claim any more than that."

"But you don't know what it feels like," I said.

"Not directly, no."

"The truth is, I'm scared of losing my memory."

"I understand that. My job here is to help you regain it afterwards. But it's inevitable that you must lose what you now have as your memory."

"Why is it inevitable?"

"It's a chemical process. To give you longevity we must stop the brain deteriorating. In the normal thanatic body brain cells never replicate, so your mental ability steadily declines. Every day you lose thousands of brain cells. What we do here is induce replication in the cells, so that however long you live your mental capacity is unimpaired. But when the replication begins, the new cellular activity brings almost total amnesia."

"That's precisely what frightens me," I said. A mind sliding away, life receding, continuity lost.

"You'll experience nothing that will scare you. You will enter the fugue state, which is like being in a continuous dream. In this, you'll see images from your life, remember journeys and meetings, people will seem to speak to you, you will feel able to touch, experience emotions. Your mind will be giving up what it contains. It's just your own life."

The hold released, sentience dying. Entry into fugue, where the only reality was dream.

"And when I come round I'll remember nothing about it."

"Why do you say that?"

"It's what surgeons always say, isn't it? They believe it comforts people."

"It's true. You'll wake up here in this chalet. I'll be here, and your friend, Seri."

I wanted to see Seri. I wanted Lareen to go away.

"But I'll have no memory," I said. "They'll destroy my memory."

"It can be replaced. That's my job."

In the fugue the dream dispersed, leaving a void. Life returned later, in the form of this calm-eyed, patient woman, returning my memories to me as if she were a hand writing words on blank paper.

I said: "Lareen, how can I know that afterwards I'll be the same?"

"Because nothing in you will be changed, except your capacity to live."

"But I am what I remember. If you take that away I cannot be the same person again."

"I'm trained to restore your memory, Peter. To do that, you've got to help me now."

She produced an attractively packaged folder containing a thick wad of partially printed pages.

"There isn't as much time as we would normally have, but you should be able to manage this during the evening."

"Let me see it."

"You must be as frank and truthful as possible," Lareen said, passing the folder to me. "Use as much space as you like. There's spare paper in the desk."

The papers felt heavy, auguring hours of work. I glanced at the first page, where I could write my name and address. Later, the questions dealt with school. Later, with friendships, sex, and love. There seemed no end to the questions, each phrased carefully so as to promote frankness in my answer. I found that I could not read them, that the words blurred as I flicked the pages across.

For the first time since sentence of death had been pronounced on me, I felt the stirrings of revolt. I had no intention of answering these questions.

"I don't need this," I said to Lareen. I tossed the questionnaire onto the desk. "I've already written my autobiography, and you'll have to use that."

I turned away from her, feeling angry.

"You heard what the doctor said, Peter. If you don't cooperate they'll make you leave the island tonight."

"I'm cooperating, but I'm not going to answer those questions. It's all written down already."

"Where is it? Can I see it?"

My manuscript was on my bed, where I had left it. I gave it to her. For some reason I was unable to look at her. As it was briefly in my hands the manuscript had transmitted a sense of reassurance, a link with what was soon to become my forgotten past.

I heard Lareen turn a few of the pages, and when I looked back at her she was reading quickly from the third or fourth page. She glanced at the last page, then set it aside.

"When did you write this?"

"Two years ago."

Lareen stared at the pages. "I don't like working without the questionnaire. How do I know you've left nothing out?"

"Surely that's my risk?" I said. "Anyway, it's complete." I described the way I had written, how I had set myself the task of expressing wholeness and truth on paper.

She turned again to the last page. "It isn't finished. Do you realize that?"

"I was interrupted, but it doesn't matter. I was almost at the end, and although I did try to finish it later, it seemed better the way it is." Lareen said nothing, watching me and manipulating more from me. Resisting her, I said: "It's unfinished because my life is unfinished."

"If you wrote it two years ago, what's happened since?"

"That's the point, isn't it?" I was still feeling hostile to her, yet in spite of this her strategic silences continued to influence me. Another came, and I was unable to resist it. "When I wrote the manuscript I found that my life formed into patterns, and that everything I had done fitted into them. Since I finished writing I've found that it's still true, that all I've done in the last two years has just added details to a shape."

"I'll have to take this away and read it," Lareen said.

"All right. But take care of it."

"Of course I'll be careful."

"I feel it's a part of me, something that can't be replaced."

"I could replicate it for you," Lareen said, and laughed as if she had made a joke. "I mean, I'll get it photocopied for you. Then you can have the original back and I'll work with the copy."

I said: "That's what they're going to do to me, isn't it? I'm going to be photocopied. The only difference is that I won't get the original back. I'll be given the copy, but the original will be blank."

"It was only a joke, Peter."

"I know, but you made me think."

"Do you want to reconsider filling out my questionnaire? If you don't trust the manuscript—"

"It's not that I distrust," I said. "I live by what I wrote, because I *am* what I wrote."

I closed my eyes, turning away from her again. How could I ever forget that obsessive writing and rewriting, the warm summer, the hillside view of Jethra? I particularly remembered being on the veranda of the villa I had borrowed from Colan the evening I made my most exciting discovery: that recollection was only partial, that the artistic re-creation of the past constituted a higher truth than mere memory. Life could be rendered in metaphorical terms; these were the patterns I mentioned to Lareen. The actual details of, for instance, my years at school were only of incidental interest, yet considered metaphorically, as an experience of learning and growing, they became a larger, higher event. I related to them directly, because they had been my own experiences, but they were also related to the larger body of human experience because they dealt with the verities. Had I merely recounted the humdrum narrative, the catalog of anecdotal details in literal memory, I should have been telling only half the story.

I could not separate myself from my context, and in this my manuscript became a wholeness, describing my living, describing my life.

I therefore knew that to answer Lareen's questionnaire would produce only half-truths. There was no room for elaboration in literal answers, no capacity for metaphor, or for *story*.

Lareen was glancing at her wristwatch.

"Do you know it's after three?" she said. "You missed lunch, and you're not allowed food after four."

"Can I get a meal at this time?"

"At the refectory. Tell the staff you're starting treatment tomorrow, and they'll know what to give you."

"Where's Seri? Shouldn't she be back by now?"

"I told her not to be back before five."

"I want her with me tonight," I said.

"That's up to you and her. She mustn't be here when you go up to the clinic."

I said: "But afterwards, can I see her then?"

"Of course you can. We'll both need her." Lareen had tucked my manuscript under her arm, ready to take it away, but now she pulled it out again. "How much does Seri know about you, about your background?"

"We've talked a bit while we were traveling. We both talked about ourselves."

"Look, I've had an idea." Lareen held out the manuscript for me to take. "I'll read this later, while you're in the clinic. Tonight, let Seri read this, and talk to her about it. The more she knows about you the better. It could be very important."

I took the manuscript back, thinking of the way my life and privacy were being invaded. In writing of myself I had exposed myself; in the manuscript I was naked. I had not written to promote or excuse myself; I had just been honest, and in the process had found myself frequently unlikable. For this reason, the very idea of someone else reading the manuscript would have been unthinkable a few weeks before. Yet two women I hardly knew were now to read my work, and presumably would know me as well as I knew myself.

Even as I resented the intrusion a part of me rushed towards them, urging them to close scrutiny of my identity. In their interpretation, passed back to me, I would become myself again.

After Lareen had left I walked across the sloping lawns to the refectory and was given the authorized pretreatment meal. The condemned man ate a light salad, and afterwards was still hungry.

Seri reappeared in the evening, tired from being in the sun all day and walking too far. She had eaten before returning, and again I glimpsed the effect of what was happening. Already our temporary liaison was disrupted; we spent a day apart, ate meals at different times.

Afterwards our lives would proceed at different paces. I talked to her about what had happened during the day, what I had learned.

"Do you believe them?" she said.

"I do now."

Seri placed her hands on the sides of my face, touching my temples with light fingertips. "They think you will die."

"They're hoping it won't happen tonight," I said. "Very bad for publicity."

"You mustn't excite yourself."

"What does that mean?"

"Separate beds tonight."

"The doctor said nothing about sex."

"No, but I did."

The energy had gone out of her teasing, and I sensed a growing silence within her. She was acting like a concerned relative before an operation, making bad-taste jokes about bedpans and enemas, covering up a darker fear.

I said: "Lareen wants you to help with the rehabilitation."

"Do you want me to?"

"I can't imagine it without you. That's why you came, isn't it?"

"You know why I'm here, Peter." She hugged me then, but turned away after a few seconds, looking down.

"I want you to read something this evening," I said. "Lareen suggested it."

"What is it?"

"I haven't enough time to answer her questionnaire," I said, fudging the answer. "But before I left home I wrote a manuscript. My life story. Lareen's seen it, and she's going to use it for the rehabilitation. If you read it this evening, I can talk to you about it."

"How long is it?"

"Quite long. More than two hundred pages, but it's typewritten. It shouldn't take too long."

"Where is it?"

I passed it to her.

"Why don't you just talk to me, like you did on the boat?" She was holding the manuscript loosely, letting the pages spread. "I feel this is, well, something you wrote for yourself, something private."

"It's what you've got to use." I started to explain my motives for writing it, what I had been trying to do, but Seri moved away to the other bed and began to read. She turned the pages quickly, as if she was only skimming, and I wondered how much of it she could take in with such a superficial reading.

I watched her as she went through the first chapter, the long explanatory passage where I was working out my then dilemma, my series of misfortunes, my justification for self-examination. She reached the second chapter, and because I was watching closely I noticed that she paused on the first page and read the opening paragraph again. She looked back to the first chapter.

She said: "Can I ask you something?"

"Shouldn't you read a bit more?"

"I don't understand." She put down the pages and looked at me over them. "I thought you said you came from Jethra?"

"That's right."

"Then why do you say you were born somewhere else?" She looked again at the word. "'London' . . . where's that?"

"Oh, that," I said. "That's an invented name . . . it's difficult to explain. It's Jethra really, but I was trying to convey the idea that as you grow up the place you're in seems to change. 'London' is a state of mind. It describes my parents, I suppose, what they were like and where they were living when I was born."

"Let me read," Seri said, not looking at me, staring down at the page.

She read more slowly now, checking back several times. I began to feel uncomfortable, interpreting her difficulties as a form of criticism. Because I had defined myself to myself, because I had never imagined that anyone else would ever read it, I had taken for granted that my method would be obvious. Seri, the first person in the world to read my book, frowned and read haltingly, turning the pages forward and back.

"Give it back to me," I said at last. "I don't want you to read any more."

"I've got to," she said. "I've got to understand."

But time passed and not much was clear to her. She started asking me questions.

"Who is Felicity?"

"What are the Beatles?"

"Where is Manchester, Sheffield, Piraeus?"

"What is England, and which island is it on?"

"Who is Gracia, and why has she tried to kill herself?"

"Who was Hitler, what war are you talking about, which cities had they bombed?"

"Who is Alice Dowden?"

"Why was Kennedy assassinated?"

"When were the sixties, what is marijuana, what is a psychedelic rock?"

"You've mentioned London again . . . I thought it was a state of mind?"

"Why do you keep talking about Gracia?"

"What happened at Watergate?"

I said, but Seri did not seem to hear: "There's a deeper truth in fiction, because memory is faulty."

"Who *is* Gracia?"

"I love you, Seri," I said, but the words sounded hollow and unconvincing, even to me.

RUSSELL HOBAN

Kleinzeit

SIX o'clock in the morning, and Hospital had had enough of sleep. Drink tea, it said. Patients sighed, cursed, groaned, opened or closed their eyes, came out from behind oxygen masks, drank tea.

The fat man in the bed next to Kleinzeit sat up, smiled, nodded over his teacup. From his bedside locker he took four fruity buns, sliced them in half, spread them with butter, loaded four of the halves with marmalade and four with blackcurrant jam, lined them up in a platoon, and ate them seriously, sighing and shaking his head from time to time.

"Interesting case," he said when he had finished.

"Who?" said Kleinzeit.

"Me," said the fat man. He smiled modestly, proprietor of himself. Behind him the shade of Flashpoint sat up, shook its head, said nothing. "I'm never full," said the fat man. "Chronic ullage. Medical science can make nothing of it. The dole can't begin to cope with it. I've applied for a grant."

"From whom?" said Kleinzeit.

"Arts Council," said the fat man. "On metaphorical grounds. The human condition."

"The fat human condition," said Kleinzeit. He hadn't expected to say that. The fruity buns had provoked him.

"Cheek," said the fat man. "Where are your friends and relations?"

"What do you mean?" said Kleinzeit.

"What I said," said the fat man. "I've been here for three visiting periods. Everyone else in the ward but you either gets visited or neglected in a bona fide way. You've seen old Griggs regularly not visited by three daughters, two sons, and fifteen or twenty grandchildren. You've seen me regularly visited by my wife, son, daughter, two cousins, and a friend. Now, what have you to say to that?"

"Nothing," said Kleinzeit.

"Not good enough," said the fat man. "Won't do. I'm not one of those who see a foreign menace lurking under every bush, mark you. Nothing like that. I don't care if you're an atheist or a communist or a wog of any description whatever. But I'm curious, you see. The more I pry, the more I want to pry. I'm simply never full. You're not visited and you're not neglected. There's something about you that's not quite the ticket, not quite the regular human condition, if you follow me."

"Not quite the regular fat human condition," said Kleinzeit. Again he hadn't expected to say it.

"Not good enough," said the fat man. He took three sausage rolls from his store, ate them judicially. "No, no," he said, wiping the crumbs from his mouth, "I'm patently too many for you, and you're simply being evasive. Childhood memories?"

"What about them?" said Kleinzeit.

"Name one."

Kleinzeit couldn't. There was nothing in his memory but the pain from A to B, getting the sack at the office, seeing Dr. Pink, coming to the hospital. Nothing else. He went pale.

"You see?" said the fat man. "You simply won't bear examination, will you? It's almost as if you'd made yourself up on the spur of the moment. It's nothing to me, really. It's only that I happen to be an unusually acute observer. Never full. We'll let it be for now, shall we?"

Kleinzeit nodded, quite defeated. He lay low, looked away when anyone passed his bed.

He left the hospital again, went into the Underground, stood on the platform, read the walls, the posters. KILL JEW SHIT. Angie & Tim. CHELSEA. My job is stultifying. ODEON. KILL COMES AGAIN. *They were all dying to come with him!* CLASSIC. COME KILLS AGAIN. *When he came, they went!* KILL WOG SHIT. My stult is ramifying. Uncle Toad's Palmna Royale Date Crunch. Whole milk chocolate, big date pieces, Strontium 91. Pretty Polly Tights. My wife refuses to beat me.

He looked into the round black tunnel, listened to the wincing of the rails ahead of the oncoming train, saw the lights on the front of the train, then windows, people. NO SMOKING, NO SMOKING, NO SMOKING, NO NO SMOKING. He got in, smoked. ARE YOU SITTING OPPOSITE THE NEW MAN IN YOUR LIFE? said an advert. Trust Dateline Computer to find the right person for you. The seat opposite Kleinzeit was empty. He declined to look at his reflection in the window.

He came out of the Underground, turned into a street, walked up a hill. Gray sky. Chill wind. Brick houses, doors, windows, roofs, chimneys, going slowly up the hill one step at a time.

Kleinzeit stopped in front of a house. Old red brick and rising damp. An old shadowy ocher-painted doorway. Old green-painted pipes clinging to the housefront, branching like vines. Old green area railings. Worn steps. The windows saw nothing. Crazed in its brick the old house reared like a blind horse.

Be the house of my childhood, said Kleinzeit.

Wallpapers wept, carpets sweated, the smell of old frying crusted the air. Yes, said the house.

Kleinzeit leaned on the green spikes of the area railings, looked up at the gray sky. I'm not very young, he said. Probably my parents are dead.

He went to a cemetery. Old, askant, tall grass growing, worn-out stones. A dead cemetery. I'm not that old, he said, but never mind.

The grayness had stopped; the sunlight was coming down so hard that it was difficult to see anything. The wind seethed in the grass. The letters cut in the stones were black with time, dim with silence, could have spelled any names or none.

Kleinzeit stood in front of a stone, said, Be my father.

Morris Kleinzeit, said the stone. Born. Died.

Be my mother, Kleinzeit said to another stone.

Sadie Kleinzeit, said the stone. Born. Died.

Speak to me, said Kleinzeit to the stones.

I didn't know, said the father stone.

I knew, said the mother stone.

Thank you, said Kleinzeit.

He went to a telephone kiosk. Good place to grow flowers, he thought, went inside, put his hands on the telephone without dialing.

Brother? said Kleinzeit.

Nobody can tell you anything, said a voice from the suburbs.

Kleinzeit left the telephone kiosk, went into the Underground, got into a train. An advert said, YOU'D BE BETTER OFF AS A POSTMAN.

He came out of the Underground, turned into a mews occupied by two E-type Jaguars, a Bentley, a Porsche, various brightly colored Minis, Fiats, Volkswagens. He stopped in front of a white house with blue shutters. Black carriage lamps on either side of the front door.

Not yours anymore, said the blue shutters.

Bye-bye, Dad, said two bicycles.

Kleinzeit nodded, turned away, passed a newsstand, scanned headlines. SORROW; FULL SHOCK. He went back to the hospital.

The curtains were drawn around the fat man's bed. Fleshky, Potluck, and the day sister were with him. Two nurses wheeled in the harbinger. Kleinzeit heard the fat man wheezing. "I feel full," gasped the fat man. Silence.

"He's gone," said Potluck. The nurses wheeled away the harbinger. The curtains opened on the side away from Kleinzeit. The day sister came out, looked at him.

"I was . . ." said Kleinzeit.

"What?" said the sister.

Was going to tell the fat man, thought Kleinzeit. Tell him what? There was nothing in his memory to tell him. There was the pain from A to B, getting the sack at the office, seeing Dr. Pink, coming to the hospital, and the days at the hospital. Nothing else.

This is what, said Hospital. And what is this. This is what what is.

STEVE ERICKSON

Days Between Stations

HE woke nine years later remembering nothing. Not his name, nor what he was doing in a room in Paris, nor whatever it was that had occurred before he went to sleep that blotted out his identity. That was what it was, the obliteration of self-sense more than of mere memory; it wasn't so much that he couldn't remember, but rather as though it was gone, his life before that morning. He lay there quite a while looking around the room, his eyes traveling the ceiling to the corners, and listening to the traffic outside. Water dripped in the sink. The walls were pale and unadorned. There was a book by the side of the bed, *Les grands auteurs du cinéma*. He finally stumbled to the window and looked onto the street below.

He did hold on to one memory, going over and over it. He did this not out of any real panic or confusion; he was amazed, instead, by the sense of relief he felt, though of course he had no idea what it was that so relieved him, unless it was the obliteration itself. What he saw in his mind were twin boys, blond, standing on a stage before an auditorium of people. Lights were cast across their figures, and their hair shone. Their mouths were small and their eyes wide, and their hands, held before them, were shaking. Seated to the rear were several men and women, watching the two children and waiting. The audience was waiting.

He found an American passport in the drawer. He opened it and looked at the picture, and then looked at the face in the mirror. They were the same face, the same black hair. The name on the passport was Michel Sarasan. This surprised him, because a second before opening the passport the name Adrien ran across his mind. Even now, after reading Michel Sarasan, the name Adrien resounded. It felt familiar to him, as though it should have been written on the passport. Sex: M.Wife/husband: XXX. Age: 29. Birthplace: France. Bearer's address: Los Angeles.

A week later Jack Sarasan, a film producer in California, received a phone call. He immediately left the studio, got in his limousine, and went home. At this moment, always conscious of those things that were his, he realized that one of the reasons he had never liked his nephew was that Michel wasn't his—not the way the chauffeur, or the limousine, or the house were his. Jack Sarasan drew the line on how far people could go and still be his, and the ones who slipped over the line he cut loose; but his nephew had cut himself loose long before. Jack was trying to calculate exactly how long by the time he got to the house. "Eight," he concluded aloud, to the stairs, lighting a cigar.

"Eight what?"

Jack looked up at the doctor coming toward him. He never liked the doctor either, but his wife claimed to trust him.

"Eight what," the doctor said again, taking his coat from the chair.

"Eight years," said Jack, after studying the doctor. "Since Michel disappeared."

"Well, he's back," said the doctor, glancing upstairs.

"I know he's back. What I want to know is why."

Michel had shown up at the door, which the maid answered. The maid had stood gawking at him until Judith Sarasan came up behind, who in turn gawked at the eyepatch Michel was wearing. He had gotten it that first day in Paris, after waking, and put it on so the anonymity of his face would match the anonymity of his memory. He had worn the patch in the streets, along the boulevard Saint-Michel, in restaurants and cafés, in shops and in the Métro, on the trains and on the airplane coming back; and somehow came to feel more and more assured when no one seemed to know him. To the recurring vision of the twin boys in the auditorium, he switched the patch from eye to eye, first watching one boy and then the other, dividing everything he saw in half. It was on the plane that a stewardess, more alert than the others, noted the patch covering the left eye when sometime earlier it had covered the right. She notified the pilot, who notified officials at LAX when the plane landed, who questioned Michel for three hours before allowing him to go. When he walked up the long drive from the taxi at the bottom of the hill, he stood at the door asking tentatively of his aunt, Do I know you? And do you know me?

Why are you wearing that patch? she wanted to know, and called the doctor.

"Why *is* he wearing a patch?" said Jack. "Is there something wrong with his eye?"

"No," the doctor said. He mulled it for a while, there in the entryway.

"Well?"

The doctor put his hand to his chin. "Nothing physically wrong with him at all," he said, shaking his head.

"What's that mean? Has he finally gone completely crazy?"

"He seems to have amnesia."

"Amnesia!"

The doctor put on his coat.

"Did somebody bump him on the head?"

"That happens in the movies."

"I know what happens in the movies," Jack said tersely.

"More likely to be emotional trauma," said the doctor. "A confrontation, a startling revelation. Something that makes the mind wipe everything out."

"He doesn't remember anything?"

"He talks about twins. You know anything about that?"

Jack was visibly stunned. He took the cigar from his mouth.

"You know anything about that?" the doctor repeated, peering at him.

Jack shrugged, and now he too looked upstairs. He shrugged again. "It's nothing, I suppose—"

"Of course it's not nothing. Of course it's something. So what is it?"

"Well, he had two older twin brothers," said Jack, "who drowned in France when Michel was very small. That was when his mother—my sister—sent Michel here to the States. I would have thought Michel was too young to remember any of that."

The doctor started for the door. "Well, I told your wife that my guess is it will all come back to him if and when he uncovers the trauma. I'm not an expert. You may want to get some help."

"Is your guess the best you can do?" Jack said.

"I know he's not physically affected. That's what I *know*," the doctor said. "Except the stuttering."

"What's that?"

"Your wife said he used to stutter."

Jack recalled this with distaste.

"Well, I've been talking with him for an hour, and Mrs. Sarasan has talked with him several hours, since he arrived. And neither of us has heard him stutter once."

Michel stood on the balcony upstairs looking over the grounds in back of his uncle's house. Since the doctor left he had been alone, and now he put the patch back on. He knew, of course, that nothing was wrong with his eyes; but he didn't suppose anything was wrong with his mind either. When the patch covered one eye he saw people all over the lawn: a nude woman on a huge turtle riding into the swimming pool, and horses on the far knoll screaming past in a herd. When he changed the patch over to the other eye no one was to be seen except the nude woman lying at the bottom of the pool and the turtle by the side, and a bloodied white horse lying dead beneath a tree. He kept changing the patch back and forth, watching the progression or, as it were, the deterioration.

When he walked down the marble stairs into the living room he saw his uncle sitting in a large stuffed lavender chair, puffing on his cigar and surveying him. Michel didn't remember his uncle's face at all, and it seemed different from eye to eye, features broadening and the light changing, shifting from mundane to something unpleasant—a face out of kilter. Watching his nephew move the patch back and forth, Jack said, "What are you doing?"

"Uncle Jack?" said Michel, and it sounded false to him. He couldn't imagine having ever called him Uncle Jack. He was correct, it turned out.

"I thought your eyes were all right," said Jack.

"There's nothing wrong with them," said Michel.

There was a time, thought Jack, when it would have taken Michel a full minute just to spit out that one sentence. The words would have bounced around in his mouth like a pinball. "Can't you remember anything?" said Jack.

"Twins."

Jack nodded.

"Adrien."

"Adrien who?"

"I don't know. Just the name Adrien." Michel didn't need to remember anything to realize his uncle didn't like him, but because he remembered nothing he couldn't realize why. The following days he sat in his room staring out the doors that opened onto the balcony, watching the shadows that loomed over the yard. He became depressed and then slightly desperate; and the panic he'd warded off that first morning in Paris finally found him. He had come to California because the passport said to; he had expected, he thought it wasn't unreasonable to expect, that he'd be welcomed here, that he'd find the things he expected a home to offer him—answers and the immediate, insistent belonging that went with a family. But he was still left faceless by the hostility he felt from his uncle. It would have been enraging had he been equipped for rage. Because he was not equipped for rage, he wore the patch; he realized the things it made him see weren't really there, but he also realized that those things had been there once, that his eyepatch provided him glimpses into his own past. So he kept the patch because, branded faceless by something that had happened to him before he woke in Paris, he decided he should be faceless on his own terms, not until he remembered who he was but until he *knew* who he was, whether he remembered anything or not. His aunt could feel his despair. She didn't feel jealous of his opportunity to start over again; she was considerate enough, even perceptive enough, to understand that for someone like Michel, it wasn't an escape but a sentence—to have to start over. And the only time she ever really stood up to her husband, in over twenty-five years of being married to him, after the mistresses and the indifferences and the loud tawdriness of the marriage (she wasn't a loud tawdry woman at all), was a week after Michel had returned, and she caught Jack scowling at the image of his nephew standing on the balcony at night, Michel's one eye staring at the black of the sky and the other eye staring at the black of the patch that covered it. She said, "He's your sister's son."

"He's not my son," said Jack.

"That's not his fault. You hate him because he's like your father."

He was stunned to hear her talk to him like this. "Fuck you," he sputtered, as though that could deny it. Watching her turn and walk from the room, he thought to himself he'd about had enough from all of them, Michel and the doctor and now his wife. He looked once more at the form of Michel on the balcony and then called out after her: If he starts screaming I'm going to throw him out. But he didn't suppose Michel would scream anymore. It first happened the day Michel arrived from France as a little boy, sent by his crazy mother from a small French village on the Atlantic coast. Jack hadn't seen his sister since they themselves were children, long before the twins; but he'd happily anticipated in her son Michel a protégé of his own, to be groomed by the studios as Jack himself had been. The boy, however, was odd right off, like his mother, from the moment he came walking down the ramp of the plane too shy to even look up; his aunt took him by the hand and tried talking to him, though Michel understood only French. Jack hadn't spoken French in a long time, so the conversation among the three of them was limited to broken attempts at the language and the boy's frantic, painfully stuttered replies. The boy said very little at all, in fact; but that first afternoon, after arriving home, they could hear the child talking to himself up in his room in a torrent of discussion among myriad voices. When he talked to himself he didn't stutter at all; in fact he didn't sound like the same person. The two adults looked at each other; each had grave concern about anyone who talked to himself, particularly a child, as if the stuttering weren't disturbing enough. That night they got a much worse shock. Jack was throwing a little party for a number of people whose favor was important to him; the party was held on the back lawn. It was a warm pleasant evening, and everything was going along smoothly when a sound came from the house. The small boy was standing on the balcony in full view, staring not at the lawn but the night, spewing a stream of verbal abuse at something or someone; Jack remembered enough French for his hair to stand on end. The guests just looked up at the boy in awe and consternation; and Jack scrambled inside, located the hired help, and instructed one woman to shut the boy up by whatever means were necessary. She ran up the stairs, followed by Michel's aunt; and the guests watched as the child was plucked from the balcony and disappeared from view.

This happened several more times: in school, the shy, deferential student would be suddenly seized by a compulsion to scream whatever French obscenities he was capable of conjuring at the age of seven or eight. The teachers were always shaken by the transformation; the tirades were always in French, even when he was otherwise speaking English; the violence of what he was saying was clear in his tone and his eyes. Finally the aunt and uncle took him to a number of doctors. They talked with the boy but didn't seem to find any answers. Though the stuttering was always evident, Michel never screamed for them. Jack told the doctors the stuttering was making the boy crazy; the doctors could find no indication the boy was actually insane, but there was something deep inside tormenting him, and it was this making him stutter, not the other way around. Rather than inhibit the boy and his conversation by making him more conscious of the stammer, the doctors felt the child should be encouraged to talk, stutter, even scream, in order to release whatever had a hold on him. By now the idea of listening to Michel at all drove Jack wild.

An incident later in the school auditorium was the last straw. That was when Jack did what he should have done all along, which was come down on the boy hard. The boy didn't scream after that. Jack's wife was worried that Michel became despondent, perhaps broken, but Jack knew that was a lot of nonsense. Nevertheless, it was true that as Michel grew up, their relationship decomposed, and along with it Jack's hopes of molding an heir—a situation marked by constant disagreements and fights, and culminating in the boardroom confrontation they still whispered about around the studio. In Jack's boardroom, before Jack's directors, Jack's nephew exploded in the stammering, word-wrenching fury of his childhood, lacerating his uncle with his own wild spastic tongue that somehow rendered what he said not ridiculous but all the more humiliating. Absolutely shaking then, face stricken, Michel burst out the door and was gone. Over the next few years Michel made a small student film that won a prize in a festival, and then disappeared.

So if Michel began screaming there on that balcony, or so much as stuttered to his uncle once, Jack would cast him from the house. Michel was left to pursue his own discoveries as best he could. If he had in fact lost who he once was, there was no percentage in it for Jack to help Michel regain that past. Michel began wandering the city in the afternoon, peering in windows he supposed would remind him of something, looking in every face to see if that face recognized him. He still wore the eyepatch, unwilling to discard it. He walked along Hollywood Boulevard and Sunset Boulevard, through Venice, where the carnival would seem likely to yield at least one sign of the past. He waited for someone to call to him, for someone to grab him by the shoulders and shake him. He spent days in Echo Park walking across bridges, looking for his name among the graffiti on the walls.

He started going to movies.

One day he passed a theater on Wilshire Boulevard near Lafayette Park, and he looked at the billboard and something stirred. He realized then that he'd been avoiding the movie marquees out of some aversion more eloquent than disinterest—now this billboard was the first familiar thing he had found since waking in Paris that morning. He paid his money and bought a ticket, and went into the theater and sat, alone in his row, waiting for the lights to fall and the screen to flicker for him, and he knew that it was this moment he had avoided—that if this moment were to mean nothing to him, he would have felt more utterly lost than ever, he would have felt isolated in a way the preceding days could not even imply. So it was a moment of wild exhilaration for him when, as the film began, he felt great excitement and passion. But something even more remarkable took place. The credits rolled by and he watched them carefully, something turning behind his eyes, and the story started, and he remembered it. He remembered all of it. He knew, not out of cleverness or precalculation, that the man Joseph Cotten came to Vienna to find was not dead at all, but alive; he remembered Orson Welles in the doorway with the cat at his feet, and in the Ferris wheel musing over the insignificance of the people below him, and running through the sewers with the police at his heels. And he remembered in detail, painfully as though it was some recast shard of his own childhood, Alida Valli walking down the road with the leaves falling around her passing Joseph Cotten in cool disdain, too violated by his treachery to acknowledge he was waiting for her. This all came to Michel there in the theater, within the first few minutes of the picture.

He went to another movie that evening but the same thing did not happen, and it dropped him into a sort of depression—but not enough to wipe out what had happened that afternoon. He learned that not all movies would do this to him. But he always had an inkling for the ones that would; he would pass a poster or a title and something would stir, like it had that first time, and he followed his hunches. He was almost always right. He remembered everything, and most clearly he remembered the faces: Oskar Werner's stunned expression when his best friend and the woman they loved drove off the bridge into the water; the electrifying close-up of Falconetti in her trial, sentence, and martyrdom; and most of all Chaplin, the look of humiliation and ecstasy, rose between his fingers, before the woman who'd gained her sight and lost her innocence; and like her, Michel wondered if, when he could see it all again, it would make him regret the squandered virginity of his instincts.

Where he had lain in the bedroom of his uncle's house feeling like a man without a persona, passive and unmoved and uninterested, now he was equipped for the thing he'd been so inadequate for: the rage, which he needed. Whether he remembered anything at all, he was still who he was, and now he felt the flashes of rebellion and intensity that had always come so easily to him, no matter how obstructed by the stuttering the expression of those things had been. Of course he didn't know he had ever stuttered, he didn't know those things had come so easily. He raged first of all at himself. It was his natural inclination to do this, and he didn't know that either.

One night he went into Venice to see some student films. He sat through the first four or five without feeling anything whatsoever. Only a minute or two into the sixth, he was overcome with nausea. He didn't know why he felt this way. There was not, apparently, anything on the screen that would cause this reaction. The film was about an old woman who lived in a house somewhere in France; this was clear from the subtitles. She wandered from room to room, up and down the stairs, and outside the window one could see the sea. The entire film was of the old woman talking about her feelings in this house. She pointed out the rooms where her children had lived: three sons, she noted. The two oldest, who were twins, died when they were small. They went swimming one night where there was no moon, and in the morning she found the bodies on the beach. She went into town and bought two coffins, and put the bodies in the coffins herself; she showed with her arms how she lifted them up. Then she asked the men from the town to help her bury them. The old woman explained all of this in a monotone. Now she went on, she said, "Living in the window, waiting to die in the window"—there was no window in the room, however, when she said this. Toward the end of the film, Michel thought he was going to be sick; nothing he saw before had affected him this way, his innards were churning. He was in a cold sweat when the picture ended, and the credit came on, "A film by Michel Sarre," and he sat stunned in the seat still watching the white screen even as the lights went up, because though the last name was different, he instinctively understood that this was his film.

On his way to the house that night, after leaving the theater, the streetlights went out one by one. At the top of the hill, he looked out over the basin of the city to see, suddenly, the rest of the lights vanish in a single moment. It was as though the earth itself had disappeared. The lights of his uncle's house went as well. He walked up to the dark porch, and felt a pang of loneliness at the realization that movie screens from one end of town to the other were black at this moment, and when he opened the door, his aunt was there to greet him with a burning candle in her hand. She held it up to his face, looking to see if he was still wearing the patch; and as the patch did for him, the candle illuminated everything around her only a little at a time; in this sense his perspective was no longer unique, at least not at that moment. "The lights have all gone out," he said, and she smiled. "What's funny?" he said. "You used to have so much trouble saying your *l*'s," she answered. He didn't know what she meant. "It's the second time this year," she went on. "They'll be going out a lot."

"A lot?"

"From here on out."

From here on out? He didn't understand it was the last twenty years of the twentieth century. She lit another candle for him and he went up the stairs to his room. He stood on the balcony and now noticed, over in the yard behind the next house, a small, half-completed bridge that stretched across one of the knolls and ended in midair. Other nights he would see the bridge progress until it completed its arc. Across the hills other people were building bridges; and later, as the lights went out more often, as more nights lapsed into blackness, more bridges were built. Someone was to explain to him that these bridges were built for following the passage of the moon at night, that as more nights passed lightless, the moon was the only light there was; and in that light Michel could see the moon-glistened figures on the moon-bridges in their backyards, staring into the night, following the white globe's journey. This is why all the bridges were built the same direction, because everyone watched the same journey; and across the city people stepped in time to the slide of the moon across the sky.

VLADIMIR NABOKOV

"That in Aleppo Once . . ."

DEAR V.—Among other things, this is to tell you that at last I am here, in the country whither so many sunsets have led. One of the first persons I saw was our good old Gleb Alexandrovich Gekko gloomily crossing Columbus Avenue in quest of the *petit café du coin* which none of us three will ever visit again. He seemed to think that somehow or other you were betraying our national literature, and he gave me your address with a deprecatory shake of his gray head, as if you did not deserve the treat of hearing from me.

I have a story for you. Which reminds me—I mean putting it like this reminds me—of the days when we wrote our first udder-warm bubbling verse, and all things, a rose, a puddle, a lighted window, cried out to us: "I'm a rhyme!" Yes, this is a most useful universe. We play, we die: *ig-rhyme, umi-rhyme*. And the sonorous souls of Russian verbs lend a meaning to the wild gesticulation of trees or to some discarded newspaper sliding and pausing, and shuffling again, with abortive flaps and apterous jerks along an endless windswept embankment. But just now I am not a poet. I come to you like that gushing lady in Chekhov who was dying to be described.

I married, let me see, about a month after you left France and a few weeks before the gentle Germans roared into Paris. Although I can produce documentary proofs of matrimony, I am positive now that my wife never existed. You may know her name from some other source, but that does not matter; it is the name of an illusion. Therefore, I am able to speak of her with as much detachment as I would of a character in a story (one of your stories, to be precise).

It was love at first touch rather than at first sight, for I had met her several times before without experiencing any special emotions, but one night, as I was seeing her home, something quaint she had said made me stoop with a laugh and lightly kiss her on the hair—and of course we all know of that blinding blast which is caused by merely picking up a small doll from the floor of a carefully abandoned house: the soldier involved hears nothing; for him it is but an ecstatic soundless and boundless expansion of what had been during his life a pinpoint of light in the dark center of his being. And really, the reason we think of death in celestial terms is that the visible firmament, especially at night (above our blacked-out Paris with the gaunt arches of its boulevard Exelmans and the ceaseless alpine gurgle of desolate latrines), is the most adequate and ever-present symbol of that vast silent explosion.

But I cannot discern her. She remains as nebulous as my best poem—the one you made such gruesome fun of in the *Literaturnie Zapiski*. When I want to imagine her, I have to cling mentally to a tiny brown birthmark on her downy forearm, as one concentrates upon a punctuation mark in an illegible sentence. Perhaps, had she used a greater amount of makeup or used it more constantly, I might have visualized her face today, or at least the delicate transverse furrows of dry, hot rouged lips; but I fail, I fail—although I still feel their elusive touch now and then in the blindman's buff of my senses, in that sobbing sort of dream when she and I clumsily clutch at each other through a heartbreaking mist and I cannot see the color of her eyes for the blank luster of brimming tears drowning their irises.

She was much younger than I—not as much younger as was Nathalie of the lovely bare shoulders and long earrings in relation to swarthy Pushkin; but still there was a sufficient margin for that kind of retrospective romanticism which finds pleasure in imitating the destiny of a unique genius (down to the jealousy, down to the filth, down to the stab of seeing her almond-shaped eyes turn to her blond Cassio behind her peacock-feathered fan) even if one cannot imitate his verse. She liked mine though, and would scarcely have yawned as the other was wont to do every time her husband's poem happened to exceed the length of a sonnet. If she has remained a phantom to me, I may have been one to her: I suppose she had been solely attracted by the obscurity of my poetry; then tore a hole through its veil and saw a stranger's unlovable face.

As you know, I had been for some time planning to follow the example of your fortunate flight. She described to me an uncle of hers who lived, she said, in New York; he had taught riding at a southern college and had wound up by marrying a wealthy American woman; they had a little daughter born deaf. She said she had lost their address long ago, but a few days later it miraculously turned up, and we wrote a dramatic letter to which we never received any reply. This did not much matter, as I had already obtained a sound affidavit from Professor Lomchenko of Chicago; but little else had been done in the way of getting the necessary papers, when the invasion began, whereas I foresaw that if we stayed on in Paris some helpful compatriot of mine would sooner or later point out to the interested party sundry passages in one of my books where I argued that, with all her many black sins, Germany was still bound to remain forever and ever the laughingstock of the world.

So we started upon our disastrous honeymoon. Crushed and jolted amid the apocalyptic exodus, waiting for unscheduled trains that were bound for unknown destinations, walking through the stale stage setting of abstract towns, living in a permanent twilight of physical exhaustion, we fled; and the farther we fled, the clearer it became that what was driving us on was something more than a booted and buckled fool with his assortment of variously propelled junk—something of which he was a mere symbol, something monstrous and impalpable, a timeless and faceless mass of immemorial horror that still keeps coming at me from behind even here, in the green vacuum of Central Park.

Oh, she bore it gamely enough—with a kind of dazed cheerfulness. Once, however, quite suddenly she started to sob in a sympathetic railway carriage. "The dog," she said, "the dog we left. I cannot forget the poor dog." The honesty of her grief shocked me, as we had never had any dog. "I know," she said, "but I tried to imagine we had actually bought that setter. And just think, he would be now whining behind a locked door." There had never been any talk of buying a setter.

I should also not like to forget a certain stretch of highroad and the sight of a family of refugees (two men, a child) whose old father, or grandfather, had died on the way. The sky was a chaos of black and flesh-colored clouds with an ugly sunburst beyond a hooded hill, and the dead man was lying on his back under a dusty plane tree. With a stick and their hands the women had tried to dig a roadside grave, but the soil was too hard; they had given it up and were sitting side by side, among the anemic poppies, a little apart from the corpse and its upturned beard. But the little boy was still scratching and scraping and tugging until he tumbled a flat stone and forgot the object of his solemn exertions as he crouched on his haunches, his thin, eloquent neck showing all its vertebrae to the headsman, and watched with surprise and delight thousands of minute brown ants seething, zigzagging, dispersing, heading for places of safety in the Gard, and the Aude, and the Drôme, and the Var, and the Basses-Pyrénées—we two paused only in Pau.

Spain proved too difficult and we decided to move on to Nice. At a place called Faugères (a ten-minute stop) I squeezed out of the train to buy some food. When a couple of minutes later I came back, the train was gone, and the muddled old man responsible for the atrocious void that faced me (coal dust glittering in the heat between naked indifferent rails, and a lone piece of orange peel) brutally told me that, anyway, I had had no right to get out.

In a better world I could have had my wife located and told what to do (I had both tickets and most of the money); as it was, my nightmare struggle with the telephone proved futile, so I dismissed the whole series of diminutive voices barking at me from afar, sent two or three telegrams which are probably on their way only now, and late in the evening took the next local to Montpellier, farther than which her train would not stumble. Not finding her there, I had to choose between two alternatives: going on because she might have boarded the Marseilles train which I had just missed, or going back because she might have returned to Faugères. I forget now what tangle of reasoning led me to Marseilles and Nice.

Beyond such routine action as forwarding false data to a few unlikely places, the police did nothing to help: one man bellowed at me for being a nuisance; another sidetracked the question by doubting the authenticity of my marriage certificate because it was stamped on what he contended to be the wrong side; a third, a fat *commissaire* with liquid brown eyes, confessed that he wrote poetry in his spare time. I looked up various acquaintances among the numerous Russians domiciled or stranded in Nice. I heard those among them who chanced to have Jewish blood talk of their doomed kinsmen crammed into hell-bound trains; and my own plight, by contrast, acquired a common-place air of irreality while I sat in some crowded café with the milky blue sea in front of me and a shell-hollow murmur behind telling and retelling the tale of massacre and misery, and the gray paradise beyond the ocean, and the ways and whims of harsh consuls.

A week after my arrival an indolent plainclothesman called upon me and took me down a crooked and smelly street to a black-stained house with the word *hotel* almost erased by dirt and time; there, he said, my wife had been found. The girl he produced was an absolute stranger, of course; but my friend Holmes kept on trying for some time to make her and me confess we were married, while her taciturn and muscular bedfellow stood by and listened, his bare arms crossed on his striped chest.

When at length I got rid of those people and had wandered back to my neighborhood, I happened to pass by a compact queue waiting at the entrance of a food store; and there, at the very end, was my wife, straining on tiptoe to catch a glimpse of what exactly was being sold. I think the first thing she said to me was that she hoped it was oranges.

Her tale seemed a trifle hazy, but perfectly banal. She had returned to Faugères and gone straight to the Commissariat instead of making inquiries at the station, where I had left a message for her. A party of refugees suggested that she join them; she spent the night in a bicycle shop with no bicycles, on the floor, together with three elderly women who lay, she said, like three logs in a row. Next day she realized that she had not enough money to reach Nice. Eventually she borrowed some from one of the log-women. She got into the wrong train, however, and traveled to a town the name of which she could not remember. She had arrived at Nice two days ago and had found some friends at the Russian church. They had told her I was somewhere around, looking for her, and would surely turn up soon.

Sometime later, as I sat on the edge of the only chair in my garret and held her by her slender young hips (she was combing her soft hair and tossing her head back with every stroke), her dim smile changed all at once into an odd quiver and she placed one hand on my shoulder, staring down at me as if I were a reflection in a pool, which she had noticed for the first time.

"I've been lying to you, dear," she said. "*Ya lgunia.* I stayed for several nights in Montpellier with a brute of a man I met on the train. I did not want it at all. He sold hair lotions."

The time, the place, the torture. Her fan, her gloves, her mask. I spent that night and many others getting it out of her bit by bit, but not getting it all. I was under the strange delusion that first I must find out every detail, reconstruct every minute, and only then decide whether I could bear it. But the limit of desired knowledge was unattainable, nor could I ever foretell the approximate point after which I might imagine myself satiated, because of course the denominator of every fraction of knowledge was potentially as infinite as the number of intervals between the fractions themselves.

Oh, the first time she had been too tired to mind, and the next had not minded because she was sure I had deserted her; and she apparently considered that such explanations ought to be a kind of consolation prize for me instead of the nonsense and agony they really were. It went on like that for eons, she breaking down every now and then, but soon rallying again, answering my unprintable questions in a breathless whisper or trying with a pitiful smile to wriggle into the semisecurity of irrelevant commentaries, and I crushing and crushing the mad molar till my jaw almost burst with pain, a flaming pain which seemed somehow preferable to the dull, humming ache of humble endurance.

And mark, in between the periods of this inquest, we were trying to get from reluctant authorities certain papers which in their turn would make it lawful to apply for a third kind which would serve as a stepping-stone toward a permit enabling the holder to apply for yet other papers which might or might not give him the means of discovering how and why it had happened. For even if I could imagine the accursed recurrent scene, I failed to link up its sharp-angled grotesque shadows with the dim limbs of my wife as she shook and rattled and dissolved in my violent grasp.

So nothing remained but to torture each other, to wait for hours on end in the Prefecture, filling forms, conferring with friends who had already probed the innermost viscera of all visas, pleading with secretaries, and filling forms again, with the result that her lusty and versatile traveling salesman became blended in a ghastly mix-up with rat-whiskered snarling officials, rotting bundles of obsolete records, the reek of violet ink, bribes slipped under gangrenous blotting paper, fat flies tickling moist necks with their rapid cold padded feet, new-laid clumsy concave photographs of your six subhuman doubles, the tragic eyes and patient politeness of petitioners born in Slutzk, Starodub, or Bobruisk, the funnels and pulleys of the Holy Inquisition, the awful smile of the bald man with the glasses, who had been told that his passport could not be found.

I confess that one evening, after a particularly abominable day, I sank down on a stone bench weeping and cursing a mock world where millions of lives were being juggled by the clammy hands of consuls and *commissaires*. I noticed she was crying too, and then I told her that nothing would really have mattered the way it mattered now, had she not gone and done what she did.

"You will think me crazy," she said with a vehemence that, for a second, almost made a real person of her, "but I didn't—I swear that I didn't. Perhaps I live several lives at once. Perhaps I wanted to test you. Perhaps this bench is a dream and we are in Saratov or on some star."

It would be tedious to niggle the different stages through which I passed before accepting finally the first version of her delay. I did not talk to her and was a good deal alone. She would glimmer and fade, and reappear with some trifle she thought I would appreciate—a handful of cherries, three precious cigarettes, or the like—treating me with the unruffled mute sweetness of a nurse that trips from and to a gruff convalescent. I ceased visiting most of our mutual friends because they had lost all interest in my passport affairs and seemed to have turned vaguely inimical. I composed several poems. I drank all the wine I could get. I clasped her one day to my groaning breast, and we went for a week to Caboule and lay on the round pink pebbles of the narrow beach. Strange to say, the happier our new relations seemed, the stronger I felt an undercurrent of poignant sadness, but I kept telling myself that this was an intrinsic feature of all true bliss.

In the meantime, something had shifted in the moving pattern of our fates and at last I emerged from a dark and hot office with a couple of plump *visas de sortie* cupped in my trembling hands. Into these the U.S.A. serum was duly injected, and I dashed to Marseilles and managed to get tickets for the very next boat. I returned and tramped up the stairs. I saw a rose in a glass on the table—the sugar pink of its obvious beauty, the parasitic air bubbles clinging to its stem. Her two spare dresses were gone, her comb was gone, her checkered coat was gone, and so was the mauve hairband with a mauve bow that had been her hat. There was no note pinned to the pillow, nothing at all in the room to enlighten me, for of course the rose was merely what French rhymesters call *une cheville*.

I went to the Veretennikovs, who could tell me nothing; to the Hellmans, who refused to say anything; and to the Elagins, who were not sure whether to tell me or not. Finally the old lady—and you know what Anna Vladimirovna is like at crucial moments—asked for her rubber-tipped cane, heavily but energetically dislodged her bulk from her favorite armchair, and took me into the garden. There she informed me that, being twice my age, she had the right to say I was a bully and a cad.

You must imagine the scene: the tiny graveled garden with its blue Arabian Nights jar and solitary cypress; the cracked terrace where the old lady's father had dozed with a rug on his knees when he retired from his Novgorod governorship to spend a few last evenings in Nice; the pale-green sky; a whiff of vanilla in the deepening dusk; the crickets emitting their metallic trill pitched at two octaves above middle C; and Anna Vladimirovna, the folds of her cheeks jerkily dangling as she flung at me a motherly but quite undeserved insult.

During several preceding weeks, my dear V., every time she had visited by herself the three or four families we both knew, my ghostly wife had filled the eager ears of all those kind people with an extraordinary story. To wit: that she had madly fallen in love with a young Frenchman who could give her a turreted home and a crested name; that she had implored me for a divorce and I had refused; that in fact I had said I would rather shoot her and myself than sail to New York alone; that she had said her father in a similar case had acted like a gentleman; that I had answered I did not give a hoot for her *cocu de père*.

There were loads of other preposterous details of the kind—but they all hung together in such a remarkable fashion that no wonder the old lady made me swear I would not seek to pursue the lovers with a cocked pistol. They had gone, she said, to a château in Lozère. I inquired whether she had ever set eyes upon the man. No, but she had been shown his picture. As I was about to leave, Anna Vladimirovna, who had slightly relaxed and had even given me her five fingers to kiss, suddenly flared up again, struck the gravel with her cane, and said in her deep strong voice: "But one thing I shall never forgive you—her dog, that poor beast which you hanged with your own hands before leaving Paris."

Whether the gentleman of leisure had changed into a traveling salesman, or whether the metamorphosis had been reversed, or whether again he was neither the one nor the other but the nondescript Russian who had courted her before our marriage—all this was absolutely inessential. She had gone. That was the end. I should have been a fool had I begun the nightmare business of searching and waiting for her all over again.

On the fourth morning of a long and dismal sea voyage, I met on the deck a solemn but pleasant old doctor with whom I had played chess in Paris. He asked me whether my wife was very much incommoded by the rough seas. I answered that I had sailed alone; whereupon he looked taken aback and then said he had seen her a couple of days before going on board, namely in Marseilles, walking, rather aimlessly he thought, along the embankment. She said that I would presently join her with bag and tickets.

This is, I gather, the point of the whole story—although if you write it, you had better not make him a doctor, as that kind of thing has been overdone. It was at that moment that I suddenly knew for certain that she had never existed at all. I shall tell you another thing. When I arrived I hastened to satisfy a certain morbid curiosity: I went to the address she had given me once; it proved to be an anonymous gap between two office buildings; I looked for her uncle's name in the directory; it was not there; I made some inquiries, and Gekko, who knows everything, informed me that the man and his horsey wife existed all right, but had moved to San Francisco after their deaf little girl had died.

Viewing the past graphically, I see our mangled romance engulfed in a deep valley of mist between the crags of two matter-of-fact mountains; life had been real before, life will be real from now on, I hope. Not tomorrow, though. Perhaps after tomorrow. You, happy mortal, with your lovely family (how is Ines? how are the twins?) and your diversified work (how are the lichens?), can hardly be expected to puzzle out my misfortune in terms of human communion, but you may clarify things for me through the prism of your art.

Yet the pity of it. Curse your art, I am hideously unhappy. She keeps on walking to and fro where the brown nets are spread to dry on the hot stone slabs and the dappled light of the water plays on the side of a moored fishing boat. Somewhere, somehow, I have made some fatal mistake. There are tiny pale bits of broken fish scales glistening here and there in the brown meshes. It may all end in *Aleppo* if I am not careful. Spare me, V.; you would load your dice with an unbearable implication if you took that for a title.

JOHN FRANKLIN BARDIN

The Deadly Percheron

THEY let me up and around but would not let me shave myself. They gave me an old pair of corduroy trousers, the ones I had been wearing—I was told—when they found me. I held them up with my hands. I could not have a belt because I might hang myself with it. There was no mirror, and I was not allowed to leave the ward. I could not see what I looked like now.

By running my hand over my head I could tell that my hair was more closely cropped than it used to be. It felt short and bristly like an undergraduate's. I began to feel like a different man, a poor man, a sick man.

I grew friendly with the young intern. His name was Harvey Peters. We talked together whenever he could spare the time. I argued with him again and again. But it never did any good.

On the second day—

"Doctor, I tell you my name is Matthews! I am married and I live in Hackensack, New Jersey. I want you to get in touch with my wife."

"I'll try if you want me to."

"There must have been some mistake about the other. The telephone company's error. But reach my wife, please! She'll be worrying about me."

"I'll try—"

The third day—

"My wife's coming to see me today? You got in touch with her, didn't you? She'll be coming to take me home today?"

He shook his head. "I'm sorry, fellow. I tried. But I could not reach your wife."

"She wasn't in? She was out shopping most likely. Sara likes to shop. But you'll try again? She'll be in the next time you call."

"There is no Mrs. George Matthews in the Hackensack telephone book."

"But, Doctor, we have a phone. I know we have a phone."

He kept shaking his head. I could see he pitied me now. "There is no Mrs. George Matthews in Hackensack, New Jersey, who is a doctor's wife. That Mrs. George Matthews moved away. She left no forwarding address. I know because I've checked with the post office."

"Doctor, there must be some mistake! She wouldn't leave like that—without a word!"

"I'm sorry, old man. You're mistaken."

"I'm not mistaken. I am George Matthews."

"You must not get so excited. You must rest."

Another day—

"Doctor, how long have I been here?"

"About two weeks."

"What is the diagnosis?"

"Amnesia, with possible paranoid tendencies."

"But I know who I am! It's just that I can't prove it!"

"I know. I know that's the way it seems." He was humoring me. A mild-mannered, kind, young man who was almost a doctor was humoring me. He pitied me. He had not as yet developed the necessary callousness, and the aberrations of his more intelligent patients still dismayed him. He wanted to let me down gently. I knew he would comply with all my requests (or pretend to comply), because he felt that my interest in my former life—in any former life, even a mythical one—was an encouraging symptom, a sign of possible improvement.

I continued to batter my hopes against this blind construction of theory and tradition, this man for whom I was mad because my history sheet said I was—and if I were not psychotic, why then was I in the psychopathic ward of the hospital?

"But, Doctor," I said, "I know who I am. A man suffering from amnesia does not know who he is. All, or a part, of his past life is lost— he has misplaced his identity, his personal history, even his habits. That isn't a description of me!"

He answered me patiently. He talked while his eyes looked past me, remembering the definitions and practices learned by rote, mechanically interposing the logical objections, the proper refutation to all my proposals. A neurotic catechism—a litany for the irrational!

"You do not recognize your identity. You do not recognize your name—worse!—you refuse to accept it as yours. You put forward instead another man's name, a dead man's name, and claim it as your own. You claim his wife, his profession. And, building on this delusion, you begin to think that all of us are persecuting you, holding back what is rightfully yours. That is paranoia."

"Doctor, do me a favor?"

"What is it?"

"Call the police. Headquarters. Ask to speak to Lieutenant Anderson of the Homicide Division. Tell him I am here. Describe me to him. Tell him that there has been a mistake—that something has gone badly wrong."

"But the police brought you here. You were charged with vagrancy. The police know all about you."

"Just this one last favor, Doctor. Please, call Lieutenant Anderson!"

He went away. This time I did not pretend to myself. This time I knew that it would do no good. Although I might still have him call my club and some of the medical societies I belonged to, I suspected that the response would always be the same. This was the last time I would try. After that I could do nothing but wait.

He returned, stood at the foot of my bed, hesitant, sorry for me. "Lieutenant Anderson knew Dr. Matthews well," he said. "He committed suicide last year. His body was found in the North River. The lieutenant said that you must be an imposter."

After that I began to believe it myself.

It was terrifyingly easy for me to believe that the past that I remembered was unreal. I had been lifted out of my life as totally as a goldfish is dipped out of an aquarium; more so, for when a storekeeper scoops a fish he soon places it again in a paper bucket of water—the fish remains in its element. I was not so fortunate. I lived and breathed, but in an entirely different fashion, horribly unfamiliar.

They wake you early in a mental hospital, at about six o'clock. They feed you prunes, oatmeal, wholewheat bread, butter, coffee. Then you help clean up the ward until nine o'clock. You make your bed, you push a mop, you scrub toilets. There is enough for an hour's work, but you have until nine o'clock to do it. But that is not too long. After a while, it takes you until nine o'clock because from nine until twelve is the rest period. That means you have nothing to do between nine and twelve but rest. You sit. You listen to the radio. Sermons, recipes, the news every hour on the hour. If there is an old magazine or newspaper around, you read it even if you have read it from cover to cover ten times before. What is left of it, that is. All items that might have an exciting or depressing effect on the patients have been removed.

The big room is clean. It is warm. There are comfortable wicker chairs (made by the patients—occupational therapy), and outside the sun is shining.

This is all necessary. I knew it to be necessary, knew for a fact that I was in a model institution, but knowing it did not help me to accept. After a week, two weeks, more weeks of sitting and listening, you get so you listen, wait to hear a sound different from the rest. The sense of hearing is the last to give up hope. But you know that time will never end, and you begin to scheme against this fact, to plan lovely lies of escape and the return to a life that probably never existed. For after twelve comes lunch, a stew of meat and potatoes, wholewheat bread, butter, Jell-O. And after lunch you clean the toilets again, push the mop (if you have mechanical aptitude you can go to the shop) until three—and after three there is a rest period until five. Then you have supper, a piece of beef or a bowl of soup, wholewheat bread, butter, rice pudding. And after supper you go to bed and tell lies to yourself until you go to sleep.

On Thursdays I saw the psychiatrist—a pleasant woman, Dr. Little-field, a behaviorist. She gave me tests. Fit the little pegs into the little holes, the big pegs into the big holes. Turn the discs over and put them back in place—one side red, one side white—see how quickly you can do it! Answer the questions, as many as you can. A king is a monarch, serf, slave, hedonist, a lucky man. Underline the one you think is more nearly right: $2 \times 2 + 48 = 54, 62, 57, 52$.

She was a small woman with a bun of neat brown hair. Her eyes were blue and she had a tidy smile. I guessed she was about my age. The first time I did the tests, she studied my paper carefully, biting her lip as she evaluated it. I waited eagerly to hear her say: Why, there must be some mistake! Why, nobody in a mental hospital should do this well!

I should have known better. She looked up at me and smiled politely. "You show ready understanding. I think you have no trouble learning. But there is a certain instability indicated—a compulsion?"

A sane man could have taken the same tests and made the same answers. A sane man? I was a sane man. But did I think so? Could I really be deluding myself?

I wanted to tell her what I knew, prove to her that I, too, could give Stamford-Binet tests, make a prognosis, indicate treatment. I wanted to be a bright student. I wanted to outwit Teacher. But I knew I did not dare.

There was only one way I could get out. I must show "improvement." It did not matter what the truth was. I could never prove to them that my name was George Matthews, that I was a doctor, a psychiatrist, a married man with a bank account. Or if I could it would take a very long time. I knew that what I would have to do would be to break down all the individual, carefully constructed ramparts of science and knowledge—I would have to prove to Dr. Littlefield, Dr. Peters, Nurse Aggie Murphy, that I was a man and not a case history, a human and not a syndrome. And I could not allow myself a short time. I had to get out tomorrow, or the day after, or the day after that!

I realized this when Peters reported my own suicide to me. He told me that Anderson had said I died last year—*last year*. I took that piece of information, so casually dropped, and with equal calm stored it in a cranny of my mind. I must have lost months! When I looked outside I saw that it was summertime. I must actually have had a loss of memory (that rushing blackness in the subway seemed yesterday or last week, not last year—but I knew it had happened on a rainy fall day, the twelfth of October). The problem was: had I forgotten the same period they thought I had? Amnesia cuts two ways. You can forget your remote past, your early years, childhood, youth, young manhood, or you can forget a piece of your maturity.

I knew now that I had forgotten some things—I did not realize how much.

But I could lie. I could build a past that was not true but which fitted the role I had been given. I could report the fictional history of a destitute man, and I could do it well because I had studied and put to heart many such case histories.

They expected me gradually to recover my memory. Harvey Peters said that I showed improvement. Dr. Littlefield gave me tests each Thursday and told me that I showed less fear, less anxiety. But they would never, or only after too long a time, know me for the man I was. Or had been.

Why should I be Dr. George Matthews any longer? What was wrong with being John Brown? Someone wanted me to be John Brown. Why should I fight him?

Was identity worth slow decay?

No. I would lie.

I had made up my mind.

A year contains 365 days. I died last year. Dr. George Matthews died this minute. John Brown is born. John Brown will escape. John Brown will find the one who wanted to obliterate Dr. George Matthews—and who played with him first, twitting him with comedy!—and John Brown will destroy him.

"I was born in Erie, Pennsylvania. My father worked in the mills. I had seven brothers. My mother died. My sister ran away. I joined the army under another name."

"You remember now?"

"It comes back slowly. I was hurt—somewhere in France. I came home. There were no jobs. I was on relief. I went from town to town. I worked on farms up and down both coasts. Then I was away for a while."

"Away? Just away?"

Slick, glib lies. I had to hide something. I had to make my story fit the pattern she expected, and she expected me to try to hold back some part of the whole.

"I got married. Down South. I worked for a real estate office. Then times got hard again. She was having a child. She should have had an operation. We waited too long. We didn't have the money for the operation. She died."

"I'm sorry."

A facile lie told slowly—a typical syndrome of self-pity. This was what was expected. This was what she was going to get.

For a few moments I said nothing. Dr. Littlefield was respectfully silent. I wanted to laugh deeply. Life was bitter and good and I hated all of them. I was glad I knew how to lie.

"Then what happened?" Tentatively. Ready to take it back with silence if her timing was off. She did not want to precipitate an emotional block. This bland little trained priestess of scientific black magic thought she could steal my story from my unwilling mind. And it was I who was doing the embezzling!

"I left town. I went the rounds again. Things got worse. You know how it was during the Depression? In season I became a harvest hand. In the winter I stayed in cities—the relief is better there. I worked on the PWA, the WPA. I bummed around . . ."

Looking down, as if I were ashamed. I was not ashamed. Even if this had been my life, I would not have been ashamed.

"Yes?"

"I drank."

"Much?"

"A lot."

She did not say anything. Had I overplayed my hand?

"It's funny but I never want a drink anymore."

That ought to do it!

"No?"

"No, not since the bust on the head . . ."

I hoped the location was right. It was usually the head.

"When did you hurt your head?" she thought she was helping me remember! It was working!

"Before I came here. I had a fight. Over a woman. He came at me with a bottle. That's all I remember."

A classic tale. Cribbed from a million sordid lives. But it would do.

Of course, they did not let me go right away. I had to run the gauntlet every day for a week. Dr. Littlefield saw me again, then Dr. Smithers and Dr. Goldman. Harvey asked me sly questions. I fed them all the same pap. A detail here, a detail there. Careful parallels drawn from selected casework. Never too close, but always the pattern they had been taught to expect.

It worked. One day Dr. Littlefield told me, "You are much better. We think you are almost well. How would you like to leave us this week?"

A carefully nurtured smile. Must not be too much of a shock, but at the same time patient should be made to feel the doctor is pleased with his recovery.

"That would be nice. You really mean it?" Equally carefully contrived incredulity. Doctor must be made to feel patient's relief and pleased amazement, but doctor must not be allowed to perceive that the game has become very, very boring.

"Friday. You're to see Miss Willows today. I think she has a surprise for you."

I was not surprised to find Miss Willows fat and sloppy. Social workers so frequently are. This was the woman who was to rehabilitate me! Well, I was willing.

"I've talked with Dr. Littlefield about you," she said. "She tells me that you are thinking of leaving us?"

"Yes, ma'am." I knew enough to be humble with her. Caseworkers like humble people.

"We don't want you to go out and lead the life you've led before. Not that it's your fault. But if you will help yourself, we can help you."

"Yes, ma'am."

"A job in a cafeteria—not a very big job—but one with a good chance for advancement."

"You're very kind, ma'am."

"And if you work hard, and be sure to remember to report back to us every month the way Dr. Littlefield told you—why, there's no telling where you might end up!"

"Yes, ma'am. You're very kind, ma'am."

On Friday, July 12, 1944, John Brown stepped onto a crosstown bus. In his pocket was the address of a Coney Island cafeteria where Miss Willows had told him to apply for a job as waiter and busboy. His clothes were cheap and new. His face was studiously blank. If you had looked at him closely, you would have said that he had once seen better days.

. . .

From then on my name was John Brown. I could not explain, even to myself, the process by which I came to refute my identity. Not so long ago I had been a specialist with a comfortable living, a wife, and a certain amount of status in the community. Now the world knew me only as a counterman in an all-night Coney Island cafeteria.

I had not intended to take the job Miss Willows offered me when I left the hospital that warm July day; there had been still some fight left in me. For weeks I had been shamming, assuming a false character, because I knew this to be the quickest way to return to what most of humanity considers sanity. I had been bitter during those weeks, cynical enough to adopt a fictional character and to play a hypocritical charade; but I had not lost hope. I might well have despaired if once in that time I had been allowed to look in a mirror.

I had noticed the lack of mirrors in the ward, but I had decided that this was a precaution similar to the banning of belts and braces: a mirror can be broken into sharp shards which can be employed to slit throats. Added care must have been taken to prevent my self-inspection in the last days of my convalescence; however, if it was, I was unaware. I do not blame Dr. Littlefield for not letting me have a mirror, although if I had been in her place, I might have considered a confrontation a necessary part of my patient's adjustment. But, perhaps, this judgment is unfair; Dr. Littlefield probably did not realize that I had not always been that way . . .

As it was I first caught sight of myself while having a Coke in a drugstore, just after I descended from the bus that had taken me crosstown. Behind this soda fountain was a mirror, fancily decorated with gaudy signs urging the purchase of egg malted-milks and black-and-white sodas. I glanced up and looked into it without knowing what I was doing. My mind read the signs first, felt good at seeing a familiar sight while being as usual a little critical of the advertising profession. Then, when the signs were read, my consciousness became curious about the horribly disfigured man who must be sitting next to me. He was not old—about my age, now that I studied his face—although he had seemed older at first glance. This was because his short-cropped hair was gray streaked with white and his jaw, that showed the remains of strength, trembled spasmodically. But what made him really fascinat-

ingly ugly was the wide, long, angry red scar that traversed his face diagonally from one ear across the nose and down to the root of the jaw at
the base of his other cheek. It was an old scar that had knit badly and in
healing had pulled and twisted at the skin until the face it rode had the
texture of coarse parchment and the grimace of a clown. One cheek,
and the eye with it, was drawn sidewise and upward into a knowing
leer—the other drooped, and with it a corner of the mouth, as if its
owner were stricken with grief. The skin's color was that of cigar ash,
but the scar's color was bright carmine. I pitied the man, then was
embarrassed to look around at him; surely, he must have seen me staring at his reflection! But as I had this thought I noticed that his glass
emptied itself of Coca-Cola just as I sucked noisily at my straw, and a
suspicion crept into my mind. I fought it back, silently scoffed at it, and
kept my eyes averted while I waited for my neighbor to go. How long I
might have continued this self-deception I shall never know since I was
soon forced to admit that the horribly mutilated face I had been staring
at was my own. A little boy came in and sat down on the empty stool
next to mine—it had been occupied only in my imagination—giggled,
and said to his perspiring mother, "Oh, Mama, look quick at the man!
Mama, how did he get like that?"

I fled with the child's taunt ringing in my ears. How did I get to be
like this? I asked myself. And then, before I tried to answer that: How
can I return to Sara like this?

I stopped in my tracks, stood staring out into the traffic. It would be
so easy to run out into the street, to feel the crushing weight of a bus or
truck, a blinding instant of pain, and then oblivion! My legs twitched
with this necessity, a great hand pushed relentlessly at my straining
back—I took two halting steps to the curb, hesitated at its edge as if it
were a precipice. My mouth went slack and the trembling of my jaw
increased. Sweat trickled down my sides from under my armpits.

Then, slowly, I turned and walked down the street towards a subway
kiosk. John Brown, waiter or counterman or busboy in a Coney Island
eatery, belonged to that face. For the time being, I was John Brown. Dr.
George Matthews would remain in hiding at least a while longer. I did
not know who had persuaded my wife that I had died, but she must
have had good reason to think I had or else she would never have left
the city. Perhaps it was better that way. Sara had a small income of her

own, enough to take care of her. In the meantime I would have a chance to think things over. I laughed. Once I had been a psychologist and had thought myself capable of adjusting to any predicament. I fingered my scar, its treacherous smoothness—well, I was capable of an adjustment. In fact, I had already adjusted so completely that I was incapable of remembering the face that had preceded that tortured grimace seen in a fly-specked mirror. I had forsworn any personality other than "John Brown, homeless, picked up wandering."

I took the B.M.T. to Coney Island.

Mr. Fuller was a small seedy-looking man with a scrubbed-pink face and bleary blue eyes. He looked like he might take one drink too many too often. The shirt he had on had probably been worn more than once; his tie was of sleazy imitation silk. His shoulders drooped, he looked harried. I know he did not mean to be unkind to me.

We sat down at one of the tables in the front of the cafeteria. It was the middle of the afternoon and the place was nearly empty. Outside the calliope of a merry-go-round wheezed and clanged and banged. A barker farther down the street exhorted a straggling, sweaty crowd of passersby to "Step right up and pay a dime to see Zozo, the beautiful, delovely Latin who lives with a boa constrictor." Mr. Fuller paid no attention to these sounds. He fingered my slip of paper, studying it as if it were a text. He regarded it for such a long time that I began to debate the possibility that he would ever look up again; whereupon he coughed once, squirmed, blew his nose.

"Ever work in a cafeteria before, Mr."—here he glanced at the slip of paper—"Brown?"

"No, sir." I had better say "sir." Now that I had decided to remain John Brown, I would have very little money. Dr. George Matthews' resources were no longer open to me—if they ever had been—and getting this job was all-important.

"How do I know you can do the work? I'm not used to inexperienced help," he complained.

"I'm good with people. I know how to talk to them. I have patience." As soon as I had said these words, I was sure they were the wrong ones and my heart sank.

"There's more to the job than that," he said. He looked at me inquiringly. "You gotta be careful, you know? I been having too much breakage lately. They don't like too much breakage."

"'They'?" I asked.

"The company," he explained. "They come in a couple of times a week and look around. Once a month they take inventory. If there's been too much breakage I hear about it. I'd like to put you on, but I can't be too careful . . ."

I spoke slowly and distinctly, trying desperately to sound sincere. "I'd be very careful," I said. "I wouldn't break anything."

He looked at me for a long time, queerly. At first I did not understand what he was looking at. Then came the shock of recognition—my hand clutched at my face.

"People hardly notice it," I said quickly, as the tortured image rose in front of my eyes and partially obscured his face. "I don't think your customers would mind. They haven't on other jobs," I lied.

He thought for a moment. I could see that the effort needed to make a decision was great for him. "I admit it's hard to get a good, steady man these days. Maybe a fellow like you has a hard time getting jobs? Maybe, if you got a good job like this, you'd be steady?"

"I'll be steady."

He thought again. He squirmed around in his chair. He blew his nose.

"Well, I'll try you for a week. If you work hard and apply yourself, you may have a steady job. That is, if the customers don't complain."

He stood up and walked to the rear of the cafeteria. I followed him. He gave me two clean aprons, a pair of white duck trousers, and a black leather bow tie. Then he told me to report for work at six o'clock that night. My hours would be from six until two, when I would be relieved. We shook hands and I thanked him. Then I left the place to go look for a room.

During the next month, the sultry, crowded days of August, I worked at the cafeteria six nights a week, slept or sat on the beach and read in the daytime, existed. I would be lying to say that this was an unhappy period. Indeed, I might say the opposite. I had no desire to do anything else. The books I read were adventure stories and the like. I did not dream of my former life, or of an impossibly satisfying one to come. I made no friends or enemies. Yet—if a form of contentment that was not unlike a drug-induced stupor can be called happiness—I was happy.

I had promised myself a period of time "to think things over." Yet I thought nothing over, made no decisions. Someday I might try again to be Dr. George Matthews, the eminent young psychiatrist. Someday I would return to Sara—Sara, my heart quickened at the thought of her. Yet day after day went by, and I did nothing.

Several times in the first weeks I worked at the All-Brite I experienced recurring fits of self-consciousness. I would suddenly become acutely aware of my disfigurement (perhaps, a customer would stare at me too long), and I would leave my work, go to the lavatory and peer at my face in the looking glass. In time, though, the first horror of my discovery passed and there came in its place a peculiar, perverted sense of pride in my distinction. No other quality of my adopted personality differed in the least from that of any man I might meet on the street or find sitting on the beach. In all other ways I was cut out of the same bolt of cloth as everyone else: I had a small job, I was lonely, I had little security. But I did have a bright scar on my face, and this disfigurement soon stood in my mind as a symbol of my new identity. I was John Brown, and as John Brown I had a scar that ran from my ear across my face diagonally. It was a strangely satisfying attribute.

There were times when a little of my old objectivity returned to me and I stood aside and looked at myself in self-appraisal, but these times were rare and soon they stopped altogether. I knew that being proud of a defect was a defense, a stepping-stone to neurosis, but I did not care. I concentrated on my tasks, saw to it that there was always one piece of each variety of pie on the counter, sufficient shaved ice on the salad trays, and that the water was changed every hour in the percolators. I waited on trade and learned to be obsequious to get nickel and dime tips. And in all this time the thought of Sara, the home that had been ours, my practice and former prestige, was only a faint and annoying memory that came in the night like the ache of a hollow tooth and which I dismissed easily from my mind, ignored as I would any petty distraction. My life had become the product of my own distorted imaginings, and I did not dare let visions of a former reality disturb my precarious equilibrium, even though in my secret mind I may have longed for my former life.

Nor did I allow myself to think of Jacob Blunt. The whole warped history of Dr. George Matthews' last day remained a forgotten thing. There are some memories we have, and which we are aware of, but never allow to become entirely conscious. Such memories are always lurking directly beneath the surface of our reason, and in times of crisis certain of our actions can only be explained in terms of these remembered experiences; yet they never become tangible and we never allow ourselves to speak of them in telling of our past. So it was with me regarding the details of Jacob Blunt and his "little men" and the other vicious nonsense of that last day which may or may not have resulted in the death of Frances Raye and my accident in the subway. I knew they had happened but I chose to forget them. They were no part of my present life.

I even became proficient at my craft, if you can call being a counter-man in a cafeteria a craft. There were three of us to a shift and each of us had a particular section of the counter to care for. The coffee urn, the salad table, and the desserts were my province; it was my responsibility to see that the kitchen kept a sufficient quantity of these items on hand for me to replace the empty dishes as soon as the customers deplenished the stock. A simple job, but one that had its difficulties. Some of my troubles lay with the customers; patrons would insist on handling each of the sweets before choosing one or would demand special orders that took extra time to prepare and then get testy because they had to wait. Often it was the cook who was slow in preparing foods that were the most popular, while flooding me with huge quantities of the slower-moving delicacies. I worked out systems by which I could balance supply and demand, push butterscotch pie and sell less apple, get rid of the avocado salad when the avocados were not all they should be—systems that worked so well that the day came when Mr. Fuller had a little talk with me and gave me a raise.

He stood behind me, watching me work and making me nervous. I heard him snuffle and blow his nose. He even cleared his throat before he said, "They're pleased with the way you've turned out, Brown. Mighty pleased. Along with me they felt that maybe the customers would complain, but we haven't had any complaints. The breakage is down this month, too. You've turned out pretty well."

"I try my best," I said.

"They told me to tell you that they wanted you to stay with us, and not to get any foolish notions in your head about working someplace else. We're going to raise your salary two dollars a week."

He snuffled again and wiped his nose on an unclean handkerchief. Why should Fuller or his ever-present "they" fear my leaving? Why should I look for another job? I was satisfied where I was.

The two dollars more a week meant nothing to me. I had been living on what I earned, spending it all on food, shelter, an occasional clean shirt, but needing nothing more. Now that I had it, I did not know what to do with it. Eventually, I put the extra money in my top bureau drawer, adding to it each week, not saving the way a cautious man saves with a goal in mind or for a prudent principle, but only putting it away because I had no desire to spend it and the bureau drawer seemed a more appropriate place than the wastebasket.

During the day and early evening the cafeteria was patronized by ordinary people out for a good time: small businessmen with their families, clerks with their girls, bands of teenage youngsters who dropped in for a hamburger and a Coke and stayed long enough to be a nuisance. But after ten o'clock the character of the clientele changed radically. It was at this hour that the carnival people began to appear.

They were of all sorts and all kinds. Gaunt, undernourished men would sidle up to the counter, order coffee and rolls, take their orders to a table, and sit there the rest of the night. These were the less prosperous ones, the "drifters." They earned their livings by taking tickets, operating rides, selling hot dogs and floss candy, by doing odd jobs. They sat with each other and did not mingle with the second group, the "artists."

Brassy blondes, flashily made-up redheads, rarely a glossy-headed brunette, showgirls, wives of entrepreneurs, lady shills—all of these were considered "artists"; as well as their masculine counterparts in checked suits and pointed-toe shoes, barkers, grifters who operated the "sucker" games, pitchmen and the "big boys" who owned the concessions. The "artists" came in later than the "drifters," spent more money, and were more convivial. They were a society to themselves, but a friendly, open-handed one; I learned that the "drifters" did not mingle with them of their own choosing, not because the "artists" were snobbish.

There was also a third group that kept partly separate, but also sometimes mixed with the shills and showgirls. Zozo, "the delovely Latin who lives with a boa constrictor," was a member of this clique, as was a man named Barney Gorham who kept a shooting gallery. Barney interested me very much. He was a great ape of a man with smoothed-back, glistening black hair and a half-grown beard. As he walked his shoulders would sway involuntarily; watching him one was always conscious of the movement of muscles beneath his rough flannel shirt. He would give the impression of having money when first met, and yet if one talked to him for any length of time he would invariably try to borrow a dollar or two. He pretended to be a painter, and it was true that he did paint in his spare time. Several times, when he brought them to the All-Brite, I saw some of his daubs; badly designed seascapes, highly romanticized pastoral scenes, and gaudy portraits of those of the showgirls he had slept with. For Barney was successful with the "ponies," as the chorines were called. Usually, he had one or two girls with him, talking vivaciously, while he sat slumped in his chair glowering at the room.

I called these last the "characters" and there were many of them, yet, of the three groups they were the most difficult to define and limit. A few of them were intellectuals or pseudointellectuals, and what they were doing at Coney Island I could not understand. Others were freaks; dwarfs and bearded ladies, the pin-headed boy who was really a cretin yet was accepted as a member of this loosely knit society—he was always accompanied by a large, motherly-looking woman with a monstrous goiter—a man who owned a motion picture theater, and a girl who ran a photographer's studio. I decided at last that what they all had in common was a sense of dissatisfaction. Both the "drifters" and the "artists" were content with their life, but the "characters"—although many of them were successful financially—were malcontents. They were not peculiar to Coney Island except in their concentration; you might find small groups such as these in the theatrical district of any middle-western city. However widely they might be separated during the winter months, as each sought a way of earning a living (some by touring the South with a carnival, some by doing odd parts on Broadway or at Radio City, others by touting the racetracks or taking any "rube" job they could find), they always returned to this place in the summer, met at this cafeteria, considered this the center of their lives.

I supposed it was only natural that after a time I came to be a part of this last group. John Brown was homeless too, and like everyone else needed to feel that he belonged. It cost nothing to sit down at one of the tables that had been designed to seat four, but around which six or seven were sitting, and soon I found myself joining in the conversations. These, instead of being confined to carnival gossip as I had guessed they might be, were about almost anything. I was surprised at how learned Barney was, for example, and both amused and frightened at the thought that Zozo, who lived with a boa constrictor, had not only read Kant but also Fichte and Spinoza. One of the favorite topics of discussion was psychoanalysis (it usually came up when one of the group would remember the time when the Wild Man from Borneo with Sells-Floto—"a quiet type who liked Guy Lombardo and Wisconsin lager"—went berserk on the midway and killed three men—"the show did great business for the rest of the stand; we made all the dailies and that year we went way over our nut"), and I astonished them with my knowledge of the field. While I restrained my memory of my past life, I seemed to have no compunction about using information I had gained during that life—in fact, one of the reasons why I was soon so fascinatedly a member of this odd group was because I was pleased to find so many neurotic personalities at one time. The All-Brite was a veritable game preserve for the psychiatric sportsman. Yet by the time I had worked in the cafeteria a month, I knew several of the "characters" well enough to consider them my friends, and also to forget that I had once considered them eccentric.

Sonia Astart was one of my friends. She entered the cafeteria at the same time each night, a few minutes after twelve. She would walk between the tables, speaking to this person or that, finally making her way to the counter, where her order was always the same: a pot of black coffee. Then she would go sit with Barney or Zozo.

I joined Barney's table more often than I did the others, and Sonia was the reason for this. She seldom had much to say, but one never noticed her silence. When I was near her, I felt her presence and it was far more stimulating than words. Yet she had few of the standard hallmarks of womanly beauty. She was tall, and her features were irregular—she was not even especially fastidious. Often she was without lipstick or powder, sometimes the sloppy shirts and slacks she wore were badly in need of a pressing.

I am certain that there were times when Sonia did not know how she would manage to scrape enough money together to live the week. She was usually between jobs. And it was at these times that she would change from a listener to the most talkative of all those present. She had a marvelous fund of stories about the carnival folk, and she would talk politics or sex or a theory of art for hours on end with Zozo or myself or anyone who would argue with her, interrupting the discussion frequently to get up from the table, corner a prosperous-seeming friend who had just come in the door, speak long and earnestly with him for a few minutes, borrow money from him. It was as if she could not carry off the necessary wheedling, the tale of sudden, unexpected misfortune but certain better luck to come, without first plunging into the fever of argument. And when I considered the content of these conversations later, I realized that they were only word games, intellectual puzzles that aborted thought.

Sonia and Barney were among the more complex of the "characters." There were others more obviously and conventionally neurotic. One of these was the Preacher, an extremely tall man who dressed in cowboy boots, riding breeches, a flannel shirt, and a Stetson hat. He would stride into the cafeteria, walk up to the first people he encountered, and begin to exhort them to leave the city.

"Go find yourself a home on the plains!" he would shout. "A free place in a wide space where you won't be bothered with no taxicabs tootling their crazy horns at you, where you can cross a street and take your time—Gawd's Country!" He would orate like this on his one and only subject, the West, oblivious to the fact that no one listened, until suddenly for no visible reason he would stop talking, stare belligerently about for a moment, and then stalk angrily out. I never saw him sit down at a table or join in a conversation even with the "drifters," nor did I ever meet anyone who knew anything about him.

. . .

I would sit with these people for hours every night, afterwards going home to my sleeping room not to leave it until late in the afternoon of the next day. I cannot say I looked forward to these social hours (they were not in any way compared to the chosen leisure of a healthy man; they were only another form of my somnambulism). When I was not actually asleep, I submerged my personality in the mechanical compulsions of my job, or in an equally mechanical participation in this society of misfits. It was a complete negation of everything that had gone before.

I suppose it was inevitable that I should sleep with Sonia, although I can say honestly that at no time did I calculate it. First we fell into the habit of sitting next to each other, an accident in the beginning and then a not unpleasant institution. Later, we would walk home together in the early hours of the morning—she lived near me. During these walks we talked little, but there existed a common feeling between us which I cannot define except to say that when I was near her in this way was the closest I ever came to awaking. Then one night by mutual consent, without a word of love being spoken, we walked by her boardinghouse and went to my room. From then on, although it was never a constant procedure and there were many nights when she went to her place and I went to mine, we considered this a part of our relationship and I believe we both found solace in it.

One night Sonia did not come to the All-Brite and I walked home alone. This, in itself, was not unusual. Sonia often missed a night a week at the cafeteria, and I never questioned her as to her whereabouts on these nights. I cannot say that I felt lonely that night either; as a matter of fact it was a beautiful night in early September, there was a blood-red harvest moon, and I took a long walk along Surf Avenue, exploring all the many side streets I had never ventured down before.

Coney Island is a terrifyingly empty neighborhood late at night. By two o'clock in the morning most of the concessions are closed, except for a few dance halls and bars and one merry-go-round that goes all night. A few roistering sailors staggered, yipped, and brawled a short way up the street that night, the three sheets and gaudy sideshow signs gleamed red in the rich moonlight, the twisted skeleton of the roller coaster stretched its conjectural latticework up towards the pitch-black sky.

I felt exhilarated, almost as if I had been drinking. I remember I stood in front of a fun house, the façade of which featured roly-poly clowns with starchy faces and huge grinning lips, and bent double with laughter at my own crazy reflection in a distorting mirror. That, I know, was the first time I had looked into a mirror with equanimity. But the distortion of this flawed surface was so grotesque that it relieved the natural horror of my face, and by making it ridiculous enabled me for an instant to accept it. I was still laughing at the insanely contorted self I had seen as I turned down my own street and started for my rooms.

Except for the main stem, Coney Island streets are dark at nights— and in 1944 they were doubly dark because of the blackout. Still the moon supplied a neon light of its own. I had walked this street many times and I had grown to like its ramshackle air; even the occasional rumble of the elevated seemed reassuring. Then, all of a sudden, I was afraid.

I do not know for how long I had been aware of footsteps sounding behind me, but at that moment I realized that they did not belong to a casual pedestrian but rather to someone who was following me. Trembling, I stood aside to let this person pass—sure that he would not.

When I turned around no one was there.

I was childishly panic-stricken. I experienced an irrational attack of terror. I remember that I put my hand up to my face to feel my scar, automatically, as if it were in some way connected with my phobia. I stood there for several minutes, holding my breath, feeling my heart hammer at my ribs and my blood freeze in my veins, ready to flee at the sight of a shadow or the sound of an echo. But no one came.

I started for home again.

And the sound of footsteps followed me! Whoever it was must have hidden in a doorway when I stopped and turned around. On the blacked-out street I did not discover his presence. I knew now that whoever it was intended to do me harm—why else hide? I walked fast.

The person behind me walked fast, too. I began to run. He ran. I ran as fast as I could, and by then I was only a block from my house. If I could reach my door, would I be safe? All I could hear was the sound of those feet. He seemed not ten paces behind me. Then I became aware of an automobile coming down the street towards me. I ran out into the street in front of it, waving my arms frantically to flag it down. I could see that its headlights were mere glowing slits, but I preferred the known danger of being run over to the unknown danger the footsteps implied . . .

The last person I thought of before the car hit me was Sonia. For some reason her hair was slicked back like a man's and she had a mustache. I hated her.

KELLY LINK

Carnation, Lily, Lily, Rose

Dear Mary (if that is your name),

I bet you'll be pretty surprised to hear from me. It really is me, by the way, although I have to confess at the moment that not only can I not seem to keep your name straight in my head, Laura? Susie? Odile? but I seem to have forgotten my own name. I plan to keep trying different combinations, Joe loves Lola, Willy loves Suki, Henry loves you, sweetie, Georgia? honeypie, darling. Do any of these seem right to you?

All last week I felt like something was going to happen, a sort of bees and ants feeling. I taught my classes and came home and went to bed, all week waiting for the thing that was going to happen, and then on Friday I died.

One of the things I seem to have misplaced is how, or maybe I mean why. It's like the names. I know that we lived together in a house on a hill in a comfortably mediocre city for nine years, that we didn't have kids, except once, almost, and that you're a terrible cook and so was I, and we ate out whenever we could afford to. I taught at a good university, Princeton? Berkeley? Notre Dame? I was a good teacher, and my students liked me. But I can't remember the name of the street we lived on, or the author of the last book I read, or your last name, which was also my name, or how I died. It's funny, Sarah? but the only two names I know for sure are real are Looly Bellows, the girl who beat me up in fourth grade, and your cat. I'm not going to put your cat's name down on paper just yet.

We were going to name the baby Beatrice. I just remembered that. We were going to name her after your aunt, the one that doesn't like me. Didn't like me. Did she come to the funeral?

I've been here for three days, and I'm trying to pretend that it's just a vacation, like when we went to that island in that country. Santorini? Great Britain? The one with all the cliffs. The one with the hotel with the bunkbeds, and little squares of pink toilet paper, like handkerchiefs. It had seashells in the window too, didn't it, that were transparent like bottle glass? They smelled like bleach? It was a very nice island. No trees. You said that when you died, you hoped heaven would be an island like that. And now I'm dead, and here I am.

This is an island too, I think. There is a beach, and down on the beach is a mailbox where I'm going to post this letter. Other than the beach, there is the building in which I sit and write this letter. It seems to be a perfectly pleasant resort hotel with no other guests, no receptionist, no host, no events coordinator, no bellboy. There is a television set, very old-fashioned, in the hotel lobby. I fiddled the antenna for a long time, but got no picture. Just static. I tried to make images, people out of the static. It looked like they were waving at me.

My room is on the second floor. It has a sea view. All the rooms here have views of the sea. There is a desk in my room, and a good supply of plain, waxy white paper and envelopes in one of the drawers. Laurel? Maria? Gertrude?

I haven't gone out of sight of the hotel yet, Lucille? because I am afraid that it might not be there when I get back.

Yours truly,
You know who.

The dead man lies on his back on the hotel bed, his hands busy and curious, stroking his body up and down as if it didn't really belong to him at all. One hand cups his testicles, the other tugs hard at his erect penis. His heels push against the mattress and his eyes are open, and his mouth. He is trying to say someone's name.

Outside, the sky seems much too close, made out of some gray stuff that only grudgingly allows light through. The dead man has noticed that it never gets any lighter or darker, but sometimes the air begins to feel heavier, and then stuff falls out of the sky, fist-sized lumps of whitish-gray doughy matter. It falls until the beach is covered, and immediately begins to dissolve. The dead man was outside, the first time the sky fell. Now he waits inside until the beach is clear again. Sometimes he watches television, although the reception is poor.

The sea goes up and back the beach, sucking and curling around the mailbox at high tide. There is something about it that the dead man doesn't like much. It doesn't smell like salt the way a sea should. Cara? Jasmine? It smells like wet upholstery, burnt fur.

Dear May? April? Ianthe?

My room has a bed with thin, limp sheets and an amateurish painting of a woman sitting under a tree. She has nice breasts, but a peculiar expression on her face, for a woman in a painting in a hotel room, even in a hotel like this. She looks disgruntled.

I have a bathroom with hot and cold running water, towels, and a mirror. I looked in the mirror for a long time, but I didn't look familiar. It's the first time I've ever had a good look at a dead person. I have brown hair, receding at the temples, brown eyes, and good teeth, white, even, and not too large. I have a small mark on my shoulder, Celeste? where you bit me when we were making love that last time. Did you somehow realize it would be the last time we made love? Your expression was sad: also, I seem to recall, angry. I remember your expression now, Eliza? You glared up at me without blinking and when you came, you said my name, and although I can't remember my name, I remember you said it as if you hated me. We hadn't made love for a long time.

I estimate my height to be about 5'11", and although I am not unhandsome, I have an anxious, somewhat fixed expression. This may be due to circumstances.

I was wondering if my name was by any chance Roger or Timothy or Charles. When we went on vacation, I remember there was a similar confusion about names, although not ours. We were trying to think of one for her, I mean, for Beatrice. Cara, Jasmine? We wrote them all with long pieces of stick on the beach, to see how they looked. We started with the plain names, like Jane and Susan and Laura. We tried practical names like Polly and Meredith and Hope, and then we became extravagant. We dragged our sticks through the sand and produced entire families of scowling little girls named Gudrun, Jezebel, Jerusalem, Zedeenya, Zerilla. How about Looly, I said. I knew a girl named Looly Bellows once. Your hair was all snarled around your face, stiff with salt. You had about a zillion freckles. You were laughing so hard you had to prop yourself up with your stick. You said that sounded like a made-up name.

Love,
You know who.

The dead man is trying to act as if he is really here, in this place. He is trying to act in as normal and appropriate a fashion as is possible. He is trying to be a good tourist.

He hasn't been able to fall asleep in the bed, although he has turned the painting to the wall. He is not sure that the bed is a bed. When his eyes are closed, it doesn't seem to be a bed. He sleeps on the floor, which seems more floorlike than the bed seems bedlike. He lies on the floor with nothing over him and pretends that he isn't dead. He pretends that he is in bed with his wife, and dreaming. He makes up a nice dream about a party where he has forgotten everyone's name. He touches himself. Then he gets up and sees that the white stuff that has fallen out of the sky is dissolving on the beach, little clumps of it heaped around the mailbox like foam.

Dear Elspeth? Deborah? Frederica?

Things are getting worse. I know that if I could just get your name straight, things would get better.

I told you that I'm on an island, but I'm not sure I am. I'm having doubts about my bed and the hotel. I'm not happy about the sea or the sky either. The things that have names that I'm sure of, I'm not sure they're those things, if you understand what I'm saying, Mallory? I'm not sure I'm still breathing, either. When I think about it, I do. I only think about it, because it's too quiet when I'm not. Did you know, Alison? that up in those mountains, the Berkshires? the altitude gets too high, and then real people, live people forget to breathe also? There's a name for when they forget. I forget what the name is.

But if the bed isn't a bed, and the beach isn't a beach, then what are they? When I look at the horizon, there almost seems to be corners. When I lay down, the corners on the bed receded like the horizon.

Then there is the problem about the mail. Yesterday I simply slipped the letter into a plain envelope, and slipped the envelope, unaddressed, into the mailbox. This morning the letter was gone, and when I stuck my hand inside, and then my arm, the sides of the box were damp and sticky. I inspected the back side, only to discover an open panel. When the tide rises, the mail goes out to sea. So I really have no idea if you, Pamela? or for that matter, if anyone is reading this letter. I tried dragging the mailbox farther up the beach. The waves hissed and spit at me, a wave ran across my foot, cold and furry and black, and I gave up. So I will simply have to trust the local mail system.

> Hoping you get this soon,
> You know who.

The dead man goes for a walk along the beach. The sea keeps its distance, but the hotel stays close behind him. He notices that the tide retreats when he walks towards it, which is good. He doesn't want to get his shoes wet. If he walked out to sea, would it part for him like that guy in the Bible? Onan?

He is wearing his second-best suit, the one he wore for interviews and weddings. He figures it's either the suit that he died in, or else the one that his wife buried him in. He has been wearing it ever since he woke up and found himself on the island, disheveled and sweating, his clothing wrinkled as if he had come a great distance. He takes his suit and his shoes off only when he is in his hotel room. He puts them back on to go outside. He goes for a walk along the beach. His fly is undone.

The little waves slap at the dead man. He can see teeth under that water, in the glassy black walls of the larger waves, the waves farther out to sea. He walks a fair distance, stopping frequently to rest. He tires easily. He keeps to the dunes. His shoulders are hunched, his head down. When the sky begins to change, he turns around. The hotel is right behind him. He doesn't seem at all surprised to see it there. All the time he has been walking, he has had the feeling that just over the next dune someone is waiting for him. He hopes that maybe it is his wife, but on the other hand, if it were his wife, she'd be dead too, and if she were dead, he could remember her name.

Dear Matilda? Ivy? Alicia?

I picture my letters sailing out to you, over those waves with teeth in them, little white boats. Dear reader, Beryl? Fern? you would like to know how I am so sure these letters are getting to you? I remember that it always used to annoy you, the way I took things for granted. But I'm sure you're reading this the way that, even though I'm still walking around and breathing (when I remember to), I'm sure I'm dead. I think that these letters are getting to you, mangled, sodden, but still legible. If they arrived the regular way, you probably wouldn't believe they were from me, anyway.

I remembered a name today, Elvis Presley. He was the singer, right? Blue shoes, kissy fat lips, slickery voice? Dead, right? Like me. Marilyn

Monroe too, white dress blowing up like a sail, Gandhi, Abraham Lincoln, Looly Bellows (remember?) who lived next door to me when we were both eleven. She had migraine headaches all through the school year, which made her mean. Nobody liked her, before, when we didn't know she was sick. She broke my nose because I pulled her wig off one day on a dare. They took a tumor out of her head that was the size of a hen's egg, but she died anyway.

When I pulled her wig off, she didn't cry. She had brittle bits of hair tufting out of her scalp, and her face was swollen with fluid, like she'd been stung by bees. She looked so old. She told me that when she was dead, she'd come back and haunt me, and after she died, I pretended that I could see not just her, but whole clusters of fat, pale, hairless ghosts lingering behind trees, swollen and humming like hives. It became a scary fun game I played with my friends. We called the ghosts loolies, and we made up rules that kept us safe from them. A certain kind of walk, a diet of white food—marshmallows, white bread rolled into pellets, and plain white rice. When we got tired of the loolies, we killed them off by decorating her grave with the remains of the powdered donuts and Wonderbread our suspicious mothers at last refused to buy for us.

Are you decorating my grave, Felicity? Gay? Have you forgotten me yet? Have you gotten another cat yet, another lover? or are you still in mourning for me? God, I want you so much, Carnation, Lily? Lily? Rose? It's the reverse of necrophilia, I suppose—the dead man who wants one last fuck with his wife. But you're not here, and if you were here, would you go to bed with me?

I write you letters with my right hand, and I do the other thing with my left hand that I used to do with my left hand, ever since I was fourteen, when I didn't have anything better to do. I seem to recall that when I was fourteen there wasn't anything better to do. I think about you, I think about touching you, think that you're touching me, and I see you naked, and you're glaring at me, and I'm about to shout out your name, and then I come and the name on my lips is the name of some dead person, or some totally made-up name.

Does it bother you, Linda? Donna? Penthesilia? Do you want to know the worst thing? Just a minute ago I was grinding into the pillow, bucking and pushing and pretending it was you, Stacy? under me, sweet fuck, it felt good, just like when I was alive, and when I came, I said, "Beatrice." And I remembered coming to get you in the hospital after the miscarriage.

There were a lot of things I wanted to say. I mean, neither of us was really sure that we wanted a baby anyway, and part of me, sure, was relieved that I wasn't going to have to learn how to be a father just yet, but there were still things that I wish I'd said to you. There were a lot of things I wish I'd said to you.

You know who.

The dead man sets out across the interior of the island. At some point after his first expedition, the hotel moved quietly back to its original location, the dead man in his room, looking into the mirror, expression intent, hips tilted against the cool tile. This flesh is dead. It should not rise. It rises. Now the hotel is back beside the mailbox, which is empty when he walks down to check it.

The middle of the island is rocky, barren. There are no trees here, the dead man realizes, feeling relieved. He walks for a short distance — less than two miles, he calculates, before he stands on the opposite shore. Before him is a flat expanse of water, sky folded down over the horizon. When the dead man turns around, he can see his hotel, looking forlorn and abandoned. But when he squints, the shadows on the back veranda waver, becoming a crowd of people, all looking back at him. He has his hands inside his pants, he is touching himself. He takes his hands out of his pants. He turns his back on the shadowy porch.

He walks in the direction opposite to the one chosen the day before. He is going to sneak up on the hotel, which might logically expect him to continue to explore the portion of the island so far unexplored. What he finds is a ring of glassy stones, far up on the beach, driftwood piled inside the ring, charred and black. The ground is trampled all around the fire, as if people have stood there, waiting and pacing. There is something left in tatters and skin on a spit in the center of the campfire, about the size of a cat. The dead man doesn't look too closely at it.

He walks around the fire. He sees tracks indicating where the people who stood here watching a cat roast walked away. It would be hard to miss the direction they are taking. The people leave together, rushing untidily up the dune, barefoot and heavy, the imprints of the balls of the foot deep, heels hardly touching the sand at all. They are headed back towards the hotel. He walks back in their footprints, noticing where his own track, doubled over, comes and goes, back to the hotel. Above, in a line parallel to his expedition and to the sea, the crowd has also walked this way. They are walking more carefully now; he pictures them walking more quietly.

His footsteps end. This is where the hotel was waiting for him. The hotel itself has left no mark. The other footprints continue towards the hotel, where it stands now, down by the mailbox. When the dead man gets back to the hotel, the lobby floor is dusted with sand, and the television is on. The reception is slightly improved. But no one is there, although he searches every room. When he stands on the back veranda, staring out over the interior of the island, he imagines he sees a group of people, down beside the far shore, waving at him. The sky begins to fall.

Dear Araminta? Kiki? Lolita? Still doesn't have the right ring to it, does it? Sukie? Ludmilla? Winifred?

I had that same not-dream about the faculty party again. She was there, only this time you were the one who recognized her, and I was trying to guess her name, who she was. Was she the tall blonde with the nice ass, or the little blonde with short hair who kept her mouth a little open, like she was smiling all the time? That one looked like she knew something I wanted to know, but so did you. Isn't that funny? I never told you who she was, and now I can't remember. You probably knew the whole time anyway, even if you didn't think you did. I'm pretty sure you asked me about that little blond girl, when you were asking.

. . .

I keep thinking about the way you looked, that first night we slept together. I'd kissed you properly on the doorstep of your mother's house, and then, before you went inside, you turned around and gave me such a look. You didn't need to say anything at all. I waited until your mother turned off all the lights downstairs, and then I climbed over the fence, and up the tree in your backyard, and into your window. You were leaning out of the window, watching me climb, and you took off your shirt so that I could see your breasts. I almost fell out of the tree, and then you took off your jeans and your underwear had the day of the week embroidered on it. Friday? and then you took off your underwear too. You'd bleached the hair on your head white, and then streaked it with blue and red, but the hair on your pubis was black and soft, layered, when I touched it, like feathers. Like fur.

We lay down on your bed, and when I was inside you, you gave me that look again. It wasn't a frown, but it was almost a frown, like you had expected something different, or else like you were trying to get something just right. And then you smiled and sighed and twisted under me. You lifted up smoothly and strongly like you were going to levitate right off the bed, and I lifted with you like you were carrying me and I almost got you pregnant for the first time. We never were good about birth control, were we, Eliane? Rosemary? And then I heard your mother out in the backyard, right under the elm I'd just climbed, yelling "Tree? Tree?"

I thought she must have seen me climb it. I looked out the window, and saw her directly beneath me, and she had her hands on her hips, and the first thing I noticed was that her breasts were nice, moonlit and plump, pushed up under her dressing gown, fuller than yours, and almost as nice. That was pretty strange, realizing that I was the kind of guy who could have fallen in love with someone after four weeks, really, truly, deeply in love, the forever kind, I already knew, and still notice this girl's forty-five-year-old mother's boobs. That was the second thing I learned. The third thing I saw was that she wasn't looking back at me. "Tree?" she yelled, one last time, sounding pretty pissed.

So okay, I thought she was crazy. The last thing, the thing I didn't learn, was about names. It's taken me a while to figure that out. I'm still not sure what I didn't learn, Aina? Jewel? Kathleen? but at least I'm willing. I mean, I'm here still, aren't I?

Wish you were here,
You know who.

At some point, later, the dead man goes down to the mailbox. The water is particularly unwaterlike today. It has a velvety nap to it, like hair. It raises up in almost discernible shapes. It is still afraid of him, but it hates him, hates him, hates him. It never liked him, never. "Fraidy cat, fraidy cat," the dead man taunts the water.

When he goes back to the hotel, the loolies are there. They are watching television in the lobby. They are a lot bigger than he remembers.

Dear Cindy, Cynthia, Cenfenilla,

There are some people here with me now. I'm not sure if I'm in their place—if this place is theirs, or if I brought them here, like luggage. Maybe it's some of one, some of the other. They're people, or maybe I should say, a person I used to know when I was little. I think they've been watching me for a while, but they're shy. They don't talk much.

Hard to introduce yourself, when you don't know your own name. When I saw them, I was astounded. I sat down on the floor of the lobby, I was that surprised. A wave of emotion came over me so strong, I didn't recognize it. It might have been grief. It might have been relief. I think it was recognition. They came and stood around me, looking down. "I know you," I said. "You're loolies."

They nodded. Some of them smiled. They are so pale, so fat! When they smile, their eyes disappear in folds of flesh. But they have tiny soft bare feet, like children's feet. "You're the dead man," one said. It had a tiny, soft voice. Then we talked. Half of what they said made no sense at all. They don't know how I got here. They don't remember Looly Bellows. They don't remember dying. They were afraid of me at first, but also curious.

They wanted to know my name. Since I didn't have one, they tried to find a name that fit me. Walter was put forward, then rejected. I was un-Walter-like. Samuel, also Mike, also Rupert. Quite a few of them liked Alphonse, but I felt no particular leaning towards Alphonse. "Tree," one of the pinkies said.

Tree never liked me very much. I remember your mother standing under the green leaves, which leaned down on bowed branches, dragging the ground like skirts. Oh, it was such a tree! the most beautiful tree I'd ever seen. Halfway up the tree, glaring back at me, was a fat black cat with long white whiskers, and an elegant sheeny bib. You pulled me away. You'd put a T-shirt on. You stood in the window. "I'll get him," you said to the woman beneath the tree. "You go back to bed, Mom. Come here, Tree."

Tree walked the branch to the window, the same broad branch that had lifted me up to you. You, Ariadne? Thomasina? plucked him off the sill and then closed the window. When you put him down on the bed, he curled up at the foot, purring. But when I woke up, later, dreaming that I was drowning, he was crouched on my face, his belly heavy as silk against my mouth.

I always thought Tree was a silly name for a cat. He ran out in front of my car, I saw him, you saw me see him, I realized that it would be the last straw—a miscarriage, your husband sleeps with a graduate student, then he runs over your cat—I was trying to swerve, to not hit him. Something tells me I hit him.

I didn't mean to, sweetheart, love, Pearl? Patsy? Portia?

You know who.

The dead man watches television with the loolies. Soap operas. The loolies know how to get the antenna crooked so that the reception is decent, although the sound does not come in. One of them stands beside the TV to hold it just so. The soap opera is strangely dated, the clothes old-fashioned, the sort the dead man imagines his grandparents wore. The women wear cloche hats; their eyes are heavily made up.

There is a wedding. There is a funeral, also, although it is not clear to the dead man, watching, who the dead man is. Then the characters are walking along a beach. The woman wears a black-and-white striped bathing costume that covers her modestly, from neck to mid-thigh. The man's fly is undone. They do not hold hands. There is a buzz of comment from the pinkies. "Too dark," one says, about the woman. "Still alive," another says.

"Too thin," one says, indicating the man. "Should eat more. Might blow away in a wind."

"Out to sea."

"Out to Tree." The loolies look at the dead man. The dead man goes to his room. He locks the door. His penis sticks up, hard as a tree. It is pulling him across the room, towards the bed. The man is dead, but his body doesn't know it yet. His body still thinks that it is alive. He begins to say out loud the names he knows, beautiful names, silly names, improbable names. The loolies creep down the hall. They stand outside his door and listen to the list of names.

Dear Daphne? Proserpine? Rapunzel?

Isn't there a fairy tale where a little man tries to do this? Guess a woman's name? I have been making stories up about my death. One death I've imagined is when I am walking down to the subway, and then there is a strong wind, and the mobile sculpture by the subway, the one that spins in the wind, lifts up and falls on me. Another death is you and I, we are flying to some other country, Canada? The flight is crowded, and you sit one row ahead of me. There is a crack! and the plane splits in half, like a cracked straw. Your half rises up and my half falls down. You turn and look back at me, I throw out my arms. Wineglasses and newspapers and ribbons of clothes fall up in the air. The sky catches fire. I think maybe I stepped in front of a train. I was riding a bike, and someone opened a car door. I was on a boat and it sank.

This is what I know. I was going somewhere. This is the story that seems the best to me. We made love, you and I, and afterwards you got out of bed and stood there, looking at me. I thought that you had forgiven me, that now we were going to go on with our lives the way they had been before. Bernice? you said. Gloria? Patricia? Jane? Rosemary? Laura? Laura? Harriet? Jocelyn? Nora? Rowena? Anthea?

I got out of bed. I dressed quickly, and left the room. You followed me. Marly? Solange? Karla? Kitty? Soibhan? Marnie? Lynley? Theresa? You said the names staccato, one after the other, like stabs. I didn't look at you; I grabbed up my car keys and left the house. You stood in the door, watched me get in the car. Your lips were still moving, but I couldn't hear. The roof was down.

Tree was in front of the car, and when I saw him, I swerved. I was already going too fast, halfway out of the driveway. I pinned him up against the mailbox, and then the car hit the lilac tree. White petals were raining down. You screamed. It felt like I was flying.

I don't know if this is how I died. Maybe I died more than once, but it finally took. Here I am. I don't think this is an island. I think that I am a dead man, stuffed inside a box. When I'm quiet, I can almost hear the other dead men scratching at the walls of their boxes.

Or maybe I'm a ghost. Maybe the waves, which look like fur, are fur, and maybe the water which hisses and spits at me is really a cat, and the cat is a ghost too.

Maybe I'm here to learn something, to do penance. The loolies have forgiven me. Maybe you will too. When the sea comes to my hand, when it purrs at me, I'll know that you've forgiven me for what I did. For leaving you after I did it.

Or maybe I'm a tourist, and I'm stuck on this island with the loolies until it's time to go home, or until you come here to get me, Poppy? Irene? Dolores? which is why I hope you get this letter.

You know who.

When the sky changes, the loolies go outside. The dead man watches them pick the stuff off the beach. They eat it methodically, chewing it down to a paste. They swallow, and pick up more. The dead man goes outside. He picks up some of the stuff. Angelfood cake? Manna? He smells it. It smells like flowers; like carnations, lilies, like lilies, like roses. He puts some in his mouth. It tastes like nothing at all.

AN INCOMPLETE ANNOTATED
BIBLIOGRAPHY OF AMNESIA FICTION

A. A. Aattanasio, *Solis*

Kobo Abe, *The Box Man*

Paul Auster, *In the Country of Last Things*

J. G. Ballard, "Notes Toward a Mental Breakdown"

Ian Banks, *The Bridge*

John Franklin Bardin, *The Last of Philip Banter, Devil Take the Blue-Tail Fly,* and *The Deadly Percheron* — Bardin's first three novels (available once upon a time as *The John Franklin Bardin Omnibus,* from Penguin) are brilliant and ludicrous amnesiac puzzle stories. *The Last of Philip Banter* involves the amnesiac equivalent of a locked-room mystery: the protagonist discovers a manuscript, written in his own hand but which he can't remember writing, which correctly predicts the events of the following day.

Samuel Beckett, *The Lost ones, Krapp's Last Tape* — see Introduction.

Boileau and Narcejac, *Vertigo*

Italo Calvino, *Invisible Cities,* "World Memory"

Jonathan Carroll, *Voice of Our Shadow*

Richard Condon, *The Manchurian Candidate*

Douglas Cooper, *Amnesia*

Philip K. Dick, *Valis, Eye in the Sky, A Scanner Darkly, Time Out of Joint, Flow My Tears, The Policeman Said, A Maze of Death,* "We Can Remember It for You Wholesale," "The Electric Ant," "Imposter" — with Steve Erickson and John Franklin Bardin, Dick is the writer who has mined amnesia most persistently. A master of disorientation, he numbers among his motifs infectious delusions that spread from one character to another; *world amnesia,* where a character finds himself written out of the universe; and a whole host of implanted or faked memories. In the latter part of his career Dick dwelled more and more on his concept of *anamnesis*—the sudden and overwhelming recollection of a lost or suppressed body of knowledge.

Samuel R. Delany, *Dhalgren*—*Dhalgren,* and Kazuo Ishiguro's *The Unconsoled,* are possibly the two most remarkable examples of amnesia fiction *not* represented here. Though completely different in tone—*Dhalgren* experimental, ribald, and realistic; *Unconsoled* dreamlike and decorous—both are hugely encompassing and discursive novels, nearly impossible to describe or excerpt. But if you're reading the fine print because you've been left wanting more, seek out these two books and—presto!—this anthology is instantly 1,413 pages longer.

Don DeLillo, *The Names*

> *Air travel reminds us who we are. It's the means by which we recognize ourselves as modern. The process removes us from the world and sets us apart from each other. We wander in the ambient noise, checking one more time for the flight coupons, the boarding pass, the visa. The process convinces us that at any moment we may have to submit to the force that is implied in all this, the unknown authority behind it, behind the categories, the languages we don't understand. This vast terminal has been erected to examine souls.*
> *. . . All of this we choose to forget. We devise a countersystem of elaborate forgetfulness. We agree on this together. And out in the street we see how easy it is, once we're immersed in the thick crowded paint of things, the bright clothes and massed brown faces. But the experience is no less deep because we've agreed to forget it.*

Thomas M. Disch, *Amnesia*

Stanley Ellin, *Mirror, Mirror, on the Wall*

Steve Erickson, *Arc d'X, Rubicon Beach, Amnesiascope*—Erickson is building a shelf of amnesia fiction all his own, and is in a sense the genre's great integrator, as he lucidly glides back and forth between the Orwellian "amnesia-as-historical-catastrophe" and Dickian "amnesia-as-personal-breakdown" modes.

Philip Jose Farmer, "Sketches Among the Ruins of My Mind"

David Goodis, *Nightfall*

William Linsday Gresham, *Limbo Tower*

Charles L. Harness, *The Paradox Men*

Patricia Highsmith, *A Tremor of Forgery, Edith's Diary* — Highsmith's great theme is the transfer, evasion, and externalization of guilt. Moral amnesia pervades her work; she'd be a cornerstone of the *Vintage Book of Denial*.

William Hjortsberg, *Grey Matters*

Evan Hunter, *Buddwing*

Kazuo Ishiguro, *The Unconsoled* — see Delany.

Franz Kafka, *The Trial* — Kafka's masterpiece is among other things the emotional X-ray of every "what if I did something bad I don't remember" story, from Schnitzler's *Dream Story* to a thousand and one film noirs — take for instance *Road to Alcatraz*, whose poster reads: "Suspected by the Police . . . Haunted by Fear . . . HOW COULD HE BE CERTAIN HE HAD NOT MURDERED HIS OWN PARTNER!!!?")

Anna Kavan, *Ice*

D. H. Lawrence, *The Man Who Died*

Stanislaw Lem, *The Futurological Congress, The Investigation, Memoirs Found in a Bathtub*

Jonathan Lethem, *Amnesia Moon*

Joseph McElroy, *Plus*

Brian Moore, *Cold Heaven*

Vladimir Nabokov, *Bend Sinister, Despair, Pale Fire*, "Signs and Symbols" — Nabokov's work, so full of projected and imaginary persons and piecemeal identities, verges frequently on amnesia.

Richard Neely, *Shattered*

> *I gasped as she enveloped the pulsating tumescence that now achingly demanded release. I reached for her shoulders to hoist her to me, to contribute to the foreplay and balance our passion. But at the touch, she came up fast, bestriding my hips. Expertly she guided the penetration . . .*
>
> *As I surfaced, her cheek now pressed to mine, her body arched and still in the dominant position, I thought: It must have been like this at Puerto Vallarta. The thought brought a tingle of alarm.*
>
> *She whispered, "Now do you remember?"*
>
> *I felt gutted and alone. "Part of me remembers," I said, and realized my tactlessness.*

Cees Nooteboom, *The Following Story*

George Orwell, *1984*

Arthur Schnitzler, *Dream Story*—see Kafka.

Sarah Smith, *The Vanished Child*

Walter Tevis, *Mockingbird*—a poignant version of postapocalyptic amnesia, where characters pick through ruins and attempt to remember their world—which is nearly always our world. Others include Walter Miller's *A Canticle for Leibowitz*, Clifford Simak's *City*, Brian Aldiss's *Hothouse*, George Stewart's *Earth Abides*, Richard Brautigan's *In Watermelon Sugar*, and Russell Hoban's *Riddley Walker*.

Rupert Thomson, *The Insult*

A. E. Van Vogt, *The World of Null-A*—Van Vogt's specialty was the amnesiac superman, who must attain self-realization in order to save the universe. His narratives are brilliantly dreamlike and discombobulated, thanks to a strict policy of introducing a new plot twist every three hundred words. Van Vogt fan Philip K. Dick took this ball and ran with it—or rather, slowed it down, to the point where it could bear real emotional weight. Van Vogt himself joined Dianetics, a pop cult in which a vast amnesia narrative serves as gospel.

Marianne Wiggins, *Almost Heaven*

> *"Youth isn't erotic in and of itself," Alex tells him without answering his question. "Hell, youth's too undiscerning to be seriously sexy: it's empty, that's its musk. It offers an illusion that a man can re-invent himself—start clean, start over. It's classic. A classic turn-on . . . Melanie is one hell of a case history. I don't deny I haven't thought of her as my passport to renown, a chance to do an Oliver Sacks, if not a Freud. Whereas for you, I think there must be an erotic charge to your samaritanism. I think what turns you on about her isn't her—wife, mother, woman with a decade of mothering behind her—I think what intrigues you about her is the sexiness of her condition, her absence from history, her non-being, her nullity . . ."*

Gene Wolfe, *Soldier in the Mist*

CONTRIBUTORS

Martin Amis was born in 1949. His books include *Money, Dead Babies, The Rachel Papers, The Moronic Inferno, Einstein's Monsters, London Fields, Time's Arrow, Visiting Mrs. Nabokov, The Information, Night Train, Experience,* and *Heavy Water,* a collection of stories. He lives in London.

John Franklin Bardin was born in Cincinnati in 1916. After an unhappy childhood he left the University of Cincinnati in his first year to find a full-time job. He became a ticket-taker and bouncer at a local roller-skating rink and educated himself by working at night, reading and clerking in a bookstore. He moved to New York near the age of thirty, and served as an executive at an advertising agency for nearly twenty years. In addition to his various journalistic endeavors, he taught advertising and creative writing at the New School for Social Research from 1961 to 1966. He is the author of ten novels, including *The Deadly Percheron, The Last of Philip Banter, The Case Against Butterfly, Christmas Comes But Once a Year, A Shroud for Grandmama,* and *Devil Take the Blue-Tail Fly.* He died in 1981.

Donald Barthelme was born in 1931 in Philadelphia. He was a longtime contributor to *The New Yorker,* winner of a National Book Award, a director of PEN and the Author's Guild, and a member of the American Academy of Arts and Letters. His sixteen books—including *Snow White, The Dead Father,* and *City Life*—substantially redefined American short fiction for our time. In 1972 he won the National Book Award for children's literature for *The Slightly Irregular Fire Engine or the Hithering Thithering Djinn.* He died in 1989.

Jorge Luis Borges was born in Buenos Aires in 1899, and was educated in Europe. His first book, *Fervor de Buenos Aires,* appeared in 1923. While his output steadily increased, it did not secure him an income, and in 1937 he accepted a job as a municipal librarian. Fired from his post by the Péron regime in 1946, he was offered a post as "Inspector of Poultry and Rabbits in the Public Markets," followed by fifteen years as a professor of literature at the University of Buenos Aires. After Péron's deposition, Borges was appointed Director of the National Library of Argentina, where he served until 1973. Meanwhile his reputation as a poet, essayist, and short story writer grew to an international scale. In 1961 he shared the International Publishers Prize with Samuel Beckett—the first of many prizes and honorary degrees awarded him. Borges suffered from a congenital eye problem, which resulted in total blindness in his last decades. He died in 1986 in Geneva.

Julio Cortázar was born in Brussels of Argentinean parents in 1914. He worked for several Argentinean publishing houses translating the works of Edgar Allen Poe, André Gide, Walter de la Mare, Daniel Defoe, and G. K. Chesterton. He moved to France in 1951, and became a citizen at President Mitterand's invitation in 1981. He remained active in Latin American politics, donating the 1973 Prix Médicis prize money for *Libro de Manuel* to the United Chilean Front. He is the author of numerous short stories and poems and achieved an international following with his 1963 novel *Rayuela* (translated into English as *Hopscotch*). He died in 1984.

L. J. Davis is a contributing editor for *Harper's* magazine and a reporter, critic, and commentator. His work appears regularly in *Mother Jones,* and he won the National Magazine Award for predicting the stock market crash of 1987. Davis has authored four novels and three works of nonfiction, *Bad Money: Big Business Disasters in the Age of a Credit Crisis, Onassis,* and *The Billionaire Shell Game.* He lives in Brooklyn, New York.

Philip K. Dick was born in Chicago in 1928 and lived most of his life in California. He briefly attended the University of California, but dropped out before completing any classes. In 1952 he began writing professionally and proceeded to write thirty-six novels and five short-story collections. He won the Hugo Award for the best novel in 1962 for *The Man in the High Castle* and the John W. Campbell Memorial Award for best novel of the year in 1974 for *Flow My Tears, the Policeman Said.* His novel *Do Androids Dream of Electric Sheep?* was adapted into the film *Blade Runner* by Ridley Scott. He died in 1982.

Thomas M. Disch is the author of numerous novels, story collections, books of poetry, criticism, children's literature, libretti, and plays. His most recent book is *The Sub,* published by Alfred A. Knopf. He lives in New York City and upstate New York.

Steve Erickson was born in 1950 in Los Angeles, and has lived in Paris, Amsterdam, Italy, and New York. He has written on a variety of topics for *The New York Times, Esquire, L.A. Weekly, Rolling Stone,* and contributes regularly to *Salon*. He is the author of the novels *Days Between Stations*, *Rubicon Beach*, *Tours of The Black Clock*, *Arc d'X*, and *Amnesiascope*, as well as two books of nonfiction, *Leap Year* and *American Nomad*. He lives in Los Angeles.

Brian Fawcett was born in 1944 in British Columbia. He has worked as an urban planner and a journalist. He is the author of *My Career with the Leafs & Other Stories*, *Cambodia: A Book for People Who Find Television Too Slow*, *The Secret Journal of Alexander MacKenzie*, *Public Eye: An Investigation into the Disappearance of the World*, *Capital Tales*, and *Gender Wars: A Novel and Some Conversation About Sex and Gender*. He lives in Toronto.

Karen Joy Fowler was born in Bloomington, Indiana, in 1950, but moved to California when she was eleven years old. She decided she wanted to be a writer on her thirtieth birthday and published a collection of short stories entitled *Artificial Things* six years later. Her first novel, *Sarah Canary*, was published in 1991 and received the Commonwealth silver medal for best first novel by a Californian that year. In 1995 she published her second novel, *The Sweetheart Season*. Both novels were selected by *The New York Times Book Review* as notable books for their year. Her most recent book, published in 1998, is a collection of stories entitled *Black Glass*. She lives with her husband in Davis, California.

David Grand attended the New York University Creative Writing Program, where he was awarded the program's Creative Writing Fellowship for Fiction. He is the author of *Louse*. He lives in Brooklyn.

Russell Hoban was born in 1925 in Pennsylvania. He worked as a freelance illustrator and advertising copywriter before turning to writing fiction. He has published over fifty books for children, including the perennially popular series featuring Frances, the badger. His adult novels include *Riddley Walker*, *The Medusa Frequency*, *Fremder*, *Kleinzeit*, *Turtle Diary*, and, most recently, *Angelica's Grotto*. Hoban has lived in London since 1969.

Shirley Jackson was born in San Francisco in 1916. She graduated from Syracuse University in 1940, and married classmate and later literary critic, Stanley Edgar Hyman, the same year. She is perhaps best known for "The Lottery," first published in *The New Yorker* in 1948, and sparking widespread public outrage. Jackson's six finished novels, *The Road Through the Wall*, *Hangsaman*, *The Sundial*, *We Have Always Lived in the Castle*, *The Bird's Nest*, and *The Haunting of Hill House*, further established her reputation as a master of gothic horror and psychological suspense. She is also the author of *Life Among the Savages* and *Raising Demons*, fictionalized memoirs about raising her four children. She died in 1965.

Anna Kavan was born in France in 1901, and raised in Europe and California. During her lifetime, which included two marriages, extended periods of illness and addiction, and the publication of several early works including the novel *Ice*, her work was known primarily in England. The posthumous publication of many further books, including *Julia and the Bazooka*, *Asylum Piece*, and *Sleep Has His House*, brought her wider acclaim and publication in America. She died in 1968.

Jonathan Lethem was born in New York and attended Bennington College. He is the author of the novels *Gun, with Occasional Music*; *Amnesia Moon*; *Girl in Landscape*; *As She Climbed Across the Table*; and *Motherless Brooklyn*, winner of the National Book Critics Circle Award for Fiction; as well as a collection of short stories, *The Wall of the Sky, the Wall of the Eye*. He lives in Brooklyn, New York.

Kelly Link was born in 1969 in Miami, Florida. She is a graduate of Columbia University and the University of North Carolina at Greensboro. Her short fiction won the James Tiptree, Jr. Award in 1997 and the World Fantasy Award in 1999. She lives in Boston and works in a bookstore.

Haruki Murakami was born in Kyoto in 1949. The most recent of his many honors is the Yomiuri Literary Prize, whose previous recipients include Yukio Mishima, Kenzaburo Oe, and Kobo Abe. He is the author of the novels *Dance, Dance, Dance*; *Hard-Boiled Wonderland and the End of the World*; *A Wild Sheep Chase*; *South of the Border, West of the Sun*; *The Wind-Up Bird Chronicle*; *Norwegian Wood*; and of *The Elephant Vanishes*, a collection of stories. His work has been translated into fourteen languages. He lives near Tokyo.

Vladimir Nabokov was born in St. Petersburg in 1899. He studied at Cambridge, then spent the next eighteen years in Berlin and Paris, respectively. While supporting himself by giving lessons in tennis and English, he began writing under the pseudonym Sirin, mainly in Russian. In 1940 he moved to the United States, where he pursued a literary career while teaching literature at Wellesley, Stanford, Cornell, and Harvard. The monumental success of his novel *Lolita* in 1955 enabled him to give up teaching and devote himself fully to his writing. Recognized as one of this century's master prose stylists in both Russian and English, his books include *The Defense*, *The Gift*, *Bend Sinister*, *Pale Fire*, *Pnin*, and *Speak, Memory*. He died in 1977.

Flann O'Brien was born Brian O'Nolan in Ireland, in 1911. He began eighteen years' employment in the Irish civil service in 1935. During the late 1930s he embarked on a literary career, writing a bilingual column for the *Irish Times* under the pseudonym Myles na Gopaleen and publishing his first novel, *At*

Swim-Two-Birds, in 1939 under the name Flann O'Brien. He kicked off the Bloomsday tradition in 1954 together with Patrick Kavanagh, retracing the steps of James Joyce's *Ulysses'* Bloom through Dublin pubs. He is the author of the novels *An Neal Bocht* (The Poor Mouth), *The Hard Life*, *The Dalkey Archive*, and the posthumously-published *The Third Policeman*. He died in 1966.

Geoffrey O'Brien is the author of *Hardboiled America* (1981), *Dream Time: Chapters from the Sixties* (1988), *A Book of Maps* (1989), *The Phantom Empire* (1993), *Floating City: Selected Poems 1978–1995* (1996), *The Times Square Story* (1988), and *The Browser's Ecstacy: A Meditation on Reading* (2000). He is the editor in chief of The Library of America.

Thomas Palmer is the author of two novels, *The Transfer* and *Dream Science*. Since writing *Landscape with Reptile: Rattlesnakes in an Urban World*, he has put aside fiction writing in favor of what he calls the "rewarding mudwrestling" of environmental activism. He lives with his family in Milton, Massachusetts.

Walker Percy was born in Birmingham, Alabama, in 1916, graduated from the University of North Carolina in 1937, and became a Doctor of Medicine at Columbia University in 1941. *The Moviegoer*, his first novel, was awarded the 1962 National Book Award for Fiction. Mr. Percy's other novels include *The Last Gentleman, Love in the Ruins, Lancelot, The Second Coming*, and *The Thanatos Syndrome*, and two volumes of essays, *The Message in the Bottle* and *Lost in the Cosmos: The Last Self-Help Book*. He died in 1990.

Dennis Potter was born in 1935 in a village in Gloucestershire, England. His first book, *The Glittering Coffin*, was published in 1960. He appeared regularly on the BBC book review program Bookstand, and wrote scripts for the satire series *That Was the Week That Was*. He is the author of twenty-eight original plays for television production, eleven serials, nine screenplays, the stage play *Sufficient Carbohydrate*, the short story "Last Pearls," and the novels *Ticket to Ride* and *Blackeyes*. He is perhaps best known for the television serial *The Singing Detective*, and the films *Pennies from Heaven, Brimstone and Treacle*, and *Gorky Park*. He died in 1994.

Christopher Priest is the author of ten novels and two collections of short stories. His last novel, *The Prestige*, won the 1995 James Tait Black Memorial Prize for Best Novel, The World Fantasy Award, and was shortlisted for the Arthur C. Clarke Award. His novel *The Glamour* won the 1988 Kurd Lasswitz Best Novel award. He lives in Hastings, England, with his wife and twin children.

Oliver Sacks was born in London in 1933. He trained as a neurologist in Oxford and California. Since 1965 he has lived in New York, where he is clinical professor of neurology at the Albert Einstein College of Medicine. He is the author of many books, including *Awakenings, The Man Who Mistook His Wife for a Hat, An Anthropologist on Mars,* and *The Island of the Colorblind.*

Lawrence Shainberg was born in Memphis, Tennessee. His books include *One on One, Memories of Amnesia, Brain Surgeon: An Intimate View of His World,* and *Ambivalent Zen: One Man's Adventures on the Dharma Path.*

Robert Sheckley was born in Brooklyn, New York, and has lived at various times in London, Paris, and Ibiza. Beginning in the mid-fifties he established himself as one of the finest and most mordantly funny short story writers in or out of science fiction, the genre with which he is most closely associated, though he has also written mysteries, westerns, and screenplays. His many books include *Untouched by Human Hands, Can You Feel Anything When I Do This?* and *The Tenth Victim.*

Edmund White was born in Cincinnati in 1940. His fiction includes the auto-biographical trilogy *A Boy's Own Story, The Beautiful Room is Empty* and *The Farewell Symphony,* as well as *Caracole, Forgetting Elena, Nocturnes for the King of Naples* and *Skinned Alive.* He is also the author of a highly acclaimed biography of Jean Genet, a short study of Proust, a travel book about gay Amer-ica—*States of Desire*—and *Our Paris.* He is an officer of the Ordre des Arts et des Lettres and teaches at Princeton University. He lives in New York City.

Cornell Woolrich was born in 1903, and began writing while at Columbia University in the 1920s. Throughout the 1930s and '40s, he emerged as one of the forerunners of the *noir* genre. He is the author of more than one hundred stories and novelettes. His work has been dramatized on classic radio shows such as *Suspense,* and adapted into numerous motion pictures, including *The Bride Wore Black, Phantom Lady,* and *Rear Window.* He died in 1968.

Valentine Worth received his degree in neuroscience from the University of Genoa in 1936. He immigrated to the U.S. in 1939, and served as a captain in the Army from 1941 to 1945. Between 1956 and 1977 he was the director of the East Central Florida Memory, Sleep, and Dream Disorder Clinic. He has been a member of the American Association for Motor Neuron Disease, the American Society for Memory Disorder, the American Association for Oblis-cence Study, and was a founding member of the Alliance for the Prudent Use of Antibiotics. With his wife, Eloise, he has established the fourth largest pri-vate collection of printed and illustrated works on memory in the continental U.S. This collection is now housed in their Melbourne, Florida, home and is known as the Eloise Mobile and Valentine Worth Mnemonics Library.

PERMISSIONS ACKNOWLEDGMENTS

Grateful acknowledgment is made to the following for permission to reprint previously published material:

Martin Amis: Excerpt from *Other People* by Martin Amis. Reprinted by permission of the author.

John Franklin Bardin: Excerpt from *The Deadly Percheron* by John Franklin Bardin. Copyright © 1946 by John Franklin Bardin. Reprinted by permission of Franklin Clark Bardin as Executor of the Estate of John Franklin Bardin. Grateful acknowledgment is made to Canongate Books, Lennart Sane Agency, AB, Poisoned Pen Press, and Rita Rosenkranz Literary Agency.

Donald Barthelme: "Game" by Donald Barthelme. Copyright © 1982 by Donald Barthelme. Reprinted by permission of The Wylie Agency, Inc.

Jorge Luis Borges: "Funes, His Memory" from *Collected Fictions* by Jorge Luis Borges, translated by Andrew Hurley. Copyright © 1998 by Maria Kodama. Translation copyright © 1998 by Penguin Putnam Inc. Reprinted by permission of Viking Penguin, a division of Penguin Putnam Inc.

Julio Cortázar: "The Night Face Up" from *The End of the Game and Other Stories* by Julio Cortazar, translated by Paul Blackburn. Copyright © 1967, copyright renewed 1995 by Random House, Inc. Reprinted by permission of Pantheon Books, a division of Random House, Inc.

L. J. Davis: Excerpt from *Cowboys Don't Cry* by L. J. Davis. Copyright © by L. J. Davis. Reprinted by permission of the author.

Philip K. Dick: "I Hope I Shall Arrive Soon" by Philip K. Dick. Reprinted by permission of the author and the author's agent, Scovil Chichak Galen Literary Agency, Inc.

Thomas M. Disch: "The Squirrel Cage" from *Fun with Your New Head* by Thomas M. Disch. Reprinted by permission of the author c/o Writers' Representatives, Inc.

Steve Erickson: Excerpt from *Days Between Stations* by Steve Erickson. Copyright © 1985 by Steve Erickson. Reprinted by permission of Melanie Jackson Agency, LLC.

Brian Fawcett: "Soul Walker" from *Public Eye: An Investigation into the Disappearance of the World* by Brian Fawcett. Copyright © 1990 by Brian Fawcett. Reprinted by permission of Grove/Atlantic, Inc., and the author.

Karen Joy Fowler: Excerpt from *Sarah Canary* by Karen Joy Fowler. Copyright © 1991 by Karen Joy Fowler. Reprinted by permission of Henry Holt and Company, LLC.

David Grand: Excerpt from *Louse* by David Grand. Copyright © 1998 by David Grand. Reprinted by permission of Arcade Publishing, New York, and John Hodgman, Writer's House, as agent for the author.

Russell Hoban: Excerpt from *Kleinzeit* by Russell Hoban. Copyright © 1984 by Russell Hoban. Reprinted by permission of Harold Ober Associates Incorporated.

Shirley Jackson: "Nightmare" from *Just an Ordinary Day: The Uncollected Stories* by Shirley Jackson. Copyright © 1996 by The Estate of Shirley Jackson. Reprinted by permission of Bantam Books, a division of Random House, Inc.

Anna Kavan: "The Zebra-Struck" from *Julia and the Bazooka* by Anna Kavan. Reprinted by permission of David Higham Associates Limited.

Jonathan Lethem: "Five Fucks" from *The Wall of the Sky, the Wall of the Eye* by Jonathan Lethem. Copyright © 1996 by Jonathan Lethem. Reprinted by permission of Harcourt, Inc.

Kelly Link: "Carnation, Lily, Lily, Rose" by Kelly Link. Reprinted by permission of the author.

Haruki Murakami: "The Fall of the Roman Empire" from *The Elephant Vanishes* by Haruki Murakami. Copyright © 1993 by Haruki Murakami. Reprinted by permission of Alfred A. Knopf, a division of Random House, Inc., and International Creative Management.

Vladimir Nabokov: "That in Aleppo Once . . ." from *The Stories of Vladimir Nabokov* by Vladimir Nabokov. Copyright © 1995 by Dmitri Nabokov. Reprinted by permission of Alfred A. Knopf, a division of Random House, Inc.

Flann O'Brien: Excerpt from *The Third Policeman* by Flann O'Brien. Copyright © 1967 by Evelyn O'Nolan. Copyright © The Estate of the Late Brian O'Nolan. Reprinted by permission of Brandt & Brandt Literary Agents, Inc., and A. M. Heath & Company Ltd. on behalf of the Estate.

Geoffrey O'Brien: Excerpt from *Notes Toward a History of the Seventies* by Geoffrey O'Brien. Reprinted by permission of the author.

Thomas Palmer: Excerpt from *Dream Science* by Thomas Palmer. Copyright © 1990 by Thomas Palmer. All rights reserved. Reprinted by permission of Houghton Mifflin Company.

Walker Percy: Excerpt from *The Second Coming* by Walter Percy. Copyright © 1980 by Walker Percy. Reprinted by permission of Farrar, Straus and Giroux, LLC.

Dennis Potter: Excerpt from *Ticket to Ride* by Dennis Potter. Copyright © 1996 by Dennis Potter. Reprinted by permission of Faber & Faber, Inc., an affiliate of Farrar, Straus and Giroux, LLC.

Christopher Priest: Excerpt from *The Affirmation* by Christopher Priest. Copyright © 1981 by Christopher Priest. Reprinted by permission of the author.

Oliver Sacks: "The Last Hippie" from *An Anthropologist on Mars* by Oliver Sacks, M.D. Copyright © 1995 by Oliver Sacks, M.D. Reprinted by permission of Alfred A. Knopf, a division of Random House, Inc.

Lawrence Shainberg: Excerpt from *Memories of Amnesia* by Lawrence Shainberg. Copyright © 1988 by Lawrence Shainberg. Reprinted by permission of Gelfman Schneider Literary Agents, Inc., for the author.

Robert Sheckley: "Warm" from *Is That What People Do?* by Robert Sheckley. Copyright © 1953 by Robert Sheckley. "Warm" originally appeared in *Galaxy* Magazine. Reprinted by permission of the author.

Edmund White: Excerpt from *Forgetting Elena* by Edmund White. Copyright © 1973 by Edmund White. Reprinted by permission of Random House, Inc.

Cornell Woolrich: Excerpt from *The Black Curtain* by Cornell Woolrich. Copyright © 1941 by Cornell Woolrich. Copyright renewed 1969 by The Chase Manhattan Bank, N.A., as Executor of the Estate of Cornell Woolrich. Reprinted by permission of Sheldon Abend.

Valentine Worth: from *Geoffrey Sonnabend's Obliscence: Theories of Forgetting and the Problem of Matter—An Encapsulation* by Valentine Worth. Reprinted by permission of The Museum of Jurassic Technology.